RACHEL ~~ ~~ T

INCRIMINATING
EVIDENCE

JANUS PUBLISHING

This one is for Jocelyn,

Because she goes to Cross-Fit even though she hates it, has vehement opinions on which Doctor is the best Doctor, and knows how to answer the question, "What is the airspeed velocity of an unladen swallow?" Plus, she loves cats.

CHAPTER ONE

Tanana Valley State Forest, Alaska
September

IT WAS A show tunes kind of afternoon, which was unusual for Isabel, but the words to the old songs came to her effortlessly as she walked downslope, deep in the Tanana Valley State Forest. Loud, full-voiced singing was necessary to warn bears she was working in this remote Alaskan wilderness and was intended to scare the creatures away. Given her off-key voice, singing pretty much guaranteed humans would stay away as well. A decided bonus.

Although, now that she was on day four of the timber sale survey, she was ready to be done. She'd had enough solitude this week and wouldn't mind meeting up with Nicole for a beer at the Tamarack Roadhouse. It was getting late, already after five p.m., and she was still a two-hour hike from her truck, but her extralong lunch excursion put her behind schedule and she had one more parcel to inspect before she'd be done with the archaeological survey. It was worth the long day to avoid hiking all the way back here tomorrow.

Most of this week's survey soundtrack had been sad songs, but yesterday had been Vincent's birthday, so her melancholy was understandable. Then suddenly, this afternoon Rodgers and Hammerstein popped into her head. She'd started with *Oklahoma!*, continued with *The Sound of Music,* and now she'd moved on to Gilbert and Sullivan's *The Pirates of Penzance*, specifically, "I Am The Very Model Of A Modern Major-General."

She'd feel ridiculous singing at the top of her lungs, except after months of working in Alaska, she'd grown used to the need to make noise while conducting pedestrian survey. She'd found straight-up talking to herself disconcerting, so she'd taken to singing. Now it was second nature. She barely even heard her own voice as she studied the ground for telltale signs of prehistoric human activity.

She paused, taking a deep breath, preparing for the next rapid verse, when she heard a branch crack, followed by a grunt.

Not the grunt of an animal, but one of a human. In pain?

She stopped. With her head cocked toward the wind, she listened. Again she heard a sound. Faint. Human. Definitely not happy.

She scanned the woods. The underbrush was thick and mosquitoes vicious. Whenever she stopped walking, they swarmed. She fought the urge to wave her arms to shoo them away so she could listen.

But all she heard was wind. Birds. Buzzing mosquitoes as the bloodsucking females feasted on her cheeks and arms. Normal forest sounds.

She slapped away the biters. Maybe she'd heard a wolverine. Their grunts could easily be mistaken for human. Shaking off the foolish notion she'd cross paths with another person out here on the edge of the bush, she resumed walking and singing, but the happy beat was lost. Now she sang solely to ward off bears. She scanned the ground as she walked, looking for signs of prehistoric occupation or use. Her job was to find archaeological sites that would be destroyed by the coming timber harvest. That was what she was here for. She needed to focus on what paid the bills.

The ground sloped at a grade above fifteen percent. Poor conditions for finding a site, because the ground was too steep for occupation. If there were a site in the vicinity, she'd find it at the base of the slope. She continued in that direction, determined to do a good job for her employer, the Alaska Department of Natural Resources.

Branches snapped below her, to the right.

She stopped signing midword.

Any number of fauna could have triggered it. She hadn't seen any scat, at least nothing fresh and therefore worrisome, for the last half mile. But still, she dropped a hand to the grip of her pistol while the other grabbed the bear spray. Of the two, the pistol was the least effective, but the noises had her on edge. While a pistol wasn't good defense against a bear, it was excellent for dealing with humans.

These woods, remote, abundant with resources, yet marginally accessible due to logging roads, could be a gateway to the bush for people on the run. Maybe she'd been foolish to brush off the noise as a wolverine.

Another sound carried on the breeze, and she ducked behind a tree to listen and wait. In her gut, she knew she wasn't about to face down a bear. She held the gun in front of her, pointed upward, clasped between both hands like a prayer. Her heart pounded, but she had no real understanding why. This just didn't feel *right*.

She couldn't stay behind a tree gripping a gun forever and eased out from her feeble hiding spot. Slowly, silently, she crept down the hillside toward whatever—or whoever—had made the sounds.

She spotted him immediately. Sunlight filtered between the leaves, highlighting the red splatter of blood that covered the man's face. He lay still. Unconscious or dead?

She'd heard of archaeologists finding bodies on survey before, but the accounts always had the earmark of urban myths—two people removed from the teller of the tale. She'd never met anyone who'd actually encountered a corpse themselves. She supposed she'd considered how scary such a find would be, but hadn't really thought beyond that, because really, it just didn't happen.

It was like planning for a head-on collision. She'd been certain that sort of thing would never happen to *her*. Car accidents, kidnappings, tornados, and random bodies in the woods were all on the list of things that happened to other people.

And yet here she was. Adrenaline flooded, frozen with shock, and facing a body in the deep, bear-infested woods.

Her past speculation had been wrong. It wasn't scary; it was utterly terrifying. Worse than facing down a bear, a pair of rattlesnakes, and a brown recluse all at the same time. Nature, she could handle. This wasn't nature.

This was murder.

She glanced left and right. She would never hear anyone approaching over the roar of her racing pulse. She stepped toward the man, slowly. Gun out. Pointed at the body.

As she neared, she caught the slightest rise of his chest. He was alive.

Not murder, then. Attempted murder? Assault?

His face was swollen. He'd taken several blows in addition to the gash on his temple that bled profusely. She dropped to her knees at his side. She had no choice but to holster the pistol to check his vital signs.

His pulse was solid even though his breathing was shallow. It was likely a blessing that he was unconscious, because if he were awake she'd bet his head would hurt like a sonofabitch.

What to do? Whoever had done this to him could return. But if she left him here, unconscious, vulnerable, he could die. No. *Would* die. There were too many scavengers and predators in the area to believe he could survive, bleeding, unconscious, and alone.

But then, he could be the villain in this. Drug dealer. Poacher. Criminal on the run. This could be his just reward. She searched his pockets for a wallet with ID, but came up empty. His clothing didn't argue for poacher. His clothing—business casual slacks and a blood-saturated button-down shirt—didn't belong in these woods at all.

She checked his mouth, looking for rotting teeth, signs of drug use, anything that would indicate she had something to fear from helping him. But his teeth's perfect alignment could only be attributed to orthodontia. Bright white and nary a silver filling.

She opened his shirt, searching for other causes for his blood-soaked clothing besides the gash on his temple. All she found was hard muscle. Whoever this man was, he took good care of himself.

Given his build, in spite of his city clothes, he could be a Raptor operative who'd strayed from the compound. That thought had her considering leaving him. The bears and wolves could have him. Or whoever had done this to him could come back and finish the job.

She shook her head, knowing her thoughts were unfair. Not all the operatives on the Raptor compound were rotten. She got along with most of them and was even drinking buddies with Nicole. But she knew without a doubt a few operatives were up to no good, and she had a serious problem with their boss. But then, it was hard to have kind feelings for the person who might have covered up her brother's murder, especially when yesterday would have been that brother's thirty-fourth birthday.

She had to assume, given this guy's condition, he could be one of the operatives involved in dirty deals. The fact that she didn't recognize him only made him more suspicious.

She stood and slowly turned in a circle, scanning the woods. What should she do?

It was a five-mile hike—at least half of that uphill—to her truck. No way could she carry an unconscious man that far. Hell, there was no way she could carry him thirty feet.

She pulled out her first aid kit and dropped to his side again. She'd tend the head wound while she decided what to do. Using precious water from her water bottle, she dampened a pack towel and cleaned the gash on his temple. Given the blood, bruises, and welts, she'd have trouble recognizing him even if he were a regular at the Roadhouse, but she was fairly certain she'd never seen him in town, nor was he one of the operatives she'd met when she'd interrupted the live-fire training exercise and been arrested.

Her hands shook as she cleaned the gash, and she paused to steady her breathing and get the trembling under control. She scanned the woods, wondering if this man's attackers lurked nearby. Every instinct said to flee, but she couldn't abandon him.

He couldn't be a soldier attending a Raptor training, because after months of effort, she'd successfully gotten the government to shut down the compound's military training program while they investigated the company's safety measures. The weekly influx of soldiers had halted two months ago. But still, to be certain, she checked for dog tags and confirmed he wasn't wearing any.

Breathing under control, she swabbed his cut with alcohol again and applied antibiotic ointment. She closed the gash with three butterfly bandages.

Unless he had internal injuries she wasn't aware of, he'd probably be okay—as long as he wasn't left to die unconscious and alone.

She considered her options. She had plenty of parachute cord and a small but sturdy tarp in her backpack. With long, strong branches, she could build a travois-type stretcher and drag him to shelter.

But still...five miles, much of it uphill. She closed her eyes, thinking of the surrounding area. After surveying this parcel of woods for the last four days, she knew this section of forest. Where could she take him?

There were a few very old caches, but she could no more haul him up into a cache than drag him five miles to her truck. However...Raptor land abutted the state forest about a half mile away.

She pulled out her USGS quadrangle map of the survey area and studied it. She'd checked the state database for historic and prehistoric sites on Raptor land as part of her search for Vincent's cave and had recorded all known sites—of which there were pathetic few—on her field maps, including this quad.

According to her map, there was a 1906 settler's cabin about a mile away.

She'd never been to that part of the compound; the closest she'd come was about a mile west. She couldn't be certain the cabin was still there, but she'd managed to find a few previously recorded sites in the parts of the compound she had explored, giving her hope that the historic cabin would also be extant.

After the live-fire training incident, the company CEO, Alec Ravissant, had acquired a restraining order to prevent her from stepping on Raptor land. But surely she wouldn't get in trouble for bringing an injured Raptor operative to the cabin, especially if the action saved his life? Of course, she couldn't admit how she knew the cabin existed, but she'd deal with that little problem if the time came.

But what if this man's attackers were in the cabin?

She didn't really have a choice. The cabin was his best hope. There was no cell coverage out here, and satellite phones were so horrifically expensive, she couldn't afford one. The hike to her truck plus the drive to where she could get a signal would take more than two hours. Help, in the form of emergency responders, would take another two hours to return. She had a feeling this guy didn't have that sort of time. Especially given his head wound and the evening wind, which was just beginning to kick up.

She dropped her hand to the gun at her hip. If there were men in the cabin, she wouldn't be helpless.

Before she could drag him a mile, she needed a travois. She set to work building it. Because she had a tarp, she didn't need most of the crosspieces; she could get by with one near the top and one at the bottom.

First, she used her knife to strip two six-foot-long branches, then she rolled the prepared branches into the opposite sides of the tarp at an angle, so it flared out, making it wider at the bottom, like a traditional travois. With the parachute cord, she lashed a short crosspiece to the top and a much longer one at the bottom, stretching the tarp tight in both places. The process took far too long for her peace of mind, but in the end she'd created something between a travois and a litter and could only pray the contraption would work.

She muttered an apology to the unconscious man as she rolled him onto the makeshift stretcher and strapped him between the poles using more rope, running it under his arms and over his shoulders. It would pinch and probably hurt like hell, but it was better than being left for dead, so he'd have to forgive her.

The man didn't make a sound, which increased her anxiety over his condition. With one last check of his pulse—still strong, thank goodness—she picked up the end of the travois and dragged him the first few steps.

Holy hell, he was heavy. She adjusted her grip and pulled another few feet, then stopped. She'd positioned him too high on the tarp, forcing her to lift too much of his weight. The poles should act as sled runners of sorts, but couldn't at the current angle.

She set him down and adjusted his position, lowering him until his legs hung off the tarp and the travois only supported his head down to his hips. Good thing he was unconscious, because he was about to be dragged across a whole lot of rocky ground, with nothing but a pair of cotton slacks to protect his skin.

After a hundred yards, she hit a snag. His sleeve had caught on a root because his arms dragged on either side of the tarp. With a short piece of cord, she secured both hands to his hips, running the thin rope through his belt loops instead of winding it around the travois and potentially causing even more hitches.

She stopped to rest often and quickly ran out of water. At least she could refill her water bottle from a stream indicated on the map—*please let it still be running this late in the summer*—and she had plenty of purification tablets. The aching, miserable, difficult, one-mile trek took two hours, but at last she reached the small meadow and spotted the cabin twenty yards away.

She paused on the edge of the woods. She was an archaeologist, not a police officer or Raptor operative. How should she handle this? Scout the cabin first with her gun drawn? Or was she *more* likely to get shot if she crossed the meadow obviously carrying a gun?

She decided to leave the gun in her holster and walk up to the cabin casually—a curious trespasser, not a suspicious vigilante.

The cabin was empty, and, given her difficulty in opening the door on rusted hinges, it had been for some time. But still, it had a floor—even if wavy, uneven, and soft—and a roof. One window held intact glass, but the other was broken. The single room was completely bare except for a stone fireplace on the back wall, and the hearth appeared sound. If she needed to, she could build a fire.

Most important, a crystal-clear mountain stream flowed ten yards away.

Shelter and water would get her and the injured man through the coming cold night.

She always carried the ten essentials and then some in her pack, so she had emergency rations to see her through the next twenty-four hours. Of course, if the man woke and was hungry, she'd run out of food much sooner. But then, if he woke, he could walk his own sorry ass out of the woods.

She settled him on the wooden floor in front of the hearth, still strapped to the travois, then went to the stream to refill her water bottle. She splashed the chilly water on her face, overheated from the exertion of dragging a two-hundred-plus-pound man nearly a mile across hilly terrain.

Her shoulders burned, her knees ached, and her head throbbed with dehydration. She dropped a purification tablet into her water bottle but only waited a minute of the required thirty for the purification to take effect. She'd take her chances.

The water was crisp, cold, and tasted like iodine, but it was still the most refreshing drink she'd had in forever.

It was now after eight, long past the time she should have called the office to let them know she'd completed her survey for the day. Would anyone notice she'd failed to call in? Would anyone in the DNR office care if they did notice?

She pulled out her phone and typed out a quick text message. It failed to send; not enough signal. She'd expected that but knew there were places on the compound where the signal was too weak for voice calls, but texts still went through. She believed Vincent's last text message had been sent from such a place. For that reason, she always sent herself a text when she managed to stray onto a new area of Raptor land.

A noise in the woods—a stick cracking as if it had been stepped on?—startled her. She set down her phone and reached for the bear spray.

What the hell was she doing? The wind was kicking up as evening settled in, and she was stuck in the woods in one of the most remote forests in the United States. Worse, she was trespassing on the primary training ground of a paramilitary mercenary organization—which happened to be the one place on earth she was forbidden by court order from entering—and she had an injured stranger to watch over. Her first aid skills were rudimentary at best, and she didn't even know if the man was worth saving.

She studied the woods beyond the stream. Porcupine, wolf, caribou, bear, or any of a dozen other animals could have caused the sound. But there was also the chance it was a human predator.

It was a few weeks before the fall equinox, so even though the sun would set in a few hours, it wouldn't get completely dark, which meant if she built a fire in the hearth—and a clogged chimney didn't smoke them out—the smoke would be visible to anyone searching the area.

Which meant she couldn't build a fire for warmth, no matter how cold it got.

She toyed with the idea of leaving the man here and going straight to her truck. By herself, she could make it in two and a half hours. Three at most.

Isabel tucked her water bottle into the side pocket of her pack and stood with the bear spray still in her hand. Her knees wobbled, weak from the exertion of dragging the man through the woods. No way could she hike another six miles tonight. She'd go back inside the cabin, get out of the chill wind, check on the man, and rest for a few hours. She needed sleep. When her brain was clear and her head didn't throb so much, she'd be able to figure out what to do.

IT HAD TAKEN all of Alec's will to feign unconsciousness when he first came to as he was being dragged across jagged ground. His head hurt like hell, and he couldn't open one eye.

Who was pulling him? Where were they taking him?

How had he gotten here to begin with?

He thought back, trying to remember. He wasn't in Maryland. He'd gone on a business trip. Not for the campaign. It was Raptor business.

Where?

Not Hawaii.

Alaska. Yeah. Alaska. He peeked through one slitted eye and glimpsed a blurry forest canopy.

Definitely Alaska.

The compound was set to reopen. Next week.

That's right, I'm here to oversee the first training.

How long had he been here?

One day.

Had he even gone to the compound yet?

He didn't remember being there. He'd had a meeting scheduled, a one-on-one with Nicole, followed by a meeting with Falcon Team.

He remembered arriving in Fairbanks and driving south. And…that was it. Nothing after that. One moment he was driving, the next he was here, being dragged through the woods, none too gently.

His captor stopped at several points, but he didn't dare open his good eye when he was lowered to the ground. His one advantage was the fact that his captor had no clue he was conscious. It slowly dawned on him that his abductor was a woman, identifying the grunts and groans and curses as she struggled to haul his deadweight as that of a woman's voice.

What the hell?

Why was a woman hauling him through the woods? Why had she attacked him to begin with?

How had she attacked him?

The throbbing in his head told him whatever she'd done, it had been effective.

Tied down and being dragged, this wasn't the time for him to make a move. He'd wait, bide his time. Strike when just the thought of moving didn't make him want to vomit.

At last she dropped him inside a small, ancient, rotting cabin, and stepped outside. Once he was certain he was alone, he gingerly moved his arms and legs. No problem there. He turned his head. The room swam and nausea rose, but he could do it.

He felt at the ropes. He was tied to a tarp on a tree-branch frame. Clever. But she'd made a mistake. His hands, while bound, weren't immobilized. It didn't take much effort for him to slide free of the binding at his belt and work the knots that secured him to the travois until he'd freed himself.

Slowly, he rose, his balance wobbly, like a damn newborn colt, but again, he could do it.

"You sonofabitch! You made me drag you a mile when you could walk the whole time?"

Dammit! He'd been so focused on getting upright, he hadn't heard her approach. His Ranger buddies would laugh their asses off over this fuckup.

To hell with the throbbing in his head. This wasn't a time to hesitate. This was a time to fight through the nausea and pain. He lunged for her, grabbing her by the throat.

It didn't matter that she was a woman. No room for mercy given what she'd done to him.

She screamed, but the sound cut off as his grip tightened.

Blinding pain seared his good eye. His lungs burned. Then she landed a blow to his nuts. He released her, falling backward.

He doubled over and tried not to puke.

CHAPTER TWO

ISABEL KEPT THE bear spray out, ready to zap the bastard a second time should he so much as twitch in her direction. He'd been so close to her, she'd gotten a whiff of the painful pepper and struggled to get air into her burning lungs. She should have gone for the gun, but at least the spray—combined with her knee to his balls—had been effective.

"I should have left you in the woods to die," she said, after she was able to breathe again. Her voice shook. Badly.

She'd been a fool to rescue him. She could have hiked back to her car, called 9-1-1, and gone home for the night. If she'd done the smart thing, she'd be in the Tamarack Roadhouse right now enjoying a beer with Nicole.

Instead she was six miles from nowhere stuck in a rotting cabin with a man who'd just tried to kill her. She rubbed her throat. She bruised easily, and this was likely to be an ugly one.

"Who the hell *are* you?" she choked out.

"Right." He coughed and struggled to breathe. "As if"—another cough—"you don't know."

"I found you five miles deep in the Tanana Valley State Forest. You were beat to hell and don't have ID on you. I have no frigging clue who you are."

He'd rolled onto his back on the uneven floor, just a few feet from the travois where she'd originally left him. Slowly, his coughing abated, and he took in deep, wheezing breaths. After several minutes, he cocked his head toward her and squinted, then swore. Squinting must have caused the pepper to burn his eye again. "Do you have pepper spray wipes, so I can clean my eye?"

"Are you going to try to strangle me again?"

"I don't know."

"Then no."

He turned his face toward the ceiling, keeping both eyes closed. "Who are you? Why did you drag me here? Are you working for Stimson?"

Stimson? What was he talking about?

The sun had dropped behind a ridge, and the inside of the cabin was dark, shadowy. Some of the welts had subsided, and she could only see the good side of his face, without the swollen eye. For the first time, she saw his profile without being distracted by welts, bruises, or blood.

She knew who Stimson was, and suddenly this man's profile was familiar. Stimson was the hint she'd needed.

Dread washed through her, causing her to suck in a sharp breath. Instinctively, she scooted backward, increasing the distance between them until her back hit the log wall. "Holy shit. You're Alec Ravissant."

ALEC FORCED HIS burning eye open to get a good look at her face. Her shock appeared real. But he didn't know her. She could be an excellent actress. But he had nothing to gain by not playing along, and maybe if he pretended to believe her, she'd let her guard down. He could take her out and make a break for it.

Hard to believe he'd been taken down by this woman, who didn't appear to be an operative of any sort. From the weapons on her belt and her heavy backpack, he'd guess she was some sort of forest ranger. Except she wasn't in uniform. Maybe she was a hiking guide?

Christ, he was a frigging Army Ranger and he'd been beaten and abducted by a woman half his size? She must have had help. He couldn't imagine any scenario where she'd have been able to overpower him.

Except she just had.

Well, he was wounded already, she'd hit him with bear spray, and she'd had an open shot at the family jewels.

But how had she taken him down the first time? Maybe her car had been broken down by the side of the road, and he pulled over to help her? Vision in the one eye sucked, but he could still see she was pretty enough. She looked almost fragile with sweet, delicate features and full lips. He could have been a fool who fell for the oldest trick in the book—damsel in distress who didn't know spark plug from dipstick.

Well, it was clear he was the dipstick for underestimating her—twice. He wouldn't make that mistake a third time. "Yeah. That's me. Alec Ravissant, at your service." He again shifted to his back and closed his eyes.

Something plunked on the wood floor. From the sound, the object was moving closer. He cracked the one good eye open and turned his head to the side. Her lightweight aluminum water bottle slowly rolled toward him.

"It's water from the stream," she said. "I used a purification tablet, but given how cold the stream water is, it hasn't been long enough to eliminate giardia or cryptosporidium. Also, don't drink it if you're allergic to iodine."

He sat up and took the bottle. The room lurched again, but not as much as it had the first time. Condensation had built up on the battered metal cylinder. He pressed it against his swollen eye. The cold eased the pressure in his head just a tiny fraction, and even that small bit was a huge relief. "Thanks. I'll take my chances with the crypto."

He opened the bottle and first poured a small amount of cold water over both eyes, then downed half the bottle in one long drink.

"Finish it," she said. "I have plenty of purification tablets." She rummaged in her pack and tossed something else in his direction. Lightweight, the item landed in the no-man's-land midway between them. "That's a pepper spray wipe. For your eye."

"Thanks," he said again. He slowly scooted toward the packet, being careful not to make any sudden moves to startle her. It hadn't escaped his attention that she kept one hand on the canister at her belt. The wipe removed the burning oil from his skin, and at last he could really see again. He splashed more water on his swollen eye and was able to open it a bit as well. With some ibuprofen for the swelling and pain, he might be fit for human company. "Do you have any ibuprofen?"

"Yes. And I can make a cold compress—with stream water— for your eye as well. I have an emergency cold pack, but we should save it. The stream water is cold enough." She paused and studied him. "If you roll the water bottle to me, I'll toss you the ibuprofen, then go to the stream to refill the bottle."

It was a fair prisoner exchange, especially since he didn't have anything else to trade. But it was going to be a long-ass night if they both had to stay awake in an *Enemy at the Gates* sort of standoff.

He rolled the water bottle toward her, and she tossed him a pill pack. After extracting his promise not to follow her outside, she took her backpack and left him to get more water.

He didn't have much choice but to make that promise, and he would even keep it, although she was a fool for trusting him with nothing more than his word. As soon as he got his various aches under control, he'd turn his brain to seriously considering the matter of who she was and what she wanted from him. But right now, every time he started to follow that line of thought, his physical needs—splitting headache, near-blindness, what have you—took over and demanded attention.

And he still had no clue how he'd gotten into this situation.

ISABEL RETURNED TO the cabin, relieved to see he'd kept his word and hadn't moved from his ceded territory in the small, rectangular room. He had the back half; she'd taken the front. At least she had the only door. But she also had the broken window. Her territory would be colder.

She shivered as she stepped inside and pushed the heavy door closed. The swollen wood dragged against the floor, scraping off a layer of rotting timber. That the cabin was still standing was a testament to old-growth trees. The logs were so thick, the cabin would last another hundred years before it faded from existence. Then the only evidence a cabin had once stood here would be a moss-covered river-rock chimney tower, standing as proudly as its white spruce neighbors.

The wind had kicked up substantially, and she was chilled from those few minutes outside. Thank goodness they had four walls and a roof, because there was no way in hell she could share her emergency shelter tube tent with Alec Ravissant. The man was an injured bear with opposable thumbs, and he believed *she* was the person who'd beat the crap out of him.

As if she could take down a former Ranger like him all by herself. If he hadn't been hit so hard in the head, he might see how ridiculous the idea was. But then, maybe he did see and assumed she had an accomplice.

The problem was, if he knew her name, he'd never believe she was innocent. Her name would only convince him of her guilt. She had, after all, declared it her life's mission to get his precious compound shut down. And she'd succeeded—even if only temporarily.

Now it was about to reopen again, and he could easily assume this situation was her last desperate act to prevent the trainings from resuming.

She *did* have a beef with the man and the compound, but beating and abduction was a tad far-fetched, even for her.

"What's your name?" he asked.

Evasive answers would only make him suspicious. Lying was her only option. "Jenna," she said, thinking of a server at the Tamarack Roadhouse.

"Jenna what?" he persisted.

"Hayes," she said without hesitation. Hayes was her mother's maiden name and Isabel's middle name. Even if Alec Ravissant had read the most detailed dossier on her, he wasn't likely to remember that detail or, if he did, make the connection now.

"What were you doing—five miles, you say?—deep in the woods, when you found me?"

This was tricky. She couldn't admit to being an archaeologist, because odds were, he *would* make that connection. Most non-archaeologists didn't know a ton of archaeologists in their day-to-day lives, and whenever she mentioned her profession to someone, they immediately told her about every archaeologist they'd ever met or heard rumors about. But if she said she was just out on a day hike for fun, she had a feeling that would raise his suspicions even further. Few people hiked in bear country alone for fun.

Hell, few people hiked alone in bear country for work. Isabel was unique in that way. Her bosses didn't mind because it was cheaper to pay one person to survey rather than two—but she'd had to sign a dozen different release forms before they'd allowed it—and she didn't mind because being alone meant she had the freedom to stray onto Raptor land to look for the cave Vincent had told her about. If she could find the cave, she could prove his death was no accident.

Her brother had been murdered on Raptor land, by Raptor operatives. His death had been ruled a training accident, but what she knew of the incident, and what Vin had told her in his emails in the months before his death, didn't add up, and she believed the wounded man lying on the floor eight feet away may well have covered up Vin's murder.

"I'm waiting, Jenna."

Pushy bastard. For someone who'd been beat to hell and who probably couldn't take her in a staring match right now, he sure sounded confident. "I'm a geologist. I work for the Alaska Department of Natural Resources. There have been reports of poaching on some DNR mining claims." This was true; it just hadn't happened in this part of the forest.

"You were out looking for poachers *alone*?"

"No. I was looking for *evidence* of poaching, signs of recent digging and minerals taken. I didn't expect to run into anyone. But I found you."

"And you thought I was a poacher?"

"No. If I had, I wouldn't have dragged you here. I'd have left your sorry ass to die and returned to the office."

"Why didn't you think I was a poacher?"

"Your clothes. You're wearing slacks, and mineral thieves don't wear button-down, going-to-business-meeting shirts. But the kicker is your shoes. Any man who planned to walk this deep in the forest would wear a decent pair of hiking boots. Those shoes"—she twisted her lips in derision—"probably cost four times what my hiking boots cost, and they'll fall apart at the first drop of rain. Forget hiking across a glacier in them. Or, better yet, sell tickets. I'd pay good money to watch you ruin designer shoes and break your ass traversing a glacier in your metrosexual lame excuse for footwear."

Alec's mouth curved in a vague smile. "These are my campaign shoes."

Isabel snorted. "Good thing you're running for office in Maryland, because in Alaska, expensive shoes with no sole will get you laughed out of contention."

He wiggled his feet as he studied his footwear with his one good eye. "I hate these shoes. I wore them on the flight and planned to change as soon as I got to the compound. I didn't bring a suitcase, because I keep a full wardrobe—not the campaign kind—at the compound."

"So you just flew in today?"

His brow furrowed. "I think so. What day is it?"

"Thursday." She glanced at her watch. "Eight forty-three p.m., Alaska time."

"My plane landed in Fairbanks at eleven. Today."

"Is that the last thing you remember?"

His fingers drummed against the soft, rotting floorboards. "I remember driving. I was heading toward the compound. Then…nothing." He met her gaze. His one eye was clearer and the other opened slightly. She realized she'd never given him the promised cold cloth for his eye. "When and where did you find me?" he asked.

She inched forward. "If I give you a cold compress for your eye, do you promise not to hurt me?"

He held her gaze for a long moment, then slowly nodded. "I don't know what I believe—if you're innocent, or if you somehow abducted me—but I know I need you to survive. Even if I escaped here—from you—I don't know where I am. I could step outside and walk for five days in the wrong direction. So yes, I promise I won't hurt you."

His words were honest. Those of a soldier used to assessing threats and making the logical decision. Vin had been like that. She remembered it well, Vin's inner determination to do the smart thing, even if it didn't seem like the right thing.

Hell, that type of decision making was what led Vin to join the Army in the first place. And later, it was why he took the job with Raptor.

She swiped at her eye. Now was not the time to get caught up in messy emotions over her big brother. Right now, she needed to deal with Vin's former boss, who had just admitted that no matter what his suspicions were, not hurting Isabel was the smart thing.

She could live with that.

She grabbed the pack towel, which she'd doused in stream water, and her compass, and approached him, slowly, as she would a feral cat.

It was a good analogy. Alec Ravissant reminded her of a tiger, all sleek muscle and coiled energy. He was power and ferociousness in one beautiful package. Best to approach with caution.

He reminded her of Richard Parker, the tiger on the boat in *Life of Pi*. Alec needed her to survive. Lashing out, as he'd done earlier, had been instinctive. His nature. But now that he understood the situation, he'd scare her to bend her to his will, but he wouldn't rip open her throat. Not yet, anyway.

He was a Ranger. He knew how to bide his time.

And she'd better not forget it.

She stopped just out of his reach and dropped the damp towel on the floor. "For your eye." She lowered the compass more carefully, dangling the long lanyard from her fingers. "There is a mirror there, if you want to check out your cuts. Be careful with the compass—it's our only one, our only hope to find our way out of these woods."

She retreated quickly, resuming her seat with her back braced against the log wall. He took the towel first and pressed it to his eye, then took up the compass. He studied his reflection in the small mirror. "It's too dark in here to see much."

"If I build a fire, whoever assaulted you might see the smoke."

He shrugged. "I'm cold. It's a risk I'm willing to take."

As if to prove his point, the wind whistled through the broken window. It *was* cold, and would only get colder as the night wore on. But still, his request was shortsighted and proved he still believed *she* was his only threat. The risk involved in proving him wrong was too much. "Yeah, well, I'm not. I found you and dragged you here because, for some stupid reason, I couldn't let you die, but that doesn't mean I'm willing to risk more for you."

He shrugged and studied his reflection in the mirror, making her wonder if she'd passed or failed some sort of test. "Butterfly bandages?" he asked.

She nodded. "You were bleeding pretty badly."

"Probably why my head hurts like hell, but the ibuprofen is helping."

Would it kill him to say thank you? She'd not only bandaged him and given him the painkiller; she'd also dragged all two hundred pounds of him a mile through the forest. Every muscle in her body ached from the effort, and his first greeting was his hands on her throat.

Ungrateful bastard.

She pulled a trail mix energy bar from her backpack and broke it in two. She paused before tossing him half. "You'll get this after I get my compass back."

He slid her compass across the floor. "You think I can't navigate by stars?"

She laughed. His temper or his headache had gotten the best of him. He wasn't thinking. "Go ahead and try it. But it's early September. You won't see a star in the sky for another week. The sun doesn't go low enough below the horizon for full darkness. Plus tonight—it's cloudy, with a bitter wind. You want to leave? Be my guest. But I'm staying here until morning."

She tossed him the energy bar, then draped her compass around her neck. "I'm going to sleep. Keep in mind, I'm jumpy when I'm stuck sleeping on a hard rotting floor not far from an idiot politician whose life I saved—who hasn't even bothered to say 'thank you' yet—and who may still be in danger. In such situations, I sleep with my pistol in one hand and bear spray in the other. So if you don't want to suffer, leave me the fuck alone." With that, she pulled out her emergency shelter and slipped between the thin Mylar sheets. If he was cold, he could cuddle with his stupid, expensive shoes.

She was off duty for the night.

CHAPTER THREE

ALEC WANTED TO laugh and groan and maybe even punch something. At least the pressure in his head had eased. The ibuprofen had helped a lot, and the cold compress soothed in a way that almost tipped the scales from pain to pleasure.

Jenna Hayes. Just looking at her could give a man pleasure. Funny that it took him so long to notice that, but then, aside from being in agony and even blinded for a while, he wasn't exactly inclined to find her attractive. She might have beaten the shit out of him and abducted him. That sort of diminished a woman's overall appeal.

Did he believe she'd somehow done this to him?

The jury was still out on that question, but as his head cleared, he could admit to having doubts.

He shivered as another gust of wind rattled the unbroken window. The broken pane was leeward, but with the way the wind whipped around the cabin, some gusts still found the opening. He studied the travois. Clever of her to have built it. It was the sort of thing he'd learned to make in survival training, but he'd never needed one until today.

Holes had worn through the tarp from being dragged across acres of rock with his weight pressing down. He had scratches on his lower back and butt in matching locations. Knowing how she'd struggled to pull his weight, it was no wonder she'd been pissed to discover he could've walked—the last quarter mile or so, anyway. He could have made the journey a hell of a lot easier on her if he'd admitted to being awake.

He reached for the travois and stood.

"What the hell do you think you're doing?" she asked.

"I'm going to wedge this in the window, to block the wind."

She sat up, grabbed her pack, and scooted away from the broken window, giving him wide berth. She nodded her permission for him to approach.

Yeah, he'd been an asshole for trying to strangle her. He'd

earned her distrust. But he wasn't exactly thinking straight at the time.

He shoved the narrow edge of the travois through the broken pane. He considered pocketing a shard of glass for a weapon, but what would he do with it? He wouldn't cut her. For all he knew, she really had saved his life.

He pushed the contraption upward until it was wedged tightly in the opening, the top half of the travois outside the cabin, the wider, flared end inside, with the gaping opening blocked by the tarp. The wind wouldn't dislodge it, and only slight drafts would enter the cabin around the edges.

They wouldn't be warm, but they wouldn't freeze either.

He returned to his spot on the floor in front of the cold hearth. "I don't suppose you have another emergency blanket?"

"No." She pulled the shiny blanket tighter around her. It flashed and crackled as she rolled to her side and presented her back to him.

He smiled. That answered any question he might've had about sharing. He eyed the tarp. He'd just used *his* blanket to block the wind. Well, he'd sure as hell had worse nights' sleep in the Army, both during training and on ops. He lay down and closed his eyes.

This felt like an op. Like the old days, before bullshit campaigning and politics. He'd been reluctant to run for the open senate seat in Maryland, but Curt Dominick had convinced him he could do more good as a US senator than as Raptor's CEO. Curt had honed his persuasive skills in the courtroom, where he'd been a hell of a prosecutor before being appointed US Attorney for the District of Columbia and eventually US Attorney General. He'd been damned convincing, but Alec had doubted his decision to run for office just about every day since throwing his hat in the ring.

The shit of it was, as much as he hated campaigning, it turned out he was *good* at it. He'd won the primary, and, with a little more than sixty days left in the campaign, it was too late to back out now.

He studied the woman curled up in the emergency blanket. Survival, Evasion, Resistance, and Escape Training—better known as SERE—had never covered this situation.

He couldn't help but wonder if this was somehow related to the campaign. But that made no sense at all. He was running for office in Maryland, not Alaska. And he might be fuzzy on the details of how he got here, but he'd seen enough of the woods to know he was definitely in Alaska.

Maybe tomorrow, today would make more sense.

ISABEL FELT A little guilty keeping the blanket when the man was injured. But still. He'd tried to strangle her. No blanket seemed a fitting punishment.

She closed her eyes. She was exhausted, and the evening had been tense, scary, and confusing. She just wanted the oblivion of sleep. Hard to believe that a few hours ago, she'd been singing happy show tunes. The soundtrack for the night was vastly different. Unsettling. Discordant. Instrumental, it had no hook to hold on to, no familiar bridge or melody. Useless for scaring away bears, because there were no words to sing.

Did one sing to ward off tigers, or was that just a bear thing? Bears, she could handle—or rather, she knew what to do—but she had no knowledge or skills with tigers. She'd never imagined being stuck on a life raft with one. Or stuck in an old, musty, decaying cabin. Whatever.

She dozed lightly, never quite sinking into deep sleep. Sometime after one a.m., she felt compelled to check on Alec. He'd had a nasty blow to the head, and she'd never really examined him to see if he had a concussion.

She set her gun next to the backpack—so he couldn't grab it from her—but kept the bear spray in hand—just in case—and silently crawled toward him.

She paused just out of his reach and studied him. His face was relaxed in sleep. The swelling around his eye had gone down, so there was just a slight bulge around the lid and cheek. When it disappeared completely, he'd be every bit as handsome as the campaign photos she'd seen.

She could see why he'd been so successful. He had the polish of a politician and the rugged edges of a soldier, and it translated well in TV interviews. Up close and personal, he had presence even when wounded. He was big, imposing, and at least one reporter—who, Isabel had figured, had a crush on him—had described his eyes as a clear, compelling topaz blue. She'd have to take the reporter's word on that, because she'd only gotten a glimpse of burning, puffy, red eyes.

But then, she wasn't exactly seeing him on his best day.

She touched his forehead. His skin was cold. Scary cold. She immediately checked for a pulse and found one, thank God.

But still, he was too cold for comfort.

Shit. There was only one solution. Well, two. Either give him her blanket, or share it with him.

The smart thing would be to share it. They'd both be warm. They'd both get the rest they needed to face the hike to her truck tomorrow.

But sharing a blanket, getting up close and personal with Alec Ravissant, definitely didn't feel like the right thing.

The right thing would be to give him the blanket and get the hell out of the cabin, head back to her truck alone. When she arrived home, she could call Raptor and tell them where they could find their boss.

The smart thing, or the right thing?

"If you're trying to decide if you should give me your blanket," Alec said softly, "forget it. I won't take it from you. I can handle a little chill."

Crap. He was awake, meaning the right thing wasn't an option. If she tried to leave, she had no doubt he'd follow her. And he was in no condition to traipse six miles through the windy woods in the middle of the night.

"No, I was debating sharing it with you."

His mouth curved in a slow smile. "You wanna get close to my body, Jenna?"

She rolled her eyes at his tone even as she stiffened at the fake name. He was going to be so pissed when he found out who she really was. "No, but I don't want you to die after I worked so hard to save your ungrateful life. It would be disappointing to know my shoulders ache for nothing." She stood. "Can I trust you not to hurt me if we share the blanket?"

"Yes."

She'd just have to take him at his word, because there was no way she'd bring the bear spray into the tube tent with her. Not when he could grab it the moment she drifted to sleep. She set the spray next to the gun and grabbed the Mylar tent.

"It's not a regular emergency blanket, it's the tent kind—a long tube. We'll have to shimmy into it."

"No problem," he said.

Yeah, no problem for one person, but a little awkward for two, especially when she didn't want to touch him. The tube tent crackled as he slid in first, making even more noise when she followed. He was a big man, with wide, muscular shoulders. No matter how much she tried to avoid him, her body brushed against his.

"I'm not contagious, Jenna."

"I know, but I'm not in the mood to be strangled again."

"I'm sorry," he said, his voice quiet and sincere. "I wish I hadn't attacked you. It hadn't occurred to me that you were helping me, not abducting me."

She rolled over and faced him. "You honestly thought I'd be capable of abducting you—a former Ranger—all by myself?"

"I have no memory of what happened to me. For all I knew, you had accomplices. Plus, my brain wasn't exactly clear at the time. But for what it's worth, I'm sorry."

"It never crossed my mind that you might not remember what happened to you, so I never considered that you'd think I was somehow the villain here."

He reached toward her, and she stiffened, but then his fingers gently probed her neck, caressing the skin he'd bruised. A strange, fluttery feeling started low in her belly. A sensation she didn't like at all. Not when Alec Ravissant was the person who caused it.

"If you hadn't found me," he said in a low, warm tone, "who knows how long I would have remained unconscious? I'd have lost a lot more blood and wouldn't have shelter. Thank you for saving my life. I'm in your debt."

She realized she was staring into two eyes, not just the one good one, and while it was too dark to gauge if they were indeed a crystal topaz blue, she couldn't deny they were compelling. And she was glad his condition had improved.

Also, after hours of waiting for him to acknowledge what she'd done for him, he'd done a rather nice job of it. She gave him a soft smile. "You're welcome. Now, let's get some sleep so we can hike out of here tomorrow." She rolled over, presenting her back to him and maintaining as much distance as the tube tent would allow.

His arm snaked around her waist and pulled her back against his chest. He tucked his knees behind hers and her butt pressed snugly against his crotch. "We'll be warmer if we spoon. One of those things you learn in survival training."

She snorted. "Yeah, I bet you Rangers all snuggled up tight."

"If it were a matter of survival, we would."

His breath tickled her ear, causing more unwelcome flutters in her belly. But damn, he did feel nice and warm at her back. She'd been colder than she wanted to admit.

"Do you have a husband or boyfriend, Jenna?"

She stiffened. Was he going to hit on her now?

"Relax. I'm just asking because I want to know if anyone is going to hear about this and demand an explanation. As it is, if the press gets wind of this, they're going to have a field day."

Oh God. There would be a massive media frenzy. And when the press learned her name…*oh shit.*

She probably should tell him right now.

But if she did, this fragile trust would go away. And he might just try to strangle her again.

Face it, the only good time to tell him would be via telephone.

"You haven't answered my question."

"No. No boyfriend. No husband." *No brother. No family.* "Just me," she added.

"Well then, maybe to thank you for saving my life, you'll let me take you out to dinner."

She knew he expected a teasing rejoinder. Something about getting off cheap if all she got was a lousy meal, but her throat had gone dry, and she couldn't muster the words.

Dinner with Alec Ravissant? Not just no, but hell no. And if he knew who she was, he'd feel the exact same way.

Finally, she found enough voice to say, "Go to sleep, Alec."

He chuckled, tightened his arm around her, and did exactly that.

OF COURSE, THIS morning of all mornings, he'd wake with a morning missile. But then, he had a soft, warm woman's round ass pressed up against said missile, and he was only human.

God how he wanted to rock his hips and rub his erection against that ass. She smelled good too—warm, earthy, with a hint of yesterday's shampoo. Her hair was carrot orange laced with blonde streaks. It was bound in a loose braid, and just enough strands had escaped to make him think she had wild curls, the corkscrew kind that would wrap around his fingers as he cradled her head and kissed her.

Whoa. Time to put on the mental brakes. That fantasy would be all too easy to make happen. But he couldn't go there. Not until he was certain she really was an innocent geologist who was in the right place at the right time to save his life.

But if she *were* an innocent geologist… Well, that changed things. His campaign manager had put the kibosh on dating during the campaign, but surely dinner with the woman who'd saved his life was the exception. Hell, the press would go nuts for it.

Plus, he'd always had a thing for redheads. Sunlight filtered in through the intact dirty glass pane, revealing hundreds of adorable freckles he hadn't seen in the shadows last night. Curls, freckles, and full lips that begged for attention. Plus she'd saved his life. No wonder he had a hard-on.

However, if she woke up and felt his erection at her back, she'd likely freak out, and rightly so. Spooning for warmth wasn't tacit agreement for anything more, and he hoped to hell she'd understand that *he* knew that. The erection wasn't anything more than a basic biological reaction, no matter how much he wanted to grind into her.

He ran through a litany of non-sexy thoughts, realizing, as he did so that he'd been so focused on the almost painful erection, it hadn't registered that he felt much better this morning. His head still throbbed, but nothing like last night.

Thinking about his injuries was the perfect cure for the inconvenient erection, and he turned his thoughts to yesterday and how he'd ended up here with Jenna.

He remembered a bit more. He was driving, heading toward the compound, nearing the turn off to Tamarack, when a light flashed into his eyes. Repeatedly. Not a trick of the sun. Deliberate.

Then a moose had darted into the road.

THANK GOD HIS erection went down, because it had felt far too good against Isabel's ass. It had taken some serious willpower to feign sleep and not let on she was aware of the hard man with the even harder prick pressed against her. She'd wanted so badly to grind her butt against him and see what happened.

Guilt stabbed her.

The man she'd wanted to grind against was *Alec Ravissant*. What the hell was wrong with her?

She rolled forward, to put some space between her and the man who might have covered up her brother's murder to save his business. To save his *campaign*.

Behind her, the coldhearted politician cleared his throat. "Sorry. It happens. Bad morning for it."

She pressed her face into the floor and shook her head, unable to speak. She didn't blame him. Couldn't blame him. At least, not for *that*. That was just biology and proximity.

"Jenna, I wouldn't have touched you. I promise."

The hell of it was, she couldn't tell him why she was upset. She finally had Alec Ravissant's undivided attention and couldn't tell him what she thought of him. She certainly couldn't admit that being turned on by his erection had triggered a deep wave of self-loathing.

She cleared her throat. "I know." She rolled over to face him, the Mylar enclosure crackling with every movement.

Sunlight sparked across the shiny tent and glinted in his dark hair. Those clear blue eyes were no longer bloodshot. He sported a day's worth of dark stubble on his firm, square jaw and was more handsome than was reasonable, given the situation.

She had never quite registered how handsome he was. Figures she'd notice upon waking up after spending the night in his arms, even if it had been purely for survival reasons. "I need to tell you something. I didn't tell you last night because you tried to strangle me, and I was afraid of your reaction."

His jaw tightened. "I'm sorry about that. I don't think I can ever apologize enough—"

She pressed her fingers to his lips to stop him. "I—"

The front door burst in at the same time the intact window shattered. All at once, men sporting forest camouflage and toting big guns poured into the cabin from both openings.

They circled her and Alec, but every gun pointed at her.

She met the gaze of the leader. Brad Fraser, one of the operatives she sometimes hung out with at the Roadhouse. She had no idea if he was friend or foe at this moment, but the gun pointed at her head argued for foe.

His brow furrowed in confusion. "Isabel? What the fuck? *You* kidnapped Rav?"

CHAPTER FOUR

"ISABEL?" ALEC ROLLED backward, splitting the Mylar tent along the taped seam. *"Isabel Dawson?"* He swore. Holy shit. He'd been ready to believe she was the innocent geologist she'd claimed to be, but she was the nut job archaeologist with a vendetta against his company. A vendetta against *him.*

He jumped to his feet, ignoring the ache the movement triggered behind his eyes, and faced Brad Fraser, who was one of his top operatives and the leader of Falcon team. "How did you find me?"

"It took half the night, but we finally found your car in the woods. There were all-terrain vehicle tracks from there, which we followed until they disappeared. It took us a while to pick up the trail again, but finally, we found a pool of blood." He looked down. "Shit, Rav. That scared us. We feared the worst. But there were tracks extending directly from the blood, and it was easy to follow."

Yeah. The travois trail may as well have been lit with neon. He'd figured that was to his advantage, and he was right. Stupid of Isabel not to realize that.

But then, it was stupid of her to pull this crazy stunt at all.

He reached out a hand to Fraser. "You have cuffs?"

"Yes, sir." He dropped a pair in Alec's outstretched hand.

Alec turned to Isabel, who'd stood while his back was turned, and grabbed her arm, pulling it behind her. "What the hell? I saved your *life!*"

"Sure you did, *Jenna.*" He took her other wrist and locked the cuff around it.

"I was about to tell you! I lied because you tried to *strangle* me. You made it clear you thought I'd abducted you. I was afraid of what you'd do—what you'd believe—if I told you my name."

"Good call. But then, I've always heard you're crazy, not stupid." He pushed her toward one of the operatives behind

Fraser. The guy looked familiar, but at the moment, Alec couldn't come up with a name. Hell, he considered himself lucky he could stand without the room spinning. "Take her to the compound and put her in one of our holding cells."

"No," a uniformed officer said as he stepped into the cabin. "She's coming with me."

Alec faced the officer and was relieved it only took a moment to pull a name out of his throbbing brain. "Lieutenant Westover?"

The officer nodded.

If Alec remembered correctly, the man had worked for Raptor but took the job at the new state trooper post around the time Alec acquired the company. Alec had all employees vetted when he took over—weeding out those who were loyal to Robert Beck, the former owner who was now sitting in a federal prison—but Westover had escaped that scrutiny, leaving Alec to wonder if the man could be trusted.

Not that he had a choice. Westover was the only law in Tamarack. As much as Alec wanted Isabel Dawson in his custody, he didn't have any legal standing to detain her. "You're arresting her?" he asked.

"She abducted you?"

Alec hesitated. A light in his eyes. A moose on the road. Then…nothing. "She tied me up and brought me here. I don't know how, or why, or if she had help. I don't remember."

"*Tied you up?*" she shrieked. "You ungrateful ass!" The high pitch disappeared as her voice shook with anger. "I tied you to the *travois*, so I could drag you to shelter. You'd have died exposed in the wind last night if I hadn't done that."

Westover frowned. "I can detain her. But we'll need more. A search warrant of her cabin could get us what we need to charge her."

Fraser leaned toward Alec. "Rav, we've got her on the restraining order."

"What do you mean? The restraining order is to keep her off Raptor land—not away from me."

"We're on Raptor land right now," Fraser said.

Surprise rippled through him. He'd try to figure out what she was doing here later. For now, it gave him the leverage he needed. To Westover, Alec said, "Book her on the restraining order violation, then see if you can get a search warrant for her cabin."

Westover bristled, probably at Alec's commanding tone, but he ignored the officer's irritation. He was used to giving orders and didn't see a reason to change now. Westover turned to Isabel and launched into her Miranda rights.

Isabel glared at Alec, interrupting the speech to say to him, "You're every bit as vile as I've always believed." Her eyes teared. "I'm on Raptor land because this was the only shelter for miles. I should have left you to die." She turned and headed for the open door. "C'mon, Westover. Take me to jail."

"THE ATV TRACKS ended on the other side of the hill about two hundred yards from here. Given the terrain, it took some time to find the blood trail, but once we did, it led us here." Fraser pointed to a glacier-smoothed bedrock outcrop heavily splattered with blood. A pool of it had gathered in a bowl-shaped depression in the stone.

Not just any blood. Alec's blood. From an injury he didn't remember receiving, in an assault he didn't remember happening. He must have lain on the rock for a long time for that much blood to have pooled in the depression. That argued for Isabel's claim she'd found him.

He touched the butterfly bandages on his temple. Had she built the travois while he lay bleeding and then bandaged him? Somehow, he couldn't imagine that.

She wouldn't even let him drink stream water without warning him about iodine allergies and the risk of crypto in the water. She wouldn't have left him to bleed, not even while she built the life-saving travois.

He picked up shavings she'd created while stripping the poles. He was impressed that she not only had the tools, she had the knowledge necessary to figure out how to haul all two hundred and fifteen pounds of him a mile through the forest. It would have been far easier for her if she'd left him, hiked out, then called for help.

But he could well have died before help arrived if she'd made that choice.

He turned to Fraser. "How well do you know Isabel Dawson?"

The operative shrugged. "Pretty well. We have a beer together every few weeks."

An unpleasant feeling dangerously close to jealousy settled in his gut. "You ever go out with her?"

Fraser tipped his head back and laughed. "Hell, no. Isabel

doesn't date Raptor operatives. Period."

His relief was just as unwelcome as the jealousy. He felt strangely possessive of her after sharing her body heat, but she was so far from being his, the notion was laughable.

"She mostly hangs out with Nicole at the Roadhouse. Nic probably knows her better than anyone in Tamarack."

"Seriously? The woman who's been trying to shut down the compound hangs out with the compound director?"

"Yeah. They liken it to the wolf and the sheepdog in the Warner Brothers cartoons. Battle each other all day, but at night, they clock out and have a beer."

How did he not know Nicole Markwell, the Alaska Compound's executive director, was drinking buddies with the woman who'd caused so many problems for him these last months? He'd been busy with the campaign, but this indicated he'd been more out of touch than he'd thought. Proof that stepping down so he could focus on the election was the right choice for the company.

He touched his throbbing temple. He'd planned to tell Nic about the CEO change first, then Falcon team, but it was Friday morning and he hadn't even made it to the compound yet. His replacement, Keith Hatcher, would arrive tomorrow. Hell, given his disappearance, for all he knew, Keith was already en route to Tamarack.

One thing at a time. Right now he had a decision to make about Isabel. To Fraser, he said, "What's your take on her? Do you think she did this?"

Fraser sat on a downed log, likely the same spot where Isabel had sat to strip the poles for the travois. "Honestly, Rav, I was shocked as hell to see her in the cabin with you. Isabel Dawson is a zealot for her cause, but I don't think she'd ever deliberately hurt anyone."

"Then why did you mention the restraining order? I didn't know we were on Raptor land." A corner of his mouth kicked up. Of course she hadn't told him that useful piece of information. If he'd known where he was, he might have tried to steal the compass and head to the training ground.

Fraser shrugged. "No matter what I think, her being there was suspicious. She needs to be investigated, and it'll be easier if she's locked up. If we don't find anything, you can withdraw the restraining order violation complaint. Her excuse that the cabin was the only shelter for miles is reasonable. It's also true." He shook his head. "Makes me wonder how she knew about it. None of us knew it was there."

The operative had a good point. The trail cut by the travois had been as straight a line as the terrain allowed. She'd known about the cabin.

Fraser met Alec's gaze. "The question is, what do you believe?"

"I think she saved my life, and I thanked her by having Westover arrest her."

"Do you want to go to town and post her bail?"

He rubbed the back of his neck. "Yeah. I do."

"You should probably go to the compound first. Get a shower. We tried to keep a lid on it, but your disappearance hit the wire. National reporters could already be in town."

Alec frowned. *Shit.* This would be all over the news in Maryland. But Isabel was locked up because of him, because he'd lost his head when he discovered who she was and allowed himself to forget everything she'd done for him.

She believed her brother's accidental death had been deliberate and his people had covered up the crime. As far as he knew, she hated him with every fiber of her being. No wonder she'd been upset when she woke up with his erection pressed to her spine. His touch probably made her skin crawl, and yet, knowing exactly who he was, when she'd discovered he was cold in the middle of the night, she'd shared her blanket and body heat with him.

Because that was who she was.

She didn't deserve to be in the cell in Tamarack, and if he made her sit there for another minute because he needed to shower to put on a polished face for the press, he didn't deserve the senate seat he was running for. "No. I want to go to town now."

ISABEL PACED THE tiny jail cell, anger coursing through her. This was the most ridiculous, outrageous outcome for being a Good Samaritan that she could imagine. Another show tune came to mind, this one "No Good Deed" from *Wicked.* Even worse than the anger was the fear that lurked behind it. What if…what if because she was in custody, the police didn't bother to search for the real culprits? What if the prosecutor filed assault and abduction charges?

What if she was convicted and went to prison for abducting

Alec Ravissant?

Surely that couldn't happen.

She'd been arrested for violating the restraining order. There was no way around that. She was guilty. Hell, if Alec Ravissant knew exactly how many times she'd violated the order, she'd be facing serious jail time for that alone.

At least because the order wasn't stalking or domestic violence related, there was a simple bail schedule, with a hearing to follow. She'd probably need a lawyer for that—at least in this one instance, she'd had good reason to be on Raptor land—and shuddered to think of the cost. Even more daunting than the financial burden of bail and attorneys was that there was no court in Tamarack, just a small state trooper post with a two-cell jail. Westover had explained on their long hike out of the forest that some of the remote jails could accept bond payments, but Tamarack wasn't one of them. Everything had to be processed at the Fairbanks courthouse, which was two hours away by car.

Isabel didn't know anyone who could drive to Fairbanks and post her bail with the promise that she'd pay them back the five hundred bucks as soon as she was sprung.

Her closest friend in Tamarack was probably Nicole Markwell—Alec's top employee. It was pretty damn unlikely Nicole would give up her career to help Isabel. Second to Nicole was Jenna, the waitress whose name she'd borrowed. Jenna might do it, but she probably didn't have the money, plus she worked Fridays at the Roadhouse. It was too much to ask a woman who lived paycheck to paycheck, especially when they weren't *that* close.

But still, with no other choice, she'd called Jenna and left a message, asking if she knew anyone who could discreetly make the trip to Fairbanks, because if no one posted her bail before close of business, the court would close for the weekend and she'd be stuck in this jail until Monday.

She shuddered.

As far as jails went, she supposed it was fine—it was hardly ever used and therefore clean, and she wasn't likely to have company—but she wasn't a fan of the being-locked-up part. She was a hiker. She chafed at being indoors unless she was safe and warm and dry in a cozy cabin while weather raged outside. Being confined to a cold cell was just about her worst nightmare. A taste of what she would face if no evidence was found to exonerate her.

Given her history with Raptor, she was guilty until proven innocent.

Alec had said his plane landed at eleven. She'd found him after five. During that whole period of time, she'd been in the woods by herself, out of reach by cell phone. No alibi. Nothing. Her future hinged on whether or not the man she'd stupidly declared her own private war on suddenly remembered what had happened to him. Except, given that private war and the blow to the head he'd taken, he could just as well "remember" her attacking him. Head-trauma injuries and memory were tricky things. She'd researched that enough in the months since Vin's death.

Officer Paul Westover stepped into the outer room of the two-cell block. "It's your lucky day, Isabel. I just received notice from the court in Fairbanks that you made bond."

"Really? Jenna found someone?"

The officer shrugged. "I don't know. I just have the bond receipt, which means I can release you."

He unlocked the cell, and she followed him into the room where she'd been photographed and fingerprinted.

Joyce Bowman, the post administrator, smiled at her tentatively. "If you want, you can go out the back door, sugar. I think every gossip in town has stopped in to say hi today, wondering who we had in custody for abducting Alec Ravissant." Joyce's Texas drawl sounded out of place in Tamarack, but then, Isabel had learned not long after moving here that most people were from somewhere else. Only about half the town's three-hundred-plus residents were actually from the area. Others were called here, tourists who came to Alaska for a week, then returned a month later, almost in a daze, not quite understanding their rash decision to move, yet knowing they'd at last found home.

Joyce was one of those.

Having come to Alaska for an entirely different reason, Isabel didn't quite understand. She usually got the itch to move after living in a new place for eight months. Unless she was in school and required to stay, she rarely lasted a full year at one address. There was much she loved about Alaska—and even Tamarack in particular—but she'd been here nearly ten months. If it weren't for her quest to prove Vin had been murdered, she'd probably already be gone.

She cleared her throat. "You didn't mention me?"

"I told them the truth. The FBI is investigating Alec

Ravissant's disappearance, and we don't have anyone in lockup charged with anything related to his abduction."

She winked at Isabel, who felt both relieved and grateful. If her boss learned about her arrest from the news, the man would flip. He'd lectured her about Raptor often enough. If he guessed she'd visited Raptor property during her solo surveys in the area—including yesterday—it wouldn't matter that she'd done it during her lunch breaks, she'd be fired.

"Wait here, sugar. I'll get your backpack." A moment later, Joyce returned with Isabel's pack and about three dozen zipper-top bags containing everything that had been inside. "Because you have pending charges, we have to keep the gun and bear spray. But this is the rest of it. Just sign the bottom of the inventory form, and you'll be all set."

Isabel scanned the list. The loss of the gun was annoying but understandable. Besides, she had a shotgun and more bear spray in her cabin. She was relieved to see her special Rite in the Rain notebook in a sealed bag. That notebook held enough incriminating evidence to nail her on the restraining order violation, making her very glad she used UTM coordinates in her notes instead of wordy descriptions of the locations she'd visited.

She frowned, noticing one important item not on the inventory, and paused before signing her name. "Where's my cell phone? You can't confiscate that, can you?"

"No."

"Then why isn't it here?"

"It wasn't in the pack." Joyce tapped the list. "This is everything that was inside."

Isabel didn't want to accuse the woman of stealing a smartphone, but where could it be? Then her eyes widened as she remembered. She'd left it by the stream. She'd set it down when she heard a noise in the woods.

But later, she'd gone back to the stream to get Alec more water. If her phone had been there, she'd have seen it.

CHAPTER FIVE

OFFICER WESTOVER WASN'T impressed with Isabel's theory that whoever had assaulted Alec might have taken her phone. "Why would they take your phone? And if they'd left him for dead as you say they did, then once they realized he was still alive, why not go after you in the cabin?"

She shrugged, irritated the man didn't recognize this for the startling clue that it might be. "Maybe because I had a gun and bear spray and was on alert?" She looked down at the water bottle, remembering the feel of it in her hands as she sat by the stream yesterday. "I heard a noise and grabbed the spray immediately."

"I'd add it to your statement, Isabel, but you refused to make a statement." Westover gave her a nasty grin. He'd been pissed she actually understood what "the right to remain silent" meant, because this was likely the biggest crime he'd ever get to investigate—since he'd flat-out refused to investigate her brother's murder, following the company line and saying it was an accident—and he was no doubt bummed he'd be out of the loop of the FBI investigation.

As if the kidnapping and attempted murder of a US Senate candidate who was also the wealthy CEO of a mercenary organization would be investigated by Tamarack's finest. And by finest, she meant *only* police officer.

She crammed all fifteen thousand plastic bags Joyce had separated her stuff into inside the backpack and headed for the back door of the post, bracing herself for a long walk. She'd left her truck deep in the woods two miles from town, but according to Westover, it had been impounded and would be searched for evidence that she'd kidnapped Alec.

Her cabin was five miles from Tamarack, on a lonely, ten-acre parcel that bordered the Raptor compound on one side and the state forest on the other. She was exhausted, but dammit, she had no other way to get home. She couldn't exactly call Nicole and ask her for a ride. Asking Raptor's compound director for a ride home from jail fell in the same category as asking for bail money.

So she'd walk, even though it meant five miles—she glanced out the window—in the rain, after an exhausting twenty-four hours in which she'd been assaulted, arrested, and had very little sleep.

Joyce patted her on the back as she unbolted the rear door. "If you wait at the Roadhouse, I can give you a ride when I clock out in another hour."

She glanced out at the rain again, considering the offer. An hour at the Tamarack Roadhouse. A beer sounded good right now, but she was a wreck. She hadn't showered since yesterday morning and had slept in a rotting cabin. She was tired to her bones, and hanging out in the Roadhouse was difficult for her on a normal night. She was fine once she settled in; it was that first ten minutes she struggled with, entering the room and the sudden quiet that inevitably greeted her—*the crazy woman who wants to destroy the biggest employer in town has arrived*—before conversation resumed. Her basic need to be among people usually forced her to face that initial discomfort, and in spite of her crusade, she'd made friends who made her forays into public enjoyable. Worth the anxiety and risk.

But tonight would be worse than usual. She'd bet she was on everyone's shortlist of people most likely to abduct Alec Ravissant. Showing up grubby from the field would only confirm their beliefs.

"Thanks, but I think I'll walk."

"But sugar, you don't have bear spray or ana'thing. Given where your cabin is, that's dangerous."

Isabel grimaced. "In all my months of hiking the forest, the first time I ever needed the bear spray was last night, when Alec Ravissant tried to strangle me. I'll be fine."

"Call me when you get home?"

She shrugged. "No phone." But she was touched. She'd never been particularly close to Joyce, but then, she wasn't particularly close to anyone. It was surprising and rather sweet to know the woman considered her a friend, that she would worry about her.

She opened the back door just as the sky opened up, and the light rain turned into a downpour. Five miles in a downpour. Not even Isabel was up for that tonight.

Behind her, Joyce said, "Go to the Roadhouse. I'll pick you up in an hour."

On impulse, Isabel turned and hugged the woman, surprising them both. She wasn't a hugger, and pretty much everyone in town knew it.

At least the rain washed some of the forest grime from her skin as she darted down the alley behind the jail to the back door of the Roadhouse. She pounded on the service entrance—it was raining too hard to waste time walking around to the front—and was relieved when Jenna opened the door.

"Isabel!" she said, ushering her in out of the rain. "How did you make bail?"

She stepped inside, shivering, and dripping enough water to form a pond in the commercial kitchen. "I thought you...?"

"No. I called a few friends in Fairbanks, but no one answered. Maybe one of them got my message in time?" Jenna handed her a stack of kitchen rags. "I've got an order up. Get dried off and head into the taproom. I'll bring you some salmon chowder."

She left Isabel to load a tray and deliver it, while Isabel blotted rainwater from her clothes and hair. Finally marginally decent, she headed for the front of the house. Soup sounded like the greatest, most wonderful food on the planet, and the owner's salmon chowder was her favorite.

Entering the taproom from the back, she was halfway to a table before the usual and accustomed hush fell. First a logger seated at the bar saw her, then he tapped the shoulder of his friend, and it snowballed from there. Tonight's hush was worse than usual, as half of Falcon team sat at a table in the middle of the bar—the same men who'd been in the cabin this morning—and gazes darted from Isabel to the team and back, as if everyone expected a scene.

She dropped into a chair at a table on the edge of the room, catching Brad Fraser's gaze as she did so. She glared at him.

He stood and crossed the room to her, a beer in his hand and an apologetic smile on his handsome face.

"Go away, Brad. I have nothing to say to you."

He pulled out a chair and sat down. "Tough. I've got lots to say to you."

Months ago, she'd considered getting involved with an operative to glean information, but the very idea had made her queasy, so she'd dropped the plan. But if she'd gone through with it, Brad would have been on her shortlist of candidates. He'd been in the Army, and like most of Falcon, he'd served on one Special

Forces team or another. Green Berets, if she remembered correctly. He was tall—at least six-two, she guessed—fit, and handsome. The only operative who might be better looking was Ted Godfrey, but Godfrey wasn't nearly as friendly as Brad, and even more important than his looks and background, she'd *liked* Brad. Which made his betrayal this morning even worse.

"I *had* to tell Rav you were on Raptor land. I didn't know how you were involved with his disappearance, and if I didn't tell him then, my ass would've been fired. And I like you, Isabel, but not enough to lose my job."

"I spent several hours in *jail*, Brad." She crossed her arms and glared at him. "After I saved your boss's life."

"You're out now—"

Another hush fell over the crowded taproom. Isabel glanced up to see Alec Ravissant in the Roadhouse doorway.

Crap. She knew she should have walked home, screw the rain.

ISABEL WAS IN the Roadhouse, just as the woman at the jail had said she'd be. Alec had intended to make a beeline for her table, but between the glare she cast him, and the fact that she was seated with the leader of Falcon team, he decided to grab a table and bide his time. He needed to talk to Isabel and didn't want an audience.

He was in the midst of ordering a beer when his compound director appeared next to the chair opposite him. "A beer, Rav? Really?" Nicole took off her damp coat and draped it over the seat, then dropped into it. "I haven't laid eyes on you since you returned from the land of the lost, and I find you here." Nicole glanced at the waitress, "Jenna, I'll have a whiskey sour, please."

Alec noted the waitress's name. No wonder Isabel had been so smooth with the first name. In filling out the paperwork to pay her bail, he'd noticed Hayes was her middle name. The real Jenna left to fill their orders, and he faced his director, to whom he *did* owe an explanation, as he'd purposefully avoided her when he was at the compound earlier. He'd wanted to deal with Isabel before diving into the massive workload that had only gotten worse thanks to his unscheduled campout with Isabel. No doubt Nicole had followed him into town.

"I'm tired and hungry, and the last day and a half have been brutal." He grimaced. Given his aches and pains, brutal was likely an apt description of his missing hours. "I decided to stop for a bite because I hear they have good burgers here."

"Bullshit. The burgers are lousy. It's the chowder that's good." Her wide, toothy grin always reminded Alec of Julia Roberts's megabucks smile. "And Joyce told me you followed Isabel here."

He shrugged and let out a small laugh. Small towns. So much for keeping secrets. "You went to the jail?"

"I was going to bail her out."

"Ballsy move, considering what she was arrested for." The words were said with admiration, not judgment. Nicole was the highest-ranking woman in Raptor and earned the position by being tough as hell. Tall, blond, and striking, there was much about her that probably set other men's hearts racing, but he didn't fool around with employees, and he respected her too much to think of her as anything other than the highly skilled director of his favorite sector of the company—the military training division.

She shrugged. "I know her well enough to believe she's innocent and couldn't stand the idea of her being stuck in the lockup all weekend."

Alec didn't know Isabel at all, but he'd come to the same conclusion. "Why didn't I know you and she are drinking buddies?"

Nicole met his gaze head-on, no intimidation, which was one of the things he liked about her. "Because I didn't want you to know."

"Were you concerned I'd question your loyalty?"

"No. I was worried you'd want me to use the friendship to have her declawed."

Alec leaned back in the chair and considered Nicole's statement. If he'd known, would he have asked her to figure out Isabel's weaknesses to disarm her and send her packing?

He didn't think so, but it was possible.

The waitress arrived with their drinks. As soon as she left, Nicole leaned forward and spoke softly under the din of the noisy taproom. "I'll be honest. I first became friends with her for just that reason. I figured I'd determine if she was nuts or grieving or vindictive. Then I got to know her and…I *like* her. I can't really help but feel protective of her. I'm sorry she managed to halt the trainings for two months, but given how her brother died, the closure probably should have happened sooner, and at least that gave us the opportunity to retool the simulated village and upgrade the shoot houses."

Yes, Nicole had found a way to make lemonade out of that fiasco, yet another reason he liked her. He had yet to tour the village and God's Eye to inspect the improvements, but tomorrow, with Keith's help, he'd get this trip back on track.

Alec watched Isabel over Nicole's shoulder. "Is there anything between Isabel and Fraser?" he asked. Sure, the operative had denied it, but seeing them together had triggered another twinge of jealousy.

The blow to his head must've messed with his brain.

"No. Isabel doesn't go out with operatives." Nicole shrugged. "Since moving to Tamarack, Isabel hasn't gone out with anyone. And it's not for lack of offers; the ratio of single men to single women here is four to one."

It was a really bad sign that this news pleased him. And yet, it did.

CHAPTER SIX

ISABEL'S SEAT FACED Alec. He boldly stared at her, which both unnerved and excited her. And that was just plain wrong. *The man had me arrested.* She twisted in her seat and met the gaze of one of the operatives Brad had abandoned at the other table. Chase Johnston. Unlike Alec, the young man's stare gave her the creeps.

"Chase's watching me again," she said to Brad. "I thought you were going to talk to him."

"I did. He both denied it and said he'd stop. He's just a puppy with a crush, Isabel. He can't help it."

"I think he's the one who's been stalking me, and he's probably the guy who shot off bear bangers outside my cabin when the compound was first closed." She met Brad's gaze, daring him to deny—*again*—that anyone had been stalking her, let alone had shot off the loud noisemakers designed to scare bears away.

Being a wise man, Brad just smiled and sipped his beer. "How's the chowder?" he asked.

She rolled her eyes. "You're lame at deflecting conversation."

"So we'll talk about how lame I am instead." He winked at her.

She couldn't help but laugh. "You're taking a chance sitting with me in front of the big boss."

He shrugged. "Rav's cool."

"Cool is not the word I'd use to describe Alec Ravissant. Ungrateful is more like it, followed by ass."

"Speaking of," Jenna said as she set a beer—which Isabel hadn't ordered—in front of her. "Did you *see* Ravissant's ass? Ohmygod, he is ten times hotter in person than in pictures. I think he's even hotter than Ted." She plopped into the empty seat next to Brad.

Isabel laughed. "Eh, his ass is okay, but his chest is better." She secretly agreed he was hotter than Ted.

"Go ahead, have your girl talk," Brad said. "Pretend I'm not here."

Jenna playfully punched him in the shoulder. "If you ever get off your ass and take me out on a real date, I'll stop treating you like one of the girls." Jenna had never made a secret of her crush on Brad. She turned back to Isabel. "Seriously, isn't he smokin'?" She fanned herself with the laminated bar menu, which was a bit over-the-top considering the room was anything but hot, with the heavy rainstorm raging outside. But then, she clearly wanted to make Brad jealous.

Brad's eyes narrowed on cue. It was equally well known that he enjoyed Jenna's crush—they were Tamarack's very own star-crossed lovers. Isabel had long suspected they were secretly screwing each other's brains out, a suspicion that only solidified with the hot look he cast Jenna's way.

It was rather sweet, seeing the sparks between them.

"Jenna! Order up!" the bartender shouted.

Jenna bolted to her feet and took off across the bar.

"Why do you two keep it a secret?" Isabel asked.

Brad grinned. "She gets better tips if guys think she's single."

"Does watching other guys flirt with her bother you?"

"It used to. But we're solid. I trust her, and she needs the money to support her dad."

Isabel nodded. Jenna's dad was disabled, living off Social Security and his Alaska Permanent Fund dividend—which didn't go far when milk was eight dollars a gallon.

Brad's gaze was on Jenna as she served drinks to a table of loggers. "Plus, she enjoys sneaking around. It amuses her."

"And you?"

"Yeah. It amuses me too. We pretend it's not serious, but she's the real deal for me."

Given the way his gaze followed her around the taproom, Isabel believed him.

He stood and picked up his beer. "We cool?" he asked.

She nodded. She didn't really blame Brad for getting her arrested. He'd been smart to include Westover in the search team, and he'd had no way of knowing what—or who—they'd find in the cabin. No, her ire was all reserved for the ungrateful ass across the room. "We're cool."

Brad retreated to the table of operatives, which included Nate Sifuentes, Dev Kalla, and Chase Johnston, who was *still* staring at her.

Unfortunately, Isabel had learned, after attempting to file her first complaint, there was no law against staring.

The oddest part was Chase had never—*not once*—spoken a word to her. She would suspect him of being part of what happened to Vin, except he was hired by Raptor only four months ago. Vin had died eleven months ago.

She returned her attention to her chowder and beer, wondering if she'd be charged for the unordered drink, which had been a ploy for Jenna to banter with her secret boyfriend. Knowing Jenna, she'd put it on Brad's bill.

A shadow fell across her table, and for the third time that evening, a hush fell over the bar. She slowly lifted her gaze, knowing in her gut exactly who was standing over her.

Her body flushed with anger, adrenaline, and something even more disconcerting as she looked into topaz-blue eyes.

ALEC GUESSED ISABEL itched to slug him in his swollen eye, and couldn't really blame her. He suspected she refrained simply because she was under suspicion of having kidnapped him and didn't want assault added to the charges. Not that he'd pursue it if she did. He had it coming. Big-time.

"We need to talk."

"Go away."

"Hear me out, Isabel."

A loud seventies tune suddenly blared through the taproom sound system. He glanced toward the jukebox and saw Nicole, browsing the playlist and feeding the ancient machine coins. The woman more than deserved the raise that was coming her way.

Isabel stood and spoke softly under the music. "What's your game here, Ravissant? Are you hoping I'll kick you in the nuts in front of all these witnesses so you can have me locked up again? News for you, much as I'm tempted, I'm not that stupid. I made bail. I'm out. There's nothing you can do about it."

"I'm the one who posted your bond."

She took a deep breath as if she was about to say something loud and angry, but his words stopped her. After a moment of frozen silence, she let out the breath. "Are you here, then, expecting me to say thanks? To you? After you choked me, waited hours to say thanks for all I'd done to help you, and then had me arrested? I don't think so." Her eyes scanned him from head to foot. "I see *you* got to shower, while I got to hang out in a six-by-six cell with a stainless steel toilet with attached sink to wash up in."

He deserved her anger and more, but he would still present his case. "Once I realized how badly I screwed up, I went straight to the post to bail you out, and found out the bond had to be paid at the Fairbanks courthouse. I sent one of my employees to handle it." He'd tried to talk Westover into letting her out sooner, but the officer wouldn't budge, and Alec couldn't hang around at the jail waiting for her release. He'd been in Alaska for over twenty-four hours at that point and hadn't even made it to the compound yet. He had an investigation to start and had no intention of leaving it up to the police to find out who had gotten the best of him.

He'd gone to the compound to be checked out by the staff physician, a former ER doctor, who'd documented his injuries for the FBI investigation. Abrasions around his wrists indicated he'd fought against restraints at some point, and a long bruise across his stomach argued he'd been beaten with some sort of rod. Doc Larson had cleaned and rebandaged the gash on his temple, giving Isabel praise for her application of the butterfly bandages as he did so, as the wound had already begun to knit.

After seeing the doctor, he'd taken a shower and returned to Tamarack. "I deserve your anger, your derision, and another kick in the balls should you want to deliver it, but I got you out of there as fast as I could. I hired a lawyer for you too. She's in Fairbanks and will contact you tomorrow."

"It might have been nicer if you didn't have me locked up to begin with. Then I wouldn't need your damn lawyer."

At least she was smart enough not to refuse the legal aid he was offering.

She grabbed her coat from the back of her chair and picked up her backpack. "I've lost my appetite. I'm leaving." She pulled out a clear plastic bag containing cash from the backpack and took out a twenty, which she dropped on the table.

Alec pulled out his wallet. "Let me pay for your dinner and give you a ride home." The woman at the jail had explained why Isabel had gone to the Roadhouse, which had triggered more guilt. Thanks to Alec, she was without a car. He'd assured the woman he'd get Isabel home safely.

"Keep your money and your ride. I don't want anything from you." She turned and headed for the front door.

Alec returned to his table and grabbed his coat. To Nicole, he said, "I want a meeting with Falcon in two hours." He nodded toward the table of operatives in the center of the room. "Tell them I'm sorry to spoil their night off, and pay their bill with the company card."

She nodded, leaving him free to chase after Isabel. He pulled on his coat as he ran down the street. Half a block away, he caught up with her and grabbed her arm. "Isabel, wait. I'm sorry. Please let me give you a ride home." It was still raining, not as hard as it had been when he first arrived, but it wasn't a light sprinkle either. She was soaking wet and shivering.

"Get your hand off me. I have nothing to say to you." Her voice caught. She was on the verge of tears.

Shit.

She'd been chatting and smiling at Fraser and Jenna; he hadn't guessed it had been an act. Now he realized she'd been banking her emotions, probably intending to let them out when she was alone.

And he hadn't even allowed her that.

He released her arm. The blow to the head must have done more damage than he'd thought, because he was screwing this up badly. He might be a novice politician, but he was better than *this*.

Isabel, apparently, brought out the ass in him.

"Please let me give you a ride home, because *I* have a lot to say to *you*. Starting with thank you and ending with I'm sorry. But in between, I need to know everything about when you found me yesterday. I need to find who did this to me. I need your help."

"You've had my help. You're on your own now." She stepped around him and started down the sloppy, wet street.

There was only one thing he could offer that she wanted. "Isabel, if you'll hear me out, if you'll help me, then I'll hear you out. I want to know why you think my men killed your brother, and why you blame me for it."

She froze. "I told you all that in my letters. The ones you never responded to."

"I read every word. I looked into your claims. My investigators didn't find anything. The police didn't find anything. My lawyers said responding to you would be a mistake. Here's your chance to tell me. Face-to-face. Everything. I'll listen."

She took another step away from him.

Rain soaked his hair and dripped between his coat collar and his skin. "I've figured out one thing since having my ass handed to me yesterday." He paused and waited. He'd laid the bait. She'd bite. This was one skill he'd mastered in his months on the campaign.

"What's that?" she asked, her voice low. Reluctant.

He smiled and mentally turned the reel, setting the hook. "You've been right all along. There's something bad going on inside the compound. Odds are, my men—my own employees— did this to me. I can't trust them to investigate. The way I see it, the only person I can trust right now is you."

CHAPTER SEVEN

"I'M SURPRISED TAMARACK hasn't been flooded with reporters," Isabel said as Alec drove down the main highway that cut through town. It looked like a typical rainy Friday evening to her.

"My campaign put out a statement that my disappearance began with swerving to avoid a moose and running off the road. I was unconscious for a number of hours. It is unknown whether or not foul play was involved or if I wandered in the woods after the accident, seeking help—which I found in the form of a female hiker."

"And the press bought it?"

"No idea, but I booked and paid for every motel room in Tamarack and the two nearest towns to make coming to Tamarack unappealing to the press. The statement also said that given the ongoing investigation, no interviews would be granted, period. I think the rain has played in our favor. No one wanted to get stuck in Tamarack with no good leads and no place to stay."

"Was I named as the 'female hiker'?"

"No."

"I'm worried that whoever beat the crap out of you might think I can identify them."

She caught his grimace at her wording, but he didn't deny it. "You're safe as long as they don't know who found me."

"But they already do." She told him about her cell phone disappearing from the side of the stream during the fifteen minutes she was inside the cabin with him.

"You're certain?"

"Yes. The only other possibility is I tucked it in my pack without thinking, and Westover or Joyce stole my phone. Paul Westover is kind of an ass, but I don't see him running a stolen cell phone racket." Outside the vehicle, trees sped by, blurred by streaks of water. She mentally added the price of a new phone to the tally of what helping Alec Ravissant had cost her.

The car took an unexpected right turn, and her body flushed

with adrenaline. She'd been waiting for this moment for months. "You're taking me to the compound?" Her throat was so dry, she'd barely been able to say the words.

"No. We're going the back way to your cabin. The perimeter road is faster."

Disappointment settled in, and she wondered if she could get the restraining order dropped simply because he'd taken this shortcut. Probably not.

"Don't get any ideas. The restraining order is to *protect you*. I'm not about to let it go. But right now I've got problems, and I need your help."

Was she about to become…*allied* with Alec Ravissant? An insane notion if ever there was one.

"If you suspect your own people of running you off the road and leaving you for dead, should you even stay on the compound? Isn't that the lion's den?"

"Yeah, but I'm the lion *king*. It's my den. There's a reason I was attacked before I reached my compound." He glanced at her askance, his focus on the road ahead, and she caught his wry smile. "Despite what you might think given the condition you found me in yesterday, I'm a damn good soldier. They caught me off guard, which won't happen again. Anyone who attacks me or what's mine will pay."

He made the turn to the compound, but before they reached the intersection with the perimeter road, he pulled to the side and put the SUV in park. They were probably less than a mile from the concertina-wire-topped fence that surrounded the structures that were popularly referred to as "the compound," but in actuality, Raptor's entire thirty-thousand-acre swath of pristine wilderness was the true compound. The hundred or so enclosed acres were only a tiny portion of Alec's vast holding.

What must it be like to be Alec Ravissant? To drive down this road and be the lion king—although after last night, she'd always think of him as the tiger king—knowing everyone on his land must answer to him, and his backyard was a paltry thirty thousand acres in the heart of Alaska. And this was just *one* of Raptor's five compounds.

He pulled his cell phone from his pocket and dialed a number, then hit the speaker button. A man answered right away. "Alec, good to hear from you—you had us all scared for a bit."

"Thanks, Lee," Alec said, "Listen, I need a favor. I need you to find a cell phone that disappeared last night."

"That happens to be one of my specialties, but I'm curious why you aren't having Mothman do it."

Mothman was the nickname of the compound tech wizard. He handled all the computer systems. Openly gay, not former military, and not an operative, he missed social cues because he probably was on the mild end of the autism spectrum, and he had a good heart even if he was condescending at times. He didn't fit with the other employees who hung out at the Tamarack Roadhouse, but he went anyway because, like Isabel, he had trouble connecting with people but still felt compelled to be among them. Mothman was Isabel's litmus test for who the bigoted pricks were among the operatives.

Anyone who was a dick to Mothman was beneath contempt.

She bristled even at the suggestion Mothman could somehow be part of the corruption within the compound, but knew ruling him out was her own foolish bias. Everyone was a suspect. Including Mothman and Alec Ravissant.

"I vetted Mothman's work when I was there last month," the man on the phone—Lee, Alec had called him—added. "His code is solid."

"I'm not sure if I can trust Mothman, but I know I don't trust others who have access to the server," Alec said. "I don't want any of my people to know about this search."

"Fair enough. What's the number?"

Alec met Isabel's gaze and raised an eyebrow. "Iz? What's your number?"

Something strange settled in her belly at his casual shortening of her name. It implied friendship. A peculiar notion. She cleared her throat and recited her number for Lee.

"What type of phone, and who is your service provider?"

She gave him the necessary information.

"Can you estimate when you used it last and where you were?"

She frowned. "The last call I made was Wednesday night—I called the Alaska DNR, Fairbanks office, to check in after surveying by myself all day. I keep it turned off when I'm surveying, and there's no ready cell coverage—so the battery won't drain. I turned it on last night around eight thirty p.m. I didn't have any bars, but I sent myself a text to see if there was even faint service. It didn't go through."

"Do you know what happens with your phone when texts

don't send? Do they wait in a queue for a signal, or do they sit in drafts until you hit Send again?"

"They wait in a queue for the next signal. I sometimes set it to send me a text when I'm out of range, so my phone will buzz the moment I've got coverage." She'd done that on some of her illegal forays onto Raptor land—trying to narrow down the area where Vin might have been when he sent his last text. It was more efficient than stopping every hundred feet and checking for service.

Lee let out a low whistle. "Perfect. Unless whoever has your phone deleted the text, it'll go out the next time it's in range and turned on. It may already have been sent. I'll see what I can find."

"Thanks, Lee," Alec said. "Call me if you get a hit."

"Will do."

With that, Alec hit the End button and set the phone in the console. "Don't tell anyone you noticed your phone is missing."

She shifted uncomfortably. "I, um, already did. I told Westover. And Joyce."

Alec shrugged. "Westover probably won't do anything about it. Will Joyce talk?"

"I have no idea." She frowned. "I don't know her that well, but she was nice to me today. A surprise, because she's never been very friendly before, but then, I'm not the most popular girl in town." She cleared her throat. "Trying to shut down the largest employer within fifty miles tends to piss people off."

"I can imagine," Alec said dryly.

She grimaced. "Exactly how much do you hate me?" She meant it as a joke, but her question didn't sound funny even to her ears.

Those jewel-toned blue eyes met hers and were every bit as compelling as described. "I don't hate you at all. I've been angry with you. Frustrated. I was scared as hell when I heard you interrupted a live-fire training exercise, but I've never, ever hated you."

"I didn't know it was live fire," she admitted in a soft voice. When it happened, when she'd disrupted the training and was arrested—the first time—it had been easier to let everyone think she'd done it on purpose. Better than admitting she was an idiot. It was effective, adopting the zealot's mantle because it got the attention of Alec's political opponent, who up to that point had ignored her plea for help.

But the politician had glommed on to the story of the sister so determined to prove Raptor was negligent in her brother's death, she was willing to risk her life to force an investigation. Norm Stimson, a congressman from Maryland, seized the opportunity and pushed for closure of the compound while safety procedures were checked. After all, he'd argued, if an unarmed fool of a woman could infiltrate a live-fire training exercise, so could ISIS or al Qaida militants who wanted to know exactly what Alec Ravissant was teaching American soldiers about how to fight terrorist groups.

She wanted Alec to know she didn't have a death wish. He'd called her crazy this morning, and it had bothered her. A lot. "I didn't know you had live-fire trainings and I didn't know I was down range during such a drill."

"I'd wondered," he said. "Especially after meeting you, seeing how well prepared you are for the wilderness. It didn't mesh with the conventional wisdom—that you were determined to martyr yourself for your cause." He frowned. "For national security reasons, we keep a pretty tight lid on the types of training we do here, which is why it isn't commonly known we have live-fire zones."

"Was live fire part of Vin's last training?"

"No. Vin took off during a straight survival training."

She stiffened and reached for the car door. "Vin didn't simply 'take off,' and I thought you were ready to believe that."

He put out a hand to stop her. "Poor choice of words. For the last year, I've believed that's exactly what happened, and my brain hasn't caught up and changed verbs yet. I'm sorry."

She met his gaze. He looked sincere, but what did she know of Alec Ravissant and his expressions? She settled back in her seat; the rain had lightened to a sprinkling mist, but she still didn't want to walk in it.

He put the car in gear, and they continued down the road. "I met your brother, you know."

She nodded. She knew all about Vin's meeting with the tiger king.

"Will you tell me about him?"

She glanced at his handsome profile. She wanted to say no. She wanted to shut him out. To not give him a piece of Vin to hold on to, because he'd refused her all those months ago when she'd first reached out to him. Yet, he was here now, asking the questions she'd wanted all along. "You didn't come to his funeral."

"I regret only three things in my life. Not attending your brother's funeral is one of them."

She cocked her head to the side. "What are the other two?"

He shook his head.

"Then tell me why you didn't show."

He tapped the steering wheel and focused on the road in a way that made her think he wasn't going to answer. Finally he said, "The campaign had only just started. I didn't plan to run. But then, no one expected the Maryland Senate seat to be up for grabs. Everyone figured the woman who'd filled Talon's open seat would run again when the term expired." He paused. "Basically, I was roped into running before I'd even decided if running for the Senate was what I wanted to do. I was stupid and listened to the advisor my father hired, and my attorney, rather than my own gut." He paused again, this time meeting her gaze. "I should have been there to pay my respects to a fine soldier, who never should have died."

They turned off the perimeter road and onto the narrow dirt track that would eventually meet up with the road to her cabin. She'd rented the cabin when she first moved to Alaska because it was adjacent to the compound. That it was isolated in the middle of the most beautiful wilderness on earth had been a bonus.

"You like it out here?" Alec asked.

"Yes. For now." But she'd been here for nearly ten months. The nomad in her was ready to move again.

He pulled up in front of her carport—empty thanks to her truck being in the impound lot. "I'm working on getting your truck back for you. It will be a few days."

She should probably say thank you, but it was his fault she didn't have her truck to begin with, so instead she just nodded.

Alec gazed at her small log cabin, then glanced around. To one side, evening sun broke through the clouds and glinted on the solar panels on the roof. To the other, a faint rainbow arced across the meadow. "If you put this place on a postcard, people would think it was too picturesque to be real."

She smiled. The late summer wildflowers were in full bloom across the meadow, and even in the light rain, a pair of caribou had settled down in the tall grass, their large, fuzzy antlers giving away their position. Caribou were terrible at hide-and-seek.

She grabbed her backpack from the backseat and climbed out

of the car.

"No power lines?" Alec asked, following her to the front door.

"No. Completely off the grid. The solar panels provide limited power for Wi-Fi, my computer, things that must run on electricity, but the big stuff—refrigerator, range, furnace, water heater, washer, and dryer—those are all gas powered. Even the light fixtures are gas."

It had taken some getting used to—electricity as a luxury item—but she'd come to appreciate the quiet and lack of lights on appliances that broke the darkness. Before she'd moved to Alaska, even her toaster oven had had a clock and red glowing light. Now she used the camping toaster rack on the gas cooktop if she wanted crisp bread.

Chores took longer, but the trees were too tall for a satellite dish, so she had no TV. It wasn't like she was in a hurry to finish washing the dishes so she could sit on the couch and do nothing. Instead she listened to audiobooks from the library on her battery-powered CD player as she did chores. Her life was solitary but busy, and at least one night a week, she found herself in the Tamarack Roadhouse, because even she could have too much solitary.

Inside her cabin, while she lit the gaslights, Alec circled the small living room, stopping in front of the mantel, where a picture of Vin and her had pride of place. He wore his Army dress uniform, with his arm draped around her shoulder. To even the casual observer it would be clear they were siblings—he had the same green eyes, obnoxious orange hair, curls, and freckles—although his military buzz meant he lacked the curls in that snapshot.

Growing up, more than one person had tagged them Raggedy Ann and Andy—they'd both hated the comparison—but at least with a four-year age difference, they'd been far enough apart in school that it hadn't been a big issue.

"I'd like to read the emails he sent you," Alec said. "The ones about Raptor."

She nodded. "They're on the computer. Let me shower, then I'll pull them up for you."

"I could read them while you shower. It would save time."

She frowned at him. Did she really want to give him access to her computer while she was in the shower? There were at least a dozen files that contained incriminating evidence—her notes and map database detailing her forays onto Raptor property searching for Vin's cave—that he could use against her.

But surely, if he believed her, he'd understand *why* she'd repeatedly violated the restraining order. And letting him read the emails would be the key to convincing him.

She could skip the shower and go over everything with him now. But she felt rancid after hiking for an entire day, hauling him, fighting him, sleeping on a rotting wood floor, hiking to Westover's patrol car—in handcuffs no less—then spending the day in a jail cell. Add to that getting rained on. She was chilled and damp, even though Alec had turned up the heat in the car.

She wanted a shower so badly, she could cry.

And she really didn't want him to wonder why she was reluctant to leave him alone with her computer.

She sighed and set her laptop on the coffee table. "They're all in the mail directory called 'Vincent.' Do you want a drink or anything while I clean up?"

"No. I'm fine. Take your time."

She nodded and left him alone with her computer, well aware that if he peeked in other files, he'd have everything he needed to send her right back to jail.

CHAPTER EIGHT

ALEC WATCHED HER leave, fully aware she'd been reluctant to give him access to her computer. He couldn't really blame her, but at the same time, he was curious if it was a generic discomfort or if there was something specific that put the worry lines between her brows.

He rubbed his own forehead. The pain had faded hours ago, and the swelling around his eye was almost gone. He was stupidly eager to see her after she'd showered. With her hair no longer confined to a wilting braid, he'd at last find out if her hair was as curly as he suspected.

He was an idiot for even wondering. He shouldn't give a crap what she looked like, and he certainly shouldn't give a damn about what she thought of him. But he did. And it wasn't for any good reason. In fact, it was for the worst reason he could imagine.

Put simply, he wanted her in a very raw, coarse, and basic sort of way.

But there was nothing simple about wanting Isabel. His campaign manager would freak, for starters. She'd insisted he not date at all until after the election. They didn't need the extra scrutiny. Carey was cautious and hated surprises, but she was a damn fine campaign manager, so Alec put up with her edicts.

Isabel was Carey's worst nightmare—she'd already derailed the campaign once when she got his opponent to demand an inspection of the safety procedures of all the trainings conducted on the compound. Now Isabel was under suspicion of having abducted Alec—which was completely his fault—and for violating the restraining order—also his fault—he had obtained to protect her from her own foolishness. When the press got the full story, unless he'd untangled Isabel's legal problems, he'd look like an ungrateful ass. Which, if he remembered correctly, was exactly what Isabel had called him.

She would wreak havoc with his campaign, but he wanted her anyway. A sure sign he'd been a fool to give in to his dad's pressure to run for office. He wasn't cut out for playing by any rules except the rules of engagement in warfare.

He dropped onto the couch, clicked on the mail directory, and found the subfolder she'd indicated. He scrolled to the bottom of the email list, looking at the dates. Vincent Dawson had emailed his sister regularly when he was in the Army, and then more frequently after he left the service fifteen months ago. Alec opened a few emails from Vincent's last months in the Army, finally finding one the soldier had sent when he'd visited the Alaska compound for specialized combat training sixteen months ago.

Izzy,

In all my years in the military, this is the most intense training I've ever attended. I could swear, sometimes, when we're deep in the woods, it feels like I'm in Afghanistan. It's hard to describe because the landscape is different, but the woods are just as freaking cold. Mountains are mountains. And I don't know how they do it, but damn if some of the houses in the simulated village don't smell like that shithole place. I think they pump in the smell to mess with our minds.

Some of the newbies are so damn jumpy, as if they really believe the Taliban is in the foothills, ready to blow us away. Thank God we don't have live rounds—a rookie shot me today when we ran an Afghan military trainee/traitor scenario. He thought I was the enemy.

Alec Ravissant is one cool dude. Since I was dead, my team had to recover my body. Surreal, let me tell you. But after my body was safely returned to the field HQ, I got to hang with Rav in the control booth and watch my team continue to screw up.

Everyone calls the control booth God's Eye, because there are about a hundred monitors that show the action in the training areas. You can see everything—it's like something out of a futuristic movie.

Rav said I'd been doing a good job—until I got dead—and asked why I never applied for Ranger school. I told him I had a bratty little sister who would have freaked if I did. I told him how I'd been your guardian since you were fourteen, and that you're all grown up and working on your PhD but are still a handful and I won't stop worrying about you until I marry you off.

I don't know if you've heard of Alec Ravissant (Rav to the troops), but he's like, legendary. He's apparently from some snotty, rich family back east. Dude went to Harvard. He's got like a genius IQ and was being groomed for politics. When he was twenty-one, he'd been accepted at Harvard Law, but he ditched it and joined the Army. His family tried to pull strings to keep him out of combat. His response was to apply for Ranger school. He served with the Rangers for years, deployed on lots of special ops missions. After he left the service, he bought Raptor with pocket change.

Knowing the guy is rich, smart, and can hold his own in a firefight, I asked Rav if he was in the market for a wife. He laughed and said he had enough on his plate and couldn't handle the troublemaker I'd described. Sorry, sis. I tried. But then he surprised me by asking if I was planning to reenlist. He said he liked the way I worked with the soldiers, and—holy shit—he offered me a job.

I'm stunned. I've always figured I'd be a career enlisted man. Without college, what else am I good for? I know. I know. You've nagged me about the GI bill often enough—but I don't want to go back to school. Shit. Can you see me in a classroom full of nineteen-year-olds? After two tours of duty in Iraq and three in Afghanistan, I don't think I could handle being in a classroom again. Honestly, I don't understand how you put up with the academic bullshit.

I'm thinking about the offer. I like Rav and the work Raptor is doing now that he's running the place—although I have to admit, some of the training is a bit too damn real. Everything here is done to simulate the real thing, to trick us into panic mode, so those who shut down will learn how to pull out of it. It's scary and intense, but valuable, especially for the kids fresh out of boot camp who've never seen combat.

I hope the meeting with your shithead advisor went well and your dissertation flies through all the hoops they throw at you. I can't wait to start calling you Doc Izzy.

Love,

Vin

P.S. Email me a photo of you. If I end up dead in God's Eye again with Rav, I'll check email and make sure he sees your picture. If I have to, I could throw myself on a dummy grenade... I'm looking out for you, Sis.

Alec couldn't help but smile. If Vin had flashed Isabel's picture his way, he wondered if he'd have asked for her number. Maybe. Probably. Superficial, sure, but also, Alec remembered the pride in Sergeant Vincent Dawson's voice as he described his little sister. Alec *had* been intrigued.

Vin had told Alec how he became Isabel's guardian. He'd been a freshman in college and Isabel a freshman in high school when their parents died in a car accident. With no other family to turn to, Isabel would have gone into foster care, but eighteen-year-old Vin dropped out of school and joined the Army so he could support her.

It was no wonder the two had been fiercely close, and Vin was especially proud that his brilliant little sister was just a year away from obtaining her PhD in archaeology.

Except she didn't have a PhD. As far as Alec knew, she'd dropped out of the program when Vin died. He suspected her decision had more to do with her crusade against Raptor than a change of academic plans, which made Alec's skin crawl with shame. He'd let Vincent Dawson down in a way that would have mattered to the soldier very much.

He shook his head. He was supposed to be reading Vin's emails about Raptor, looking for hints as to what had happened to him and connections to what had happened to Alec yesterday, not looking for insight into the soldier's little sister's psyche.

He knew the basic timeline of Vin's last months. Two months after sending Isabel that email, Vin received an honorable discharge from the Army and started the job for Raptor less than a week later—Alec had paid him a huge bonus for starting so quickly, because between purging the roster of employees loyal to Robert Beck and having Apex, a rival private security company, headhunting his best operatives, he'd been dangerously short-staffed at the Alaska compound.

Vin's first emails after moving to the compound were as expected. He shared his sister's love of the outdoors and described Tamarack and the surrounding taiga forest in detail only another avid hiker would appreciate.

The fourth email—sent about a month after Vin moved to the compound—held the first hint that things weren't perfect in his new northern home.

Izzy,

Sorry I haven't emailed in a while. I was down with a nasty bug. I'm fine now—nearly 100%—or I wouldn't tell you about this at all, because I know how you worry.

The bug was bad, knocked me on my ass for a few days. I don't know if I've ever been so sick. I was out in the woods, hiking on my day off, when it hit me. Explosive pain in my head. Nausea. I passed out—I think I was only out for a few seconds, but it scared the shit out of me. I thought I was going to die.

I finally got the strength to get up and walk. It took me three hours, but I made it back to the compound. Went straight to the infirmary. They ran a gazillion tests—checking for stroke or anything else that can explain it—but came up with nothing. Doc thinks it was a virus. He's warned me not to go hiking alone anymore.

I wish you'd come visit. You'd love the hikes, and I could use the company. No one here is into hiking, and I just reach a point where I'll go crazy inside the compound. I need to get out. The simulated settings are just too much like a war zone for me I guess. The noise, the smell, the intensity.

I need to hike to escape it.

I know what you're thinking—PTSD. I'm dealing with it, I promise. Rav made it a condition of employment—all vets see a shrink who drives up from Fairbanks twice a month whether we show signs of PTSD or not. Some of the guys resent the hell out of it. Others give lip service to hating it, but I think are secretly glad it's required. I'm probably one of those, but don't tell anyone.

Also, the shrink is kinda hot. It's a shame she's all loaded down with no-dating-patients ethics.

Miss you.

Vin

Alec had read both the doctor's report on Vin's sudden illness, and he'd reviewed the psychiatrist's notes. Vin had signed a release upon employment to allow human resources and senior staff access to all medical records including mental health. It was vital for Alec to know the mental state of the men and women who were training soldiers for combat.

Vincent Dawson passed every psych evaluation given him.

Two weeks after his illness, Vin had gone back to the woods alone. When he failed to return to the compound that evening, two operatives set out to find him. In deference to the doctor's orders about not hiking alone, he'd left a map indicating the area he intended to explore. He was out cold when the operatives found him, and it appeared he'd suffered a fall from a short but steep hillside and hit his head.

His next email to Isabel after that held the same degree of reassurance as before—he was fine, his injuries minor—but he also described a dream he'd had while unconscious. He'd said it had the feel of a night terror. He'd felt like he was awake, but couldn't move, couldn't talk, couldn't scream, and everything felt as though it was happening in real time. In the dream, he'd been dragged into a cave by two masked men. It had been so real, he'd believed he'd somehow gotten caught up in a Taliban hostage-taking scenario that was being run for a small group of soldiers on the compound.

Inside the cave, the terrorists tested his ability to withstand torture, and he no longer thought it was part of a Raptor training exercise.

On the ceiling of the cave, Vin saw a petroglyph. A lynx, identifiable due to the feline's distinctive ear and beard tufts. He'd focused on the etched cat while they tortured him, fiercely holding on to sanity by reciting aloud all he knew about big cats followed by everything Isabel had taught him about petroglyphs and archaeology. By fixating on the lynx, he'd stopped himself from divulging classified information about his tours in Afghanistan.

The experience had been terrifying, but when he came to after being found, aside from a few bruises from his fall and a concussion from hitting his head, there'd been no bruises on his body from the torture, telling him it had all been a horrific, vivid dream.

Nicole pulled him from the trainings and gave him a desk job for three weeks, as was their standard concussion protocol. He passed the next psych eval with no red flags indicating he wasn't fit for full duty, but he didn't tell the psychologist about the dream. He only shared that tale with Isabel.

Six weeks after his fall while hiking, in the middle of a survival training exercise in a remote part of the compound, Vincent Dawson disappeared. His body was found three days later. There wasn't a mark on him to indicate he'd died of anything other than exposure.

The day he went missing, Isabel received a text from her brother, which she'd shared with the Raptor search party as soon as she learned he was missing. His final message to his sister: *Oh shit. I found the lynx cave.*

After his body was found, the area was scoured for caves. No caves, and certainly no lynx petroglyphs were located.

The FBI, the local police, and Alec's own men conducted a full investigation, finding no sign of foul play. It appeared Vincent had either suffered a mental break—perhaps he'd crossed paths with a lynx, which were known to inhabit the area—and it had trigged memories of the dream, or maybe his mental constructs had crashed during the tense survival training. Whatever had happened, it appeared he'd gotten lost and forgotten the very survival skills he was imparting to a team of soldiers.

He'd gotten wet crossing a river and lost his pack midstream—it was found several days later, having caught on a beaver dam—and he'd died from hypothermia a day or two after he'd gone missing.

The insurance company claimed his death was a suicide, but Alec's lawyers had used the loss of the pack to argue for accidental death. In the end, because he'd been on the clock when he disappeared, his death was deemed a training accident.

Alec had visited those woods himself, had searched both where Vin had disappeared from and where he was found. There was nothing to indicate Sergeant Dawson's death was anything other than a tragic accident due to a mental breakdown.

At first Alec's lawyers thought Isabel had protested because her brother was mentally unfit for duty but had been put back in the field. They thought she was angling for a bigger payout than the accidental death policy she'd already received.

But she'd surprised everyone with her own narrative—that Vin had actually been taken into a cave and tortured, and during the training, he'd stumbled upon the cave again, and whoever had tortured him the first time had somehow managed to lure him across the river and left him to die.

Her theory was nutty on every level. There was no cave for Vin to stumble upon in the area where they'd conducted the survival training, and there hadn't been a mark on Vin's body to indicate he'd been tortured the first time, let alone had somehow been coerced into crossing a frigid river in late fall. Vin was, first and foremost, a soldier. Alec had seen the man in action and knew he was as fit as any Ranger he'd fought beside.

Vin was also a hiker and outdoorsman, as proficient in the woods as his little sister. It was hard to imagine a man like Vin could be forced to cross a river, hike a mile, then lie down and die, without leaving a mark on the man.

Vin would have fought like hell.

Unless his only opponent was his own inner demons.

At least, that was what Alec had believed, until he woke up deep in the forest with a splitting headache and no memory of how he got there. Now he didn't know what to believe.

A noise came from the kitchen, and he set the computer on the coffee table to investigate. Before he rose from the couch, the culprit came to him in the form of a fluffy gray cat. It must've entered the cabin through a pet door.

The cat looked too sweet and fuzzy to survive being an outdoor cat in the middle of the Alaskan wilderness, but he had a feeling the creature was a lot like its owner, tough as hell under a beautiful, fragile exterior.

The cat stared at him in that assessing way cats do, and finally deigned to jump up on the couch. Then it walked across his lap, without stopping before it settled in the corner, just out of Alec's reach. Of course it could have just jumped to that end of the couch, but where was the not so subtle message in that?

He'd always been a dog person and suspected this cat knew it.

The cat held his gaze, and he wondered if it was choosing which part of him to shred first.

"You two fighting over which one is the alpha cat?" Isabel asked.

Alec startled at her voice and had a feeling he lost status with the cat when he broke the staring contest and faced Isabel. He caught his breath. Even damp, her red-and-gold locks formed tight spirals that appeared intent on doing whatever they pleased. She had gorgeous, obstinate hair, which he found entirely fitting.

"Gandalf, meet Alec Ravissant. Alec, meet Gandalf the Grey," she said.

He grinned. She was a *Lord of the Rings* fan, which almost made up for her being a cat person.

She frowned. "Is something wrong?"

"No. Why?"

"You're staring at me. Kind of like a tiger ready to pounce."

"Sorry. I just... Your hair is—"

"A pain in the ass."

He stood and slowly crossed the room. As he drew near, she took a surprised step backward. He continued forward until he'd backed her into the wall. He planted a hand by her ear and leaned over her. "Your hair is gorgeous. It's the most beautiful hair I think I've ever seen."

Her eyes widened as she stared up at him, and her breath hitched, proving she was as stirred by him as he was by her. Good.

A drop of water gathered at the end of a ringlet. He watched it fall, landing in the hollow of her collarbone. He wanted to lick the moisture from her skin.

This was foolish as hell, yet he didn't want to be anywhere else.

The pulse at the base of her throat jumped. Maybe he'd start there instead. He lowered his head.

"This isn't the smart thing," Isabel said, her voice so soft it was almost a whisper.

"The smart thing?" he asked.

"Sometimes you have to make a choice between the smart thing and the right thing. This isn't the smart thing."

He grinned, liking very much the option she left open. "But it definitely feels like the right thing." He leaned down and pressed his mouth to hers, not hard and fast, but soft, testing. Giving her a choice. She leaned forward, into him. He took that as a good sign and slid an arm around her waist, pulling her against him as he slipped his tongue between her lips.

The slide of her tongue along his triggered a current that coursed through his body. *Absolutely the right thing.*

She was every bit as sweet as he'd imagined when he woke with her in his arms this morning.

She dropped back to her heels, introducing space between them when he craved the exact opposite. He wanted to demolish all distance and give her nothing but pleasure. Erase pain and conflict with an act as old as humanity. Older than war.

"We shouldn't—" she said.

"I'm finding it hard to give a damn about shoulds and shouldn'ts."

She gently pushed at his chest. "Then I will for the both of us."

He leaned back and held her gaze. What he saw gave him

hope. Not rejection. Caution.

He rubbed a thumb across her full bottom lip. "Fair enough." He stepped back. She was right to be cautious. Hell, he needed to think before he jumped in too. Just this morning, he'd been certain she'd orchestrated his abduction as some sort of twisted revenge for her brother.

She pushed off the wall and straightened her shirt—even though his hands hadn't strayed and messed with her clothing. He only wished they had.

She looked cute in the blue flannel top and faded, worn jeans that adhered perfectly to her curves. Comfortable, relaxed. But he'd probably think she looked cute no matter what, because something had happened to his brain when he was hit over the head, and he found himself focusing far too much on her hair, body, and lips than a responsible man ought to.

He should be asking her about the forest yesterday, probing for missed clues. Her cell phone was missing. She'd found him on the rock, stewing in a pool of his own blood. What else? "Was I faceup or facedown on the rock when you found me?"

"Up," she said immediately, and he had a feeling she was relieved he was getting down to business. "I wasn't sure if you were dead or not, but then I saw you breathe." She crossed the room and dropped onto the couch and pulled Gandalf to her lap. The cat settled in like a blanket.

"You bandaged me right away?"

She nodded. "I cleaned your cut while figuring out how to get you out of the forest." She stroked the thick gray fur, and he found himself stupidly jealous of the cat.

"Doc Larson says you did a good job." He touched the fresh bandages on his temple. "How long did it take you to build the travois?"

She bit her bottom lip as she considered his question. Finally she said, "Thirty, maybe forty-five minutes? It felt like forever—I was scared whoever had hurt you would return."

He frowned, knowing she'd risked a lot in helping him, and he'd assaulted her and had her arrested. He had a hell of a lot to make up for.

"It took about two hours to drag you to the cabin," she continued. "You are ridiculously heavy." She scanned him from head to toe, and he very much enjoyed the appreciation she didn't bother to hide.

"The cabin… How did you know it was there? *I* didn't even know it was there, and it's my land." It might be marked on the title maps stored in his office at the compound, but it wasn't something he'd have noticed when he purchased the company and all its assets after it had been seized from Robert Beck.

"I copied the locations of all known historic and prehistoric sites on my USGS quad maps. I received the data from the state historic preservation office in Juneau. The settler's cabin was recorded decades ago."

"I understand why you'd mark sites on state forest land, but why note historic properties on my land?"

She hesitated. "It's always good to know where shelter is in the woods. Last night proved it."

"I can't argue with that but…" His blood pressure rose as understanding hit him. "Shit, Iz, you've been looking for the cave, haven't you? That's why you interrupted the live-fire training. You were searching for a cave with a lynx petroglyph."

Her gaze flicked to her computer. Was that why she'd been nervous earlier? Was there evidence on the hard disk of her illegal forays onto his land?

Jesus. Searching for the cave was spectacularly foolish for the careful, prepared hiker that she was. In the case of the live-fire training, it might have gotten her killed. She'd wandered onto the range and could easily have been shot before the instructors saw her. All because she was determined to find a cave that might not even exist.

She frowned and stopped petting Gandalf. "No. That would be impossible. Thirty-thousand acres is too large an area for one person."

"Don't lie to me, Iz."

The cat opened its eyes and glared at Alec, likely recognizing the source of her irritation. "Listen, I've had a crappy twenty-four hours and don't enjoy your company." She lifted Gandalf from her lap and stood. "It's time for you to leave." She crossed the room and opened the front door.

Alec let out a sharp laugh, making no move for the exit. "Two truths and a lie."

Her mouth flattened. "Three truths."

He stepped up to her and took her hips between his hands. Again her breath hitched. "No. You only wish it were three." He released her and turned toward the open door. "Tomorrow we're going back to where you found me in the woods."

"Tomorrow I need to get my truck back from impound and drive to Fairbanks to buy a new phone. I don't have time for a trip down memory lane with you."

"You won't get your truck back until Monday at the earliest, but I'll lend you a Raptor vehicle. And I'll give you a phone, so there's no need for a trip to Fairbanks. I'll pick you up at eight. Be ready to hike." With that, he stepped outside and pulled the door closed.

CHAPTER NINE

SOMETHING NAGGED AT the back of Alec's mind as he drove to the compound. It had to do with Vin's emails, but he couldn't quite place it. When he arrived inside the compound, he made arrangements for a car and cell phone to be delivered to Isabel and confirmed with Nicole's assistant that she and Falcon team were meeting in the northwest conference room in thirty minutes, then he went to his suite.

He yanked off his tie—which he'd worn in case he had a run-in with the press in Tamarack—and unbuttoned the top buttons of his shirt before settling in front of his laptop to email Isabel. He grimaced at the huge volume of emails that had arrived during his involuntary Internet hiatus. Apparently, disappearing for sixteen hours could make an in-box explode.

He dropped about twenty emails into his personal directory, then moved the rest into his DC office administrator's folder. His assistant could read them and let Alec know which ones were worth responding to. Chore complete, he emailed Isabel, asking her to forward several of Vin's emails, specifically requesting the one that described his illness when he'd been hiking alone, and the one in which he described his night-terror-like experience.

She responded almost immediately, and he couldn't help but smile, imagining her sitting in front of her computer, her wild curls now dry, and he itched to run his fingers through them.

Shit, he had it bad.

He emailed her again: *What are you wearing?*

Her reply: *Pervert.*

He grinned and typed another message: *FaceTime with me?*

She responded: *Hell, no.*

He knew in his gut she was grinning as she typed each reply. His next message: *Fine. I was going to tell you I'm sending two of my men to your place to drop off a car and a cell phone. I don't like you being stranded without either. Please don't run them off with a shotgun. It's bad PR.*

A minute later, he received her reply: *Spoilsport. Can I at least tase them?*

He laughed. *No. Bad Isabel.* He hesitated, then typed his phone number and added: *That's my private cell. If you need anything, call.*

She sent him one last message: *I'm fine. See you tomorrow. Wear boots or I will mock you mercilessly.*

Alec smiled as he switched from her reply to the first email she'd forwarded from Vin. He reread Vin's description of the sudden, incapacitating headache he'd experienced while hiking alone, and Alec felt a flash of sympathetic pain.

And then he knew the feeling wasn't sympathetic. He'd experienced the exact same thing yesterday. That was what had been nagging at him earlier.

A moose appeared out of nowhere, and I swerved and slammed on the brakes. The moose passed within inches of the front of the car as it darted across the road. I pulled off to the side to ride out the adrenaline.

Again, something flashed in my eyes. Deliberate. A signal mirror? Some asshole playing tricks?

The windshield shattered, and then my head felt as if it could explode. Nausea. Pain that started around my ears but settled in the gut. Agony ratcheted until I was certain I would die. Then nothing. Blessed oblivion.

Alec's heart raced. He was panting just at the faint memory.

He'd read reports on various nonlethal experimental weapons and knew of one that could cause that sort of pain. It was theorized that it could be directional and wouldn't penetrate glass. But it had never been effectively weaponized. The theories had never panned out.

Until now?

One way or another, he was certain he'd been incapacitated by infrasound.

ALEC DROPPED INTO the visitor's chair in front of Nicole's desk. "For the record, I like Isabel too. I'm not pro-declawing."

Nicole leaned back and smiled. "You made peace?"

"More or less." *Probably less, but hoping for more.*

"Did you talk to her about Vincent Dawson?"

"I did."

"Are you thinking her theory of what happened to Dawson has merit?" she asked.

He wondered what Nicole expected him to say almost more than he wondered what she wanted him to say. "I have to consider it, given what happened to me."

Nicole cocked her head. "You think you were dragged off into a cave and tortured?" There was a hint of alarm in her gaze, but she hid it well. He had no doubt if he said an emphatic yes, she'd say she believed him, even as she mentally composed her report to the company shrink.

"No. But something happened to me, and I ended up deep in the woods with a blow to the head, and I can't remember it." He wouldn't mention the potential for infrasound now. He wanted to talk to Keith and maybe even Curt first.

"I bet Barstow or that weasel Stimson is behind it."

"Norm Stimson is a shit and a dirty politician, but I don't think he's *that* dirty. Simon Barstow on the other hand… I think he'd kill me in a heartbeat if he thought he could get away with it."

"Shit, Rav. Do you really think it was attempted murder?"

"Unless they knew Isabel would find me and had the skills to stop the bleeding and get me out of the cold, yes. I probably would have died if not for her."

"You seem so fine now. It's hard to imagine it was that bad. What if you'd come to on your own? You could have stopped the bleeding and hiked out to the road."

"I had no clue where I was. I could just have easily hiked for days in the wrong direction. I had no supplies. I'd have been screwed without her."

"Can you get your buddy Dominick to investigate Barstow?"

"Curt is aware of my suspicions of Simon Barstow, but he can't simply sic the FBI on the bastard because I'm mad his company is swiping my best operatives. Nothing Apex has done is illegal." *That we know of.*

Nicole opened her mouth to speak, but at the same time, her assistant knocked on her open office door. "Falcon team has gathered in the northwest conference room."

He thanked Hans and headed to the meeting with Nicole. When he reached the open double doors to the conference room, he frowned. Seven operatives sat around the table. He glanced sideways at his director. "Three down? I thought it was only two."

"Ted Godfrey tendered his resignation yesterday afternoon. I was just about to tell you. Barstow again."

"Apex made him an offer he couldn't refuse?"

She nodded.

Alec cursed. The rival company had been cherry-picking his best operatives for eighteen months. He didn't know what the hell

Simon Barstow could be offering, because Alec paid top dollar, and in exit interviews, his former employees never uttered a complaint about Raptor, work at the Alaska compound, Nicole as director, or anything that explained why they'd chosen to leave the company. But he suspected Barstow made his employees sign a confidentiality agreement that was even stricter than Raptor's.

He entered the conference room and paused by his seat at the head of the table, nodding to the men already seated, among them Brad Fraser and the others who'd invaded the remote cabin just twelve hours ago. Three of them had been with Brad at the Roadhouse earlier. Nicole took her customary seat at the opposite end of the table.

"Because this has been a long day for most of us, I'm going to keep this short and sweet." He'd intended to tell Nicole before announcing to Falcon, but he'd spent precious minutes looking up infrasound, and by the time he made it to her office, there hadn't been time. It was entirely possible he'd made a subconscious choice, knowing this would upset her, but she'd keep her cool in front of Falcon. "Tomorrow, Keith Hatcher, a former Navy SEAL I worked with on several ops when I was a Ranger, will arrive at the compound. Keith is coming here to tour the facility, meet my top operatives, and observe the training, because when I return to Maryland, I will officially step down as CEO of Raptor and Keith will take over."

A few operatives allowed surprise to show on their faces, but only one, a young man Alec couldn't name, made a low whistling sound as his gaze darted from Alec to Nicole in shock.

For her part, Nicole sat in stone-faced silence.

"I wanted Falcon to know before anyone else, and I ask that you all refrain from sharing this information until the official announcement."

"Is this because of the campaign?" Nate Sifuentes, an operative who'd been on Falcon team since before Alec bought the company, asked.

"Yes. If I win, all my financial assets will be folded into a blind trust. Physical assets, like Raptor, remain my property, but because of Raptor's government contracts, I'll be forbidden from being involved in any management decisions. I've decided to step down early so I can focus on the campaign during the final days."

"And if you lose?" Dev Kalla asked. Kalla was from India and a relatively new hire. He was the first Raptor operative to come from a foreign army.

"Then Hatcher's tenure as CEO will be short," Alec said.

"So, wait…" the operative who'd whistled asked. "Then who's running the training this week? You? This Hatcher guy, or Markwell?"

Nicole stiffened and cast a glare at the young operative.

"I'm afraid I don't know your name?" Alec said to the man.

"Johnston, sir. Chase Johnston."

Alec remembered him now. One of the few hires who didn't have a military background. He'd gone through police academy training and was waitlisted for a job in Anchorage when he'd applied to Raptor. That someone without combat experience sat on Falcon was telling. Simon Barstow had swiped too many experienced operatives. "Director Markwell will remain in charge of the compound. There are no changes planned for the structure and running of this facility," Alec said.

Nicole stood again. "Is that all, Mr. Ravissant?" Nicole hadn't mistered him in a long time. She was well and truly pissed.

"Yes."

"Great. We'll gather again as soon as Mr. Hatcher arrives. Dismissed." She stood and headed for the door.

"Nic. Wait. I need to speak with you."

She stopped dead in her tracks and spoke with her back to him. "Yes, of course, Mr. Ravissant."

The members of Falcon team couldn't escape the room fast enough. In a flash, only Nicole and Alec remained in the conference room.

"Sit down, Nic."

Even though she was no longer in the Army, Nicole knew when to comply with a direct order. She sat.

"You're angry," Alec said.

"Damn right I am. You know I wanted that promotion. Dammit, Rav. You led me to believe—"

"No. I didn't. I told you I was looking outside the organization, because I need you to continue as compound director. I said that if I *couldn't* find a replacement from outside, you topped my list of internal promotions."

"I could sue. Sex discrimination—"

"Don't threaten me, Nicole. You know it's not true. The simple fact is, there's a lot of upheaval going on in the organization. We've lost too many key operatives to Apex; if things don't turn around in Texas, that compound will be closed. And, I'm leaving. I want you to continue as Alaska compound director to ease the transition. I've already completed the paperwork with human resources to raise your salary. You're being given the title Vice President of Operations in addition to compound director."

"But my duties won't change."

"Not really. Not for the first six months anyway. We'll see what happens with the election. If I win, Keith will be calling the shots, and he knows how valuable you are to the company."

She pursed her lips then asked, "How big is my raise?"

Alec smiled. Retaining her would cost him, but he was ready to pay. "Two grand a month."

The rigidness of her posture slipped a fraction. "I suppose that eases the sting a bit." She glanced around the conference room. "Although I have no idea what I'm going to do with extra money when I live in a windowless monstrosity in the middle of a frigid wasteland."

"Vacation in Hawaii?"

She leaned back in her seat and looked at him speculatively. "You have a house there, right? I'm not talking about at the compound on Oahu, but on Kauai. The beach house. The one that was in *Architectural Digest.*"

Alec smiled, knowing where this was going. "Yes."

"I want the house for a two-week vacation. In February— when this place is so damn cold I feel like I'm going to lose my fucking mind."

"No problem. I'll have HR add the stipulation to your contract."

"Not just this year. Every year."

He laughed. "Deal." He rarely visited the Kauai house anyway, and if offering it as an employment perk helped retain a valuable employee, so be it. He'd do anything to keep Apex from stealing Nicole too.

"Fine. When, exactly, do I get to meet my new boss?"

"Tomorrow afternoon."

She drummed her fingers on the tabletop. "Maybe *he'll* agree to change the format of the hostage scenario…"

Alec smiled. "A week from Monday, you can collude with Keith to change my scenarios all you want, but until then, we do the trainings my way."

CHAPTER TEN

ISABEL JOLTED AWAKE, unsure what had pulled her from sleep. Then she heard it again. Someone was shooting bear bangers outside her cabin. Her first reaction was irritation that the Raptor boys were messing with her again. They'd shot off bear bangers a few times in the past. The first time happened right after a congressional committee investigating safety measures at the compound voted to close the facility for two months so they could evaluate the training safety procedures.

She'd reported the harassment, and Officer Westover had conducted a halfhearted investigation. Alec had made a statement through his attorney that there was no evidence his men had trespassed on her property or, for that matter, that anyone had shot bear bangers outside her windows at all. And that was it.

Now they were at it again. The dregs of sleep left her as they fired a third shot. A loud report, like an M-80 firework, it was designed to startle bears—but it worked equally well on humans, and Isabel couldn't help but feel more than a little freaked out.

Why would Raptor operatives do this to her *now*? She had a truce with Alec, and the compound was set to reopen in a few days.

For the first time, she considered that it might not be Raptor who'd been harassing her, and the idea that some unknown person or group wanted to scare her sent an extra chill down her spine.

She grabbed her shotgun from the closet and went to the living room to grab the cell phone that had been delivered several hours ago. Her cabin was dark inside, but outside, the gray light of the late summer night made it all too easy to see across the meadow to where a man stood. He reloaded his bear banger pistol, and pointed it directly at her.

She lunged for the phone, then dropped to the floor, scooting backward, away from the window, wondering if the man had seen her, or if he'd just been aiming for the single front window.

If she called 9-1-1, Westover would take his sweet time in getting here. Alec was closer. She hit the Call button as another banger sounded.

His voice was groggy. "I hope this is a booty call and not an emergency, Iz."

"There's someone in the meadow shooting bear bangers again."

He didn't respond, and she wondered if he didn't believe her. He never had before, why should this be any different?

"I saw him—" Before she could finish, the window shattered. "Oh my God! The front window—"

Pain exploded in her head. Had she been hit by whatever shattered the window? She groaned as nausea settled in her belly.

"Iz, are you okay? What's happening?"

"H-hh-hurts. S-s-ooo much…"

ISABEL LET OUT another groan—the kind Alec had heard in combat, when a soldier was in serious pain. Infrasound again? He pulled on his jeans as he kept the phone pressed to his ear. "I'm coming, honey. Hold on. I'll get there as fast as I can."

"Gonna be s-s-ick."

"I know. Hang on. Stay with me. Keep talking if you can."

"W-wh-what's that?" She gasped, and the next sound wasn't a high-pitched screech. It was a low wail of torture.

A crashing boom sounded; then he heard nothing at all.

HURLED BY AN explosion, Isabel flew backward as a scream erupted from her throat. She slammed into the rear door of the cabin. Pain shot from her wrist, along her arm, and across her shoulder. She grunted and twisted to see the devastation that had been her living room and was stunned to see the room wasn't filled with smoke.

There was no shrapnel, no smell of gunpowder. Not even a wisp of flame. However, some sort of shock wave had upended her furniture—a 9.0 earthquake confined to her living room.

What the hell was that? First she'd been struck by pain that made her think her head would burst, and then her cabin was hit with a flameless explosion? Indoor windstorm?

Again, her head started to throb. Just like right before the shock wave, pain shot down her spine. She dropped to the floor, doubled over with nausea. Cold sweat broke out on her skin. She couldn't breathe.

She was going to die.

ALEC DROVE FAR too fast on the rutted dirt road and arrived at Isabel's cabin less than twenty minutes after their call had abruptly cut off. After he lost connection with her, he'd dialed Nicole and instructed her to rouse Falcon and send them to Isabel's. He estimated the team was five minutes behind him.

The night was still and quiet at her cabin. The only indication something had occurred was the shattered front window. A breeze stirred the wildflowers as he climbed out of the vehicle, causing them to ripple in a shadowed, sepia-hued wave. The calm normalness of it set his nerves on edge.

He scanned the area, then decided to approach the cabin head-on. With his pistol in a two-handed grip, he darted for the front door. He should wait for backup but feared Isabel didn't have that sort of time. "Isabel?" he shouted through the shattered window.

No hurled rock had broken the double-pane window. The glass had fractured across the entire surface—just like his car windshield. A high-pitched sound wave had probably shattered it—similar to infrasound but a different frequency.

With his back to the wall, he twisted the knob on the front door—it was unlocked—and shoved it open. He entered, gun out, shifting from target to target until he was certain the room was clear.

There was no sign of Isabel, but the room was a wreck. The couch was on its side, lodged in the archway between living room and kitchen. Bookshelves lay facedown on the floor, with the contents scattered beneath.

What the hell?

"Isabel?" he called out again.

An eerie screech came from the corner, behind an overturned end table. Alec crouched down and saw wide, glowing eyes. Gandalf. Cowering. Was he injured?

He reached toward the cat, slowly, tentatively. "Where's Isabel?" he asked the cat, feeling foolish even as he said the words. Gandalf didn't hiss or strike out, and Alec stroked the soft fur. The cat mewed in a way that seemed to signal Alec's touch was okay. He wanted to pull the creature out and check for injuries, but he needed to find Isabel first.

He stood and hit the Redial button on his cell, hoping to hell she'd answer this time. He startled when the tinny notes of a muffled song—he recognized the tune as "Call Me Maybe"—filled the cabin. The chorus repeated. The song was a ringtone.

She'd had the phone for only a few hours, and she'd downloaded "Call Me Maybe" for his ringtone. He was fairly certain he knew what that meant. He'd celebrate that little victory as soon as he knew she was okay.

He followed the music, but it cut out before he could find the phone. He dialed again and searched the kitchen, which looked normal in comparison to the overturned living room.

The sound came from under the range.

He plucked out the phone. The screen was cracked. It must have taken a fall before it slid beneath the appliance.

Where the hell was Isabel?

CHAPTER ELEVEN

ISABEL JOLTED AWAKE, unsure what had pulled her from sleep. Then she heard it again. The song was playing again. Someone was calling her. Not just someone. Alec. That was his ringtone.

She groaned and rolled over in her bed, then yelped at a sharp pain that shot up her wrist. What the hell? Her wrist throbbed. She was bleary and her head hurt as if she'd had too much to drink, and she couldn't remember how she'd injured her wrist. Her stomach rolled. Had she vomited?

How much did I drink?

She'd had half a beer at the Roadhouse. Given the pain in her head, she felt like she'd had several. Maybe she'd opened a bottle of wine after Alec left? It seemed like she'd remember that.

"Isabel?" someone shouted from the living room.

She pulled her pillow over her head and groaned. Bad enough he'd called and woken her, but he was *here*?

Was it morning already? The gray light through the window hadn't given much hint as to time, and she wasn't a fan of opening her eyes to check the clock.

No way could she hike out with him today. All she wanted to do was stay in bed and sleep off the worst hangover of her life. "Go away," she muttered into the mattress.

"Jesus, Iz. I was scared to death. What happened?"

"Leave me alone. I just need sleep."

"You need to tell me what happened. I heard the explosion."

He could hear her head exploding? That made no sense. "Nothing happened. I just have a hangover. Go away." She curled into a ball, then whimpered when she again put her weight on her wrist. "Why does my wrist hurt?" she whispered. She turned over and met Alec's concerned gaze. "Did I drink too much last night?"

Oh God. What if she'd had too much to drink and slept with Alec? She glanced at her alarm clock. It was just after one in the morning. Why else would he be here this time of night?

Alec swore and sat on the edge of the bed, which bounced

under his weight, causing a spike of pain in her miserable head. "No, honey. Unless you tied one on after I left, but somehow I doubt it. You called me less than a half hour ago. Someone was shooting bear bangers outside the cabin. Then the window shattered, and you were in pain. Our call cut out right after I heard an explosion." He took her hand and gently probed her wrist. "I drove straight here. Falcon team will be here any second. I just found your phone under the range."

"I called you?" She shook her head, but that was a mistake. Her stomach lurched again.

He brushed a loose curl from her forehead. "I think you were hit by infrasound. I suspect it's how I was attacked yesterday, and may be what happened to Vin."

She closed her eyes and tried to remember. Bear bangers, pain, and an explosion?

The pain part sounded right.

Noise in the front room indicated Falcon had arrived. Alec left her alone to get dressed and met with his team.

She could hear the low hum of intense conversation through the door, but her head hurt too much to make sense of it. Was this how Alec had felt Thursday evening when he came to? If so, no wonder he'd been disoriented and attacked her. If anything, he had to have felt even worse, given the blow to the head on top of general malaise.

And she'd really like to know what had happened to her wrist.

She drank a large glass of water, popped two ibuprofen, and entered her tiny living room, which was overrun by Raptor operatives rearranging her furniture. Even Nicole was here. The only member of Falcon missing was Ted Godfrey.

Could Ted be the man who'd shot the bear bangers? She tried to remember, but the whole event felt just beyond her reach.

Alec hung back as Nicole checked out Isabel's wrist and demanded an ice pack, which Nate Sifuentes—who'd been one of Vin's closest friends—promptly provided.

"Thanks, Nate," Isabel said. Through it all, she felt Alec's gaze, watching her interact with his team. Until he saw her talking with Brad at the tavern, he'd likely been oblivious to how well she knew everyone, and she wondered what he thought now that he knew his own people hadn't vilified her for her crusade, or declared her crazy—at least, not to her face.

"Where's Gandalf?" she asked.

"He was hiding in the corner, behind the table, when I arrived," Alec said. "But he took off through the pet door as soon as everyone showed up."

That made sense. Gandalf didn't like strangers. She'd been surprised he'd tolerated Alec earlier, but then, she'd been gone overnight, and he was late getting fed. "He was okay?"

"He was scared, but when he ran out, he didn't seem to be injured," Alec said.

That was a relief, but she would worry until she saw him for herself. She settled into the couch, listening to the operatives discuss what might have happened. Slowly, the nasty hangover feeling lifted—far faster than it would have if she'd really had too many drinks.

She rubbed her head and closed her eyes, trying desperately to remember the call she'd made to Alec. Flashes of memory returned, as he filled in his side of the conversation. The bear bangers sounded familiar—but then, it had happened a few other times—she could be remembering another night.

Her living room window was gone, now a puddle of glass that glistened in the glow of the sconce gaslights, and her furniture was all skewed, the bookshelf next to the mantle overturned. She paused, her gaze on the lights. Between the wall-mounted gaslights and her stark furnishing, there wasn't a lot that would be damaged if there'd been an explosion outside that caused the earth to shake. There were no lamps to smash or bric-a-brac to shatter. She wasn't a bric-a-brac sort of person.

In her mind, she had a déjà vu-type image of her couch mid-tumble, the shelf toppling. She'd witnessed a massive earthquake in her living room.

She slowly rose and crossed the short distance to the mantle. Conversation and speculation around her stopped as she bent down to retrieve the photo of her and Vin, which lay on the floor. She turned it to the dim light and saw the hairline crack that split the glass, a rift between siblings that hadn't been there hours ago when Alec studied the photo.

She couldn't help it; her eyes teared at the symbolic but all too real fracture. She closed them against the burn and again saw her furniture in flight. She'd slammed into the back door, her wrist taking the brunt of impact. She'd twisted to see the damage, viewing the living room through the kitchen archway. The coffee table had rolled left, the couch right.

"My computer was on the coffee table before the earthquake."

"Earthquake?" Alec asked.

"For lack of a better word. The explosion that upended the room… There was no fire. No smoke. But it wrecked the room like an earthquake. It's why the furniture was jumbled." She glanced around the room. "But where is my computer?"

CHAPTER TWELVE

ALEC FOUND THE news article on his cell phone and recited the web address for everyone so they too could load it on their phones. He then settled next to Isabel so she could read along with him.

Pentagon Eyes Nonexplosive Airwave Weapon as Nonlethal Solution

Simon Barstow, the CEO of Apex, a private security and nonlethal weapons manufacturing company based in Oregon, was in Virginia yesterday showing the Pentagon his company's latest innovation: Airwave®, a nonlethal—if used at a safe distance—weapon Barstow claims is ideal for crowd control.

Airwave, a pulsed energy projectile, shoots a plasma beam, which heats air so quickly it causes the air to "explode" without fire or spark. The exploding air is felt as a shock wave, which contains enough force to upend people and objects in its path. In a demonstration presented to military officials, a midsize sedan targeted from twenty-five feet away rocked heavily, while test dummies ten feet away were lifted and hurled up to five feet.

"I received a briefing on Wednesday, right before the Pentagon demonstration," Alec said after he finished reading. "And saw the article Thursday morning. I'd planned to discuss Barstow's experimentation with nonlethals during today's meeting with Keith Hatcher."

"If Barstow is playing with nonlethals, maybe he's working with infrasound too," Sifuentes said.

"This proves it, then, doesn't it?" Kalla added. "Barstow set off Airwave in Isabel's living room."

"Unfortunately, we have proof of nothing," Alec said. "A missing computer and overturned furniture are hardly evidence Airwave was used here. I don't even know if there's a test that would show plasma-beam superheated air particles."

"I don't understand, sir," Johnston said. "Why would Simon Barstow go after an archaeologist?" The rookie operative cast a glance in Isabel's direction, then looked down, his face flushed, making Alec wonder why. "Because she saved your life?"

"Maybe he thinks Isabel witnessed the assault on Rav," Sifuentes suggested.

"But that still doesn't make sense," Nicole said. "Why would Barstow go after Rav to begin with? He's already got Airwave in his pocket. He's hired away fifteen operatives in the last year—seven from Falcon alone—and Rav is about to step down from the company. What does Barstow have to gain?"

"I have no idea." Alec glanced at his watch. It was nearly two in the morning. Isabel looked a lot less green but no less exhausted. Hell, they were all beat after the previous night added to this one. He knew his operatives could handle it, but Isabel wasn't trained for it, and there was no need to push themselves when nothing would be solved right then. "Let's pack it in, head to the compound, get some sleep." He turned to Isabel, feeling a pleasant rush as he met her wide green eyes. "Pack a bag. You're coming with us."

ISABEL COULD HARDLY believe she was going to the compound as Alec Ravissant's guest, but then, she could hardly believe anything that had happened in the last two days. She was alone with him in one car, while Falcon team and Nicole were in the vehicles in front and behind as they drove down the perimeter road that connected her rented property to the compound. "You know bringing me onto Raptor land will void the restraining order. I'm like a vampire. You're only safe if you don't invite me in."

Alec laughed. "Screw the restraining order. It was in place to prevent you from walking into another live-fire training. Which you'll never do again, right?"

"I didn't mean to do it the first time," she said dryly. It was time to fess up. He'd already guessed anyway. "You were right. I was looking for the cave."

"Tomorrow, you and I are going for a hike."

"Back to where I found you. I know."

"No. I'm taking you to where Vin disappeared and where Vin was found. We're going to find that damn cave and figure out what the hell is going on."

She couldn't help it and threw her arms around his shoulders and pressed a kiss to his cheek.

Alec grunted. "Figures you'd finally put your hands on me when I'm driving and can't do anything about it."

She laughed, feeling a strange joy bubble up inside her. Finally. At last. She might actually get the answers she needed so desperately. She would grieve the loss of Vin every day for the rest of her life, but at least there was the possibility for a small piece of closure. She could move forward with her life, start living again, knowing Vin's murder hadn't gone unnoticed. Unpunished.

She was tempted to say something suggestive. Inviting. And then, like a bucket of ice water, exactly who the man sitting beside her was came crashing down and chilled her to the bone.

She trusted him at least seventy-two percent more than she'd trusted him yesterday, but that meant she trusted him only seventy-three percent.

The attraction she felt for him made her uncomfortable. A betrayal. He owned the company that had killed Vin.

She didn't understand it, really. She knew plenty of handsome Raptor operatives who didn't entice her in the least. Take Brad, for example. He was as good-looking as any man she knew. He made her laugh and was nice to Mothman. But she wasn't interested. She didn't mind *looking* at him. But had no desire to kiss him, no strange, fluttery feeling in her belly when she met his gaze.

It must be some sort of Florence Nightingale effect. Alec had been her patient, dependent on her to survive, and now she felt some sort of twisted affection for him.

It was the only possible explanation, because wanting Alec Ravissant was just plain wrong. "I don't think I'll feel any safer inside the compound than in my cabin," she admitted.

"My suite is secure. And you'll have me guarding you."

"I don't want to sleep in your suite." God, no. The temptation to betray everything she believed in would be too great.

His lips flattened. "Tough. If you want inside, you're stuck with me." He paused and shook his head. "Don't worry. I wasn't thinking we'd share a bed. I have a couch. You'll be in the bedroom. Alone. You can even have a canister of bear spray to snuggle with if you want."

Twenty-seven percent of her still didn't trust him, but she feared even more the dangerous joy she felt when she made him laugh, or the flutter in her belly when she met his gaze.

She was terrified of the fact that she'd woken up in his arms yesterday and had been aroused at the feel of his morning erection. Not just aroused. Eager. Needy.

Wanting Alec Ravissant wasn't the smart thing or the right thing. It was the worst thing.

Right or wrong, they were heading to the compound, and Isabel was finally going to get what she'd been angling for since she moved to Tamarack months ago—she would finally see inside the facility, explore where Vin had lived his last months, and visit the location where he'd died.

The guard inside the gatehouse waved them through without hesitation, and she wondered again what it must be like to be the tiger king. One would think having been abducted and beaten would diminish his swagger, but as far as she could tell, his swagger had suffered no shrinkage. He parked in the open space closest to the main entrance, shut off the engine, and handed her the key, because this was the vehicle that had been delivered to her cabin for her use earlier in the night. She slipped the key into her purse as he jumped out of the car with a show of energy that belied his aches and pains from yesterday.

He grabbed her bag from the trunk. She felt a twinge of worry that Gandalf wasn't with her, but she'd set out extra food for him, just in case she didn't return for a day or two.

Alec nodded to a security guard stationed on the front steps of the building, and pushed open the door, pausing to hold it open for her. He resumed his quick pace. Isabel followed, having to walk quickly or be left behind.

In the foyer, Alec nodded to the man behind a desk and kept walking. She followed him, stepping through the glass partition that separated the public front room from the forbidden zone, where yet another man sat at yet another desk. Isabel recognized Nicole's assistant, Hans. It appeared everyone in the compound had been roused by the incident in her cabin, because she highly doubted Hans was usually at the front station at two thirty in the morning.

Alec continued past. His demeanor seemed to change with the setting. He was no longer the politician, the wounded warrior, or the man with questions only she could answer. Nor was he the Ranger. Now he was the Boss. The man in charge. The alpha tiger.

A purist might point out that tigers were loners and therefore neither alphas nor betas, but to her, Alec was a tiger, and decidedly alpha.

She quickened her pace again to keep up with him. He headed down a mazelike corridor, turning sharply at intersections with the single-minded intensity of Pac-Man pursued by ghosts. Three—or was it four?—turns in, and she was hopelessly lost. There were no markers, no exit signs, nothing to aid her usually keen sense of direction. "What's with the ant-farm layout? Have you ever found someone huddled at the end of a corridor, delirious from dehydration?"

He cracked a small grin. "Extra security, courtesy of Raptor's former owner. He was paranoid the compound would be raided and designed the place to be disorienting." He glanced at her askance, and his grin widened. "It's almost like he expected *you.*"

She couldn't help but smile as she followed him through the endless maze, at last coming to a door no different from any other except it was at the end of a corridor. He punched in a code on the keypad, then twisted the knob. With a sweep of his hand, he bade her to enter a room that could house her small cabin several times over.

Alaska wasn't known for luxurious comforts, but this room ranked on an entirely different scale. This was luxurious on a sheik's scale.

"Holy crap. I didn't know former Rangers had such a big thing for marble." She crossed the room to the ornate white marble hearth. "It couldn't have been cheap to truck this monstrosity over the pass." It had Corinthian columns, for goodness' sake—tall ones that reached the ceiling flanked the short ones that held up the mantel. As if four columns weren't bad enough, there were also high-relief angels arching over the open grate.

He closed the door and leaned against it, amusement evident in his eyes. "It's the ugliest mantel I've ever seen. Apparently, Robert Beck had a thing for rococo. I have no idea why he indulged his gaudy tastes here, of all places."

"Why don't you get rid of it?"

"It's a working fireplace. To remove the piece intact would require taking out a wall; otherwise, it would have to be broken. I may not like it, but I'm not about to destroy something functional just because it doesn't suit my tastes."

She swept her arm across the room. "And the furniture? You could have switched the tables and"—she shuddered at the carved marble cherub under a lampshade dripping with glass prisms—

"lamps without destroying them."

He shrugged. "The furniture is cold, ugly, and uncomfortable, but I have better things to do than redecorate."

He pushed off the door and crossed the room. "I did change the bedroom, though. Beck's bedroom furniture was donated to a shelter in Fairbanks. I wasn't about to sleep in the bastard's bed." He opened a door, and Isabel peered into a large bedroom furnished simply with wood furniture he'd probably purchased from Walt's Designer Emporium in town. The entire name was tongue-in-cheek, considering it was a catalog shop in the back corner of the general store, operated by a woman named Doreen.

"There's a bathroom through the far door. The tub has jets and temperature controls and more gadgets than I've been able to figure out. Take a bath if you want. Or just go to sleep. That's what I'm going to do." He crossed the room and pulled open a door that revealed a walk-in closet. A moment later, he returned with blankets and sheets.

"Make yourself comfortable. You're safe here. I promise."

Safe from attack, maybe. But with Alec just outside the door, sleeping on an ugly, uncomfortable couch?

She wondered if she was safe from herself.

The moment he left the room, she plopped onto the bed.

Holy hell. Her life had certainly taken a wild turn. She dropped her head in her hands. She'd spent a lifetime constructing isolationist walls. With the exception of her brother, no one was allowed inside. She had friends, but no one closer than arm's length. Now, when she needed her barriers most, she discovered she'd built on permafrost, and her foundation was melting.

She'd hugged Joyce. She'd kissed Alec. She was becoming a regular teddy bear.

She'd been attacked in her home but didn't really remember it. What if… What if she hadn't been attacked? What if it was all Alec? He'd been there when she woke up. He'd told her she'd called and screamed and said she was in pain. But she had to take his word for it. For all she really knew, her memory of an earthquake in her cabin was a suggested memory. He could have drugged her.

She had nothing to hold on to. Nothing crystal clear to believe.

She mustn't forget everyone had an agenda. For Alec, charming politician was his primary role.

He wasn't her friend. He was a power-hungry politician who

wanted to control anyone who could tarnish his image. She'd willingly entered the alpha tiger's territory, but that didn't mean she was prey to his predator. She wouldn't let him control her. And she definitely wouldn't give in to the heat that coursed through her whenever they were alone.

CHAPTER THIRTEEN

KEITH HATCHER GRABBED his girlfriend, Trina Sorensen, by the waist and pulled her flush against him. He kissed her deeply—probably too deeply for a public display of affection, but just ten feet from the security screen at Dulles Airport, the men and women who worked for TSA were probably immune to inappropriate PDAs after repeated exposure. And Keith was hardly a public figure who needed to keep things rated G like his new boss.

"I'm going to miss you like crazy," Trina said.

"Same here, babe."

She frowned. "I know your job is dangerous, but *this* trip was supposed to be easy. I'm a little annoyed that your first trip on Raptor business feels more like you're going to Kazakhstan than Alaska."

Keith shrugged. "I've been to Kazakhstan. I'm pretty sure it was worse."

Trina's eyes widened. "Really? You've never mentioned Kazakhstan. Was it a SEAL mission? Is it classified? I'd love to hear how—"

Keith kissed her again to shush her. They'd only been going out for a month, and he was still getting used to the fact that his military historian girlfriend was more interested in his exploits as a SEAL than most veterans were curious about entire wars. At the point at which a normal person's eyes glazed over, Trina would start asking questions about troop morale or the underlying economic influences that pushed an individual to bow to a warlord's commands to storm a NATO stronghold or turn to piracy on the East African coast.

She was adorable but also a little exhausting.

She dropped back to her heels, ending the kiss. "Fine. We'll talk about Kazakhstan when you get back."

Trust Trina to remember what they'd been talking about and to see right through his deflection. He smiled. "You got it, babe."

"Don't let Alec steamroll Isabel, okay?"

Keith shook his head. "You talk about Isabel like you know her. Alec is the one you know. I'm sure you remember him. The politician? My new boss? The guy who financed your bodyguard a month ago?"

Trina smiled. "Yeah, yeah. Alec can take care of himself. Isabel's an archaeologist, and you know how the grapevine works. Erica and Mara asked around, and she's solid. A little messed up—but who wouldn't be after the way her brother died. Alec is a good guy, but he could have done more to investigate Vincent Dawson's death."

Keith grimaced. Rav might have done four hundred and twenty-eight things right in the last year, but he'd dropped the ball once, and Isabel Dawson had stepped forward and made sure the world knew it.

Because of the ongoing investigation and the campaign, only a handful of people knew the truth behind what happened to Rav—that he'd definitely been abducted, beaten, and left for dead, and that Isabel Dawson, of all people, had saved his life—but the media wasn't likely to be held at bay for long. It was only a matter of time before the full truth came out, and for the sake of the campaign, Carey, Rav's campaign manager, had floated the idea of casting suspicion on Isabel for the abduction. Carey had argued that Isabel had a well-known vendetta with Raptor and there'd been questions about her mental health.

Isabel Dawson had motive to abduct Rav, and her motive had nothing to do with politics, the military, special ops, Raptor's mercenary work, or any of a dozen other reasons someone might target Rav. Even more important, unlike a foreign terrorist group, she didn't have tools of torture or brainwashing at her disposal—and with a seven hour gap in his memory, that was a real concern—making Isabel the ideal villain as far as keeping Rav electable.

Keith had no doubt Carey wanted Isabel to be the culprit and she wouldn't bat an eye at pinning it on her if the truth would harm the campaign.

With a perfect patsy in the crosshairs, Keith feared the FBI would begin and end their investigation with Isabel Dawson. She might well be guilty, but he didn't like the idea of anyone being railroaded simply because they were politically convenient. He wanted Alec to win the election so he could stay on as Raptor's

CEO, but no job, not even this one, was worth selling his soul.

ALEC SMILED AT Isabel from his seat at the table and nodded toward the breakfast spread laid out on the marble-topped sideboard. "Help yourself," he said.

She filled her plate with scrambled eggs, bacon, and fruit and set it across from him on the small table, then turned to grab utensils. He had a tablet in front of him, the modern version of reading the morning paper with breakfast. It felt strangely intimate, sharing breakfast with him, as if this were a morning after. It didn't help that she'd dreamed about him. Not a sex dream, but the undercurrent of desire had been there, giving the dream a sexual edge. She woke fully aroused and wishing Alec were spooning with her, his morning erection pressed between her thighs.

This was a problem.

"Feeling better?" he asked.

Her dirty mind turned his innocent question into a proposition, and she shook her head to clear it of the sudden fantasy of him clearing the sideboard with the sweep of his arm, then lifting her onto it and sliding deep inside, making her feel much, much better.

"You aren't feeling better?" he asked, and she realized he took the shake of her head as a negative.

She felt her face flush, knowing she was turning a deep cherry red—the curse of red hair and fair skin. "No, I feel much better."

He studied her face, and one corner of his mouth kicked up. A little smug and a whole lot sexy. "Care to share what's making you blush?"

"Not particularly."

He stood and plucked a strawberry from her plate, then advanced on her, slowly. She couldn't help but feel like prey as the tiger stalked. She took one step back, then another, until the sideboard pressed into her spine. The same sideboard that had just played a vital role in her quick, hot fantasy. Her breathing turned shallow.

Alec paused before her, but he didn't clear the marble counter. He didn't lift her. He didn't spread her legs and fill her. Instead, he brushed the strawberry over her lips. She couldn't resist and took a small bite. The sweet juice dampened her bottom lip, and she licked it.

His gaze had fixed on her mouth; he let out a soft growl and bit into the berry himself.

He'd kissed her once, but she'd put an end to it before it could go too far. Now, here she was, wanting another kiss—and much more—so badly she could feel the flush spread from her face to dangerous, hidden regions.

"Your move, Iz."

She cleared her throat. "I can't." Not until she was certain beyond a shadow of a doubt that he hadn't known Vin was murdered and covered it up because it would have destroyed his fledgling candidacy.

"Can't, or won't?"

"Both."

He nodded and stepped back, giving her room to breathe. He popped the rest of the strawberry into his mouth. "Fair enough."

"When do we head out on our hike?"

"I'm afraid it won't be until early afternoon. With everything that's happened, we've had to rearrange the schedule. This morning, Falcon team will practice training scenarios in the simulated village and the shoot houses. I need to be there to go over the setup with them."

Vin had described how realistic the village and shoot houses were, and she'd always wanted to see them and how the trainings were conducted. "Can I join you?"

He frowned and studied her. "They'll be running through hostage-rescue drills. No live fire—but still, it can be intense. The team will be amped."

She had a good idea what that meant. After all, as a teen, she'd lived on base with Vin. She'd particularly enjoyed the times he invited his fellow soldiers over. Just watching football could send testosterone levels through the roof. Much to Vin's irritation, at sixteen she'd found it a rush to be surrounded by pumped-up nineteen- to twenty-one-year-old men in prime fighting shape. Her jailbait age combined with her brother's threats of bodily harm to any guy who touched her ensured—much to *her* irritation—nothing ever happened with any of Vin's friends.

"What does that smile mean?" Alec asked.

"I was just thinking it's been a long time since I've hung out with a group of handsome, amped-up soldiers. Pretty please can I go?"

His eyes narrowed. "I don't think I like the idea of you getting excited about watching Fraser and Sifuentes."

She couldn't help but grin. "I have a feeling you can hold your own with Brad and Nate. Besides, Brad's taken." Truthfully, she wanted to see Alec—and only Alec—in soldier mode. "I promise to stay out of the way."

His mouth quirked up at one corner. "Your reputation for getting *in* the way precedes you." His eyes were a warm blue, and she realized the swelling was now completely gone. "But this might be the only way to keep you out of trouble while I'm with Falcon." He nodded. "Fine. You can join us."

"Thank you." On impulse, she leaned in and kissed his cheek.

He slid an arm around her waist before she could slip away. "We'll set out after breakfast." His voice lowered as his eyes flared with heat. "Although I *can* delay it. One of the benefits of being the boss."

She imagined the cold marble of the sideboard under her bare ass, her head banging into the wall as he pounded into her. So very, very tempting. She cleared her throat. "No. After breakfast is fine."

"HOW MANY PEOPLE do you have to play the market crowd?" Alec asked Nicole as they strolled between the rows of wooden stalls in the fake outdoor market.

Two rows away, Isabel paused to admire the setting. The stalls were set up to simulate an open-air market in the Middle East or any of a dozen different terrorist hotspots. According to Nate, they had different "product" props to fill the tables, depending on which scenario they were running. Today the tables were empty, the props stored in Conex boxes tucked in the woods well away from the training area, so as not to interfere with the authenticity of the setting.

Nicole and Alec were conferring about the training for US Army soldiers that would begin on Wednesday as Nate gave her a tour of the facility.

"Isn't it a little cold for a Middle Eastern market?" she asked.

Nate fixed her with a look and cleared his throat. "Um, well, that's why we like to run these trainings in the *summer*, but since we were closed the last two months—"

She pursed her lips, chagrined. "My intention was never—"

Nate smiled and held up a hand to cut her off. "Wars and markets aren't confined to the summer. We're going to set this up to simulate an Afghani market, and we're going to run two different scenarios—one is going to be US soldiers in the market finding themselves targeted by Taliban; the other is going to be a hostage scenario."

Isabel gazed across the stalls to where Alec spoke to Nicole. "The soldiers, when they show up for the training, do they know what to expect?"

"No. Everyone starts out at the simulated base camp two clicks from here. Their CO will assign them all duties. Not even the CO will know exactly what we have in store. Several soldiers will be sent here with operatives who are playing the role of Afghan military personnel training under the US soldiers. While in the market, the Afghan trainees might turn traitor or be targeted by Afghan civilians, or they might come across a suicide bomber, or the Taliban can show up and take hostages."

"Who plays the villain in those scenarios?"

Nate grimaced. "Falcon team always plays the Tangos—the target, or villains. It's the price of being on the top team." He shrugged. "But we get to play good-guy roles too, so it balances out."

"When you're playing the good guys, do you know what's going to happen?"

"No. The only people who know the full details of the Tango's plan are the operatives who are given the role of Tangos, plus Nic, and Rav, if he's visiting. Sometimes Nic will assign Tangos conflicting plans—they won't be working together. Like ISIS and al Qaeda, we can have two factions who are out to screw everyone, but they haven't communicated with each other their particular plans."

"So what are you going to do here today?"

"Today we're scouting out vulnerabilities. Where the worst place to be caught in the market is, what attacks are easiest and hardest to defend. I think Nic already has this week's training outlined, but Rav always has tweaks he likes to toss in at the end."

At a sharp whistle from Nicole, Nate left her side to receive his orders. Isabel hung back, trying to stay out of the way as promised.

It was fascinating to watch Falcon work as a team as they walked through the market and discussed tactics and training measures with a level of detail that sounded like a foreign language.

Engrossed in his work, Alec seemed to have forgotten Isabel's presence, which pleased her—the last thing she wanted was to be a distraction here—plus she could study him, unobserved, as he directed the team, asked questions of Nicole, and mapped out his plans for the training.

From the market, they moved on to a brand-new shoot house. Brad had explained the purpose of the shoot houses to her about a month after she was arrested, and she knew Vin had found the shoot house trainings to be the most intense.

The shoot house was usually used for hostage scenarios. Soldiers were expected to work their way through the house, clearing each room by taking out Tangos without shooting hostages, women, or children—unless the women attacked.

They sometimes ran scenarios with Raptor operatives acting as Tangos, hostages, and innocent civilians. Those were dry-fire trainings, in which everyone used unloaded guns. When dummies or photos were used to represent Tangos and hostages, then live fire was used. The walls were constructed with a special concrete that absorbed bullets with less scarring, so the house would stand up to several years' worth of trainings.

Months ago, Isabel had been down range from a shoot house during one of the live-fire trainings, when she'd been spotted and arrested. Alec's concern was well warranted, she could see now, because while the concrete walls did stop bullets, there were windows on the south side of the building, and portions of the structure lacked a roof, so there were opportunities for strays. There was a wide buffer zone that was off-limits, and instructors watched those exercises from an observation post on a hill above the shoot house, which was enclosed in bulletproof glass, so they could watch the portions in the roofless rooms as well as a video feed of the action in the roofed sections of the house.

The video feed from the shoot house—and all the training ground settings—went to God's Eye, back at the compound, where Nicole was usually situated when trainings were in progress.

Today, Nicole divided Falcon into teams of two, and they ran practice drills with unloaded guns to rehearse and block the moves for the upcoming hostage scenario. Because they weren't using any type of ammunition, it was safe for Isabel to observe the action from a closer vantage point.

Beside her, Nicole said to Alec, "With the design of this house, we can run dry-fire exercises where the hostage is moved from room to room—doubling back into rooms that have already been cleared."

"I want to run that a couple of different ways," Alec said. "With the connecting doorways covered by tapestries, and other times with a visible opening. I also want tapestries hung on solid walls as well, so they have to find the opening."

"I think we've got enough tapestries in Conex storage. I'll have maintenance install hooks today."

"Good."

Brad and Chase finished their dry run through the building. Brad flashed a grin at Isabel and flexed a muscle. "How'd I do?" he asked with a wink. Even though it was just a demonstration for blocking purposes with invisible Tangoes and hostages, she could see he was pumped. As Alec had warned, the exercise got the adrenaline flowing.

"Not bad. But I think you took out at least one hostage in room two."

"Nah. Clearly it was a Tango."

She laughed.

"You want to st-stand in for a h-hostage, Isabel?" Chase Johnston asked.

She did a double take. It was the first time the man had ever spoken to her.

"No," Alec said flatly, before she could respond.

She turned to Alec, head cocked in question. The fact that the invitation to play hostage came from Chase, of all operatives, was admittedly, a little creepy, but the exercise could be more effective if they had a clueless stand-in for a hostage in the mix. Plus it would give her a chance to be useful. "Why not?"

"Because it's not a game. The moment we play it like a game is the moment we get sloppy and forget the stakes."

She stiffened, offended he'd assume she'd diminish the exercise with her presence. That she wouldn't take it seriously. "I didn't suggest it was a game, or that I'd play it as such."

He shook his head. "Not you, Iz." He nodded toward the members of Falcon and stepped aside. He lowered his voice, making their argument semiprivate—or at least, the others were no longer invited to listen. "The team. They wouldn't treat you how they must treat a hostage in these scenarios. Because they know you, they'd soften it up, make it less scary. Which means it would become a game, not an exercise. Exercise, to be effective, has to hurt a little bit."

She glanced at Nate and Brad. Friends, but soldiers through and through. She couldn't imagine them going easy on her, if they were instructed not to. "So tell them not to go easy on me."

Again he shook his head. "You don't get it. I can't do that. I *won't* do that. When people are assigned roles—victim, traitor, terrorist, bystander—we run it as real as possible. Every time. We never *play*. Hostages are tied up. Possibly gagged. Gun to the head. And I'm telling you right now, I will *not* allow Brad to hold a gun to your head. I don't give a fuck if I've checked it first and know without a shadow of a doubt there isn't a bullet within a hundred yards of the chamber. It's not gonna happen. Not even with a prop."

He nodded toward the shoot house. "You saw how it went. Even without ammo, a run through the house gets the adrenaline going. Add a screaming hostage into the mix, and it starts to feel too real, too fast. There are some things you don't want to experience. Even in simulation. We aim to make it feel real so it's damn scary for everyone involved."

Her throat went dry. She hadn't thought her objection through.

She'd long suspected her brother's murderer could be on Falcon—after all, Vin had been on Falcon—and the idea of one of them putting even an unloaded gun to her head gave her the creeps. She pursed her lips and gave Alec a sharp nod.

"I need you to go to the observation post while we finish this exercise. We still have a lot to do, and I need to focus."

She followed his instructions without a word. She wasn't mad—at anyone but herself. She hated being wrong and needed to collect her thoughts. The observation post was a good fallback position.

She watched from above as Alec and Nicole directed the teams to run through the house again and again. Alec's focus was razor-sharp, as intent as he'd been before their argument. She'd promised not to get in the way, and was glad to see she hadn't gotten into his mental space, not when he had an important job to do.

But he was in *her* mental space, and that was the problem.

She was becoming convinced she'd been wrong about Alec all these months. And now that she was seeing firsthand what Raptor offered soldiers in terms of combat readiness, guilt over the two months of missed trainings swamped her. Hundreds of soldiers wouldn't have the benefit of getting the crap scared out of them in Alaska, so they'd be better prepared to shake off the freezing response to fear in Afghanistan, or Somalia, or Syria, or Iraq, or wherever they were sent next.

Hadn't Vin talked about how valuable the training was, when he'd gone through it?

Wasn't that part of why he took the job? He'd been excited to have options outside the military, but he'd also been pleased with the results Raptor achieved. Her big brother had been a born teacher, and here he'd finally had his chance to teach.

She tried to shrug off the guilt. Without shutting down the compound, how else would she have gotten Alec's attention? No one believed Vin had been murdered at all. No one would listen. So she went after the compound on the grounds that it wasn't safe. She didn't get results until the shutdown. There hadn't *been* another way.

Except…she didn't get results when the compound was shut down either. The government investigators who evaluated the safety procedures didn't give her the time of day. None of the inspectors suddenly came forward and said they believed Vin had been murdered.

Alec certainly hadn't come around. He didn't hear her out, didn't start to believe, until something happened to him. Only then did he agree to listen. His abduction had finally gotten her what she so desperately wanted.

She hoped to hell that he believed her innocence now, because an outsider looking in could think she had a very strong motive for abducting him.

CHAPTER FOURTEEN

IT WAS WELL after lunch when the planning meeting wrapped up and Falcon team and Nicole returned to the main compound buildings. Alone again for the first time since their discussion earlier, Isabel was strangely nervous. Not that she feared he was angry with her, and she certainly wasn't angry with him.

It was more the suspicion. What if he remained suspicious of her? What if this slow seduction—if that was what this *thing* was between them—was all a ploy to determine if she was behind his abduction?

He could bring her anywhere on the compound and tell her it was where Vin disappeared, and she'd have no way of knowing if he was lying to her.

"We can take ATVs as far as the river. But it's too deep to cross in this area and the bridge too narrow," he said. His deep voice was a low rumble. Strangely, achingly familiar after such a short acquaintance.

Just his *voice* delivered a pleasurable chill.

What was wrong with her? She wasn't the type to get twitterpated over a handsome face with a perfect body. At least, not since she was eighteen. Not after the time the guy she had a crush on had sex with her best friend during their big graduation party, then had the gall to try to get into her pants thirty minutes later.

That was the night Isabel had sworn off handsome jocks. And confiding in girlfriends.

Alec Ravissant was far more than a handsome jock, though. To lump him in the same category with the boy soccer player from her senior year was seriously selling the man short. Alec was the full package—brains, brawn, and charm.

"Do we need ATVs?" she asked. "You miss so much, riding. Plus they're so loud."

"We can walk, but we won't have a lot of time to dally. Keith's plane should be landing about now. We've got three hours, tops.

It's a lot of hiking for three hours."

She gave him a wry smile. "Hiking in the woods is sort of one of my specialties."

He waggled his eyebrows, and his sexy voice lowered even more. "Want to know what one of *my* specialties is?"

She rolled her eyes. "Avoiding walking by getting women to drag you through the woods?"

"No fair. That was a seriously off day for me."

"Uh-huh," she said with as much skepticism as she could put in the syllables.

He lunged and scooped her up, his arms wrapped around her butt as he held her so they were chest-to-chest, face-to-face. "You want me to make up for it by carrying you today?"

It would be so easy to lean in and kiss him.

She braced her forearms against his chest; her wrists rested on his collarbones. Her fingers itched to slide up into his dark hair as she held his gaze, her mind utterly blank, snappy comebacks lost to the heat in his eyes. Finally, she licked her lips and managed to say, "I don't think so. I think I like having you in my debt."

"I believe in paying back with interest."

She slid against him as he slowly lowered her to the ground. "I'm counting on that."

She plucked her backpack from the ground and slung it over her shoulders. "Which way are we headed?"

"Northeast."

"Let's get going then, Tiger. We're burning daylight."

"Tiger?"

She had no intention of telling him where that nickname came from.

First he led her to the place where Vin had been found the day he fell and dreamed of the lynx cave. She pulled out her quadrangle map and studied the terrain, looking for landforms that could conceal caves. "Did Vin ever come back here?"

"Not that I know of. But he and the trainees camped about a half mile from here for that last survival training. They hiked through this area."

"How do you know this is where he was found?" she asked.

"The two operatives who found him that day identified the location when we investigated your theory after he died."

"Who found him?" She'd asked Nicole this question, but she'd never answered. But then, Nicole hadn't answered any questions about Vin—probably because Raptor attorneys had warned her not to.

"Ted Godfrey and another operative who left for Apex about a month before Vin died."

She stared up at the steep hillside Vin had fallen from just over a year ago. A game trail was faintly visible crossing the active talus slope. "Do you think there's a connection between what happened to Vin and Apex?"

"I don't know. The fact that your cabin was hit by Airwave last night seems damning, but also convenient, if someone wanted it to look like Apex was involved."

"I don't like it," she murmured, taking a step toward the slope.

"The Apex connection?"

She shook her head as she stepped onto the slope. She took three steps sideways, each slightly higher than the previous. As expected, the rocks rolled, and she slid down, gaining only a few inches of elevation from her starting point.

She met Alec's gaze. "I don't like this slope. Why would Vin climb it? He was alone—and had already been lectured about hiking alone by Dr. Larson—and the slope is too active. A fall would have been a foregone conclusion. It's a terrible hike with no benefit. The summit is below the tree line and from looking at the map, it appears to back up to an even bigger hill. There's no view. No way in hell did Vin climb this slope."

Alec slapped at the cloud of mosquitos that had swarmed around them as soon as they paused at the base of the steep hill. "According to his write-up of the incident, there was a rockfall trail through the talus, indicating Vin had fallen—and then rolled—about thirty feet."

She faced the slope again and kicked at the rocks, triggering a small slide. The truth settled in her gut. "Godfrey lied." She glanced over her shoulder at Alec. "Why wasn't he at my cabin last night? Or, for that matter, at the shoot house this morning? The rest of Falcon was both places. It crossed my mind last night that he could have been the one who shot the bear bangers and set off Airwave."

Alec frowned. "He quit on Thursday. He was recruited by Apex."

"So it could have been him."

He nodded. "When we get back to the compound, I'll ask the FBI to check on his whereabouts."

She reached down and scooped up a rock, then chucked it at a high point in the slope. The impact caused yet another mini-avalanche of stones. "Vin must have seen this during the training. He'd have remembered hiking this area, but because he was unconscious when he was found and didn't come to until he was inside the compound, he didn't know what hill he supposedly fell down. One look at this slope and he'd have known Godfrey lied, or that if he really *was* found here, that someone had to have dumped him at the base and made it look like a fall. It must have been jarring to realize he didn't remember what really happened that day." It had been odd enough for her last night, and she'd only lost thirty minutes.

"Tell me about it," Alec said with a hint of bitter humor. Then he sighed. "My guess is, your brother believed the dream was just that, until he returned here and things stopped adding up, or maybe being here triggered a memory. Like I was able to remember the pain of infrasound after reading Vin's description."

"And I was able to remember the earthquake in my living room after you told me you heard an explosion. It's like the memories are there, but only accessible with a trigger." Even now her recall was vague, more like snapshots in a photo album, viewed from outside, disconnected from her thoughts and experience. She glanced around and attempted to wave off a dozen mosquitos that vied for her blood. "So Vin saw this place and remembered something. Maybe."

Alec nodded. "Maybe."

🐾

"THE GROUP WAS camped here," Alec said, pointing to the spongy ground beneath a stand of tamarack trees. "According to the trainees, Vin slept over there—set off from the group. There were four of them—three trainees and Vin—and they each had a two-hour watch shift. One of the soldiers—a nineteen-year-old boy who'd yet to complete a combat tour—probably dozed on his shift. When another soldier woke to take over, they noticed Vin was gone."

Alec circled the small area. "They assumed he'd stepped away to take a leak, and made a bird call signal, one Vin should have repeated. He didn't." He paused and scanned the hills that jutted from the landscape a hundred yards away. Beyond the foothills were glacier-covered mountains, nothing but wilderness for hundreds of miles. "It dawned on one of them that Vin's gear was gone too. But instead of worrying and raising the alarm, they assumed it was some sort of test. They figured Vin had moved a distance away and was watching them to see how they'd do in survival training without an instructor." Alec rubbed a hand over his face. That first night, Vin had still been alive. If the trainees had followed protocol and radioed back to the compound, a search party would have been formed. They might have found him. But it wasn't until twelve hours after Vin had disappeared that anyone in Raptor was informed one of their own was missing.

He finally turned to meet Isabel's gaze, not knowing what he expected to see. This was different from visiting the place where Vin had supposedly fallen—which had been a puzzle with possible answers. She'd been quiet from the moment they reached this area, and now tears fell unchecked down her cheeks, and he felt like a complete and utter ass for not having made arrangements for her to visit this place months ago.

His lawyers had said many times it was unwise, and he damned himself for listening to them. One problem with growing up in an überwealthy family was the perpetual lawsuits. He'd had his own team of lawyers since he was sixteen and a fender bender—in which he'd been the middle car, rear-ended by a distracted driver and shoved into the stopped car in front of him—triggered his first frivolous lawsuit.

His father had freaked when Alec told him he intended to spend his inheritance on Raptor. Companies like Raptor were a tort lawyer's wet dream.

But Alec had moved forward, knowing he could turn Raptor into something special. The mercenary organization—and the Alaska training ground in particular—would teach soldiers, sailors, airmen, and marines life-saving skills. All branches of the military would receive specialized training that was desperately needed to defeat terrorists and insurgents and suicide bombers and all the new threats that had developed during the ongoing war on terror.

He didn't give a crap if he was sued. He didn't give a damn about his family's money. He only cared that the company and assets didn't fall into the wrong hands—as they'd been under Robert Beck's ownership.

But still, he had attorneys. Legions of them. And, to a man, they'd insisted Isabel Dawson not be taken to the place where Vin disappeared or where he died. They were certain she would try to take Alec and Raptor for everything. Not that she'd succeed, but that allowing her inside invited the threat. He was fairly certain several lawyers, eager to present her case, had approached her. As far as he knew, she'd turned down every one.

Isabel had even refused the insurance money for Vin's accidental death, because she didn't want any legal documents to show she'd even tacitly accepted Vin's death as an accident. The money sat in an escrow account, unclaimed.

Now, after meeting her, he was certain he'd never had to fear a lawsuit from her. Money played no part in her motivation.

She stared at the last place Vin was seen alive, with silent tears flowing down her cheeks. Alec crossed the soft, mossy ground and took her into his arms. She stiffened at first, but then settled against his chest. Her arms wrapped around his waist, and she let out her first audible sob.

He stroked her hair, which was every bit as soft as he'd suspected, but this was *not* what he'd imagined for the first time he tangled his fingers in her beautiful curls. "I'm sorry, Iz. I should have brought you here months ago."

She nodded. "I know why you didn't."

"Because I'm an ass."

She laughed even as she cried. "Well, sure, but I also know you were warned I'd sue you for everything if I could."

"I'm sorry I listened."

She looked up at him, her green eyes glistening and beautiful and sad. "Thank you." She rose on her toes and pressed her lips to his. A soft kiss of friendship and acceptance that gave him hope she could forgive him.

If she forgave him, maybe they had a shot at more than friendship, more than sex, which he realized in that moment was what he wanted. Last night he figured he could be satisfied with a no-strings physical relationship, but they'd passed that point. He wasn't sure when. Maybe when they flirted over breakfast, or when he'd had a visceral, negative reaction to the suggestion she play the role of hostage. Maybe *when* didn't matter.

He ran his thumb over her chin. "You ready to go to the place where we found him?"

She nodded. "I'd sort of hoped to look around—to see if we could find a cave—but I don't suppose we have time."

"Not today. I promise, we searched this area, and the area around the talus slope where Godfrey said they found him, thoroughly. There aren't any caves until you get into the higher foothills—and we didn't find any petroglyphs in those."

"I'll still want to look."

He nodded. "Maybe Tuesday. I need to finish prep for the upcoming training first."

"I could go by myself—"

"No. It's not safe."

She frowned. "I hike by myself all the time, Alec. It's part of my job."

"I'm not worried about bears. I'm worried about whoever killed Vin."

He caught the widening of her eyes. Had he not said it outright before? He wasn't sure, but even if he had, it was clear she wasn't used to hearing it. "He was murdered, Iz. And we're going to find out who did it."

She gave him a sharp nod and said, "Let's go."

They walked for nearly an hour before they reached a narrow footbridge that crossed the river. "We think Vin crossed a mile downstream the day after he disappeared. I'll take you to where we think he crossed after I show you where we found him."

"Were you part of the search team?"

"Yes. The day he was reported missing, I caught a flight from Maryland and joined the search. Brad Fraser and I found Vin."

She took his hand in hers and squeezed. "Brad never told me that."

"He wasn't under orders not to—he probably felt it would be hard for you—or that you'd pressure him to take you there."

"Probably the latter. And, honestly, I would have."

She didn't release Alec's hand, which surprised him. He had a feeling Isabel wasn't really a hand holder, but she was facing her deepest grief and needed a hand to hold. He was damn glad that he could provide it.

Mosquitoes swarmed in the late summer heat. He waved an arm to disperse them but didn't release Isabel's hand to dislodge the worst offenders. No way was he letting her go now that he had her.

They reached the glade where he'd found Vin eleven months ago. Back then, snow had dusted the ground and Vincent Dawson's body. Between the snow and his camouflage clothing, he'd blended into the landscape, and Alec hadn't spotted him until they were just yards away. Today Alec was glad for the bright afternoon sun and the late summer wildflowers, which lent the clearing a peaceful beauty.

"It was snowing when he walked here, and continued snowing for several hours after he died. There was a faint, single set of footprints leading to his body."

A granite marker rested on the exact spot where Vin had lain down and died. Isabel gasped when she saw it and dropped to her knees, tracing the letters of her brother's name etched into the stone. She looked up at Alec. "Did you…?"

"Yes."

She smiled at him, and he was surprised there were no tears. "Thank you."

"Do you want to have a ceremony here on the first anniversary? You can invite friends and family. I'll make sure my people leave you alone."

Now her eyes did tear. "Really?"

"Absolutely."

"I'd like that. We don't have any blood relatives, but there's a military family I lived with in high school, when Vin was deployed. It would mean a lot to them to be able to visit."

"I'll pay for their trip."

Her brow furrowed.

"No strings, Iz. I'm just doing what I should have done months ago."

She stretched out a hand, and he pulled her to her feet. She stood before him and slid her arms around his neck and rose up on her toes. She kissed him again, not with passion, but not exactly platonic either.

She dropped back to her heels and took a deep breath. "Okay, let's go to the river, then head back to the compound."

He nodded and took her hand again and led her toward the low, wide stretch of the river that was the only shallow crossing for a mile in each direction.

Isabel studied the rapid flow. "How high was the water when Vin crossed?"

"About the same as it is now. It snowed that first night, and again the last night, before we found him, so the ground was slick on the bank. There were footprints on the far side that indicated he'd stumbled and fell into the water."

"That's when he lost his pack?" Isabel asked.

"We think so, but continuing across after losing his gear has never made sense. He knew the compound buildings were on that side of the river. Plus, there's a prove-up cabin, where he could have gotten warm, just a half mile away."

She dropped to the damp ground above the bank and unlaced her heavy hiking boots.

"You want to cross?" he asked, surprised.

"It'll be faster than hiking to the bridge."

He wanted to caution her, but if anyone knew how to cross a rapidly flowing river in Alaska, he had a feeling that person was Isabel Dawson. She tucked her socks into her boots and tied the laces together, then draped the boots around her neck. Next she hiked her pants above her calves and cinched them in place by tightening elastic bands built into the cuffs.

Alec dropped down beside her and ran a hand up her bare left shin, loosened the band, then slid the cuff higher, above her knee. He caressed her knee before pulling the elastic through the spring-cord lock and tightening it again. "In the middle of the river, the water will reach your knees."

She chuckled. "You could have just *told* me."

"Where's the fun in that?"

The light in her eyes shifted. She leaned into him, pulled his head down, and kissed him, no hesitation, no holding back. Her mouth opened, inviting his tongue inside. He wasn't one to pass on such a sweet offer and slanted his mouth across hers, kissing her deeply as he fulfilled the fantasy he'd had yesterday morning and threaded his fingers through her curls.

The boots draped around her neck dug into his chest, and he ended the kiss with a grin. "I wonder what my employees'll say when they see your boot print on my heart."

Her eyes lit with humor as her gaze dropped to his shirt, which did indeed have her boot print stamped across his chest. "I'm sure they'll assume you had it coming." She adjusted her other pant leg and stood.

Alec hitched up his own hiking pants but left his boots on.

"You aren't going barefoot?" she asked.

"In a combat situation, you never remove your boots."

"It's at least three miles to the compound buildings."

"I've hiked farther in wet boots."

"Suit yourself." She faced the river.

The water was a heavy slate gray—opaque due to the high glacial silt content. No way to see what lurked beneath the surface. "I should go first," he said.

She shook her head and adjusted the straps on her backpack to balance the weight. "This isn't my first Alaskan river crossing. A big old Ranger like you, I'm sure I don't need to tell you to walk sideways, facing upstream?"

He winked at her. "I've crossed a few rivers in my time as well."

She stepped up to him and grabbed his shirt, pulling him down for a fast, hard kiss. "See you on the other side, Ranger." She stepped into the river, letting out a soft curse directed at the frigid water as she carefully probed for a place to plant her bare foot.

Alec watched, impressed with her surefooted confidence as she inched into the deep murky center of the glacier-fed river. He followed a few feet behind her, keeping her within arm's reach.

At the midpoint, her foot slipped and she sucked in a sharp breath as the water reached her upper thighs, soaking her hitched-up hiking pants. She glanced sideways, a half smile on her face, and he expected a quip about how he'd been wrong, but all at once her face fell and she let out a low wail of agony.

Pain stabbed at Alec's head.

Holy fuck. He grabbed Isabel's shoulder. "Infrasound waves can't go through water." He shoved her down, into the icy river.

CHAPTER FIFTEEN

DAGGERS OF COLD sliced into Isabel, taking her breath away, but surfacing was not an option. She'd been facing upstream, so she twisted and tried to swim across, but the current was too strong. Her side slammed into a rock just beneath the surface. Shooting pain radiated from her ribs as she swallowed silty water.

She surfaced and took in a lungful of air, then dove under again, but this time twisted to go with the flow, feet first, the only safe way to ride a rushing river.

Alec caught her wrist and pulled her across the current, slightly changing their trajectory. The water was so brutally cold, she couldn't hold her breath—it rushed out the moment she submerged. She needed air but was terrified of surfacing and being hit by infrasound again. They reached a stretch of rapids. Her back scraped rocks that lurked below as she tried to stay under the surface.

She lifted her head and took another deep breath and glanced downstream. The current had carried them farther than she expected. Ahead was a boulder that split the river. She tugged on Alec's hand and pointed, then angled her body to aim for the far side of the boulder.

The boulder loomed; she dodged to the side just before slamming into the face. Instead, she scraped along the edge, likely losing a layer of skin, but her body was so numb with cold, she didn't feel the abrasion. She landed in a groove and came to a stop, no longer at the mercy of the current. Alec surfaced beside her and pressed her against the stone, his body shielding her from the opposite bank.

"Fuck me," he said. "I'm the shittiest Ranger alive." He took a deep breath. "We won't last long in this water. Downstream there's a drop-off. Stay to the right."

"What's on the left?" she asked.

"Rocks, big and jagged, and not much water. To the right there's a pool. The drop is only about four feet. I think there's a beaver dam below that. We can grab it and pull ourselves out."

She shook with the cold, massive quakes that racked her entire body. She doubted she'd be able to grip the tangled sticks that made up the dam with her numb hands but didn't have a choice. "Let's do it."

"Take the drop feetfirst, toes pointed. Protect your head."

She nodded.

"I'll go first. Count to five, then follow. Got it?"

"Yes."

He captured her face in his frozen hands and kissed her. "See you on the other side." He pushed off the boulder and was gone. Isabel counted to five, sucked in a deep breath, and shoved off the boulder, torpedoing feetfirst to the right side of the drop-off.

ALEC HAD NEVER been so afraid in his life. Not when he was under fire in Afghanistan, not when conducting a covert op, not even when parachuting into live-fire zones to aid a squad of pinned soldiers.

His fear was for Isabel. Unlike the Rangers he'd teamed with, she hadn't signed up for this. She could die. Here, now.

He plunged down the drop with knees bent to prevent slamming into the rocks below with undue force. A stone gouged his calf and scraped his side, but the current quickly shoved him forward. He sucked in a breath and dropped below the surface.

The river was much deeper here, over his head. The current pushed him toward the center, but he swam to the side, aiming for the dam. His arm caught a tangle of branches and a log braced against a boulder. The tree limbs loosened under his weight, with numb fingers he scrambled for a stronger hold. Isabel slammed into him, and he nearly lost his grip. She grabbed him with one hand and the tangled limbs with her other.

He tightened his hold on the roots and branches and grabbed her pack with his free hand. "Hold on to me, and I'll pull us to the bank," he said over the noise of the rushing river.

Her fingers slipped on his shirt just as he let go of her pack, and she started to slip away. He caught her by the hair, and winced at the pain it must have caused her. She caught the waistline of his pants. He felt the tug, and she tangled her fingers through his belt loops. As soon as he knew she wouldn't be swept away, he released her curls and grabbed her arm to pull her to his chest. "Sorry, honey."

"S'okay. Too numb to hurt."

"You've got a firm grip now?"

"Yes."

They had to get out of the frigid water before their bodies completely shut down. And they had to pray that whoever had hit them with infrasound was still looking for them upstream. Iz quaked against him. "Hold on. I'll pull us to the bank," he said.

She nodded.

It was slow going with the need to make sure every handhold could support their combined weight against the current. More than one branch snapped, but he managed to get them both to the side.

He took her hands and placed them in the network of roots extending from the beaver-gnawed trunk that was firmly embedded in the bank. She'd have to find the strength to climb on her own. The roots would snap under their combined weight.

She struggled to grip the slick roots.

"You can do it, honey."

She nodded and pulled herself upward. Inch by slow inch, she emerged from the river and climbed over the log to land. Thank goodness overhanging branches shrouded them, or they'd make a clear target for whoever had zapped them earlier.

She collapsed on the bank while he pulled himself up and out, then dropped to the mossy ground beside her. The low overhanging tree provided adequate cover. They could take a moment to catch their breath before getting the hell away from the deadly river.

He pulled her against him, seriously concerned about her intense shaking. Her deathly pale face and blue lips didn't instill confidence they'd escaped the river before hypothermia had taken hold.

"I d-d-on't know w-what's worse." Her words were broken with chattering teeth and stuttering speech. "The fr-igid w-ater or the c-c-old air."

Shit. They were three miles from the main buildings. He grabbed his phone from his soaking backpack. Waterlogged and useless. "We'll go to the prove-up cabin." He touched her cheek. The half mile to the cabin might still be too far. Her boots were gone, lost to the river. "Can you hike barefoot? The cabin has electricity, a fireplace. Everything we need to get you warm." There was also a direct radio link to the compound. "I can carry you, but we'll get there faster if you can walk."

She nodded.

He dropped a kiss on her cold lips. "That's my girl." He stood and pulled her to her feet.

"W-hat if...what if wh-wh-oever z-apped us is w-w-aiting at the cabin?"

Alec drew his gun from his back holster; thankfully, it hadn't been dislodged as he slammed into rocks in the river. "Infrasound is directional. Trees—or water—can break infrasound waves. If you feel a sudden headache, or any other infrasound-like symptoms, take cover." He checked the load on his gun and chambered a round. "Leave it to me to hunt the bastard down."

Isabel proved her strength as she hiked barefoot without complaint or hesitation. She held up as well as many soldiers he knew. As soon as they were safe, he'd strip off her wet, miserable clothes and warm her.

They reached the crest of a steep hill, affording them a limited view through trees to the south and east. Twenty yards of open space separated them from the safety of the cabin. When they were inside, he could commandeer a damn tank if he wanted and take out the bastards who'd forced her to swim down a glacier-fed river—less than ten miles downstream from the actual frigging mile-thick melting glacier.

Beside him, her body shook uncontrollably. Alarmingly. The clicking of her chattering teeth rebuked him for his failure. He had to get her warm. Keeping the cabin in view, he grabbed her shoulders and positioned her against the trunk of the nearest spruce, then took her hands in his. Her fingers were ice, but his weren't much better. He lifted his shirt and placed her cold hands against his belly. His skin might be cold and damp, but she was even colder.

Her hands slid up to his chest, leaving an icicle trail in her wake. "Surprisingly, this isn't a come-on."

"I know, honey." He turned to study the structure below. "It'll take me a moment to type in my security code to unlock the cabin. While I do that, I want you to tuck in between me and the cabin, so no one can get a clear line of sight at you."

In this condition, if they were both hit by infrasound, he might not be able to hold it together long enough to get her inside. This way, only he'd take the hit. She'd be okay.

"Can you run for the door?"

She nodded.

"You are one in a million, honey. On three." He counted, and they both sprinted through the open space.

Halfway, she stumbled. He scooped her up and ran. At the door, he pressed her between the wall and his body as planned, and punched in his code.

The click of the lock releasing was the sweetest sound he'd ever heard. He lifted her again and carried her inside, then slammed the door closed with his foot. Still holding her with one arm, he slid the manual bolt home and punched in the code to arm the security system and relock the door.

Far better than the structure Isabel had taken Alec to on Thursday, the prove-up cabin had originally been a basic one-room log home built by a homesteader—a requirement to prove he would live here and work the land—but had been expanded over the years. Alec had added his own embellishments after he purchased the company. It now boasted indoor plumbing, electricity, and bulletproof windows—a necessity with the live-fire trainings. Between the thick log walls and hardy glass, they were safe.

He set Isabel on her feet and pulled the damp top from her body, wishing this were a different circumstance to be stripping her, but he was seriously worried by the bluish tinge to her skin. "Finish undressing while I build a fire," he said.

He turned to the fireplace and opened the damper, then threw in a fire-starter log and a bunch of kindling. No time to finesse the job. He lit the wrapper on the starter log, then turned to see Isabel fumbling with her pants, unable to work the button.

He helped her. The lightweight hiking pants easily came off even when wet, and were made of a special fabric that wicked away moisture and dried quickly, which was probably the only reason her body hadn't completely shut down on the hike to the cabin. There was blood on her waist. A scrape from the river. Warmth first, then he'd check out her wound.

He shucked his own shirt, then turned back to the fire. The kindling hadn't caught yet, but he tossed in a log anyway, hoping he wouldn't kill the meager flame. It was more important that he help Isabel. After she was warm, he could worry about the damn fire.

She stood in the center of the room, almost in a daze, shivering.

She was in trouble.

With the knife from his belt, he cut his bootlaces, no time to untie the wet leather. Thus freed, he stepped out of the boots and stripped out of his pants and socks. Naked but for boxer briefs, he scooped her in his arms and carried her to the bed. After pulling the thick comforter aside, he placed her in the center, then slipped in beside her, covering them both with flannel sheets, wool blanket, and down comforter.

He gathered her against him, her cold body pressed to his as he whispered encouraging words. She was a helluva hiker and outdoorswoman but lacked bulk to keep warm or the training to power through trying physical circumstances.

He held her tight while she tried to burrow into him. "Mmmm," she said. "You feel heavenly."

Hardly—his skin wasn't much warmer than hers, but being skin to skin and covered by blankets he too was beginning to warm.

He kissed her forehead as he lowered his hands to the scrap of wet fabric that covered her butt. This last bit of modesty was ridiculous in this circumstance, and he peeled off her panties, wishing the first time he got his hands on her luscious ass had been part of foreplay.

She snuggled closer with her hands pressed flat on his chest. They weren't as cold as they'd been earlier. Her cheeks were already losing the bluish tinge in favor of a pink glow, but she was sleepy, her body seeking hibernation to conserve resources. He pulled her tighter and unhooked her bra, determined to rid her of the last of her wet clothing.

Her eyes remained closed as she slid her hands over his chest in a sensual exploration, tracing muscles. She made a low purring sound and shifted to cup his ass, which was still covered by wet cotton briefs.

He wanted nothing more than to enjoy the feel of her hands on his body, but his conscience made him pull back. Her brow furrowed, but she didn't open her eyes. "Closer," she murmured.

"No, Iz. You're half-asleep and hypothermic. You don't know what you're doing."

"Please, Alec. Warm me." Her lips pressed to his chest, his throat, then moved upward and sought his mouth.

Damn, how he wanted to go there. But he wouldn't. Couldn't. Not this way. "I am, honey. But that's all I'm gonna do."

With a sleepy yet somehow wicked smile, she slid a hand between them and stroked his unwilling erection through his damp briefs. Jesus, he was hypothermic and exhausted, yet she gave him a woody that could put the Washington Monument to shame.

But this wasn't consent, and he wasn't some asshole who couldn't tell the difference. He lifted her hand from his cock and turned her over, so he could spoon against her back, keeping her warm but limiting her access to body parts that were more than eager for her touch. "Just let me hold you, Iz."

She wiggled her ass against his erection, and he groaned. He tightened his arm around her hips, limiting the friction she could create, and nipped at her neck. "If you don't stop, I'll get out of the bed."

She stilled immediately, indicating she might be more awake and aware of what she was doing than he suspected, but that didn't weaken his resolve. He held her tight, being careful to place his hands well away from erogenous zones—and slowly her body relaxed against him as she drifted into a deep sleep.

When he was certain her core temperature was near normal, he gently extracted himself from her side and the bed. He tucked the thick blankets around her. Her hair had dried and splayed across the pillow in a sexy tumble.

God, how he wanted her. She was strong and brave and smart. She made him laugh, and when he watched her kneel by the marker where Vin died, he'd wanted to cry for her too. He could fall in love with her if he weren't careful. But for now, he just wanted her. To make her laugh and take away her tears and to give her pleasure. But it would have to wait for a time when she was fully cognizant of the choice she was making.

He'd meant it when he told her it was her move. She still didn't quite trust him.

He turned to the hearth and added another log to the fire. He rubbed a hand over his face as he considered what to do next. He needed to radio the compound. Operatives on ATVs could pick them up. They both needed dry clothes and Isabel needed boots. He glanced at his own boots and frowned. He also needed laces, although the parachute cord in his pack would serve in a pinch.

Who the hell could he trust to bring them clothes and an ATV?

He and Isabel had been hit with infrasound in a stealth attack at the most vulnerable moment of the lengthy hike, leaving him to wonder if they'd been followed, or if someone had been lying in wait, knowing he'd take her to the river where Vin crossed.

Was that what had happened to Vin? Had he been chased across the river, but instead of swimming, he'd finished his crossing and tried to lose his pursuer in the woods?

On that side of the river, he'd had no cabin to escape to, and having lost his pack when he fell into the icy water as a light snow fell, his fate was sealed. Whoever hunted Vin probably didn't even have to follow to know he'd meet his death on the opposite bank, which explained the single set of footprints barely visible in the snow.

Alec was certain he, Isabel, and Vincent had all been hit with infrasound. The question was, who had done it? And why?

CHAPTER SIXTEEN

ISABEL WOKE SLOWLY, a gradual easing into consciousness. She rolled to her side to take in the room and get her bearings, gazing through lashes to hide that she was more awake than asleep. The cabin was dim, cozy, and smelled like chocolate. Alec crouched in front of the hearth, a fire poker in his hands as he rearranged flaming logs that didn't need rearranging.

She remembered everything—the kiss by the river, the frigid water, his hands on her skin as he held her tight—but most importantly, she remembered running her hands over his body, over his erection, and the intense want that had coursed through her. Even now her body hummed with need. Not generic arousal. No. She wanted Alec Ravissant, and that desire filled her with shame.

Evening sun spilled onto the floor in front of the windows. The only other light in the cabin came from the fire, which lit Alec with a warm, dancing glow. She opened her eyes fully to take in the sight. He was beautiful. Shirtless. The golden light played across his bare skin. Hard, corded muscle formed thick shoulders, and his wide chest tapered to a narrow waist. He'd been out of the Army for at least three years, but clearly he'd kept up with the hard physical training he'd maintained as a Ranger.

The display of firelight on muscle was magnificent. She wanted to grab a mug of hot chocolate—which must be the warm, sweet scent that filled the room—and watch him for hours.

He turned and met her gaze. "You're awake." The words were soft. Concerned. "How do you feel?"

"Cold." Regret shot through her. She shouldn't have been flip. What if he offered to warm her again? She couldn't say yes but didn't want to say no.

He nodded toward the hearth. "Move closer to the fire."

She gathered the comforter around her naked body and scooted to the edge of the bed. The room shifted as her head swam. Okay. She still wasn't one hundred percent. With the blanket clutched tightly around her, she approached the hearth, wondering if it was the flames or the man she was drawn toward.

Both had irresistible heat and the power to burn her.

She stopped short of the circle of heat. Alec set the poker in the rack and turned to her. He grabbed the edges of the down comforter where they met at her breastbone and stepped backward, drawing her into the warmest spot in the room.

The comforter had a slick, satiny texture against her bare skin, the pleasurable sensation intensified with proximity to Alec. She cleared her throat. "How long did I sleep?"

"About two and a half hours."

"You missed your meeting with the new guy at the compound."

He shrugged. "You needed to rest and get your core temperature up."

"I'm sorry I...came on to you the way I did." She felt her face flush; more proof her core temperature was back to normal.

Alec's carnal grin made her body flush even more. "I'm not." The hands gripping the comforter tightened, causing the cloth to rub against her nipples, igniting an ache for something more. "And I hope you didn't take my action as rejection. Make no mistake, Isabel; I want you. Very much. But you were in no condition to consent."

She'd been one hundred percent aware of what she was doing. The hypothermia had merely given her an excuse to ignore the voice of reason. Now that she was warm again, she was bereft of ways to quell her conscience. "For two people who are supposed to be enemies, we've spent a lot of time in each other's arms in the last few days."

"Darling, I'm not your enemy. I never have been." He released the comforter and stepped back, the hard line of his jaw indicating her words had irked him.

It was probably better that way. She was feeling far too close and comfortable with him. It had to stop. She faced the fire. Gripping the blanket with one hand, she slipped her other arm out, exposing a shoulder, and reached toward the flames to warm her fingers.

Behind her, Alec made a sound low in his throat. A tiger sort of noise—neither growl nor purr, but somehow, both.

She glanced over her shoulder and caught the raw desire in his eyes. She reached for the blanket to cover her shoulder, causing it to gap even more.

Alec grinned and sat on the couch. "No. Don't cover yourself. I like the way the firelight matches your hair and makes your skin glow. I can handle looking without touching."

She pulled the blanket up. "Sounds like a dangerous game."

"I'm okay with dangerous."

She turned to fully face him, and stepped forward, loosening her grip on the blanket as she moved, so it slipped down, revealing both shoulders and the tops of her breasts. "Well then, this could be fun."

Alec groaned. "I take it back. I'm not cut out for the rules you play by."

She pulled up the blanket and returned to the fire, which was strangely colder than standing bare-shouldered in front of Alec. "Without condoms, it's game over anyway."

"Honey, there's a helluva lot we can do without condoms."

Her body flooded with heat as her mind ran through all the things he could do to her with hands and mouth, and she was even more turned on by thoughts of the things she could do to him. The urge to kneel before him in the firelight and take him into her mouth was almost overwhelming. She wanted to feel his cock against her tongue, to make him groan her name as she sucked on him.

She flushed as she realized she'd just licked her lips while staring at the bulge of his sweatpants. She met his gaze, and his eyes held raw hunger. His nostrils flared. He must know what she'd imagined; he'd probably envisioned something similar.

She wanted to revel in his heat, explore every hard inch of him, and feed his hunger.

"Also...we *do* have condoms." His voice was a deep rumble of sound. She felt the vibration in her solar plexus. "In the supply closet, between the first aid kit and spare clothing."

She blew out a breath. Clothing. Yes. Focus on that. Clothing was armor to protect against base desires she'd only regret giving in to. "There's dry clothes?" But of course there were; dry, clean sweatpants tented over his erection. Her gaze traveled over his sculpted abs and hard pecs as she remembered the play of firelight across his perfect torso. "Would it have killed you to put on a shirt?"

He chuckled and stood, then scooped an item from the side table. "There was only one shirt and one pair of sweatpants, and I figured you'd want the shirt." He held up a large hooded University of Alaska sweatshirt that was long enough to reach her upper thighs. He reached for the drawstring on his sweatpants. "But we can trade if you prefer."

She rolled her eyes. "I'll take the sweatshirt, thanks."

He winked at her. "I *knew* I should have taken the shirt when I had the chance." He handed her the hoodie. "Why don't you get dressed while I heat up some soup for you?"

She nodded and turned to make a beeline for the bathroom, but he caught her around the waist. His lips brushed against her collarbone, exposed because the blanket slipped again when she grabbed the shirt. "It's just as well we won't make use of the condoms now. We need to head back to the compound. I've got work to do."

She nodded, relieved. She wasn't ready to jump into bed with Alec Ravissant, no matter how much her raging desire said otherwise. But still, she might tuck a few condoms in the pocket of the hoodie. And in her backpack. And maybe in Alec's backpack too.

ALEC CONSIDERED GOING back to the frigid river and taking another swim to cool his raging libido, but if he remembered correctly, even hypothermia hadn't kept him down when he had Isabel naked in his arms. He entered the small kitchen and grabbed a dehydrated soup packet and added the requisite hot water from the instant hot tap.

It was reasonable to let Isabel sleep until she got her core temperature up, but the verbal foreplay after she woke had been irresponsible. He had a crap-ton of work to do to figure out what was going on and he needed to ensure the compound was safe and secure for the upcoming training. He didn't have time to obsess over the woman who'd somehow managed to become the focal point of this trip.

While the soup hydrated, he used the cabin radio to contact the compound again. Isabel stepped out of the bathroom wearing the extra-large hoodie and sported a towel around her hips. One look at her and he knew staying in the cozy cabin longer than necessary would be far too tempting. He instructed the compound radio operator to send out a team on ATVs to pick them up, and told them to bring clothing and boots in both their sizes. He raised an eyebrow at Isabel, and she gave him her shoe size, which he relayed to the compound, then signed off.

Soon they'd have company, until then, he needed to keep his libido in line. "Soup's on," he said, nodding toward the kitchen.

"Thanks."

"There's also hot water for coffee or tea."

She cocked her head. "I thought I smelled hot chocolate?"

Alec felt his face flush. "Uh, yeah," he mumbled. "There's hot chocolate too."

Isabel did a double take at his stumbling response. "Alec Ravissant, are you *blushing*?"

He frowned. "Maybe."

"Because you drink hot chocolate?"

"Maybe."

"Why?"

"It's not...*tough*. You know? I'm a Ranger. Or at least, I used to be. I'm supposed to drink my coffee tar black and my whiskey neat. But I can't stand coffee. Or whiskey, for that matter."

She grinned. "I think that's sort of adorable."

"Adorable. Yeah. That's what I was aiming for." He felt his flush deepen. He didn't know why his hot chocolate addiction embarrassed him all of a sudden, but it did. Maybe it was because she'd found him in the woods after he'd suffered a major ass-kicking.

"Please tell me you put marshmallows in your hot chocolate too."

He shook his head. "Marshmallows are for sissies."

She laughed. "What other embarrassing secrets are you hiding? That you like kittens too much?"

"Shhh!" He took two quick steps, stopping directly in front of her and placed his index finger to her lips. He glanced in both directions as though suspicious. "Not so loud. You have no idea how cutthroat the dog lobby can be."

She licked the pad of his finger, then sucked it into her mouth.

Alec groaned at the heat that shot through him with the speed and combustion power of a backdraft. Without thinking, he scooped her up, and the towel fell away as her legs circled his hips. In four steps, he had her pinned against the uneven log wall, the sweatpants a thin barrier between his erection and her naked, hot center.

His tongue plundered her mouth, stroking, taking, igniting flames as he mimicked sex with thrusting hips, drawing panting gasps from her as his cock teased her clit. "I want to be deep inside you, Isabel." The words tumbled out in a low whisper against her lips. "I want your heat to surround me, to feel you clench tight as I stroke you and make you come. I want to watch you orgasm, hard and fast, then again, more slowly, in a long-drawn-out wave so intense you'll think the pleasure might break you." *I want to smash your barriers and possess you. For you to be mine. Only mine.*

She gripped his shoulders as she met his gaze, her lips open and damp from the hot kiss. Her green eyes were dilated with arousal. Her chest rose as she panted and wiggled her hips, stroking him with her clit, further stoking his intense need.

"I want you in the same way," she said in a breathy whisper.

She ground against him again, the sensation so damn hot, he locked his knees to keep his footing.

"I can't look at you without having fantasies," she said. "This morning, I wanted you to take me on the sideboard. Minutes ago, I wanted to go down on you in front of the fire. But I'm afraid when the heat is over, orgasm complete, I'll have nothing left but guilt and shame."

If there were any other words that could kill his erection faster, he didn't know what they could be. He loosened his grip, setting her gently to the floor, then stepped back, releasing her as the heat left his body as quickly as it had arrived. "Guilt and shame?" He met her gaze. "That's what you'll feel if we have sex?"

She nodded. "I—I hate myself for wanting you. It feels like a betrayal."

His eye—the one that had taken the worst of the blows on Thursday—began to throb. As if she'd hit him there again. Strange, because it should be his nuts that ached, given that was where her verbal assault had been aimed. He scooped up her fallen towel from the floor and thrust it in her direction.

"I didn't kill your brother, Isabel."

She took the towel and cinched it around her hips. "I know that."

"Your brother even tried to fix us up. He *wanted* us to meet." How desperate did he sound? It occurred to him that he'd never been rejected before. His life had been pretty charmed—born into a rich family, blessed with brains, he'd had the drive and ambition to excel in the military. While there had been struggles along the way, and he worked his ass off to be the best soldier he could be, relationships—sex—had always been easy to come by. He'd always been the one to set the rules. Who'd have guessed this woman's rejection would make him so damn pathetic?

"I *want* you, Alec. But I can't forget that you ignored Vin's murder. Your inaction helped cover it up."

She really believed he'd done that? That was an even bigger blow to the balls than the bit about guilt and shame. "I didn't cover up his murder. How can you even think that I would? I get that you might've thought that before, but now you *know* me."

"Do I really?" Her voice rose along with her anger. "I found you in the woods. I saved your life, and you attacked me. Then you had me arrested. The next time we crossed paths, you'd bailed me out of jail—probably because you realized having the woman who saved your life arrested would look bad in the polls. Then you show up at my house after *your men* attacked me in my home. Hell, for all I know, you were with them in the meadow. Honestly, Alec, you may well be the biggest threat to me here.

"I *don't* know you. All I really know about you for certain is that you want to fuck me, because I've seen evidence there you can't fake. But I can't help but wonder if even that is fueled by political motivation. Imagine the headlines if you pretend to fall for the woman who saved your life. The voting public would eat that shit up."

Politics. She honestly believed it all came down to politics for him. She was right; she didn't know him at all. He dropped down on the couch and let out a bitter laugh. "Isabel, you are my campaign's manager's worst nightmare, because Lord knows we couldn't count on you to censor your words or adhere to any party line. Sure, some voters might think it's nice if they learned we were involved, but twice as many would probably be as cynical as you are and think it was a ploy. I don't want you for political gain. I'm not power hungry enough to make decisions like that. You'll probably never believe this, but I'm not power hungry at all.

"Hell, if all I wanted was power, I'd stick with Raptor. Having your own mercenary army, now *that* is power. I stepped into the race because I believed I could *do* something. I missed serving my country after I left the Army. I thought Raptor would be enough, but it wasn't. I was trained for politics since birth, and I see a gap in political leadership really understanding what the war on terror even means. I've been to war. I understand it. And, thanks to my mother's dreams of the Ravissants becoming a Kennedy-esque political dynasty, I also understand economics, transportation, crime laws, education funding, and how political deals are made.

"The simple fact of my wanting you has no bearing on my political aspirations. I just want you. Plain and simple. Honestly, I doubt my campaign would survive Hurricane Isabel, so I'd just as soon keep you under wraps, but I'd never ask you to hide if you didn't want to, because *I* am not ashamed of wanting *you*."

Her nostrils flared at his last statement, but she said nothing. She just stood before him with a look of heartache and confusion on her face. Her anger had melted. Now she just looked...raw.

He wanted to curse and bitch and basically make an ass of himself, but she'd merely been honest with him, and on a fundamental level, he understood. She'd had eleven months of grief and anger in which he'd not only been the focal point, he'd done nothing to dispel her beliefs. Everything he'd done had only underscored her assumptions. "I suppose our best course of action is to get to know each other," he said.

She cocked her head.

"A date."

"What, you want to go out to dinner?"

"Why not? I owe you for saving my life. I even suggested it before I knew who you were."

"But you saved my life in the river. So we're even."

"Fine, then you can take me out to dinner."

"But we're *even*."

"Then we'll go Dutch."

She laughed. "And when are we supposed to go out on this date? Don't you have work to do?"

In the distance, Alec heard the low whine of an ATV engine. They had only another few minutes alone. "Yeah. So it'll have to be the week after next."

"But you'll be in Maryland then."

"So you'll fly out to Maryland." He stood and crossed the room to stand before her. "When rich guys want to impress a girl, we do over-the-top things like fly to Paris on our private jets for dinner."

"Do you want to impress me, Alec?"

"Very much. I know of a great little place in Montmartre." He gripped the zipper of the hoodie and tugged her forward. He brushed his lips over hers. "But you're paying for your half of dinner."

CHAPTER SEVENTEEN

AN HOUR LATER, Isabel was back inside Alec's suite. She was again chilled to the bone after riding on an ATV, clinging to Alec's back as he drove the quad over bumpy terrain.

Exhausted from the cold, even though it wasn't yet nine p.m., all she wanted to do was sleep, but before she could crawl into bed, Doc Larson examined her. He prescribed warm blankets and more sleep.

Two FBI agents who wanted to interview her had arrived at the compound while Isabel had recuperated in the prove-up, but Doc told them they'd have to wait until the following day, for which she was grateful. As much as she wanted to be interviewed and tell everything she knew about Alec's abduction, her brother's murder, and the two infrasound assaults on her, she was cross-eyed with exhaustion. The last three days had simply been too much.

Alec tucked her into his bed, but this time didn't linger to warm her—which was probably a good thing, because she had no doubt she'd throw herself at him again, given the chance, and she seriously needed to get her head on straight where he was concerned. He left her to meet with the new guy, or to be interviewed by the FBI. She was too tired to remember.

She closed her eyes and settled deeper in the thick blankets on Alec's bed, wishing the sheets carried his scent, but he'd spent scant few hours in this bed since his arrival. She quickly drifted into a deep and blessedly dreamless sleep.

Sometime later, she woke, feeling sleep saturated and confused. She stared at the backlit clock in the darkened room. Ten o'clock. She'd slept a little more than an hour?

She rubbed her eyes and looked at the clock again. The a.m. light was on.

Her eyes widened. She'd slept *thirteen* hours?

She couldn't remember the last time she'd slept so long. Maybe when she was five?

And yet, she felt good. Restored. Alive.

And warm. Wonderfully, magnificently, warm. She dropped into the pillows and pulled up a blanket. Maybe she should sleep for another six hours or so.

The moment she closed her eyes, guilt swamped her. She had yet to get started on her report for the timber sale. Even though her day off on Friday had been involuntary, it didn't mean it was okay for her to get behind at work. The preliminary findings were due on Wednesday, and she still needed to finish the survey. Then there was the fact that she hadn't spoken with the FBI yet. And she needed to figure out who the hell had attacked her cabin.

Much as she wanted to hide in this big warm bed for the next week, she had to face today. She crawled out of bed and entered the sitting room, not surprised to find it empty. The blankets and sheets Alec had used were neatly folded and placed on the sideboard.

He'd left a note for her on the table.

I'm meeting with Keith and Nicole all morning. Fraser is showing the FBI agents the forest—where you found me, where my car was found, and the cabin—and will be gone most of the day. Agents Crews and Upton plan to interview you this evening. Stay put in my quarters. You are not to wander the building unescorted. Dial extension three, and meals will be delivered.

She bristled at the command. He'd forgotten she wasn't one of his men and didn't have to blindly follow his orders, and she was hardly a prisoner.

Besides, she wanted to meet the new guy. Keith Hatcher. He at least couldn't be involved in whatever was going on, because not only was he new to Raptor, but up until a few months ago, the guy had been a Navy SEAL.

It was comforting to know there was someone here they could trust, because right now, everyone who worked at the compound was suspect: Nicole, Brad, Nate, Dev, even Mothman. There were a few men on Falcon she wasn't fond of, particularly Chase Johnston, but he hadn't been at the compound long enough to have been involved in Vin's death, and just because the way he looked at her gave her the heebie-jeebies didn't mean he was the culprit who'd shot her with infrasound.

She stiffened as she stared at the slip of paper.

Infrasound. She hadn't had a chance to look up infrasound on

her own and didn't like relying on what anyone from Raptor—
even Alec—told her. Aside from not having time to research, she
also no longer had a computer or smartphone.

She needed a shower, then she'd use Alec's computer and start
researching. She'd even be good and stay in his quarters. In the
bathroom, she shuddered at her reflection in the mirror. She
didn't exactly look good after taking a swim, riding on a quad, and
then sleeping for nearly twice as many hours as she usually slept.

The bathroom was as ornate and over-the-top as the rest of
Alec's suite. She'd never seen so much marble outside of the
Library of Congress. The tub was a small swimming pool with a
control panel that could launch a rocket, and the shower could
accommodate a swim team. While she longed for the tub, she
opted for the expediency of the shower, glad that yesterday
morning she'd figured out the controls so she wouldn't scald
herself again today.

The pounding hot water rejuvenated her. The seven
showerheads scrubbed her clean of glacial silt in no time, and the
spray felt so wonderful against her skin, she wanted to stay in the
shower forever. She massaged her scalp as she washed the
corkscrew curls that gave her nothing but grief.

The bathroom was heavy with steam by the time she shut off
the shower, and the heated floor and warm towel fresh from the
heated rack nearly sent her back into a sleepy stupor.

After she was dried and dressed, she set to work detangling her
hair. During a wet combing, her hair reached halfway down her
back, but as her tresses dried, they coiled upward, reaching just
past her shoulders. Without clips or hairbands, her curls stuck out
in unruly, comical ways. She'd forgotten to grab extra clips when
she hurriedly packed the other night, and she'd lost the one she
wore yesterday in the river, so she dug through Alec's drawers
seeking a hair tie or clip, anything to prevent her from sporting a
curly red lion's mane.

Vin used to tell her the mean girls in high school who mocked
her hair were just jealous. It took her a decade to realize he
might've been right. But years of being called Sideshow Bob
because she had both wild curls *and* red hair, made it hard to see
herself as anything but a clown.

Alec had no hairpins, clips, or ponytail holders, not exactly a
surprise, but still, she liked the idea that she might be the first
woman to share his suite. She gathered her hair from her temples

and twisted the locks together, then found a pen in Alec's nightstand drawer to slide through the knot, noting as she did so that a box of condoms resided in the drawer as well.

Maybe she wasn't the first woman to share his room after all. Or maybe condoms were just an item he kept on hand. After all, she had a box in her nightstand too, and she hadn't had sex since moving to Tamarack.

She lifted the box. Sealed. She checked the expiration date. Less than two years to expiration. Maybe after she looked up infrasound, she'd google the shelf life of a spermicidal condom.

Back in the main room of the suite, she planted herself in front of Alec's computer and promptly discovered she needed a password to use it. She couldn't look up infrasound or condoms. Or Apex or Airwave or any of the dozen things she really needed to know about.

Well, that sealed it. She'd just have to venture out of the suite. She'd tried to comply. Really. She took a deep breath and left Alec's quarters, hoping she wouldn't get hopelessly lost in the labyrinth.

"THAT BRINGS US to the next topic," Alec said to Nicole and Keith. "I want an operative assigned to Isabel."

"Babysitting duty? No one's going to like that. Especially not Isabel." Nicole sighed. "I don't know if her staying inside the compound is a good idea."

Alec studied his top employee, confused by her attitude. "I thought you were friends."

Keith grabbed the solved Rubik's Cube from the corner of Alec's desk and twisted the squares, his gaze on Nicole.

"We are," she said. "But right now, I'm on the clock. I'm the sheepdog, and you've brought the wolf into the pasture."

He smiled at that. "I think she sees herself as the sheepdog."

"Yeah, well, I sure as hell am not the wolf." She frowned at Alec. "She's wanted nothing more than to get inside this place for months, and now she's here, as your guest." She paused. "I hate to say it, but someone has to. We only have her word anything happened in her cabin the other night. How do we know she didn't read the news article about Airwave and make up the whole 'inside earthquake' story?" She pursed her lips. "Isabel is my friend, and I want to believe her, but her proof—a broken window and a cracked picture? Isn't it convenient that it happened to be a picture you said you'd looked at just hours before?"

Keith frowned. "Nicole's argument has merit, Rav." He tossed the now thoroughly scrambled cube to Alec.

Alec caught it with one hand and glanced at it distractedly before he began twisting to solve it as he considered Nicole's statement. "I was with Isabel when we were hit by infrasound yesterday. I felt it."

"She could have an accomplice," Nicole said.

"Swimming down the river is a risky-as-hell move. And what would the attack gain her? She was already here, on the compound. I'd already taken her to the one place she wanted to go."

"Your trust," Nicole said simply. "Look. I'm not saying this is what I believe, I'm just saying we have to consider it. If your trust is what she's after, don't give it to her."

He frowned. Nicole had a point. But trust wasn't a commodity that could be easily given and withdrawn. Trust was all about gut-level instinct. However, he wasn't entirely certain his gut was the part of his anatomy that believed Isabel was innocent. "I'll admit it's possible. Another reason to assign an operative to watch over her."

Nicole nodded. "I won't put anyone from Falcon on Isabel guard duty. We're stretched too thin as it is, what with Godfrey's resignation."

"Understood." He paused. "Speaking of, we need to promote someone from security to Falcon to replace him. Who's your top pick?"

"Shauna Wells."

Alec had three sides of the cube solved and began the turns that would complete the fourth. "Good choice. About time we had a woman on Falcon."

"She's more than qualified—" Nicole quickly added.

"I know she is. That wasn't a crack about her qualifications. Merely an observation that Falcon has been a boy's club too long."

Nicole smiled. "I'm tired of the fart jokes."

Alec hit the button on his phone for security and requested Wells come to his office immediately.

Keith leaned forward. "Rav, I have a temporary solution for the two remaining spots on Falcon."

Alec set down the solved cube and nodded for Keith to

continue.

"Sean Logan and Josh Warner."

Sean was the top operative based in the DC area, and Josh Warner was Keith's first hire—one of his former SEAL team members. With the addition of those two men to Falcon, maybe the coming training would succeed. The run-through yesterday had been hampered by the short staff. "How soon can they get here?"

"Tomorrow."

"Do it," Alec said.

"I approve of Logan—I've been trying to lure him out here for months," Nicole said. "But I've never heard of Warner. I'd like to review his personnel file before he's assigned to my team."

Alec waited for Keith's response. He'd known Nicole would attempt to assert power in this meeting, to establish herself as the sole leader at the Alaska compound. It was what any alpha dog would do in the face of a major power shift, and Nicole was as alpha as any Raptor employee.

Keith turned to the compound director, showing he knew exactly how to face down challenge to his authority—one of the reasons Alec had selected him to take the top spot. "I'll send you his personnel file, but there's no time to dick around with this decision. The training starts in three days, and you need a full team to run it. Warner is coming. He's more than qualified and has my complete trust."

"Yes, but *I* don't know him, and I have full and final say in the makeup of Falcon team," Nicole said.

"Not anymore. You've lost seven operatives to Apex in twelve months. That warrants intervention from the home office." Keith dropped a file on Alec's desk in front of Nicole. "And I want to know why a rookie like Chase Johnston is even on Falcon team. Nothing in his file shows he has the skills to warrant being named to the elite team."

Alec sat back and smiled. He should have known Keith would review all the personnel files before arriving and flag the discordant notes. Keith Hatcher might not have gone to college, but he believed in doing his homework.

"Johnston is fully skilled. He's just light on experience," Nicole responded with a defiant tilt to her chin. "I haven't had the luxury of being picky with Apex poaching our best operatives."

"I've looked at the numbers, and sixty-five percent of the

employees who've taken a job with Apex came from the Alaska compound, yet Alaska makes up only thirty-two percent of the company," Keith said.

Nicole's bristled, but not in an angry way. "We're in *Alaska*. How many men has Barstow snatched from the Hawaii compound? None?"

Keith nodded.

"There's a reason for that. Have you ever spent a winter in Alaska? The aurora borealis is pretty, but it doesn't make up for forty below. It takes a special sort of person to make the transition from chechaquo to sourdough. I've been telling Rav from the start we need to rotate operatives in and have fewer permanent Alaska employees. We'll have better retention if people know they aren't stuck here forever."

Keith turned to Alec. "Why haven't you rotated operatives?"

"Consistency. We haven't been able to work out a rotation schedule that allows for operatives to learn the training scenarios *and* build a cohesive team. Ideally, I'd like four sourdoughs," he said, copying Nicole's use of Alaskan slang for a person who'd acclimated to the subarctic climate, "and six operatives on rotation to run each training session, but we need to rebuild our core Alaskan staff first. It doesn't help that we've been shut down, and therefore lightly staffed, during the summer—the best months weatherwise."

To Nicole, Keith said, "My plan is to have Logan and Warner stay on here for the next six months. That'll get you through the worst of winter, and neither operative will be tempted by Apex."

"I get Logan for six months?" Nicole said, excitement in her voice. "What the hell did you promise him?"

Keith grinned. "I won a wager."

Alec laughed. The Rubik's cube was part of an ongoing wager between Alec and Keith, a bet Keith refused to concede. "What did you bet on?"

"He figured I was too old and too far removed from my glory days to kick his ass in a football-throwing contest."

Nicole rolled her eyes. "Men are so easily manipulated by their egos. Too bad my sport was swimming."

Outside his office, Alec heard Hans raise his voice in alarm. "You weren't supposed to leave Mr. Ravissant's suite."

"I forgot to tell Alec I'm allergic to marble," Isabel said. "And I'm seriously considering suing Raptor over the labyrinthine layout. I might have died if GI Jane here hadn't found me and led me this way."

"I didn't lead her," said a woman—probably Shauna Wells—in a defensive tone. "She followed me. I told her specifically to return to Rav's quarters and not to follow me." She paused. "You're every bit the pain in the ass I've heard."

"And here I was, hoping for this month's congeniality award."

Wells laughed. "Try again next month."

"I find it difficult to string together thirty days of good behavior," Isabel said.

Alec stood, leaving Nicole and Keith to argue over the power structure of the coming training, and opened his office door. He crossed his arms over his chest but couldn't help but smile at the sight of Isabel's gorgeous damp curls. "You can't even manage one hour."

She flashed him a sheepish grin. "I was going insane in your concubine palace. Rococo is really not my thing."

"I need to work, Iz."

She nodded. "I know that. I just want a computer. If you'd given me your password, I might have been a good little girl and stayed in the suite."

Alec frowned, considering her request. If she were given a computer, she'd have access to the network. They still didn't know who'd hacked into the system over the summer. Lee had fixed the leak, and he'd said the job was sophisticated—probably too sophisticated for the troublemaker who'd gotten the compound shut down. But still, he didn't know for certain it wasn't Isabel. And Nicole's argument *did* have merit, dammit.

Much as he wanted to, he shouldn't trust Isabel Dawson. Not completely.

Well, that answered the gut question, didn't it? "No," he said.

"Fine." She pivoted on her heel and headed for the front door of the compound. "Then I'm going home."

CHAPTER EIGHTEEN

ISABEL FELT ALEC'S distrust as a blow to the gut. She couldn't even explain why it hurt so much, considering she'd made it clear *she* didn't trust *him*. All she knew was that it rankled. Did he believe she'd actually been the person who assaulted him? Was he back to believing she'd abducted him?

Everything she'd done in the months since Vin's death was for one purpose: to prove he'd been murdered. During their hike yesterday, Alec witnessed firsthand what it meant to her. For him to doubt her now took the wind out of her, made her question what she'd thought was a budding alliance.

She reached the glass partition that separated the stark foyer from the secure interior of the training complex.

"Iz, wait!"

She stopped with her hand on the door and asked herself why.

"You're being a fool. Someone attacked you—twice. It's not safe to leave," Alec said.

She whirled to face him. "Since I was probably attacked by *your men*, I think it's not safe for me to stay."

Her voice echoed down the short corridor. Odds were, GI Jane, Hans, Nicole, and the new guy whom she hadn't even met yet, all heard her accusation. Another reason she should probably leave.

Alec's gaze narrowed. He pointed to the dome-enclosed camera mounted to the ceiling. "They don't record sound, but if you shout, there's not much we can do to keep the people we want to investigate ignorant of our suspicions."

"Our suspicions. You say that like we're a team, yet you just made it clear you don't trust me."

He crossed his arms. "You don't trust me either."

"That's different."

"How?"

She was about to point out that she'd spent the last year believing he'd covered up her brother's murder, but stopped. He'd likely spent the last year believing she wanted to sue him because she was greedy.

"Exactly," Alec said as if he could read her mind.

"So what do we do?" she asked.

"Why do you want a computer?"

"I want to google infrasound. I still don't even know what it is. And I want to know what Robert Beck was hiding here that required a stupid labyrinthine layout. And I want to know the shelf life of condoms."

Alec startled at the last item on her list.

She pursed her lips. "Forget I said that last one."

"I don't think I will." He raised a brow in question.

"You have a box of condoms in your nightstand."

"So?"

She looked down. "I just wondered how long they've been there."

Alec grinned. "Probably since I took over Raptor. I'm not even sure who stocked the suite, but it would be part of the standard kit."

"Standard kit?"

"Raptor has five compounds. I have a suite at each one. But, similar to not wasting time with redecorating, I didn't spend time stocking my quarters with toiletries. I have employees for that."

"You have people whose job it is to keep you supplied with condoms?" Jesus, she'd known the guy was rich, but her brain was just starting to wrap around exactly how privileged he was.

He laughed. "Not condoms specifically. There's a list of basic supplies. They go into everyone's quarters. Much like the condoms that were in the prove-up cabin. Why are you so fascinated by the condoms?" His eyes lit with heat. "Are they a particularly kinky style or something?"

"I just sort of wondered... You said you've taken women to Paris to impress them. I wondered if you'd ever brought a woman here."

His knowing grin made her face flush. It was irritating how easily she blushed. "I said *when rich guys want to impress a woman.* I've never actually done the private-jet-date-thing. I've never had someone I wanted to impress that much. And no, I've never brought a woman here. When I come to Alaska, it's for work, not play." He frowned. "Speaking of. I really need to get back to it. I'll have Mothman set up a login for you and you can use the computer in my suite. Then you can google me and condoms all you want."

"I googled *you* months ago."

"Learn anything good?"

She smiled. "Just that there aren't enough shirtless photos of you on the web."

Alec grinned and ran his knuckles along her jawline. "I'll give you a private viewing later, if you want."

"In front of the fire. And I want a mug of hot chocolate."

He leaned down and kissed her. "It's a date."

"Excuse me, *boss*, but this isn't the time," Nicole's voice carried down the short corridor. "Wells is waiting, and I need to rework the shifts for the training now that Logan and Warner are coming."

Alec turned to face Nicole. Isabel grinned at her from around his shoulder. "Sorry, Nic. It's my fault."

"Of that, I have no doubt." She huffed out a sigh. "You should know, Isabel, security is always watching the public spaces inside the compound." She pointed to the same security camera Alec had indicated earlier.

Isabel pushed Alec back and met Nicole's gaze with her chin raised. "Thanks for the tip."

Nicole cracked a smile. "Jesus, what am I going to do with you?"

Alec draped an arm around Isabel's shoulder and headed down the corridor. "She's my problem, Nic. Not yours."

Outside Alec's office, which was adjacent to Nicole's, Hans sat behind his desk facing the tall African-American woman Isabel had dubbed GI Jane when the woman refused to give her name. Another man Isabel didn't recognize stood in the doorway to Alec's office. He was speaking with the others but broke off midsentence when Alec returned.

Alec promptly introduced Isabel to Keith Hatcher, who gave her an assessing look as he shook her hand, but his words were friendly. "Thanks for saving Rav's life. He's an ungrateful bastard, but the rest of us are thankful." He winked at her.

She couldn't help but smile at the future CEO. "He was pretty whiney when injured too."

"Rangers." Keith scoffed. "SEALs know how to take an ass-kicking without complaint."

Behind her, Alec laughed. To Hans, he said, "Call Mothman

and tell him to set up a login for Isabel, then inform Quinault he's giving Isabel shooting lessons in the firing range in an hour."

"Shooting lessons?" She turned and gave Alec a skeptical gaze. "This is Alaska. They issue new residents a gun and NRA membership at the border. I know how to shoot."

"Are you any good?"

"No."

"Then you need a lesson. Ethan Quinault is my best firearms instructor."

"Were you hoping I wouldn't realize he's my babysitter?"

"A little," he admitted.

"I don't need a sitter."

"But you do need to learn how to shoot. You should probably carry a gun from now on." He smiled. "And bear spray too, I think."

ISABEL STARTED WITH the definition in the American Heritage online dictionary: *in·fra·sound (ĭn'frə-sound') n. A wave phenomenon sharing the physical nature of sound but with a range of frequencies below that of human hearing.*

It was a start, but rather inadequate for her needs. A general search turned up the information that elephants, whales, hippopotami, giraffes, rhinoceroses, and alligators use infrasound to communicate over distances. Interesting, certainly, but not exactly the information she was looking for. She typed *infrasound weapons* in the search bar and hit pay dirt. Most of the articles were speculative, and some included conspiracy theories, but even the most respectable sources indicated that infrasound could be used as a weapon as certain frequencies caused headaches, nausea, and people subjected to intense infrasound had been known to pass out. It was believed but not confirmed that the Nazis had tested infrasound on human subjects during World War II.

Information on infrasound and memory loss was less reliable. Not surprisingly, given the harsh effects, documented tests on human subjects were inadvertent, and not in a controlled laboratory environment, making it impossible to track the effect on human memory.

One article spelled out the basic known ways infrasound could harm humans in simple terms.

Lower than twenty hertz in frequency—the limit of human hearing—

means humans perceive infrasound as pressure rather than noise. This pressure will cause the human body to vibrate, with specific frequencies having known effects on certain organs. Fluids and gases in the body will stretch when subjected to the frequency, but organs have limits on how much pressure-induced stretching and contracting they can accommodate. Infrasound is low in hertz, but can still have a high decibel level. It is at these high decibel levels that the human body reacts to the inaudible sound waves.

At 130 decibels, the human ear will experience direct pressure distortion that can affect the ability to hear and understand speech. At 150 decibels, people experience nausea and whole-body vibrations. Above 165, vibration of the lungs triggers breathing problems. The critical point is felt around 175 decibels, when, if the hertz level is between .5 to 8, an artificial, abnormal breathing rhythm can be induced.

Isabel wasn't entirely certain she understood the difference between hertz and decibels, but figured the gist was that even though infrasound wasn't audible, it still could be loud. The louder it was, the stronger the vibration, and the worse the effects on the human body.

And someone—the CEO of Apex, Simon Barstow?—had figured out a way to make a directional silent weapon that subjected the body to the harmful low-hertz, high-decibel sound waves.

How far away did the person need to be to use the weapon? Had she been hit when she reached the middle of the river simply because it was the deepest, and therefore most dangerous point, or was that when she'd stepped into the weapon's range?

There were any number of hiding places on either bank. Anyone who was familiar with the search for Vin could have guessed Alec would take her to the river where he crossed. No need to follow them all morning. Just wait by the river—possibly in the same place they'd hidden when they shot Vin with the same infrasound weapon.

She was certain Vin had been subjected to infrasound in the river. It explained why he finished the crossing, even though it was the wrong direction—heading away from shelter.

Was Vin targeted because they'd tested the weapon on him in the cave? Was the torture he'd experienced infrasound? It would explain the lack of marks on his body, and the brief jolt of it she'd felt in the river had hurt like hell. She could easily understand why prolonged or repeated exposure would feel like cruel and unusual punishment.

She typed in Apex and Simon Barstow in the search engine but found nothing that indicated Apex was experimenting with infrasound. Given their development of Airwave, it made sense that they might be working with infrasound as well.

She read article after article about Barstow and Apex but couldn't figure out why he'd test his weapons on Vin when he had a legitimate laboratory for weapons development. Granted, human testing wasn't an option, but he wouldn't be able to use the data gathered from illegal human testing to get his weapons approved anyway.

A knock on the suite door reminded her of the time. Research hour was over; her babysitter had arrived.

THE INDOOR FIRING range was located in the lowest level of the compound, a partially underground basement—the only subterranean construction possible in the subarctic due to the hazards of building on permafrost. The floor lacked traditional corridors that could trap heat. Instead, the basement had occasional short sections of wall punctuated by thick metal posts in the otherwise vast, open space. The posts, Isabel knew, were necessary to hold the heat and pressure of the four-story structure above the permafrost, to prevent the soil from thawing, which would cause the building to buckle.

Glancing upward at the massive building, she shuddered at the thought of the structure collapsing on top of her.

"You get used to it," Ethan said. "It's better inside the range, because it isn't under the building—it's adjacent. For safety, the firing range is a big underground cavern with reinforced but natural walls. Stray bullets can hit the dirt without causing damage to the building."

She shot him a speculative glance. "I had no idea the compound had this big a footprint. A lot of earth was moved to build this place. Too bad no one did an archaeological survey first."

Ethan shrugged, too even-tempered to rise to the bait. A regular at the roadhouse, he'd joined her for drinks several times in the last few months, and she liked him. "Not my problem. The facility was built before I was hired."

True, as Ethan had joined Raptor sometime after Alec purchased the company, and, if she remembered correctly, he was from Pennsylvania, or some other eastern state. "How did you end up here?" she asked.

"Rav begged me. Made me an offer I couldn't refuse."

"You knew him before?"

"Yeah. I taught him how to shoot when he was fresh out of diapers."

Isabel laughed. "Before he joined the Army?"

"No. Right after. He joined up, then realized he couldn't shoot worth a damn. He was terrible. A menace. He was going to kill someone, and it wasn't the enemy. But Richie Rich doesn't know how to be *bad* at something. It offends him. So during his first furlough from boot camp, he showed up at my door and offered me an obscene amount of money to teach him how to shoot. Over a weekend."

"And did he learn in two days?"

"Hell, no. But he came back during his next furlough. And the next one. The man didn't take a decent break for a year. But at the end of that year, he qualified for sniper training."

"He was a sniper?"

"Nah. The Rangers had other uses for him."

"Do you like Alec? Personally, I mean?" It was a forward question, and she didn't really expect an honest answer if he didn't, but she'd gotten to know Ethan well enough over the last several months to think he might tell her the truth, and she was curious, especially because he'd known Alec for more than a decade.

"I do, actually. He was intense at twenty-two. So determined to prove himself. Prove that he earned his place in the world, that nothing was given to him because of his family's money. He's mellowed over the years. I think being a Ranger knocked that chip off his shoulder—like he'd proved it and was done. I think he's less embarrassed by the wealth now."

"And yet he wasn't afraid to use it back then—to hire you to teach him how to shoot."

"He's too smart not to use the money to his advantage. And he still had to do the learning. Money can't make you a crack shot. Only practice will do that."

At last they reached a thick steel door cut into the foundation wall. Ethan typed a code into the keypad, and the door opened, revealing another vast chamber separated into six long lanes, like a bowling alley, but these lanes were about four times longer. Ethan made a beeline for a large safe situated on this side of a counter that defined the firing line.

His fingers danced over the safe's keypad, and a buzzer sounded. A moment later, the door released.

"What's with the buzzer?"

"It means security has been alerted that the gun safe has been opened." He pointed to the dome mounted to the ceiling in front of the safe. "Security monitors this room. If they see an unauthorized person accessing the gun safe—even if the person uses a correct code—they can lock down the safe."

"That's pretty high tech."

He nodded. "Rav takes safety and security seriously."

She didn't miss the pointed comment. She had argued the compound lacked proper safety measures. Everything she'd seen since stepping inside indicated she'd been dead wrong.

Ethan handed her a pair of headphones, then grabbed a pistol from the safe.

"Is that one for me?"

"Yes."

"But it's a girly gun."

"Rav said to start you out with the Sig Mosquito."

She felt like Will Smith in *Men in Black*. "I want something…mean-looking."

"It's not the size of the weapon that matters."

She frowned. "No, it's the caliber of the bullet. I want to shoot a forty-five."

"You're starting with a twenty-two or my ass is fired."

She sighed. "Okay."

Ethan was a good sport, putting up with her petulance with nary a ripple in his easygoing manner. Here, he was in his element. He was a good teacher, all business, but knowledgeable and friendly. He quickly assessed her skills and reminded her to zero in on the finer details, like how breathing rate could affect accuracy.

Once she'd hit the bull's-eye at twenty-five yards, he moved her up to a bigger gun, but still, sadly, not a forty-five. Finally, after two hours, she could fire the heavier gun with reasonable accuracy, but her arms shook with exhaustion as she held the weapon in a two-handed grip.

"You're done," Ethan said, his voice reaching her through

speakers in the protective headphones. "Take the shot, then I'll show you how to clean the gun."

She squeezed the trigger, so glad to be done she ignored everything he'd taught her about stance, aim, and breath. The bullet went high, missing the target completely.

"Christ, Ethan, I thought you were supposed to be a good teacher." Alec's voice had a tinny quality through the speaker, and she turned—keeping the barrel of the gun pointed down the firing lane—to see he'd entered the range and donned the protective headgear with built-in microphone.

She carefully set the gun on the counter before planting her hands on her hips. "That was the first shot that *didn't* hit the target in an hour. I made confetti of the last sheet." She waved toward the shredded paper. "So don't mess with me." She twisted and picked up the gun again, and this time took careful aim, determined to impress him with her newfound marksmanship.

Her shot went low. She frowned as she heard a soft, throaty chuckle in her ear.

"Her arms are tired, boss."

She ignored the dialogue and tried again. But her arms were visibly shaking. Exhaustion had caught up with her. Her ribs ached. The bullet hit the paper but not the human outline. Arms slid along hers, and she startled. Ethan had been careful with his touches to correct her stance, always giving verbal warning, and never touching more than the joint or muscle required for her to adjust her grip, stance, or position. This was a slow, sensual caress that had less to do with teaching and was more about seduction.

Alec's hand supported her elbow as his chest pressed against her back. "Deep breath. Slow. Align the front sight with the rear sight. Watch for two or three breaths when they bounce over the center of the target. Try to anticipate the bounce. Squeeze right before the crosshairs cross over the center."

She did as he said, and fired with her fourth breath. It wasn't a bull, but she hit well within the rings.

Lips caressed her neck. "Ethan's gone," he murmured.

She set the gun on the counter and leaned against Alec. He pulled off her headphones and nibbled on her ear. "God, that was hot. I had no idea I could get so turned on watching you with a gun."

She arched her neck, giving him better access, even as she rolled her eyes and said, "Men."

He chuckled. "We're simple creatures." His hand slid up her ribs and cupped her breast as he pressed his growing erection against her spine, underscoring his statement.

She laughed and twisted in his arms until she faced him. His mouth met hers in a deep kiss that stole her breath. He cradled her ass and held her against him. Her fingers threaded through his short-cropped hair, while his tongue delved into her mouth and made her forget every unpleasant feeling she'd experienced in the last three days.

The kiss had come about so naturally, a progression, she hadn't really seen it coming. And didn't want it to stop.

She wanted him. Now. But this was wrong. When he wasn't with her—and she could think clearly—she was plagued with all the reasons she shouldn't want him. But with one kiss, logic evaporated, and guilt fled to the dark corners of her mind.

His tongue stroked hers. Heat infused her while guilt took flight and lust gathered the reins. She reached for the buttons on his shirt and had two open before he stopped her. His breathing was ragged as he pressed his forehead to hers. "Not here. Cameras. There are two in this room." He nodded to a dome mounted above the firing lane.

Her hands froze. *Shit.* His men could be watching, right now. Correction. They *were* watching.

He took a step backward, releasing her. He rubbed a hand across his face. "I'm sorry. I shouldn't have started that. Not here."

"My fault for taking it further."

He buttoned his shirt. "I wasn't supposed to touch you at all. It's still your move."

She frowned at that. To her conscience, his making a move and her accepting him was entirely different from her seeking him out. "You can't leave it up to me. I *want* you to make the next move."

He shook his head, fixing her with his tigerlike stare. "I'm not going to make this easy for you, Isabel." He stepped forward, backing her into the firing-line counter. "Make no mistake, I will make love to you, but *you* will initiate it."

His bold declaration scared her. "I…can't."

His eyes lit with blue flame, and his mouth twisted in a confident half smile. "It's not a matter of can or can't. It's only a matter of when."

His arms rested on the counter on either side of her, pinning her, yet no part of his body touched her. Mere millimeters separated them. Aroused, she sucked in a shallow breath, because a deep one would cause her nipples to skim his hard chest. She was completely turned on by his confidence and certainty.

She'd been certain about many things in her life, but never like that, and never about a man.

"I won't touch you again, not until you touch me first. You're going to come to *me*." He stepped back, releasing her from his heat. "Shooting lessons are over. I'd like you to go back to my quarters."

"I—" Her voice creaked, and she cleared her dry throat. "I need to clean the gun. Ethan said he'd show me how."

"I'll do it."

"You have work to do."

He shrugged, "Then I'll have one of my minions do it."

She couldn't help but laugh. He was the only person she knew who could say that and actually mean it. She turned to the door. "You know, you don't need to take me to Paris. I'm already impressed." She slipped through the door before he could answer, and picked up her pace as she headed across the vast underground chamber. This space still gave her the creeps.

Nearing the middle—or at least she thought it was the middle—she became disoriented. She'd thought the elevator was this way but instead found a maintenance room. She turned, scanning the space. Where the hell was the elevator shaft?

Spotting the elevator a hundred yards away, she made a beeline for it. She rounded a thick support pole and landed smack into a man's chest. She stumbled, reeling, her head spinning so it took a moment for her to recognize the brick wall who stood before her. Chase Johnston, the newbie on Falcon team who made her uncomfortable.

His feral grin said he was far too happy to see her.

CHAPTER NINETEEN

ALEC SAT ON the bench and grabbed a towel and the gun oil. He *should* let an employee clean the weapon, but he needed to think, and he was used to strategizing while cleaning guns.

He should be thinking about the training, his abduction, the campaign, or any of a dozen other things, but Isabel Dawson was first and foremost in his mind. Insane as it sounded, falling in love with her seemed like more than a possibility; he had a feeling it was inevitable. But damn if he was going to let her hide behind her reservations. She would break through them, and he'd be waiting on the other side.

The door to the firing range opened, and Ethan stepped inside. "I'll clean the guns, Rav."

Alec frowned at the pistol, then made eye contact with his employee, a man five years his senior whom he'd known since he was twenty-two and the worst shot at boot camp. "How'd she do?"

"Really well. She's methodical. Like you. With practice, she'll be a crack shot." Ethan paused. "Be careful, boss. She's more fragile than she seems."

Alec had figured that out already but was curious to know why Ethan would warn him. "What do you mean?"

"Isabel needs to be around people but holds herself back from them. She goes to the Tamarack Roadhouse every week, but more than once I've caught her hanging out front, trying to decide if she can step through the door. I figure she's afraid of connecting to people. Afraid of caring."

Ethan wasn't the first person to make that point, and yet Alec had seen little of that side of Isabel. When she was around him, she was all heat and energy.

"I'll clean the guns," Ethan said again.

Alec nodded. He really needed to meet Keith in God's Eye, to give him a brief introduction to the control room. "I won't hurt her," he said, as he opened the door. The moment the thick steel portal opened, he heard a loud, piercing scream.

ISABEL STARED IN shock at Chase as the man dropped to his knees, his hands gripping his head. He sucked in a deep breath and let out another screeching wail. He whimpered and said, "I can't! I can't! I'm sorry! I can't!"

Was he being hit with infrasound? What was happening to him?

"Isabel!" Alec's shout echoed across the basement.

Chase opened his eyes—bloodshot and watery—and met her gaze. "I'm sorry, boss!" he said through tears. "I can't do it. I won't!" Then his body convulsed three times, and he made a gurgling sound that ended abruptly as he teetered, then fell to the floor.

Isabel drew in a deep breath and shouted, "We're by the elevator!" She dropped to her knees and checked for a pulse. She couldn't find one. She pushed him over until he lay flat on his back, her heart hammering as she tried to figure out what had happened and what she should do.

One moment Chase was giving her a look of mixed fear and loathing; the next he'd seemed to argue with himself, in a freakish Gollum impersonation, if the *Lord of the Rings* character were a six-foot-tall mercenary. And now the man wasn't breathing and had no pulse.

Chest compressions first. She'd recertified in CPR last year and knew the drill. Thirty compressions and two breaths—but breathing only if she had a partner. She placed her hands in the center of his chest, one hand on top of the other, and started compressions at a hard, rapid pace, chanting "Another One Bites the Dust" to get the rhythm.

Footfalls sounded and she glanced up to see Alec and Ethan racing toward her at a dead run. "What happened?" Alec asked.

"I don't know! He has no pulse. He's not breathing." She didn't break stride with the compressions as she answered. The rhythm was fast. She'd begun to sweat as she tried to keep the young operative's heart beating.

Alec hit the intercom button next to the elevator and relayed the emergency to the communications operator. Ethan knelt beside her and touched Chase's neck with two fingers.

"You're doing good. I'm getting a pulse with each compression."

"You know CPR?" she asked.

"Yes."

"You can breathe for him, then."

"You got it." He positioned Chase's head to open his airway. "Just tell me when."

"On thirty." She'd been counting silently but now she said, "Twenty-eight, twenty-nine, thirty."

Ethan gave Chase two quick breaths, and Isabel returned to counting silently.

"Doc's on his way," Alec said as he knelt down across from her. "Do you want me to take over?"

"Not yet. Soon." She focused on Chase's face as she counted chest compressions. He was so young. Twenty-two or three? Far too young for his heart to stop. Something had been *done* to him. But what? Why? And how did it connect to what happened to Vin? To Alec? To her?

Isabel's forehead was slick with sweat by the time the elevator door opened. Doc Larson and his assistant stepped out, followed by a gurney being pushed by someone from security. The gurney was loaded with equipment.

"Keep doing chest compressions," Larson said as he grabbed his equipment from the gurney. Alec moved out of the way, and Larson took his spot. While Isabel pounded on Chase's chest, Larson used a blade to slice open Chase's thick camouflage shirt, starting at the sleeve and cutting from hem to the neckline. He repeated the action with the other arm.

Isabel reached the end of the cycle and stopped compressions so Ethan could breathe. Larson took the opportunity to pull the shirt down, exposing Chase's chest. He quickly placed a small square patch in the middle of his chest, then nodded to Isabel.

She positioned her hands again, this time above the square pad, and returned to the fast beat as Larson placed a larger square patch to the upper right on Chase's chest that was connected to the smaller one under her hands. He then placed a final large square patch on Chase's left side, just below the nipple line. He quickly placed four small electrodes—two on Chase's upper hip bones, two on his collarbones—and the monitor sprang to life.

Larson paused and studied the screen. "Patient is in V-fib. On my count, Isabel will stop compressions and switch positions with Ethan." He counted down, then nodded to Isabel, who scooted back so Ethan could take over chest compressions.

"Charging to 200 Joules... Everybody clear... Delivering shock." He pushed a button.

Chase's body contracted, his whole body jolting—almost levitating from the floor. Larson kept his gaze on the monitor. "Ethan, begin compressions," he instructed.

Ethan took over the job of pounding on Chase's chest, while Isabel moved to take over breathing, but Larson's assistant brushed her aside and put a manual resuscitator mask over Chase's nose and mouth.

She slumped backward and took her own deep breath.

When Ethan reached the end of the cycle, he counted aloud, and the assistant pumped the air-filled bag two times. Meanwhile, Doc Larson was in the process of setting up an IV. He injected something into the line.

"You both have done great," Larson said without taking his gaze from the monitor.

The minutes moved slowly, and she wasn't even doing the compressions any more. She met Ethan's gaze. With a quick nod, she indicated she could take over after the next round.

Larson's gaze never wavered from the screen. Finally, he spoke. "He's in sinus rhythm now. Stop CPR." He pressed fingers to Chase's throat. "Strong carotid." He shifted to his wrist. "Weak radial."

Instant tears sprang to her eyes. She scooted backward to get out of the way so the security officer and Larson's assistant could lift Chase to the stretcher.

"If his heart keeps going, he may be solid for airlift to Fairbanks." He nodded to his assistant, who'd been busy in the background, handing the doctor the various patches and tools necessary, and it vaguely registered that he'd been on the phone, calling for emergency airlift. She'd been so focused on Chase, the rest was a blur.

"Let's get him up to the clinic. Isabel, Ethan, Rav, ride with us and tell me what happened."

Everyone crammed into the elevator, a tight fit due to the gurney carrying Chase. Isabel gave a brief rendition of Chase's screams, disoriented speech, convulsions, and eventual collapse. The only time the doctor looked away from the heart monitor was when she mentioned infrasound and added that she thought he'd been hit with a frequency that caused an abnormal heart rate and eventual cardiac arrest.

Larson's eyes widened, and he turned to Alec with an accusing gaze. "Infrasound? I thought you stopped the experimental weapons program."

"I did. It appears someone decided to continue it without my knowledge."

The elevator doors opened, and Larson pushed the gurney into the corridor. "We'll discuss this later, Rav. Right now I have a patient to take care of." His angry tone made it clear he was as suspicious of his boss as Isabel had once been.

The elevator doors closed, leaving Isabel, Alec, and Ethan inside. No one had pushed a button. They didn't move. Isabel was at a loss for where they should go. What they should do. Alec opened his arms, and she fell into them. The tears she'd been holding back burst through her control. She had no clue why she cried. It could be the shock of watching a man collapse before her, the relief his heart had restarted, or the fear his heart would stop again.

"You did great, honey," Alec murmured as he stroked her back. "If he lives, it's thanks to you and Ethan."

She pulled back and met his gaze. "He's what, twenty-three? His heart never should have stopped. What the hell is going on?"

The intercom inside the elevator beeped. Behind her, Ethan pressed the button and identified himself.

"This is Hatcher. Is Rav with you?"

"Yes, sir."

"Tell him Markwell and I are in Chase Johnston's quarters on the fourth floor, and we need him. Now."

ALEC FLIPPED THROUGH the pages of Chase Johnston's most recent journal. Anger mixed with horror caused his stomach to clench with each turn of the page. Johnston had been stalking Isabel. For three months. Page after page showed photos of Isabel. Handwritten underneath were dates, times, and locations.

"He must have set up cameras in town," he said to Nicole and Keith. "He had to be working some of these dates and times." He closed his eyes. This was worse than bad. Isabel had claimed— several times—that in addition to someone shooting off bear bangers on her property, she was being monitored by Raptor personnel. Of course the claim made her look like a nutcase or a liar. This was proof she was neither, and the fact that one of his employees had been stalking the woman who'd been on a crusade to shut down the compound wouldn't look good, no matter what his relationship with her was now.

His campaign could well fall apart. He was already slipping in the polls. His opponent had raised questions about his missing hours, and voters were echoing them to the pollsters. Stimson had cast suspicion on the silence from the campaign on the subject, and it didn't help that Alec was still in Alaska, and not in Maryland working damage control. A full seven percent of the registered voters who'd been firmly in the Ravissant camp had moved to the undecided column.

Alec had no illusions they'd maintain the fiction that he'd hit a moose and wandered the woods until Isabel found him—for starters, that would mean letting the bastards who'd abducted him get away with their crime—and when the truth came out, voters would have even more doubts. If his employees were behind the abduction, there would undoubtedly be whispers of cover-ups and Alec's involvement in dirty deals.

Prior to seeking out Isabel in the firing range, he'd been on the phone with his campaign manager, who had not so subtly hinted that the only certain way to salvage the mess was if the FBI charged Isabel with his abduction. Carey asserted a crackpot with a baseless vendetta would be far easier for voters to accept and move on from than anything involving Raptor.

Alec had made it clear to Carey that any attempt to characterize Isabel as a crackpot wouldn't be tolerated. He'd rather lose than allow anyone associated with him to smear her.

Aside from finding the idea of pinning everything on Isabel abhorrent, it was now clear she'd been right about her stalker. She'd been right about so many things.

Had Chase stalked her because he was obsessed with her? Or did his reasons have to do with Raptor and infrasound?

A team of operatives had entered the basement from the south stairwell and searched for Chase's assailant—assuming he'd been zapped with infrasound—even as Isabel and Ethan performed CPR. But they'd found no one in the shadows of the vast basement. Security was going through all the basement camera footage, including the stairs and elevators in hopes of identifying a suspect, but any number of employees could have a legitimate reason to enter the basement, and Alec was certain the assault on Chase had been an inside job.

The deeper they looked, the more tangled the situation

became. All he knew as he stared at the journal was that he was glad Isabel was safe in his quarters, because if she saw this proof Johnston had her under surveillance, she would rightly freak out.

Would she regret administering CPR to her stalker? He doubted it. After all, she'd saved Alec's ass, taking good care of him even after she knew exactly who he was.

CHAPTER TWENTY

ISABEL STARED AT the screen of Alec's laptop, methodically picking through the results of Internet searches on infrasound and cardiac death. She rubbed her eyes and stretched her neck. Information on infrasound remained scant, and she'd learned the odds weren't in Chase's favor.

A knock on the door startled her. She heard Nicole shout, "It's Nic. I bring food and files."

Isabel slid back the dead bolt Alec had installed while they were hiking yesterday. The bolt couldn't be unlocked from the outside, ensuring she'd feel safe in his suite. It was strangely comforting to have a simple, mechanical lock in a building in which everything was controlled by electronic key codes. If the power went out, and the backup generator failed, this door would remain locked.

She swung open the door to see Nicole holding a plastic file box. Behind her stood Hans, carrying a cafeteria tray laden with food and a basket with an assortment of drinks and the necessary accoutrements. Nicole breezed past Isabel and set the file box next to the computer desk in the corner.

Hans followed her in and set the tray the table. "Do you need anything else?"

"No. Thanks, Hans. Call when the FBI is ready for Isabel, and I'll escort her to the conference room."

He nodded and left.

Isabel eyed the food, realizing she was hungry. The events of the last two days had suppressed her appetite, but the smell of steak revived it. "Aren't you a little high up in the hierarchy to be saddled with babysitting duty?" she asked.

Nicole grinned and started dealing plates and silverware. "Yes, but it's been a craptastic few days, and I wanted an hour off so I can vent about my new boss, so I volunteered."

Isabel smiled and dropped into a seat at the table, snitching a slice of garlic bread from the basket as she did so. It had been a few weeks since she and Nicole had hung out and she'd missed her. "You don't like Keith Hatcher?"

"Hatcher is fine. He might even be easier to work for than Rav. He seems open to some of my ideas that Rav has repeatedly shot down. I'm just annoyed that I *have* a new boss. I wanted the job."

Nicole had made no secret of her wish to take over as Raptor CEO if Alec won the election, but she'd also admitted it was a long shot given the difficulty she was having retaining employees at the compound.

"I heard Godfrey quit on Thursday," Isabel said, then licked garlic butter from her fingers.

Nicole made a low growling sound in the back of her throat. "I begged Godfrey to stay. Quitting without notice when the CEO was about to arrive was shitty as hell. I can't blame him for my not getting the promotion, though. Hatcher, apparently, was hired weeks ago, right after he passed the background check." She pulled a bottle of cabernet sauvignon from the basket along with two glasses. "But I can get my petty revenge against the company by drinking one of the best wines from the cellar."

"The compound has a wine cellar?" Isabel asked incredulously.

"It was Beck's." She waved an arm around the overdecorated room. "I think Beck intended to move here permanently, maybe right before he'd planned to set off an epidemic in the lower forty-eight, making Alaska a safe haven. The CEO suites at all the other compounds aren't nearly this gaudy, and Hawaii doesn't have a wine cellar or tennis courts. Beck's passions were wine and tennis." She twisted the corkscrew into the top of the bottle. "My revenge is feeble, though, since Rav instructed me to pick out a good bottle to go with our dinner." She gave Isabel a knowing smile. "It appears he's wining and dining you even when he's not here."

"More like he's placating you."

"That too. Rav is nothing if not a brilliant strategist." She pulled out the cork. "And, sadly, I can only have one glass. With everything that's going on, more would be foolish."

"Just one for me too. I've got to talk to the FBI." Isabel loaded her baked potato with butter, cheese, and sour cream, but her attention was on something else Nicole had said about Robert Beck. "What do you mean 'start an epidemic'?"

"I only know what came out in the pretrial filings. Beck

hemorrhaged money building this place—the Alaska compound ended up costing three times the estimates. He was at risk of defaulting on far too many loans, and his scheme to turn things around was to freak out the American people by committing terrorist acts that would scare the government into contracting more security work to him. There was a bill in Congress at the time that would have designated private security firms as first responders. There was some speculation that biological agents and an epidemic were involved, but none of that was presented as evidence in the filings."

Isabel knew most of that but hadn't heard the part about biological agents, but then, that had probably been kept out of the media, for good reason. "Do you think Beck was experimenting? With infrasound, among other things?"

"It's possible. With Beck, it's hard to rule anything out. But I've searched this place top to bottom. Hell, I've even paced and measured. While it's a crazy maze, there are no unaccounted-for spaces. No hidden chambers or laboratories. I always heard that if there was a lab, it was in the Virginia compound."

Isabel sliced a bite of steak—medium rare, just the way she liked it—and chewed the perfect cut slowly while considering the pieces of the elaborate puzzle. It was easy to imagine Beck had been experimenting with infrasound if he'd been dabbling in biological agents. Anyone working on that research for him would have been more than eager to cover it up to save themselves from jail. Then, six months or a year after Beck plea-bargained for a life sentence to avoid the death penalty for a vast array of crimes that included murder-for-hire and treason, whoever had been experimenting with infrasound could have resumed their research.

She nodded to the file box as she cut another bite. "What's in the box?"

"Everything we have on the search for Vin and the investigation into his death."

That fast, Isabel's eyes teared. "*Everything?*"

Nicole squeezed her hand. "Yes. Everything. Rav gave me permission to give it to you."

It wasn't wine, food, or a trip to Paris, and it proved Alec was, indeed, a brilliant strategist.

ISABEL MET WITH the two FBI agents in a small conference room on the third floor. She told them everything, starting with Vin's first email about passing out while hiking on Raptor land and ending with performing CPR on Chase Johnston. In between, she confessed to encroaching on Raptor property to find the lynx cave, her fears of being stalked by Raptor operatives, and her vague memories of being hit with infrasound and Airwave in her cabin.

In short, she finally got the FBI to listen to her, after ten months of begging them to investigate her brother's death, only to sound utterly paranoid and insane with the bizarre list of events that had occurred since finding Alec in the woods on Thursday afternoon.

She could only hope that Alec's version of events matched hers.

For their part, the agents—a white man named Upton, and an African American woman named Crews—kept their faces blank, never once indicating whether or not they thought she was nuts.

Interview complete, she shook hands with both agents and stepped into the hall. No one waited to escort her back to Alec's suite, but then, they hadn't known how long the interview would take, and everyone here was busy prepping for the training.

She went to the elevator and hit the down button. As she waited, she realized this was the same bank of elevators that went to the basement where she'd encountered Chase. The medical clinic was just down the hall, but Chase wasn't there. He'd been airlifted to Fairbanks within thirty minutes of his collapse.

Odds of surviving cardiac arrest outside a hospital were slim, but she'd started CPR immediately, and a doctor had arrived with a defibrillator within minutes. Plus, he was young, and cardiac arrest had likely been caused by infrasound or something like it.

Restarting his heart and getting it to stay beating was the first hurdle, which had been cleared. The second hurdle—getting to the hospital—had also been cleared. He had a chance, better than most.

She needed to ask him what the hell he'd meant by, *"I'm sorry, boss! I can't do it. I won't!"*

Do what? And who did he mean when he said "boss"?

Alec? Nicole? Or someone else?

The basement had been searched, and Keith and Alec had identified the spot where they suspected Chase's assailant had stood. In all probability, the acoustic weapon hadn't affected Isabel because a section of wall had blocked her from the weapon's line of sight, and only a direct hit by the sound wave was harmful.

The elevator door opened, and she stepped inside and pressed the button for the ground floor, where Alec's suite was located.

But the elevator skipped the ground floor and went straight to the basement. The doors opened.

A shiver of fear swept through her.

She was certain she hadn't hit the wrong button.

She told herself the prickles of fright were due to the basement being built into permafrost and a few hours ago she'd helped bring a man back from the dead just three feet away.

She hit the button for the ground floor again, but nothing happened. She jabbed at it three times before giving up. With a sigh, she stepped from the elevator. She'd seen a stairway sign on the third-floor corridor. It couldn't be far.

Unfortunately, the basement layout didn't match the upper floors, but she guessed she'd find the staircase to the left about fifty feet. She glanced that way, but the lit corridor faded into a dark, distant void. No convenient exit sign.

She headed that direction anyway. There had to be a sign; a short section of wall was probably blocking it from view.

Tinny musical notes—sounding just like her mother's old record player—carried from the void.

The notes took shape into a familiar tune. Shock jolted through her. The music was the opening notes to "I Am The Very Model Of A Modern Major-General"—the song she'd been singing in the forest right before she found Alec. Her heart hammered as terror rooted her to the spot.

Lights came on in a row—as if the motion sensors had been triggered—and in the distance, she saw a man. Or at least she thought it was a man. A black mask covered his face, and something—like a gas mask?—covered his nose and mouth.

Nausea hit, breaking her fear-induced paralysis. Pain exploded along her occipital nerve. She turned and launched herself toward the elevator but feared her gait was more stagger than run. Behind her, she heard footsteps. The pain in her head ratcheted higher.

The elevator door remained open, and she pitched herself inside. As if drunk, she slapped a hand against the panel of buttons, praying she'd hit one that would close the door and this time the elevator would work.

She tucked herself to the side to get out of the sound wave's path and braced both hands flat against the wall. She focused on the panel, trying to decipher the blurred controls. She remembered reading that the fluid in the eyes expanded and vibrated with the high frequency, causing pain and interrupting vision. She couldn't read but saw something red on the panel. Emergency call button? She slapped it.

An alarm sounded.

The rapid lyrics from "Modern Major-General" pummeled her, causing a spike in pressure on her brain with every note.

She was trapped in a house of horrors.

She covered her ears and screamed as the world faded to nothing around her.

Chapter Twenty-One

ALEC PAUSED IN the stairwell and listened at the door. Every cell in his body wanted to burst into the corridor, but he couldn't be stupid about this. He had no idea what was on the other side of that door. The sound of Isabel's scream through the elevator emergency intercom still rang in his ears.

He nodded to Keith, who flanked the door to the right, and they both pointed their pistols at the ceiling in a ready position. Alec kicked open the door.

In smooth choreography, they slipped through the opening, Alec first, Keith at his back. Just like they'd done in Yemen a lifetime ago.

Also like Yemen, the basement appeared empty of Tangos.

This section of basement was dark—too dark—and he glanced up at the lights. Both the corridor lights and the exit sign were out.

The elevator alarm continued to wail. Isabel lay slumped in the opening, one leg protruding, preventing the door from closing. Only years of training stopped him from diving to her side. He had to ensure the area was clear first.

Keith checked the corridor while Alec cleared the elevators. Empty. He dropped to Isabel's side. Her chest rose in a regular cadence. She was breathing.

Thank God.

"Isabel?" he said, gently tapping her cheek. He ran his hands down her body, searching for wounds, knowing he wouldn't find any. This had all the earmarks of infrasound, which meant she'd likely come to but would feel sick and disoriented. Would she remember what happened?

The alarm shut off abruptly. Alec looked up to see Keith at the controls, resetting the system. "Thanks."

Isabel groaned and rolled to her side. A good sign.

"Let's get her to the clinic," Keith said.

Alec scooped her up and stood. She lay slack in his arms as the doors slid closed.

Keith used the intercom to instruct security to send in the team waiting to search the basement. This search would likely be as fruitless as the last, and the person who'd assaulted Isabel could well be on the team, but they had to try.

Alec shifted her weight, cradling her against him. Her eyes fluttered open. She whimpered and tucked her head into his chest. "The light hurts," she muttered.

"Do you remember what happened?" he asked.

She nodded into his shirt and whispered something.

"What is it, honey?"

"Take me out of here." Her words were faint, a dry rasp.

"I'm taking you to Dr. Larson."

"No. I can't stay in the compound." Her voice rose, gaining strength. "They attacked my cabin so you'd bring me here. They *want* me here. I need to leave."

Alec wanted to deny her point, but she could be right. Why had they attacked her cabin? To steal her laptop? That made no sense. The information on her computer—evidence she'd been sneaking onto Raptor land for months—was moot now. Harmless, given that Alec couldn't press charges for the restraining order violation even if he wanted to. And he didn't want to.

"You need to see Doc Larson," he said.

"We can't trust him. We can't trust anyone. I'll be fine. I just need to sleep. Then I'll feel better."

"My quarters," Alec said to Keith. "Ground floor."

"*No*. Alec. I have to leave."

"I trust Keith and Ethan, but I can't spare them to guard you outside the compound. I have soldiers arriving in a few days. We need to be ready. You aren't safe alone in your cabin."

"I'll go to another prove-up. One no one knows about."

"You'd be isolated. Alone. Anything could happen, and I couldn't be there to help you. You'll be safe in my quarters. With me. Tomorrow we'll figure something else out."

She held his gaze, her eyes were so bleak, so tired, it broke him a little bit. Finally, she nodded.

The door slid open, and he stepped into the corridor.

"I can walk," Isabel said, and she wiggled to indicate he should set her down.

"Why walk when I can carry you? I owe you for dragging me through the woods."

"If you think carrying me through a building with elevators and smooth, level floors makes up for my dragging your heavy, ungrateful carcass across miles of woods…"

"One mile of woods."

"It felt like fifteen."

Like seeing her chest rise and fall when she'd lain on the floor in the elevator, the teasing was a relief. She wouldn't be Isabel if she didn't tease him, and he wouldn't have her any other way.

He carried her into his suite and straight to his bed. The second time he'd deposited her in a bed and wished it were for other reasons.

He nodded to Keith, who pulled out a scanner to sweep the room for listening devices. "Room's clean of bugs," Keith said.

Alec called security. "What was up with the elevators?" he asked.

"Near as we can tell, sir, the moment Ms. Dawson stepped inside, all elevators were switched to 'fire emergency lock'—they were called to the basement and locked with doors open."

"How did that happen? Someone pulled an alarm?"

"No, sir. If they had, we'd have known the elevators were offline before Ms. Dawson hit the emergency call button. It appears someone hacked our system and had access to the elevator controls."

Given that Alec and Keith had been in the security room trying to figure out what happened to the camera feed when Johnston collapsed, and that the elevator controls were in the security room, he had to agree. The two men working in security couldn't have locked down the elevators without him noticing. Could they?

"Upload the video camera feed from the elevator and the basement corridor cameras to the Raptor FTP site."

"Yes, sir."

He hung up and dialed Lee Scott, the computer security specialist who'd locked down the system after the major hack in July. He answered immediately. "Lee, there's been another breach."

"I was just on the phone with your security team and see it on the shared screen. No doubt it came from inside."

"Can you fix it?"

"Not from here."

"How soon can you get to Tamarack?"

"I'll look up flights. Tomorrow evening, probably."

Keith tapped him on the shoulder. "Josh and Sean are taking the BD-700. They were supposed to depart in an hour."

To Lee, Alec said, "The company jet is heading this way. How soon can you get to Dulles?"

"This time of night? Forty-five minutes."

"Give yourself time to pack, make it ninety. The jet will be waiting."

Alec hadn't even hung up with Lee before Keith was on his phone with one of the pilots explaining that they needed to wait for a third passenger.

Calls completed, Alec said to Isabel, "Tell us what happened."

She sat up in the bed and took a sip of water from a glass Keith handed her, then leaned against the pillows and launched into her story. When she told him about hearing the song she'd been singing in the woods, he swore. "They heard you. They were there the entire time."

And now they'd used that to torment her.

She nodded, pulling the bedding closer around her as she did so. She finished her nightmare story, and Alec itched to pull her into his arms but didn't think she'd appreciate that in front of Keith. He had to remind himself that she had a reputation for being reserved, even standoffish with others, because she wasn't that way with him.

She took another sip of water. "I'm feeling better. It seems like it's wearing off faster than when they attacked my cabin. But then, I also remember everything that happened this time around."

"Let's see what the video cameras picked up." Alec opened the feed on his laptop.

He'd spent good money on new cameras throughout the compound when he took over, and the feed was crystal-clear color. The elevator doors slid open. Several moments later, Isabel stepped out. She left the range of the first camera. Alec paused that video and switched to the corridor recording.

Isabel froze, fear plain on her face.

"I wish we had sound," Keith said. "Then we could figure out where the music came from by checking which cameras picked up the noise."

On the screen, Isabel grimaced and staggered to the elevator, and everything played out as she described. After she collapsed, nothing moved for several minutes until Alec and Keith entered from the shadows.

Alec opened the video link for the elevator. It matched the footage from the corridor camera. Isabel staggered inside and hit the buttons. She hit the red emergency button, which set off the alarm, and opened the intercom to Isabel's scream, alerting Alec in the security room.

He frowned. He'd hoped they have some glimpse of the masked man, but he'd remained in the shadows, away from the cameras.

Keith cleared his throat. "Rav, we need to cancel the training. It's not safe here. For anyone."

The words settled in the room, drifting like falling feathers, when they should have landed with the force of a brick. But deep down, Alec had known since he swam down the frigid river this was the inevitable choice.

He wasn't just going to cancel the training; he needed to close the compound. "Looks like you're getting your way after all, Isabel."

CHAPTER TWENTY-TWO

ISABEL DREAMED ABOUT Vin. She hated waking from those dreams, the abrupt return to a world in which he was gone, after she'd had moments of joy at seeing him again, of believing that the last year had been the nightmare, and the dream was real.

Now here she was again, post-dream, and depressed. No. Not depressed—at least, not this time. Tonight, she was pissed. Vin was *gone*, and the people who had stolen him from this world were messing with her. They'd hurt her, repeatedly.

They'd terrified her and made her feel helpless, exposed. Vulnerable. All the things she'd felt when she was fourteen and lost her parents. But then her big brother had changed the entire direction of his life to prevent her from going into foster care.

She was mad as hell now.

She glanced at the clock on the nightstand. One a.m. She was alone in Alec's bed; he slept on the couch in the sitting room—guarding her even in his sleep while the compound was still full of mercenaries who couldn't be trusted.

She sat up in bed, pulling her knees to her chest. She was wide-awake, riled, and a man she was intensely attracted to slept mere feet away. Would Alec be willing to engage in a bout of angry sex to break the tension coiled in her body?

Not that she was angry with Alec. Her rage was reserved for Vin's killers.

It infuriated her that she was now afraid of the basement. And the elevator. And *Pirates of Penzance*.

Masks were also on her shit list.

She opened the nightstand drawer and pulled out the box of condoms.

Angry sex could be just the thing to calm her down. Then she could sleep again.

She threw back the covers. It was her move. Alec had insisted upon it. Anger was just the excuse she needed to squelch the guilt that was holding her back.

She eased open the door and crept into the sitting room, moving slowly so she wouldn't wake him if she changed her mind at the last second.

She rounded the foot of the couch and stopped short at what she saw. Her cat, Gandalf, was curled in a ball and sleeping on Alec's chest.

"Please tell me you're here to take this damned cat off me so I can sleep." Alec's voice was a whisper in the quiet room, and she smiled, realizing he was trying not to wake said damned cat.

The angry haze that had driven her here faded as she took in the scene before her. Her cat. Asleep on the most gorgeous naked chest she'd ever seen.

She was a little jealous of Gandalf.

"Sorry, no. I came out to ask for angry sex. I didn't realize Gandalf was here."

"I sent two men from security to pick him up. I figured after what you'd been through, you needed him. You were asleep by the time they delivered him, and I didn't want to wake you." He grimaced. "He's spent the last two hours kneading me and walking across me like I'm his personal sidewalk. He finally went to sleep about a half hour ago."

She couldn't help but grin. Alec lay pinned on the couch, clearly uncomfortable. Gandalf looked light and fluffy, but he was heavier than he appeared under all that fur, and he slept on Alec's heart as if he owned it. "He's a pest when you're trying to sleep. I never let him in my bedroom at night."

"Thanks for the warning," he said dryly. He held her gaze in the darkened room. LED lights on various electronic devices provided just enough illumination. "What was that thing you said about angry sex?"

She set the condoms on the coffee table and scooped Gandalf from Alec's chest. "Forget I said anything." Gandalf made a disgruntled sound at being woken; then he must have smelled her, because he settled down and purred.

Alec took a deep breath—probably his first since Gandalf used him as a mattress—and sat up. "I don't think I will." He shifted his legs to the floor. "Why angry sex? Why not just sex?"

She dropped onto the end of the couch where his legs had been and settled Gandalf on her lap. "Because I'm mad. I dreamed about Vin again and woke up pissed. I'm so mad at everything that's happened. I'm afraid of the basement now." Her voice rose as the anger came flooding back, causing Gandalf to tense. "And elevators! I feel like a piece of my security and sanity has been stolen from me, on top of having my brother taken. I just want to punch someone."

Alec slowly rose from the couch and paused in front of her, looming in the dark room. "Here's the deal, Iz. We're taking the elevator to the basement so you can shoot the shit out of some targets and get rid of some of that rage."

He extended a hand toward her.

She hesitated but then set Gandalf aside and took his hand. He pulled her to her feet, bringing them so close she had to lean back to meet his gaze. He steadied her with an arm around her waist as he studied her face. His mouth slowly curved in a carnal smile that triggered a flutter in her belly.

"And then"—his voice deepened to a low rumble—"if you're still feeling afraid, I'm going to strip you down and fuck the fear right out of you."

HE COULDN'T BE serious. Isabel stepped into the elevator, thinking about Alec's words, an effective block to what had happened in this box hours ago.

Yeah. He must've been kidding. A distraction.

It worked.

He stood silent at her side. Scruffy, tired, tousled, and frigging gorgeous. His T-shirt hugged his muscles as if it were painted on. She was in the same elevator that was part of one of the scariest moments of her life, and all she could think of was unbuttoning his jeans and going down on him.

She'd never had elevator sex before.

He was strong enough to lift her, pin her in the corner, and…

The doors opened. They'd arrived in the basement. The scariest place in her mind.

Alec merely grinned and raised an eyebrow.

He probably knew exactly what she was thinking. She nodded for him to lead the way, wondering all the while if he'd brought condoms. The box hadn't been on the coffee table after she got dressed.

Motion sensors caused lights to flare as they crossed the vast, disorienting space. Nothing moved in the shadows beyond the light.

The compound was quiet.

But then, it was half past one in the morning.

Inside the firing range, Alec locked the door behind them and then punched numbers into the gun safe keypad. The buzzer sounded, reminding her of the cameras that watched this room, even now.

Yeah, he must've been kidding. He wouldn't touch her in here, not with the cameras rolling. Disappointment filtered through her. They should have stayed in his suite.

He pressed at least a dozen more buttons on the keypad, then turned to her. "Punch in the same code I gave you for my quarters."

She brushed against him as she reached for the keypad. Instead of moving back to give her space, he leaned a titch closer. She glanced askance and caught a wicked, sexy grin. White teeth surrounded by dark stubble. He hadn't shaved since yesterday, and his square jaw was heavy with the beginning of a dark beard. He wasn't the polished politician anymore. She was fairly certain this man was the Ranger, and she found the Ranger a decided turn-on. Somehow she managed to remember and punch in the access code. Barely.

Only one panel of the gun locker opened. Inside was an array of small pistols and racks of ammunition. "That code gives you access to the range and these weapons."

"What, no fifty-caliber sniper rifles for me?" The bigger guns were in the other half of the gun locker.

"Hell, no. Those things have a nasty kick." He leaned in close and said in a husky voice, "The cameras are off."

"You didn't."

"Lee set up a special override code that only I have. I can turn off the cameras in any room in the compound."

"Is that really safe? To shut off the cameras?"

"This room has been on lockdown since I decided to shut down the compound. Only Keith, you, and I have the access code."

"What if the power goes out? Don't all the rooms unlock?"

"Most do. But not this one. It can be unlocked manually from the inside, to prevent anyone from being trapped, but otherwise, it would take a battering ram to get in here."

She glanced at the thick steel door and guessed that even a battering ram wouldn't be enough. Heat flared in her belly. Maybe he did intend to screw her brains out here and now.

He grabbed the Sig she'd used during her lesson with Ethan and a box of ammo. "Put on headphones. If you hit the bull three times in a row with this, it's yours."

Okay. Maybe they really were here just to shoot. "You'll give me the gun?"

"Yes."

"All I have to do is hit the bull three times?" Hell, she'd hit the bull's-eye a dozen times earlier. This would be a piece of cake.

"In a row."

She cocked her head. "You have to do it too."

"It's already my gun. My compound." His gaze scanned her from head to toe. "Everything in it is mine." Clearly, his self-imposed restraint toward her was gone.

Restraintless-Alec was even hotter than his previous incarnation—and she'd found him pretty damn hot before.

"Humor me," she said in the best challenging tone she could muster.

"Fine." He pulled on a pair of headphones, rammed the magazine into the handle, and one breath later squeezed off three shots in rapid succession. He slapped the button to recall the target, and the human outline on paper floated toward them, a ghost on a wire pulley. When the target reached the counter, Isabel saw three overlapping holes in the red center circle over the chest.

"Your turn," he said as he reset the target. The paper retracted down the lane but stopped at half the distance. "Twenty-five yards."

Her first shot was good. But the second went high, and the third went low. He stood behind her and coached her on her grip. With a hand on her hip and another under her elbow, he adjusted her stance. She took another shot. Dead center.

She grinned.

Lips touched the back of her neck, and through the headphones, she heard him say, "God, that's a turn-on."

Feeling pumped, she took another shot. It went high. Off-the-target high. He chuckled.

She set the gun on the counter and faced him. Crossing her arms over her chest, she nodded to the lane next to her. "You're distracting me on purpose. Go shoot in your own lane."

He grabbed her hips and pulled her against him. His tongue traced the hollow beneath her throat. His lips trailed upward, nuzzling the sensitive skin below her ear. "How about we play a game that's a lot like strip poker, but with shooting?"

She laughed. "Since you're obviously an ace marksman, there is no way I could win."

"Honey, when I get you naked, you'll feel like the winner."

She rolled her eyes and pushed him away. "Leave me alone. I'm trying to shoot."

He dropped a soft kiss on her lips. "Fine."

Her body hummed with pleasure as she emptied the magazine into the paper man. Every time she hit within the inner circles, she felt a jolt of adrenaline and a kick in the libido.

Next to her, Alec's target had disintegrated under rapid fire.

She paused to watch, her heart rate increasing as she took in his firm profile as he gazed down the sights. The intensity of his stare as he focused on the target, well, if he wasn't trying to kill it, she'd be jealous of the poor line drawing.

Watching him shoot was an aphrodisiac.

What was she thinking? Why was she wasting her time shooting at paper when she could be in bed with this man?

She carefully set her gun aside and moved to stand behind him. She cupped his butt with one hand and supported his elbow with the other. "You need to stand up straighter," she said, giving his perfect ass a solid squeeze. "And lift your elbow."

He chuckled and did as she said. The shot went high. His first shot that didn't even hit the target, let alone the inner circles.

"That's more like it," she said, tracing a line along his arm, over his pecs, down the T-shirt, finally, finding the hem, she slid her hand up, underneath, and explored those rock-hard abs.

He set down the gun and twisted so fast her hand that had been exploring his abs now rested on his back, and the hand on his ass met his erection. His lips were on hers in a flash, his tongue thrust into her mouth in a deep, erotic kiss that made no secret of exactly where this would go.

She slid her hands under the sinfully tight T-shirt, marveling at the feel of hot skin over iron muscle. He lifted his mouth from hers. "It's about damn time," he said.

She laughed and kissed him, losing herself in the hot, knee-melting kiss. His mouth moved lower, to her neck, and a semblance of sanity returned. "Alec, the cameras."

"They're off."

"But how do we *know* they're off? What if your override code didn't work?"

His mouth remained on her neck, but his right hand darted out and grabbed the gun from the counter. In one smooth motion, he lifted his head and raised the gun. Still holding her against him with one arm, he fired off two shots in rapid succession: one at the camera by the gun locker, and one at the camera affixed in the center of the lanes fifty yards away.

His hazed, lust-filled gaze met hers. "Good enough?"

She sucked in a sharp, shocked breath as heat flooded her system. "Yes."

"Good." He set the gun on the other side of the lane divider, next to her weapon, then yanked off the protective headphones and tossed them behind him. Finally, he scooped her up and set her on the counter. "Now. I've got another gun ready to fire."

CHAPTER TWENTY-THREE

ALEC COULDN'T HELP but laugh at his own words. He had a beautiful woman splayed out on the counter before him, and he'd made a crack about his *gun*. But then, from the moment he'd decided to take Isabel here to exorcise her demons, he'd felt strangely free. He wasn't a politician right now. Or a boss. Or a Ranger. He was just a man pursuing a woman he had to have.

She'd said something once about the smart thing versus the right thing. He knew being with Isabel might not be the smart thing—politically, she could ruin him—but she was, without a doubt, the right thing. Hell, she was the *only* thing.

She tugged at his T-shirt. "Off. Now."

No sooner was the offending article gone than she was pulling apart the buttons at his fly. He stopped her. "No fair. I hit the bull's-eye more than you did, and you have too many clothes on."

"This is your reward for shooting so well. I'm going to taste you."

Her words sent heat straight to his cock. He froze while she wriggled off the counter and dropped to her knees before him. She tugged down his jeans and briefs, freeing his erection in one swift motion.

This was unreal, a thousand fantasies coming true at once. He was with Isabel. In the firing range. And she was about to give him head. This had Penthouse Fantasy Forum stamped all over it.

She cupped his balls in one hand and slid her hand over his cock with the other. He groaned. Kneeling before him, she licked his erection from base to tip, then took him deep in her mouth in one smooth stroke. Pulling back, she sucked lightly on the tip. His balls tightened, and her fingernails grazed the sensitive sac. She slid forward, again taking him deep.

"Holy hell. Iz. That's…incredible."

She gazed up at him, her beautiful green eyes lit with wicked intent. The sight of her lips wrapped around his cock was nearly as hot as it felt. He pulled out of her mouth. No way was he going to let her make him come so soon. "Naked. We both need to be naked."

He tugged her to her feet and lifted the hem of her shirt up, over her head. She wore a sexy, black lacy bra. It was almost a shame to take it off, but he needed to lick and taste every inch of her.

Bra removed, he sucked on a nipple as he unzipped her jeans and slid his hands inside, cupping her ass. She let out a sexy moan as her nipple hardened against his tongue.

Dammit, *his* clothes were in the way now. He scooted back and bent to untie his boots. In seconds, he had them off and shucked his jeans and briefs. She pushed him backward, to the bench along the wall, and knelt before him. Again she took him in her mouth. The slide of her lips was so intense. Perfect. Impossibly, his cock thickened even more.

"Iz, you're not naked yet."

Her mouth, that hot, incredible mouth, slipped off him long enough to say, "I don't care," then she took him deep, sucking all the way down.

He groaned and gripped her hair. "*I* care. Don't you dare make me come. I need to come inside you."

"No condoms. You can come in my mouth."

Her hand circled the base of his cock as he thrust into her mouth. He was so close. So dangerously close. "Condoms. In my. Jeans. Pocket."

She sucked on the tip a moment longer, then released him, still holding his rigid flesh in her hand. Her eyes were smoky. Hot. Erotic. "You really brought condoms? I figured you were joking. Because of the"—she glanced at the ceiling—"you know. Cameras."

He laughed and leaned sideways, making sure to stay within the hot circle of her hand as he reached for the packet. "You must've figured out by now that I wasn't about to let the cameras stop us." He held up the condom. "Take off your jeans."

Her smile was pure, sensual heat. She stood slowly. Her delicate hands brushed against her hips as she lowered the pants. "Wait. Turn around," he said.

She complied. With her back to him, she bent over in an exaggerated pose, pushing down the jeans with her ass high in the air. He sucked in a guttural, gasping breath. She was perfect in every way.

And he was going to fuck her brains out until she forgot every bad thing that had ever happened to her.

He reached for that beautiful ass, raised high above her head. With one finger, he slid the crotch of her panties aside. His tongue found her opening and dipped inside. She was tangy and hot. He groaned and tasted her again, then shifted his tongue forward, finding her clitoris and licking until she whimpered with need.

He leaned back. "Take it all off. Now."

She stood and kicked off her shoes and jeans. Panties dropped next. She turned to face him and he took in her beautiful, naked body. Red curls hid her hot, delicious clit. Firm, round breasts with ripe, pink nipples begged to be tasted again. He wanted to savor this, to slowly drink in every inch of her.

And he wanted to fuck her hard and fast with equal urgency.

He dropped to his knees before her. He'd take it slow. Enjoy her breasts and work his way down. But no sooner did he have his mouth over a nipple and his fingers pressed to her clit than she moaned his name and rocked her hips into the pressure of his fingers. "Alec. I want you inside me. Now."

Okay, maybe the first time would be fast and hot. They could go slow later. In his bed.

He stood. She turned, kicked down the long, low bench tucked under the shooting range counter that served as a sturdy step stool, and planted her feet on it in a wide stance. She leaned against the counter, offering her ass to him in the most glorious invitation he'd ever received.

No. This wouldn't be slow lovemaking. This was going to be a hot, hard fuck all the way. He tore open the packet and slid on the condom, then stepped behind her. With the bench, she was at the perfect height. He pressed his erection against her slick opening. "Is this how you want me?" he asked. He reached around and touched her clitoris.

She gasped and panted, "Yes. Please."

With one hand on her breast and the other at her clit, he buried his lips against her neck and thrust forward, penetrating her in one swift, intense stroke.

She felt amazing. Pure, hot, adrenaline-filled sex with the brilliant, gorgeous woman who'd saved his life. She clenched down on him, and he groaned at the sweet pressure.

"Iz...." But that was all he was capable of saying as he thrust into her tight heat again. She pressed back against him, and his fingers found the rhythm that made her moan as pleasure built.

The intensity of his feelings for her infused each sensation. This was so much more than a hot screw, but the physical thrill kept him grounded in the moment, and heightened his awareness as they rocked with their bodies locked together in the narrow, cavernous space.

Her husky moans echoed back down the lane, making him impossibly hard as he slid inside her hot body. "Come, sweetheart," he murmured against her neck.

She smelled of sweet, flowery soap, gunpowder, and sex. She fit in his arms like a dream, all soft skin and curves as he massaged her clit with his fingers. He was so damn close to coming. The buildup so intense, his orgasm would be powerful. White-hot. But he refused to come before she did. No way. The little hellcat who'd been a burr in his side for months would know satisfaction before he did.

Isabel's body began to quake with orgasm. Her moans filled the room, vanquishing the last of his control. A hard, powerful release slammed into him. He stilled his fingers on her clit, pressing to continue her climax as he thrust into her, rocked by the intensity.

Her orgasm continued long past his. Spent, he leaned down to nuzzle her neck while wiggling the fingers planted on her clitoris.

She trembled. "Stop. I can't." She gasped. "Take. Anymore."

He kissed the smooth skin at the nape of her neck. "Oh, honey, you're getting more." He breathed deep, then nipped her shoulder. "As soon as I can move again. You're getting more. Just give me four…no, make that five minutes."

She laughed. "You've impressed me already. No need to kill yourself."

"Good. Then we'll make it ten. Just enough time to get dressed and go up to my quarters so I can strip you again. I want you in my bed." He slid out from her and lifted his weight from her hips.

She twisted in his arms until they were chest to chest. Her incredible green eyes were warm with satisfied hunger, and her smile lit a fire dangerously close to his heart. She caressed his face, her fingers playing with the stubble on his cheek. "That was…something. I think you've cured my fear of basements and pretty much everything else."

He grinned. "As a politician, it's unwise for me to make promises I can't keep."

TRUE TO HIS word, no sooner were they back in Alec's suite than Isabel was drowning in pleasure. While the sex had been hot and fast in the firing range, the second time he insisted on going slow. He touched, tasted, and explored every part of her, making her come until she couldn't take any more.

After days of being the focus of his deliberate, unwavering seduction, it was no surprise to discover he made love with the same intensity he applied to everything else. Afterward, they lay chest to chest. Her heart gradually slowed as she stared into his incredible blue eyes. "Well," she said softly, "you've got my vote."

He laughed, his eyes creasing around the corners. This was a man who smiled a lot, and it was genuine, not a politician out to win over the masses. She loved his smile. His laugh. If she wasn't careful, she might start to love everything about him.

This feeling of contentment was utterly new for her. She had a bad habit of bolting after sex, developed after a life of aversion to putting down roots. But with Alec, she wanted to stay. Wanted to sleep in his bed. Wanted to face him in the morning.

It was an odd feeling, this desire for intimacy that had nothing to do with the joining of bodies. She wanted to *know* him. What made him tick? What made him laugh? What made him cry?

And, more shocking than anything, she wanted him to know her.

He was Alec Ravissant, owner of Raptor. But maybe he could be just Alec? *My Alec.* No one here called him by his first name. Calling him Alec felt intimate. Special. Akin to his calling her Iz. Vin had called her Izzy, but no one ever called her Iz—probably because she so often held people at a distance. But distance hadn't been possible with Alec.

It meant something to her that her big brother had met him and tried to fix them up, even if it had been a joke. Vin would never have made the joke if, deep down, he hadn't approved of the man.

"Why did you join the Army?" she asked, surprised to realize she honestly had no idea. He'd told her he'd been raised for politics, not the military.

He pulled her snug against his side and stared up at the ceiling as he spoke. "My mom always wanted me to get into politics. Always. It wasn't even a question. My childhood was basically 'eat your peas and study the long-term effects of the Bay of Pigs' or other political standoffs that changed the world. I hate peas, but the political history was interesting. My dad did a stint as a congressman—he served three terms when I was really young. I think my mom imagined a Ravissant dynasty, like the Roosevelts or Kennedys."

"Not like the Bushes or Clintons?"

"No. My mom had a preference for old-money dynasties."

"You come from that kind of money, don't you?"

He nodded. "Yeah. Old wealth. The railroad-baron kind. Added to and expanded thanks to smart investments in communication technology over the decades. From the telegraph to the smartphone, my family has always owned a piece." He glanced down at her. "I'm not saying that like it matters—I mean, there are plenty of people in my parents' world for whom how old the money is *does* matter. But I didn't belong in that world. I still don't."

She couldn't imagine the life he was born into. After her parents died and Vin was the lowest private in the Army, she wouldn't have had protein on a daily basis if it hadn't been for food stamps. The idea of growing up in extreme wealth—where how seasoned the money was mattered—was beyond foreign.

"Don't get me wrong," he said, stroking her back. "I'm not going to whine or complain about how difficult it was to grow up rich, because it wasn't. I had warm, wonderful parents and a great childhood. They had big dreams for me—but they were reasonable, given our means. If it hadn't been for fertility issues, there'd have been plenty of brothers and sisters to share the expectation load. I wouldn't even have been the oldest. I was my mother's fourth pregnancy but their only child."

"That must have been so hard for her."

"I think it's one of the reasons she freaked out when I joined the Army. She'd grieved so much already. She was terrified of losing me."

"So why did you join?"

"Partly to find out what struggle meant."

His answer surprised her. "What do you mean?"

"I'd lived my entire life in a protective bubble. Expectations for me were high, but I have a good brain, so I could live up to them. Academics weren't hard. I went to the right prep schools. I *earned* my place in Harvard—and no, that wasn't easy, I worked my ass off to get there—and I graduated on schedule with a degree in political science. As expected, Harvard Law accepted me. Again, I earned it, but also, without concerns about money, I could devote my time to studying. It wasn't like I had to work my way through school. My life had followed the proscribed path, without a single ripple.

"Then I woke up one day and realized I couldn't do it. I couldn't go to law school. Hell, I was a kid. Twenty-one, and I'd never made a decision of my own. I didn't even know if I *wanted* to be a lawyer. To be a politician."

"What did you do?"

"I drove to Baltimore, parked my stupidly expensive sports car—graduation present from my dad—on a city street and jumped on a city bus. I'd never ridden a bus before—not like that, anyway—not through the projects, not to truly see what life was like outside the bubble. It wasn't a field trip to a museum or a lark with friends for a night on the town, where we'd take a cab home because we could afford it. It was a city bus, taking people to and from work. To the hospital. To the grocery store. I don't think I ever realized some people had to take the bus to the grocery store. How do they carry their purchases home without a car? I did the math as I looked at grocery bags, realizing that because they had to buy the smallest size of items that were far cheaper in bulk—laundry detergent, milk, things that are *heavy*—I finally saw exactly how high the cost of living is for the people who can least afford it.

"I rode that bus all day. I talked to people. It was eye-opening. Late in the day, I gave up my seat to a seven-year-old girl who was bald. It was obvious she was in cancer treatment. The girl's immune system had to be fragile, and she had to ride the bus. I emptied my wallet, giving everything I had to her mother. Then I insisted we take the bus back to my car, so I could give it to her."

"Seriously?"

"Hell, yeah. She was nervous at first. Like she thought I was some sort of scam artist. The bus driver had gotten to know me that day, and he believed me. He switched the route indicator to 'out of service' and drove straight to my car. She sold it, bought something reliable, and with the excess rented an apartment near the hospital."

"What happened to the girl?"

"She won that round."

Isabel heard the meaning behind that. "But there were more."

"It was leukemia. There were more. She survived the next one too. But when she was eighteen, she lost the battle."

"How long ago was that?"

"Three years." His eyes glistened as his nostrils flared. He took a deep breath. She'd stumbled upon one of the memories that triggered tears. "She'd be twenty-one now. The same age I was the day we met."

"I'm sorry, Alec."

"So am I."

"None of this is in your bio."

"Hell, no. It's private. I did it for Keisha and her mom, not because it would make me look good. Keisha's mom is one of my campaign volunteers, but I've forbidden her from telling anyone how we met."

"So when did you decide to join the Army?"

"That day. On the bus. I knew, in my gut, it was what I wanted. I think I'd always known I needed to serve. I'd been given everything, and I needed to give back. Finally, after I gave away my car and my money, the bus passed a recruiting office. I pulled the cord, thanked the driver, and got off. I stepped into a new world, but it was the one I was meant for."

"So that's how you ended up in the Army, but how did you come back to politics?"

"Army life was harder than everything I'd experienced before. I mean, I'd thought Harvard was hard, but Harvard has nothing on a drill sergeant. But even so, after a certain point it became clear that I was again on the smooth, gilded path. Officer, command, even though I hadn't been ROTC in college, my parents called people, and magically, those became available to me. My parents wanted me to get a safe job at the Pentagon and avoid combat.

"So I applied to Ranger school. It took a few years to get in, but once I succeeded, they couldn't deny me combat tours. Hell, they trained me too well not to use me."

"How long were you in the Army?"

"Almost twelve years."

"How long have you been out?"

"Nearly three."

"Did you leave the Army because you wanted to buy Raptor?"

"No. I left because my mother was dying—also leukemia. She wanted me home for her final days, and I couldn't deny her that.

She passed away four months after I left the service."

She squeezed his hand. "I'm sorry for that too."

His arm tightened around her. "Thanks. She…well, we had issues because I'd joined the Army instead of following the path she wanted, but she was my mom. We remained close. " He idly traced circles on her back. "Within a month of my leaving the service, the deal for Raptor was in the works. I had money—trust fund, inheritance, investments that paid off and then some. An insane amount of money, which meant I could buy the company outright. No need for investors. I could run it my way, undo the damage Robert Beck had done."

She glanced around the room, glad it wasn't festooned with Beck's garish rococo furniture. This room, at least, looked like it belonged to Alec. "And this is all yours now."

"Yep." He grabbed her ass and pulled her closer. "And everything in it is mine."

She laughed, strangely not put off by the idea of belonging to Alec. She'd never belonged to anyone before. Never really belonged anywhere. "And the senate seat? Why politics now?"

He smiled. "I still haven't gotten to that?"

She chuckled. "No."

"A few years ago, Senator Talon resigned, causing a power vacuum. Everyone expected the woman who replaced him to run for the seat in her own right, but she declined. Finishing out his term was enough for her. Maryland has always been a toss-up state. With my background—Harvard, Army, Rangers, and Raptor business experience, a lot of people put pressure on me to run. I could draw votes from both ends of the political spectrum."

"You're young for a senator, though, aren't you?"

"If I win, I'll turn thirty-six right after the swearing in. Young for a first term, but not unheard of. And frankly, I think every three months in Afghanistan adds about three years to life experience."

"What was the kicker? It doesn't sound like you wanted politics. What made you decide to run?"

"Two things. My mom, for starters. I've always felt guilty I hadn't followed the path she wanted. Now she's gone. It was something I could do for her. Too late, but not too little."

"And the other?"

"The US Attorney General. We became friends after he vetted me to purchase Raptor. Curt called me and said he wanted, just once, for a politician he could believe in to run for office. Curt's opinion means the world to me, and he's a man who made his name going after crooked politicians. It's hard to ignore a plea like that."

She'd known he and the attorney general were friends but hadn't realized they were so close. "And now? How do *you* feel? Do you want it?"

"Honestly, Isabel, I've learned something these last few days. I thought I was doing this for my mom. But what's happened here is jeopardizing the campaign. Like everything I've ever done—with the exception of being a Ranger—politics was *mine*. A cakewalk. In the bag." He glanced sideways at her. "Until you came along and got the compound closed. That was the first ripple. Then there was that trouble with one of my campaign aides last month. Now I'm told my disappearance is being called a publicity stunt. Stimson, my opponent, is saying I'm wasting FBI resources investigating a faked abduction at the same time he's casting suspicion on me being involved in something dirty. When I announce the training is canceled tomorrow, I'll be defaulting on a government contract. That won't go over well. It costs the government a lot to pull these trainings together—and I'm not talking about the fees Raptor charges, I'm talking about the administrative end that can't be refunded. My campaign manager is freaking out. I bet there are ten messages on my phone since I checked at midnight." He grimaced. "Right now, the campaign is in havoc. I could lose this thing.

"And the one thing I've realized in all this is, I want it. Not because of my mom. Not because Curt stroked my ego. But because it's right. For me. Just like the Army was right. I *need* to serve. I served as a soldier for as long as I could. And when it was time to do something else, I thought Raptor would fulfill that need. And it does, but it's not enough. As a senator, I can serve, I can give back to this country that has given so much to me and my family."

"What will you do if you lose?"

His voice hardened. "One thing I've learned in the Army: never plan to lose. Losing is not an option."

A YELL TORE Isabel from sleep. She sat bolt upright before she was fully awake, disoriented, heart pounding. The man by her side let out another low groan. He sounded like he was in excruciating pain. "Alec," she said, gently touching his shoulder. "You're having a nightmare."

His face turned toward her. His eyes were open but eerily blank.

"Alec?"

He lunged toward her, hands reaching for her throat. She scrambled backward and fell from the bed, her feet still tangled in the bedding.

He growled—pure predator—and grabbed her ankle. She kicked upward to free herself, connecting with his chin. Freed, she crab-walked backward to escape. "Alec! Wake up!"

He froze with his head cocked, then looked to his left, as if a sound had drawn his attention. With a roar, he launched himself off the bed and landed on top of her.

She tried to knee him in the balls, but he deflected the blow.

He's going to kill me.

She shoved at him, but he was too heavy. Too strong. She swung out, aiming for the healing cut on his temple, connecting with her fist.

Alec cursed as he released her and fell backward.

Isabel scooted back until she hit the wall, wondering if she should grab the gun on the nightstand. The one he'd given her and said he wanted her to carry at all times for protection.

Tears streamed down her cheeks, blurring her vision. "Alec. It's me." She suppressed a sob. "Isabel."

She crawled toward the nightstand, then stopped, out of his reach but short of being able to grab the weapon.

This is Alec. My Alec.

She couldn't aim a loaded gun at him. Ever.

"Iz?" he asked softly. She met his gaze in the dark room, just discerning that his eyes were focused. They widened in shock. "Oh my God. Iz. I—"

He reached for her, but she held up a hand. "Prove you're awake. What did I tell you my name was when we first met?"

"Jenna Hayes."

Relief swamped her. She leaned toward the nightstand and turned the switch on the lamp.

He blinked in the sudden light. "Did I…attack you?"

She nodded.

Blood dripped down his temple. She'd reopened the gash. "Oh, Iz." He ran a hand across his face. "Honey. I'm so sorry."

He hadn't hurt her. Not really. But what did it mean? Had he dreamed he was assaulting her, or someone else?

Hard to believe that just hours ago, he'd been inside her, that she'd held his gaze until a hard, fast orgasm caused her to close her eyes as she came apart. He'd made love to her to erase her fear, but now she feared *him*.

"It's okay." She forced the words out, knowing she didn't mean them.

Losing is not an option. Even in his nightmares he refuses to lose.

"No, it's not." He stood and took a step toward her but stopped short when she backed up, remaining out of his reach.

"Was that PTSD?" Guilt swamped her. Here she was, suspicious and afraid, and the episode had probably been triggered because he served his country. Like Vin and so many others.

"Not PTSD. I've never had anything like that happen before." He shook his head as if to clear it. Again, he ran a hand over his face. "I dreamed I was in a cave, strapped to a table, in agony. No one touched me. It was eerily silent—almost like negative noise— silence so loud it blocked everything, even my ability to think.

"Then a sound broke through—ironically, the words were from a musical, the one about the hills being alive with music."

She swallowed as the meaning of that sank in. "The title song from *The Sound of Music*?"

He nodded. "You, your voice, jarred me out of my agonized trance, and I yelled out. A man wearing a ski mask and some sort of voice-altering mouthpiece came into my line of vision and hit me in the solar plexus with a thick stick, knocking the wind out of me so I couldn't make a sound." His gaze dropped to his wrists. "The restraints were simple Velcro—probably so they wouldn't leave obvious marks—but that also meant they were weak. Probably not a problem when I was being zapped with infrasound, but that pain had stopped. I was alert. And enraged."

His jaw was tight with anger. His fingers curled into a fist. He stared at his hand, then met her gaze, his eyes clear but burning with leashed fury. "I'm well trained to channel that rage into brute force. I ripped my right hand free and grabbed the stick. Using it for leverage, I got my hands on the man in the mask and pinned him to the table. I felt a blow on my temple. Then I woke up—or blacked out. I'm not sure."

She cleared her throat, about to ask if he'd seen the lynx petroglyph, when there was a sharp knock on the outside door.

Isabel glanced at the clock. Five a.m. Who the hell would come knocking at this hour?

"Shit," Alec said. "This early means it must be important."

Isabel grabbed her clothes from the floor and pulled them on, while Alec donned his jeans. He didn't bother with a shirt and wrenched open the bedroom door. Isabel followed him through the sitting room.

More pounding, this time accompanied by Nicole's sharp yell. "Alec Ravissant, you sonofabitch. Open the dammed door!"

He turned to Isabel. "Don't tell her about my dream."

She nodded. Nicole remained a suspect. "Do you think she's mad about the compound being shut down?"

"She hasn't been told yet. This could be about the cameras in the firing range."

In spite of the tension between them, Isabel smiled. Years from now, when she was feeling isolated and alone and this fling was but a distant memory, she would have the moment Alec had shot out the cameras just so he could be with her to replay in her mind. She would revel in the heat and exhilaration that infused the memory.

Alec slid back the dead bolt and opened the door.

Nicole snarled and thrust her iPad into his hands. "Explain this, you bastard."

Isabel read the headline on the screen over Alec's shoulder. *Dead Soldier's Sister is Suspect in Senate Candidate's Alleged Abduction.*

CHAPTER TWENTY-FOUR

BILE ROSE IN Alec's throat as he read the *Baltimore Sun* article—which quoted Nicole directly as having stated Isabel was suspect, in words eerily similar to those she'd said in his office yesterday. Isabel's arrest on the restraining order violation was mentioned, and the FBI was quoted as offering no comment on the ongoing investigation. But it only got worse from there. The article proceeded to neatly lay out the case against Isabel, attributing the speculation to "confidential sources within the Ravissant campaign." She was painted as imbalanced, possibly dangerously so, with a strong vendetta against Alec in particular.

The stricken look on Isabel's face triggered a fresh wave of horror. "I had nothing to do with this, Isabel."

She turned to Nicole. "Did you say what the article quotes you as saying?"

Nicole grimaced even as she nodded. Alec had to give her credit for being honest.

Isabel took a step back. "I thought we were *friends*."

"We are, Isabel. But that doesn't mean I won't consider all possibilities. Tell me you don't suspect me. I dare you."

Isabel glared at Nicole but said nothing. She turned to Alec. "And you. You've been seducing me even as you've been looking for ways to use me to get your campaign back on track?" She jabbed a finger at the offending iPad. "Don't think I don't see this for what it really is. I'm the perfect goddamned suspect, because if I take the fall, your campaign won't have to face questions of whether you have dirty operatives on the payroll. You won't be tainted by scandal."

"Isabel, I told my campaign manager in no uncertain terms you're off-limits. When I find out who did this, their ass is fired."

"Right. When they single-handedly saved your campaign with this smear piece?"

"Watch me."

"We've got other problems to deal with first, Rav," Nicole

said, her voice stiff with anger. "Someone quoted what I said in a private meeting in your office. If it wasn't you, then who was it?"

Alec was damn tempted to point a finger right back at Nicole, but exchanging suspicions would get them nowhere fast.

"Who was present when you said it?" Isabel asked.

"Hatcher, Rav, and me."

"And Hans," Alec added. "He can hear everything said in both our offices."

"Hatcher could have done it to save your campaign," Nicole said. "He needs you to win to secure the CEO position."

That balloon would never float. Alec knew Keith was adamantly opposed to using Isabel that way. He'd been outraged by Carey's suggestion. Nicole's casting suspicion on Keith hinted at her own desperation.

"I think we need to sweep my office for bugs again."

ISABEL FELT AS if she'd been hit with infrasound. Her pathetic life had been laid bare in the papers in an appalling exposé. She'd been labeled antisocial. A loner. Out for revenge. Jesus, put up a sketch of the Unabomber next to the piece, and no one would bat an eye. She'd been tried and convicted by the *Baltimore Sun*. Not too surprisingly, the paper had endorsed Alec weeks ago.

A search for bugs in Alec's office turned up a listening device. Meaning once again, *everyone* was a suspect, and yet as much as it hurt to consider it, Isabel couldn't help but wonder if Alec was behind it. He had the most to gain. She only had to remain the prime suspect until after Election Day. After that, she could be neatly cleared and he could claim no harm, no foul.

Except she'd been made to look like a bitter, grieving, vindictive sociopath in an article that was certain to go viral. All harm, all foul. Whether she was guilty or innocent didn't matter. What mattered was Alec couldn't lose with her taking the spotlight.

He was down in the polls, and he'd told her himself losing was not an option. He could have done this.

She closed her eyes and remembered last night, when she'd finally released her guilt over wanting him and enjoyed every minute of being in his arms and taking him into her body. There'd been a connection that was more that sex. More than fulfilling the need for orgasm. But what if, for him, it had just been a means to an end?

The suspicion settled in and made a home with her deepest insecurities. Seducing her could be a way to control her. To convince her to play the game, take the heat until the election.

She'd returned to his suite alone while he called his campaign manager, supposedly to demand answers. He didn't want her in the room while he made the calls. She dropped onto the couch and picked up Gandalf, who seemed annoyed to be woken, but he settled onto her lap anyway.

They hadn't had a chance to finish discussing his dream, which they both knew was memory. He'd heard her singing the title song from *The Sound of Music* in the dream. What she hadn't told him yet was she *had* sung that song on Thursday, but it hadn't been while she was working for the DNR.

She'd sung it during her lunchtime foray onto Raptor land to look for the cave.

Apparently, she'd gotten close.

ALEC HUNG UP the phone, having just granted an impromptu, angry interview to the reporter who'd skewered Isabel. He had no clue how the reporter would slant the piece. Maybe he wasn't cut out for politics, but how could he sit back and watch the press go after Isabel, all because of him?

She'd saved his life, and they'd flayed her.

It would only get worse if she were his girlfriend or wife—she would be an open target as the candidate's—or senator's—wife. As far as he could tell, only the youngest children of politicians got a free pass. And sometimes not even them.

He ground his palms into his eyes. Nearly six a.m. and it had already been a helluva day.

He'd assaulted Isabel in his sleep, and he'd yet to tell her he'd seen the lynx petroglyph in his dream. A dream that wasn't a dream at all.

He'd heard her singing, which meant she'd been near the cave as he was being tortured. If she could narrow down where she'd been when she sang that song, they'd have a starting point for the search. But the article had undermined every ounce of trust Alec had managed to build with her.

He was falling in love with her, but from the look in her eyes, she not only didn't trust him, she was back to dislike. Possibly even hate.

And he couldn't exactly blame her.

Did she once again think he might have had a hand in covering up Vin's murder? Had they gone all the way back to the start with the awful article?

He tilted back in his chair and stared, unseeing, at the ceiling. He'd had about four hours sleep, and much as he wanted to crawl back into bed with Isabel, he had a feeling she wouldn't welcome him.

I attacked her.

He feared what he could have done if she hadn't woken him with the blow to his temple.

In the cave, muscle memory had taken over, and he'd defended himself with the ferocity in which he'd been trained. The same ferocity he hoped soldiers learned here, because in the heat of battle, sometimes only muscle memory, thanks to intensive training, could see a soldier through.

The Army had taught him how to kill, and he was good at it. Very, very good.

He stiffened. A memory hovered, just out of reach.

The memory dissolved before it could solidify. He shook it off. Probably it was an op in Afghanistan. Or Pakistan.

He picked up his phone and dialed. It was time to fire his campaign manager.

ISABEL PULLED ON her hiking clothes and stuffed her pack with all the items that had been removed to dry when they returned from their swim down the river. The trail mix, jerky, and energy bars were all sealed in their packages, nice and dry, a ready breakfast on the fly.

From her rarely used purse she grabbed the phone and keys for the car Alec's employees had delivered to her on Friday night. The screen of the phone was cracked. She unlocked it to make sure it still worked and saw she'd missed some calls. Odd, since no one but Alec had this number. There was a text as well. A quick check showed the text and the missed calls were from the Fairbanks lawyer Alec had hired for her. She'd forgotten about the legal issues with everything else that had happened.

But she didn't have time or the emotional energy to face that now and tucked the phone into her backpack. She'd deal with the lawyer later. She had more important items on today's agenda.

She faltered as she made her way through the labyrinth to the front door. Should she stop and talk to Alec? Give him the chance to deny again that he was behind the article that had presented a caricature of her to the world and called it a photograph?

Could she look into his eyes and ask him point-blank what he would do if she found the cave? Given the slant of the article, at this point, finding the cave would only hurt his campaign. If she were proven right, she'd no longer be the perfect scapegoat. Even worse, he'd have to face difficult questions about his abduction. If voters believed he'd been abducted by pretty much anyone *but* her, they might have serious questions about his mental fitness for such a high-stress office.

He'd been tortured, like Vin. He'd said as much when describing the dream. This wasn't John McCain running for office years after being tortured in Vietnam. Alec had suffered through a life-altering event less than sixty days before the election.

If he wanted to win, the cave could never be revealed.

But still, she couldn't just walk out. She didn't want to believe he was the kind of man who would put his election above the truth. Above justice for Vin.

She turned down the short corridor that led to his office, thankful that this early in the morning, Hans wasn't at his desk.

She could hear Alec's voice through the door, confirming that Hans could indeed hear every word spoken in the office. She couldn't help but wonder if Robert Beck had planned that as well, and why.

"What are the polling numbers in the Piedmont region?" Alec asked. After a short pause, he cursed. "We're going to need another poll after the new ad rolls out with quotes from the *Sun,* if there's anything we can use."

She didn't know which was more appalling, that it was business as usual for him with the campaign, or that he planned to use quotes from the article in his TV ads.

Who was this man? In the last five days, she'd thought she'd gotten to know the soldier and the boss, but now she realized she didn't know the candidate at all.

She headed for the front entrance. In moments, she was behind the wheel and driving through the main gate. The security guard merely nodded as she passed. He was there to keep people out, not to trap her inside.

CHAPTER TWENTY-FIVE

"SHE LEFT. AND you just let her go." Alec stared down the security guard who'd let Isabel pass through the gate without so much as a phone call to Alec to inform him. She had at least a twenty-minute head start.

"Yes, sir. She was driving the vehicle you signed out to her on Friday night. I'm sorry. I wasn't aware she was a prisoner here. Sir." The guard said the last bit with only the slightest hint of sarcasm.

Alec was not amused.

He'd forgotten he'd given her the keys after they arrived on the compound. At the time, it had been a gesture of trust. It wasn't like she'd needed them. Or even wanted them, considering how badly she'd wanted inside the compound in the first place.

She must have gone to the forest. To find the cave. His best guess was she knew where she'd been in the forest at the time she sang the song from *The Sound of Music*. Which meant she'd been on Raptor land Thursday afternoon, searching for the cave. That she'd withheld that information from him was yet another bitter pill to swallow.

Now, like a fool, she'd gone off to find the cave by herself.
Why?

Because she feared him? Or because she didn't trust him?

There was a huge difference. The fear he could understand. He'd hurt her. Twice. And he'd feel sick about that to his dying day.

But the trust thing, this late in the game, he had a problem with that.

The idea that she believed he was behind the article made his guts clench. He'd fired Carey without hesitation and replaced her with a far less experienced aide who would spend the next week scrambling to figure out the job during the most critical juncture of the campaign.

Unless Stimson said something profoundly stupid or was caught in a sex scandal, Alec would have a hell of a time recouping his lead after this fiasco.

But while he'd been throwing away his campaign, she'd taken off to find the cave—the one *he'd* been tortured in—without him.

He'd been inside her body and had made her come as he tangled his fingers in her sexy curls. She'd tipped her head back and the sound of her orgasm echoed from the firing lanes. He'd taken and given, and he wanted to give and take more. He wanted all of her. Not just her body.

And she still didn't trust him.

He turned on his heel and marched to his quarters. He'd grab his pack and set out to find her. To hell with the compound closure and mass eviction of the staff. Keith would handle it. That was why Alec was paying him the big bucks.

His company was falling apart. His campaign was all but over. But the only thing that mattered was finding Isabel.

Actually, he had to admit this was a damn good time to search for the cave. Everyone they were suspicious of had a job to do inside the compound to manage the closure, meaning they couldn't be in the forest, hunting Isabel with infrasound.

The thought of her alone in the woods, being chased down by men with infrasound—just as Vin had been—made him sick with fear, which almost eclipsed his anger.

Almost.

In his quarters, he grabbed his cell and dialed Lee, who should be landing in Fairbanks soon. He hoped to hell Isabel had taken the phone he'd given her and Lee could activate the GPS and locate her. She was probably still in cell range, but in another twenty or thirty minutes, he'd never find her.

As he spoke with Lee, he loaded his pack with supplies. Starting with his gun and several magazines. More memories of what had happened to him in the cave returned while Alec had been on the phone with his new campaign manager. He hadn't just been tortured; he'd been interrogated. He didn't remember what he'd been asked, just that there'd been many questions, and he'd come close to breaking.

If infrasound could be used to torture and interrogate without leaving a mark, without the victim even remembering what had happened to them, then how could the Geneva Convention protect against it? It could take days, weeks, even months of torture to break a soldier, but Alec had reached that point in mere hours. He might've broken, if Isabel's singing hadn't woken him from some sort of trancelike state.

He might find himself facing a cover-up after all, but not of Vin's murder; the cover-up would be to prevent other countries from adding infrasound to their arsenal.

TODAY THERE WOULD be no singing. She'd give no warning she was coming. The bears would just have to deal. She had a bigger, scarier predator to deal with. She would find that damn cave and prove once and for all her brother had been murdered. No one would be able to cover it up. And no one could claim she was crazy or vindictive.

There would be justice for Vin at last, and she could get the hell out of Alaska and away from Alec Ravissant and his seductive lies.

She usually hated ATVs, but today she'd give anything for access to one. It would make getting to the part of the compound where the cave had to be so much faster. After all, she'd seen tracks on Thursday. It was one of the reasons her excursion lasted longer than the usual hour. She'd followed the tracks until they disappeared at the edge of the stream. She hadn't spotted similar tracks on the opposite bank, but it also hadn't been a good idea to cross. It was a small stream. Ankle to midcalf deep. But still, crossing glacial runoff in Alaska *always* held risk. No point in doing it without cause, and on Thursday she'd needed to finish her survey.

But today was different. Odds were, after today, she wouldn't have a job at the DNR anymore, but it didn't matter. She was done with Alaska.

She had no clue where she'd go next. She hadn't completely burned her bridge with the PhD program in Oregon, but at the same time, she'd lived in Portland longer than she'd been anywhere since she was fourteen.

She'd always wanted to try Montana.

But before she could head to big sky country, she needed to find the damn cave. She reached a fork in the logging road and stopped the car to study her quad map. The map was old. The logging road had been added five years ago, and it had been months since she'd driven down this road. After a while, all forest roads blurred together in her mind. If she remembered correctly, this was the closest route to that edge of the compound, but she couldn't be certain. Detailed maps drawn by the logging company were in her cabin. She'd considered going home to get them, but she'd wanted as much of a head start as she could get.

Sure as hell Alec would come after her once he guessed where she'd gone.

She pulled out the cell phone and turned it on. There was a faint signal. She'd probably lose coverage in the next half mile. She'd find the cave, get the coordinates, take pictures of whatever she found, and head back here as fast as possible. She'd send the photos to Alec's political opponent, Officer Westover, the FBI, TMZ, and whoever else she could think of. She had no intention of giving the *Baltimore Sun* the story. They could go to hell as far as she was concerned.

Her one goal was to make it impossible for Alec or anyone to orchestrate a cover-up by the time she was done. The cave existed. Vin was murdered. She'd find the proof.

It was up to the FBI to figure out who had abducted Alec, but if she handed them the cave, they'd have reason to look at someone—anyone—other than her.

"TELL ME SOME good news, Lee," Alec said after he shut off the loud engine of the ATV to answer his vibrating phone.

"I found her. She's out of cell range now, but I have a location where you can start looking. I sent the coordinates to your GPS."

"I owe you."

"No charge for this. Just find her. She's in danger, Alec."

Alec knew this better than anyone, but he hadn't told Lee the details. "What makes you say that?"

"During the flight, I went through all Chase Johnston's stalking data. He was sending reports on her activities to someone. I haven't figured out who received them yet, but this wasn't a sicko with a crush. She was under organized surveillance. Just like she claimed."

And Alec had ignored her, yet another reason for her to distrust him. For her to flee.

Another way in which he'd failed her and Vin.

She still didn't know Chase was her stalker. He'd planned to tell her after Gandalf was delivered, but she'd been asleep by the time the cat arrived. And later, well, he'd had other things on his mind.

"Have you submitted your findings to the FBI?"

"Yes."

"Good. An agent is guarding Johnston's hospital bed. When he wakes, he can tell them who he was reporting to." He said good-bye to Lee, then opened the GPS app. He tucked the phone under a strap on the console and started the engine. There were no roads between him and Isabel's last known location, but at least with the ATV, he didn't need them.

He drove in as straight a line as the terrain allowed, and an hour after he set out, he reached her car, parked at the terminus of an abandoned logging road. He circled the vehicle. The ground was still muddy from Friday's rainstorm. Easy to spot her boot prints where she'd entered the forest.

One hand on the hood told him the engine was still warm. She'd had to drive the long way around to get here, whereas his route had been more direct. He'd been delayed as he gathered his gear for the hike and contacted Lee, but he'd made up time with the ATV. He guessed she had a fifteen- or twenty-minute head start.

Isabel might know these woods, but Alec knew tracking. No way in hell was she going to find the cave without him.

ISABEL SCANNED THE thick woods. She'd been here just five days ago, but already the rain had changed things and she couldn't find the ATV tracks. In all likelihood, thanks to the rain, they were gone.

She'd searched her pack for her notebook—the one in which she noted everything about her search for the cave—and came up empty. She'd had it Friday night, after she returned home from the jail. She'd entered the data in the computer after Alec left. The notebook must have been taken at the same time her computer was stolen. But how had they known about the notebook? Or the data on her computer, for that matter?

Without her notes, she had only memory to rely on, and the area she'd covered on Thursday had been large. The lighting had been different, early afternoon versus morning, and wind and rain had shifted things around. She'd find the cave, of that she had no doubt, but she was likely to spend a fair amount of time duplicating Thursday's effort because she couldn't be certain if she'd explored a particular area or not.

This part of the subarctic taiga forest was difficult to traverse with limited sight distance due to the thick undergrowth. Bears could lurk almost anywhere, and it felt strange to hike in silence after months of mindless, endless, relentless singing.

Everything sounded sinister in the silent forest. The crack of a stick—likely an animal alerted by her footsteps—immediately brought to mind the men who'd abducted Alec.

Alec had been abducted by Raptor operatives. She had no doubt about that. Especially after being attacked inside the compound last night. She had a few key suspects, and they were all currently at the compound. They had to be, to oversee the closure. They *couldn't* be here. Which was why this was the perfect time to search for the cave.

Ahead she saw a shape that looked familiar—a moss-covered stump she felt certain she'd seen on Thursday. In fact, it might be the one where she first noticed ATV tracks on the spongy ground cover to the south of it. She aimed for the stump, skirting around a thick cluster of conifers, her gaze on the trunk ahead, wondering if it was the right tree.

If only she had her cell phone. She could check the photos she'd taken. But that, too, had been claimed by whoever had abducted Alec.

A noise to the right startled her. She turned, reaching for her bear spray.

In a flash she was on her butt on the damp, squishy forest floor, her bear spray in the grip of the man straddling her legs. Only her heavy backpack kept her from being pinned flat to the ground.

She stared into the coldest, angriest topaz-blue eyes she'd ever seen. "You are *not* nailing me with pepper spray a second time, darling."

CHAPTER TWENTY-SIX

ALEC DIDN'T KNOW whether to kiss her or handcuff her. After running off without telling him she deserved the latter, but the feel of her hips between his thighs had him more than eager for the former.

She held his gaze in a silent stalemate. "Let me go," she finally said.

"Not until you tell me why the fuck you took off."

She shoved at his chest. "Because I don't trust you not to cover up the cave."

Even though he'd expected her to say that, his anger still spiked. He released her and stood. "See now, there's a big difference between you and me, because I don't have sex with people I don't trust."

"*Angry* sex." She stood and brushed off her pants. "I don't see why trust is a prerequisite for angry sex."

"Oh, honey, you can lie to yourself all you want, but you can't lie to me. By the time I was buried deep inside you, anger was the *last* emotion you were feeling."

Her pupils dilated, but she didn't say a word, and he wondered which time she was remembering—in the firing range, when he took her from behind in the hottest, wildest fuck he'd ever had, or later, in his bed when they'd been chest to chest and she locked her thighs around him and moaned his name like it was a prayer or maybe her salvation.

He sucked in a deep breath himself. The memories were nearly as potent as the real thing.

"It doesn't matter what I felt when we were having sex, not when I woke up to discover you're using *me* to fix your campaign."

"I had nothing to do with that article, Isabel. I'm offended you'd think that given how clear I've made it that I'm nuts about you."

"I don't know what to believe when it comes to you, Alec. I was ready to believe you cared about me—I even stopped by your office before I came out here—only to hear you plan to use quotes from the *Sun* article in your ads."

Shit. Naturally, she'd heard *that* and not the conversation where he'd fired his campaign manager and thrown away his future as a senator. He growled a curse and dropped his pack to the ground. They'd talk this out if he had to handcuff her to a tree to force her to listen.

"I wasn't referring to today's article. I called the damn reporter and told him to print a statement that I did not agree with a single word in the article. I said Isabel Dawson is one of the most amazing women I know. I told him how you saved my life and I'm completely crazy about you and there is no way in hell I believe you had anything to do with my abduction. I went on to say that the concerns you raised about the safety of the compound were valid and I regret not listening to you sooner. I have no idea if there will be anything quotable in the next article, but if there is, I intend to use it because I won't let that bullshit article become the only thing the world knows about you."

He finally dared to meet Isabel's gaze. Her eyes were wide, her brow wrinkled in confusion. "Why would you *do* that? You told me losing is not an option."

He shook his head. "When I said losing is not an option, I was referring to *planning to lose.* I don't plan to lose. Ever. At anything. But I'm not going to throw you under a bus to save my campaign. I fired my campaign manager because she gave the reporter background information on you—information Raptor collected when my attorneys were certain you were gearing up to sue me. I also fired the Raptor employee who provided Carey with the data."

"You fired your campaign manager less than eight weeks before Election Day?"

"Yes."

She took a step toward him, then paused. "What about the cave itself? Say your campaign recovers from this. If the cave is found and it becomes clear that Raptor has been involved in dirty deals and experimenting with infrasound, it's hard to see a way you can recover from that. People will suspect *you.* Or they'll blame you for not knowing what your employees were doing. Plus you were tortured. Do you really think voters will be ready to accept you as fit for office?"

He shrugged. "So be it. I lose. Hell, maybe my opponent is

behind this, because it sure as hell looks like I'm in a no-win situation. But I'm not willing to change facts and cover up crimes to save my campaign. Do you really think I care more about the election than I do about the safety of soldiers who come here?

"If you think that, then you still don't know me. First and foremost, *I* was a soldier. When the bullets start flying, God and country go out the window. The truth is, I always fought for my brothers beside me. I would have died for any Ranger on my team, and they would have done the same for me. A few of them *did* die fighting to protect the rest of us. I have to live with that. Every damn day, I know that I'm here because some very good men—men far more deserving than I—are not."

He began to pace, the words pouring from him without his permission. Isabel had a way of doing that to him, triggering more emotions than he wanted to feel, making him admit more than he wanted to share. "It's too late for me to fight for Vin's life, but that doesn't mean I can't fight for the truth about his death. This isn't just your battle, Iz. He was your actual brother, but he was a soldier, which made him a brother to *me*. And he was *my* employee, which made him my responsibility. I failed him once. I won't fail him again by letting something happen to you, and I sure as hell won't let his murderers go unpunished. I don't give a flying fuck about the consequences for the campaign."

ALEC'S WORDS HIT her in the solar plexus, knocking the wind out of her.

He stood before her in the misty gray light of morning, deep in the forest, a setting so similar to where they'd first met. They'd started as enemies, become reluctant allies, then friends, and eventually—or maybe inevitably—lovers, but she wondered if this was the first time she'd truly *seen* him.

She'd been blinded by assumptions and beliefs formed when he first ignored her requests for an investigation, but now she saw the man. Wearing the same clothes he'd thrown on after he'd told her about the dream, he sported two days' worth of stubble, and his hair, dark and just long enough to show curl, was a wind-blown wreck. He wasn't the polished politician; he was disheveled, rugged, and the most impossibly handsome man she'd ever seen, let alone touched, tasted, and shared her body with. But it wasn't the exterior she found so incredibly compelling.

She stared at him in the dappled light of the forest sun. Before her was a merging of all his incarnations: Ranger, CEO, politician, but most of all, the man she'd spent the night with.

It was time to decide, once and for all, if she trusted him.

She took a step toward him—almost involuntary, like he was a magnet she was powerless to resist—and gripped his shirt, pulling his mouth down for a hard kiss.

He cupped her face but resisted the tug of her hands, halting the kiss before it got started. His eyes probed hers.

It was his move now. His turn to accept or reject.

He continued to hold her gaze, unwavering. Reading. Assessing. His jaw set in a firm line.

Heat flared in his eyes, and slowly, deliberately, his fingers slid up, into her hair. He twisted her curls around his fingers in a tight but painless grip, then slowly, lowered his mouth to hers for a hot, glacier-melting kiss.

He pushed at the straps on her shoulders, loosening her pack. She squeezed the buckle at her waist, popping it open, and let the pack drop to the ground.

In one smooth motion, he scooped her up and pinned her to the moss-covered trunk, the one she'd been walking toward. She wrapped her legs around his hips as the heat and slide of his tongue sent shivers down her spine. Thoughts of trust and reporters and campaigns evaporated as her mind went blank.

All that existed was his tongue tangling with hers. She reveled in the sweet, hot flavor unique to him and tugged at his shirt. He leaned back even as he held her pinned so she could peel his T-shirt from him, revealing a feast of muscles and skin.

He had the physique of a warrior, and the scars to prove he was no pretty-boy body builder. With her lips, she counted and traced each one, starting at his shoulder, where a thin white line bisected his clavicle.

She wiggled until he released her so she could stand on her own feet as she explored. His nipples were hard and tight against her tongue. She dropped farther, aiming for a scar that crossed his hip and disappeared under his jeans, but he caught her, pulled her upright, and pressed her against the soft moss.

"We really don't have time—" he said, even as he pulled off her top, then cut off his own words when his mouth found her breast. He brushed her bra cup aside and licked her nipple, then sucked on it. Pleasure shot straight to her sex.

He groaned and yanked open her hiking pants, while she

unbuttoned his fly and freed his erection. He pulled her pants and panties down, but they caught on her boots. He grinned, ignoring the complex bootlaces, and slipped one leg between hers, then lifted her, opening her knees wide so he could slip his other leg inside the circle created by her pelvis, legs, and pants. Her thighs wrapped around his hips as he gripped her ass and pressed her back against the trunk. She was trapped, bound at the ankles by boots and pants, her bare sex pressed against his.

She ground against him. "Condoms?"

His eyebrows dropped, then he felt below her thighs for his jeans, and grinned. He plucked out a strip of condoms. "These are the same jeans I wore last night to the firing range."

She ripped one open and handed the latex circle to him. He held her up with one hand as he sheathed himself with the other. She gripped his shoulders and pressed her center down on his hard cock. "Get inside me."

He chuckled. "Yes, ma'am."

He thrust into her in a single smooth stroke.

"Oh *yes.*" She threaded her fingers through his hair and kissed him, venting her moan of pleasure into his mouth as he thrust a second time, triggering a delicious friction she needed more than air.

He was thick, hot, and perfect in every way.

She groaned again, this time loud, wild, unrestrained.

That would scare any bears away.

This was insane. And hot. And everything she wanted. He was the CEO of Raptor, and she was taking him deep inside her body, giving him the most private part of herself without regret or reservation.

She leaned her head against the trunk and clenched tighter on his thrusting cock.

His eyes drifted closed. He tilted his head back and let out his own guttural groan. She loved watching him this way. The tension that always hovered around him momentarily gone. He wasn't thinking about his business, his campaign, his abduction, or the attacks on her. He was lost to sensation. To her. She held the power to make him surrender. And it wasn't just sex. There was more to it than that.

This was a hell of a lot more than a hot screw against a tree.

His fingers slid between their bodies and pressed against her clit. His rhythm changed from fast and urgent to a leisurely stroke that sent immediate jolts of pleasure through her. His mouth found hers, and again, coherent thought vanished.

Pressure mounted with each thrust. The friction of his fingers intensified the pleasure times a thousand. Sensation built. She whimpered and moaned in his mouth. She couldn't possibly last another second without splitting in two.

With one hard stroke, she crested. Orgasm pulsed through her. Not a short, hot flare. He kept her coming with slow, continuous caresses. His own growl of release mixed with hers as he came with a final deep thrust.

Silence descended as he held her against the trunk. He nuzzled her throat, and she felt his body shake with silent laughter. "Holy crap. I didn't think anything could beat the firing range, but I was wrong."

She laughed with him. She cradled his face, gazed into his clear blue eyes, then kissed him, sliding her tongue deep into his mouth.

When the kiss ended, he leaned his forehead against hers. "There are a whole lot of things I want to say to you, but this, unfortunately, isn't the time."

She nodded. This thing that was happening between them, she wasn't ready to put a name to it, and it was probably more than she could handle. All she knew was she simply wanted to live in this moment. Forever.

Except for the sharp knob that penetrated the thick moss and dug into her spine. She could do without that.

She wiggled, and he stepped back from the trunk to release her, but then stopped. "It was way easier to get into this position than it will be to get out of it," he said.

She gripped his shoulders as he lowered her to the ground and, with some effort, managed to extract his legs from the circle of hers. She adjusted her bra and pulled up her pants. Clothed again, she stood to gather Alec's T-shirt, which she'd tossed to the side of the stump in the heat of the moment. As she bent to pick up the shirt, something glinted in the moss, catching her eye.

She studied the ground, searching for the item that had caught the light. There weren't any ATV tracks, but she didn't expect to find tracks again after Friday's rain.

The light flashed again. There.

She dropped down and reached for the object.

"What have you got there?" Alec asked.

She frowned, staring at the chipped piece of plastic. "I think it's a broken headlight. Could be from an ATV." She explained about the tracks she'd seen on Thursday. "We're close, Alec."

He picked up her backpack and helped her slip it on. Once it was settled on her shoulders, he buckled the belt at her hips, then he kissed her. "Let's go find Vin's petroglyph."

CHAPTER TWENTY-SEVEN

ALEC FOLLOWED ISABEL, who retraced the ATV tracks from memory. Several times they had to double back and start over from the last recognizable point, because she lacked both her notes and photos from Thursday.

Alec was now certain whoever had taken her computer, notebook, and cell phone had been out to cripple her search. He was impressed as hell that she was able to retrace her steps, given how much time she spent in the woods. The terrain had to blur together in her mind. But one thing he'd known about her from the beginning, she was smart as hell and determined. He had a feeling she was a lot like her big brother, who, in a better world, Alec could have imagined becoming a friend.

Vin would probably have fit right in at the private dojo in DC. A small gym in the heart of the city owned by JT Talon, it was where Lee, Curt, JT, and Alec worked out and sparred several times a week. They'd recently added Keith and Sean to the mix, and for Alec the dojo was the one place where he could be himself. Not a candidate. Not a boss—even though Keith and Sean were there. In the dojo, everyone was equal, with the possible exception of belt ranks. The three men who'd studied martial arts the longest and had the highest belts—Curt, Lee, and JT—were also the three who'd never served in the military, which made for an interesting mix.

In a different, better universe, Vin would have lived and been transferred to the Virginia compound on rotation, and odds were he'd have hit it off with Alec, Keith, or Sean and been invited for a round of sparring with the inner circle.

In that universe, Alec would have met Isabel under entirely different circumstances, and he had no doubt that he'd have been ass over teakettle just the same.

Some things were meant to be.

He was meant to get on that bus when he was twenty-one. He was meant to be a Ranger. He was meant to buy Raptor. And Isabel Dawson was meant to come into his life with the destructive power of a tsunami.

Because even if he'd met her in a better world, he had no doubt meeting her would wreak havoc with his organized life.

"You can't remember the questions they asked," Isabel said as she pushed a branch out of the way. "But do you have a guess as to who it was? Height and build?"

Her question pulled him back to their conversation. He'd told her he was certain he'd been interrogated in the cave. "No. I think they dilated my eyes and stood behind spotlights. It was so bright, even though it was a cave. The only thing I could see was above— the petroglyph on the ceiling. A lynx with a smile like the Cheshire Cat."

"But who do you suspect?"

He ducked under another low branch. "I've avoided naming names with you, because I didn't want either of us to develop a favorite suspect, blinding us to other possibilities. I believe in suspecting everyone equally." He paused, then added, "But at this point, I think it's fair to say I believe whoever abducted me is on Falcon."

She nodded. "Yeah. Falcon has all my top suspects too. There are some I would rather it be over others. I'd ruled out Chase from the start, because of the timing."

He'd finally had a chance to tell her Chase was her stalker, but neither of them could begin to guess what it had to do with the rest, given that Chase had only been with the company for a few months. Keith felt the young man was underqualified for Falcon, but Nicole had a point about being short of options.

That both Chase and Isabel had been hit with infrasound inside the most secure building only confirmed the belief that someone within the company was behind everything.

"You think someone picked up where they left off with infrasound development when Robert Beck was arrested?" Isabel asked.

He'd thought long and hard on that point. "Yes. I had all employees vetted—weeding out those who were loyal to Beck— but obviously, a few were missed."

"Why didn't you change the name of the company, like Blackwater did, when you bought it?" she asked as she climbed up on a rock. She shaded her eyes and scanned the woods from her slightly higher elevation.

"Raptor wasn't in the same sort of trouble as Blackwater"—he allowed sarcasm to enter his voice—"or whatever the hell they're called now—was in the first time they changed the name. I felt it was important to show the company was under new ownership, but not hide from the fact that it was the same company. Raptor had good training and good rules of engagement, but was led by a corrupt man with a handful of loyal followers. With Beck and his supporters gone, there was no reason to hide. And frankly, I bought the name recognition as much as the company."

"No such thing as bad publicity?"

"Pretty much. Can you name another private security company, besides Raptor and Blackwater?"

"Apex," she said distractedly as her gaze skimmed the forest from her perch on the rock.

He laughed. He should have seen that coming. "Could you name Apex before Friday night?"

"No. I'd never heard of them." She jumped off the rock and lifted a branch that covered the path ahead. She examined the end. "It's been cut. Recently."

He studied the raw end and saw she was correct. He helped her move the long bough, and the reason for the cut branch became clear. The ATV had slipped and torn the moss ground cover. There was no way to repair the gouge without making it more obvious. Whoever had created the rut had covered it with the branch.

She pulled out her quad map and marked the location, then traced the route they'd taken with her finger. "The ATV went along this swale. The fact that there are no other permanent ruts means they don't use the same route often. So there have to be several ways to get to the cave, or they rarely come here."

She sat on the rock, her focus on the map. Alec dropped down beside her. She pointed to a dotted blue line on the map—a seasonal stream—and said, "I think this is the stream where I lost the tracks. We should find it just below that line of trees."

"If you lost the tracks in the water, they probably drove down the riverbed."

She nodded. "I think the water is low enough. So the question is, upstream or down?"

Alec studied the map. "Up. The sharp elevation drop downstream could be a waterfall."

She nodded and stood. "We'll head upstream, then."

He caught her arm when she would have started toward the

stream. "We're getting close. I go first from here on out."

She looked like she wanted to argue.

He pressed a finger to her lips. "You're a helluva hiker. And given the fact that you managed to find a piece of headlight and covered tracks in thick forest, my guess is you're a hell of an archaeologist too. But I'm the soldier here, and we're likely dealing with people who are armed and dangerous. If I didn't know you'd zap me with bear spray for suggesting it, I'd send you to the car right now."

She pursed her lips and said nothing.

"Here's the deal, Iz. You got us this far. I'm impressed you've found the proverbial needle in the haystack, but from this point forward, I'm in command. You will follow my orders, or I'll handcuff you to a tree and leave you while I search for the cave. It's that simple."

"You're bluffing. You don't have handcuffs."

"Wrong. I have two pairs in my pack. I grabbed them before I left the compound, because if there's anyone in the cave, I intend to take them alive."

She made a grumbling sound and said under her breath, "I should have known that if you remembered condoms, you'd remember handcuffs."

He laughed. "I *didn't* remember condoms. Those were already in my pocket. Lucky break. Now. Are you taking the deal, or do I need the cuffs?"

She met his gaze unflinchingly, then finally said, "Fine. But for the record, this is the *only* time you're permitted to order me around like one of your employees."

He grinned. "Honey, when we get back to my suite, you can order *me* around all you want. I'll even give you control of the handcuffs."

She paused. "What if in that situation, I *want* to be handcuffed?"

The thought of Isabel strapped to his headboard gave him an instant hard-on. "That can be arranged." The words came out huskier than he intended.

She gripped the straps of his backpack and slipped her tongue into his mouth for a fast kiss, then said, "Sounds fun. My safeword will be…tiger."

He had no clue what word he expected her to choose; all he knew was it wasn't *that*. "Tiger? You called me that before. Why?"

"Because you're the tiger king."

"Tiger king? But tigers are solitary. No pride. No kings."

"Tigers are sexier than lions, ergo, you're a tiger."

He laughed at that leap of logic and couldn't wait to get back to his suite to discuss the issue in detail. "Fine. Your safeword is tiger, but when I have you handcuffed to my bed, you won't want to use it."

"I'm counting on that."

He kissed her one more time, then took the lead in the trek toward the stream.

She was a dangerous distraction, but he'd never be this close to getting answers without her help, so he'd have to find a way to bury his libido as long as they were in this section of woods. It wasn't safe.

They found the tributary and headed upstream as planned. Following his orders, Isabel trailed right behind him. They reached a flat basalt face that had been scoured by a glacier thousands of years ago. "Alec, that's a petroglyph on the rock face."

He studied the etched lines. "Not a lynx."

"No. A hawk. I think. Ironic that it's a raptor." She paused. "It could be a prehistoric marker. A helpful note that a rock-shelter, cave, or storage pit is nearby."

"Like a road sign?"

"Sure you can call it that. Exit twenty-two, prehistorically speaking."

He smiled. They could use a sign right now.

He paced the edge of the face. Flat. Cold. No breaks, nothing to indicate a cave was nearby. He reached the edge of the sheer face, where it jutted out from a rock-sprinkled slope and rounded the bend. The face didn't project from the slope in a solid, attached wall of rock; it was a massive boulder that had been pushed from the top of the foothill by a glacier thousands of years ago. What appeared to be a face was really a flat, hundred-foot-wide boulder that rested against a rocky hillside. A deep crevasse separated boulder from hill.

Isabel gasped. "The boulder is a capstone." Astonishment filled her voice. "No wonder I missed it before. This was probably a simple rock-shelter—just a deep overhang—until the boulder landed in front of it."

She turned and gazed downslope. "We came a different route up the stream today, but on Thursday, I'm pretty sure I walked through that stand of trees." She pointed to the stand. "And I went up that ridge. Then I looked at my watch and realized I needed to get back to my survey area."

"That's when I heard you and came out of the trance."

She took a step toward the opening.

He caught her arm to stop her. "I enter first. I'll call out if it's safe for you." He could see she wanted to argue, to insist on blindly entering—as she'd have done if he hadn't been with her. "We don't know what's in there. Do the smart thing, Iz. We've come this far."

She frowned but nodded.

He took her face between his hands and kissed her. He released her and pulled his gun. Isabel pressed a canister of bear spray into his other hand. He nodded in thanks and stepped into the crevasse between boulder and hillside.

The opening was low and narrow, a tight squeeze for Alec's shoulders. An adult bear would have difficulty squeezing through, giving him hope none would have taken up residence inside. He shuffled forward in a slow, careful gait, aware that if there was a human predator inside the cave, they could zap him with a torrent of infrasound while the slim crevasse constricted him.

Finally, he made it through, facing no infrasound attack. The space to his right widened while to his left was the flat, glacially carved boulder. The cave was the shape of an open pita pocket—no walls, just floor and ceiling coming together in a sideways vee.

He ran his flashlight beam over the jagged ceiling and floor. The space was empty except for a few sleeping bats hanging from the ceiling. It smelled awful, bat guano and something else—likely the remains of a carnivore's dinner—but it looked like no human had ever been here.

"Alec?" Isabel's shout was muffled by the thick rock wall.

He tucked away his gun as disappointment filtered through him. He'd felt certain this was the place, yet it didn't look familiar. But then, there had been lights. The dream had been like an overexposed photograph, which was why he suspected his eyes had been dilated. "Come in, Iz."

A moment later, she was by his side. She explored the ceiling and floor with her own light, then stepped deeper into the cave, ducking to avoid low rock protrusions. Finally she stopped and let out a relieved sigh. "There."

Alec moved to her side, so he could see where her flashlight beam had landed. She'd found a smooth stretch of rock on the ceiling etched with a grinning catlike face.

ISABEL FELT A strange jubilation. Strange, because this room had been a torture chamber. Jubilation, because she'd found it at last.

The lynx petroglyph proved Vin's dream was real. He'd been out hiking—probably not far from here—and he'd been shot with infrasound and dragged to this cave, and they'd tested their weapons on him.

She'd excavated in a rock-shelter like this in Eastern Washington about five years ago. It had been used for storage pits thousands of years before, and there'd been very little dirt. Excavation was mostly removing cobbles from the unit one at a time. Every time she removed a rock, she'd watch the dirt slip between the cobbles below, sinking ever farther down. Taking soil samples had been nearly impossible.

If a forensic team came out to look for evidence that Vin and Alec were tortured here, they'd have a hell of a time trying to collect it.

She ran her flashlight over the ceiling, pausing on the bats, then shifted the beam to the floor, seeking some hint as to who had hurt her brother and her…she didn't really know what to call Alec.

Had Godfrey been here? He may have lied about where he'd found Vin. He'd resigned from Raptor on Thursday, leaving him unaccounted for when someone shot her cabin with infrasound and Airwave on Friday.

She took a step toward the back to see beyond the two-foot-high boulders that littered the floor. The strong stench of rotting meat intensified. She gagged and peered over a boulder to see what critter had played a fatal role in the food chain, and stumbled backward in shock.

Something—*wolf, lynx, coyote?*—had feasted here. Actually, probably several somethings, given that there was very little left. The shocking part was the prey wore clothing.

And not just any clothing. Raptor forest camouflage.

"Alec!" His name was all she could choke out. She covered her nose and mouth, desperately trying not to heave.

He stepped beside her and froze.

She managed to get her stomach under control and breathed through her mouth to avoid the smell. "Do you think it was an employee they were testing infrasound on?" The thought made her belly roll again. Another victim, like Vin. Like Alec.

Alec said nothing. He could have been made of marble as he stood staring at the mutilated remains.

"Alec?"

He met her gaze, but his eyes were blank. "No. Not a victim."

"How can you be sure?"

"It was me."

"What do you mean?" Fear spiked. He wasn't making sense.

"I mean I did it. I remember it all now. Right before I was hit in the head and knocked unconscious, I snapped this guy's neck. *I* killed him."

CHAPTER TWENTY-EIGHT

ALEC STARED AT the body. Adrenaline flooded his system. He'd killed this man. The memory punched him in the gut with enough force to make him wonder if he'd cough up blood.

He'd killed a man during the lost hours, and the memory had been suppressed, not by his own brain, but by the bastards who'd taken him. The hole in his memory was a violation. He felt no remorse over the killing. No, his outrage was over the memory gap, that something so important could be altered in his mind.

This kill had been self-defense. As a soldier, he'd killed. He didn't regret those deaths. All Tangos had been valid targets. Threats to be neutralized.

He'd compartmentalized and moved on. But this… this was an entirely different kind of compartmentalization. His memory of this had been buried. Someone had seriously fucked with his mind.

I didn't remember killing a human being.

His brain was his greatest asset. He might not be as smart as genius Curt, and he didn't doubt Lee had a few IQ points on him, but he was no dummy and had a degree from Harvard to prove it. The idea that someone had screwed around in his brain enraged him.

Fight or flight surged through him—except flight had been trained out of him, so he was all fight with no one to rip apart.

He sucked in a deep breath. Flexed his fingers. Punching the rock ceiling wouldn't do anything but break his hand and scare the shit out of Isabel.

Time to find out who this person was and get the hell out of this cave of forgotten nightmares.

In control again, he grabbed a bandanna from his backpack and crouched by the remains. There wasn't much left. The face had been chewed on to the point of being unrecognizable and the few scraps of clothing had been shredded and matted with blood. Using the bandanna, he lifted the torn sleeve, exposing flesh and bone.

Behind him, he heard Isabel gag. "Look away, Iz. Anything we find won't be pretty."

"I can take it. Or I'll puke. One or the other."

The putrid stench of rotting flesh hit him in a wave. "I might puke with you." Slowly, carefully, he lifted another section of cloth, revealing the man's wrist and gloved hand. If this crime scene weren't so damn remote—odds were more of the man's body would be eaten before a forensic team could get out here—and if he didn't know *exactly* who'd killed the guy—he'd never touch the remains. But right now he needed answers that couldn't wait for FBI crime scene techs.

He stared at the small patch of skin on the wrist. The edge of a tattoo was visible. He looked up at Isabel. "Do you recognize this ink?"

"There's not enough to be sure. A few operatives have full-sleeve tats, but only one hasn't been around the last few days."

Her words confirmed his thoughts. "Ted Godfrey."

ISABEL BACKED AWAY from the remains as the full import sank in. Her heel caught on a rock, and she stumbled, falling on her ass on the rocky floor. A stone gouged her butt, but the pain didn't register as her mind reeled from an entirely different source of agony.

Nicole, last night at dinner, her voice firm without a trace of hesitation: *"I begged Godfrey to stay. Quitting without notice when the CEO was about to arrive was shitty as hell."*

But Godfrey hadn't quit, not if he was here—and dead—which meant Nicole couldn't beg him to stay.

"Nicole is one of them." Isabel had always known it was possible, but she'd never wanted to believe it.

Unfortunately, it fit. Nicole could easily have given quotes to the *Sun*, her outrage this morning merely an act to deflect suspicion. She cleared her throat. "You need to ask Nicole to produce a letter of resignation. Proof Godfrey quit."

Alec nodded. "She won't have it. She's part of this. She's probably the leader of this whole operation."

"But why? Why would she do this?"

"I don't know, Iz. But we'll find out." He pulled out his cell phone and began snapping pictures of the remains. "We need to head to town and talk to the FBI."

"What are you going to tell them?"

Alec nodded toward the remains. "That we think it's Ted Godfrey, and I killed him while he was torturing me."

"There will be questions. Doubts. It will destroy any chance you have of getting elected." This would ruin him in a way that wasn't fair. Not that she expected life to be fair—she knew better than anyone that there was no such thing as fair in this world. But still, for Alec to lose everything because he'd been abducted was wrong.

He shrugged. "We have to tell them."

"Why do you think they left Godfrey here?"

Alec snapped another picture. The cell phone camera flash burned the grisly image of human entrails in her brain. "In two more days, there'd have been nothing left for anyone to find, and whoever was with Godfrey had to figure out what to do with me first. He—or she," he added pointedly, "probably figured no one would find this cave. They went after your computer and cell phone to make it harder for you to retrace your steps. It's even possible they planned to return to take care of Godfrey, but have been too busy at the compound to get away."

A chill shot down her spine, and she turned toward the entrance. "They could come back at any time."

"Yeah. Another reason we need to get to town and tell Agents Upton and Crews what we found." He tucked his phone in his pocket. "Let's go, Iz."

They trekked through the woods as close to a run as possible given the terrain, making it to the car in record time. Alec pulled out his cell phone and frowned at the screen. "A dozen texts just landed." He scanned the contents. "Most are from Keith. Compound evacuation is underway." He tapped the screen. "Shit. Brad Fraser quit."

Isabel's stomach—still queasy from the cave—did another flip. She *liked* Brad. Bad enough Nicole was a traitor. Were all her supposed friends involved in her brother's murder? "What do you think that means?"

"I don't know, Iz. He's been on my short list of suspects from the start."

Admittedly, hers too. But that didn't mean she'd believed it. But then, she hadn't believed it of Nicole either.

"Did Keith say why he quit?"

"No. He just said Brad's gone to Tamarack, and there was no

legal recourse to keep him in the compound or send him to Fairbanks with the others."

"Send him to Fairbanks?"

"All compound personnel are being sent to hotels in Fairbanks on paid leave. If they want to get paid, they have to stay in Fairbanks. That way we can search the compound top to bottom, without whoever is playing with infrasound getting in the way. Anyone who rejects the deal is suspect."

"And Brad didn't take the deal."

"Where would he stay in Tamarack? With the exception of the motel rooms for the FBI agents, I've booked and paid for every room in town through the end of the week."

Isabel felt the blood drain from her face in a mad dash to her heart. "Jenna's. He'd stay with the Roadhouse waitress, Jenna." She swallowed hard. "Do you think Jenna is in danger from Brad?"

"I don't know. We don't even know if Brad's involved." Alec typed a message on his phone.

"Let's go to Tamarack. I want to see Jenna. The FBI agents are there, not at the compound, right?"

He tucked his phone in his pocket and said, "Yeah. Let's go."

On the ride to town, she slumped down in the seat. She was bone tired. She'd only slept in segments—granted the middle of the night therapy session with Alec had been well worth losing sleep over—but in all she'd probably only slept four hours, then hiked several miles, and experienced pretty much every emotion a person could feel in the space of a few short hours. Lust, heartache, fear, shock, horror, something deeper that was dangerously close to caring, then right back to fear and horror again.

Anger was back too. Plus she knew an abyss of grief waited for her. Grief over what Vin had gone through, and horror that a woman she'd considered a friend was the monster she'd been seeking. "Yet another reason to avoid making friends," she muttered.

"What?" Alec asked.

"Nicole. Brad. Jenna. Two people who might have killed my brother, and a third I'm scared will get hurt. Making friends, caring about people, it's the most awful thing in the world." She closed her eyes, thinking about all the people she'd lost. After losing her parents, she'd moved so many times that by her junior year in college—after she'd transferred from community college in northern California to Washington State University—she'd decided to stop making friends. She was so sick of missing people; it was easier to have no one.

From there, she'd continued the moving pattern. Never setting down roots long enough to grow attached. Grad school had been difficult because it required staying in the same place longer than she usually allowed. But even so, she'd gotten her master's from one school and had been working on her PhD at another.

She thrived on change, plus the frequent moves made it easier to accept being alone. She didn't have to admit to being a porcupine in a human world. For six months after each move she could tell herself, *I don't have friends because I'm new here.* And it didn't even sound pathetic.

Vin had given her Gandalf five years ago, because he worried about his vagabond sister. He'd wanted her to have one constant in her life while he was off fighting for his country. When he'd taken the job with Raptor, he'd promised to stay in Alaska. Her plan had been to move to Tamarack after she had the PhD in hand. She'd finally have family again. A place to call home. A reason to make friends.

But that dream had died with the only person in the world who cared about her.

She'd moved here to find justice for him, and spent time with Nicole and Brad and the others because reaching out was necessary to make inroads into the workings of Raptor. But somewhere along the way, the friendships had become real. Not exactly deep, but genuine. She'd looked forward to the evenings at the Roadhouse with Nicole and Brad as the brightest spot in her long, isolated weeks.

And it had all been a sham.

Silent tears rolled down her cheeks. She couldn't stop them; it took all her will to keep from sobbing aloud. She kept her head averted and hands on her cheeks, wiping away the evidence that grief and anger and hurt had caught up with her.

She hated showing emotions almost as much as she hated having them. She hated being weak.

She didn't want Alec to know how fragile she was. He was the one who'd just discovered he'd killed a man. It was ridiculous for *her* to be the one breaking down.

Without a word, Alec stopped the car in the middle of the

logging road and threw it in Park. He hit the release on her seat belt. "Come here." He pulled her across the console and onto his lap.

That shattered her restraint, and a hard, pent-up sob escaped.

"Oh, honey," he murmured against her hair as she pressed her face into his chest. "Caring about people is what makes life worthwhile."

"That's because you have people who care about *you*. Since my parents died, I haven't had anyone but my brother."

One large hand cradled her cheek, holding her against his beating heart. "You have me."

She pushed off his chest and swiped at a tear with the palm of her hand. "I wasn't fishing for that."

A smile warmed his eyes even as his lips barely shifted. "I know."

"You just like having sex with me. This isn't *real*. You're leaving in a few days. This—whatever it is between us—will be over."

"Honey, I don't *like* having sex with you. I *love* it. And no way in hell does this end when I return to Maryland, because this isn't just about spectacular sex. Five days ago, I met this amazing woman. She dragged my sorry, beaten ass across a mile of forest and saved my life. Even after she realized she'd rescued the person she probably hated most in the world, she took care of me. Since then, I've gotten to know her. She's dedicated and strong and fierce and bold. Add to that brilliant and funny, and how could I not fall in love with her?"

"You don't—"

"Hush. I've been practicing delivering speeches a lot lately and think this one is pretty good for being off-the-cuff, but you're ruining it by interrupting."

She laughed even as more tears fell.

"I'm falling in love with you, Isabel Dawson. I wish to hell we'd met in a different time, a different place. I wish I'd asked Vin for your phone number when I had the chance. But we can't go backward and all I know is I don't want to move forward without you. This has happened fast, but then, when I know something is right, I move quickly. Like when I joined the Army. And I know in my gut this is the right thing."

Tears ran freely as she held his gaze. Both fear and elation gripped her. "I don't know how to do this. To love. To care. What if I'm not built for it?"

"Honey, you underestimate yourself so much. You care more about people than anyone I've ever met. The way you took care of me that first night proves it. And now your heart is breaking because you've been betrayed by at least one friend and maybe another, and you're scared for a third. You have a bigger heart than you know."

"It doesn't freak you out that I'm not saying the words back to you?"

"I can wait. I love you. Now. Today. Just the way you are. My feelings aren't dependent on you loving me back."

"And if I can't handle this and leave you tomorrow?"

"I'll be devastated and miserable, but I won't stop loving you." He wiped her cheeks with his fingertips. "This isn't a marriage proposal—it's way too soon for that. It's a relationship proposal. I want you in my life, by my side, to be the anchor that holds you in one place. Secure."

His choice of words was perfect. She'd been adrift for so long, she needed an anchor. But not just any man could be that for her. Only one who was strong, determined, and focused. He needed to be a brilliant strategist, and someone who wasn't put off by her prickly ways. Willing to hold her when she was sad, and make love to her when she was afraid. She needed a tiger with a weakness for hot chocolate. "Okay," she said.

He tilted his head back and laughed. "Good thing I'm the only one in this relationship who needs to make speeches."

A new fear gripped her, drying tears of joy and grief. "You don't want me to campaign for you, do you? Because I'd be terrible at that."

"The campaign is so shot to hell, I doubt it will matter. But no, if I somehow manage to salvage it, politics is my thing. It doesn't have to be yours."

"But isn't politics all-consuming? A way of life?"

"That's why I need you. If I win, you'll keep me grounded. Prevent me from getting an overinflated idea of my own importance, and stop me from letting the politician become everything I am."

She shifted in the seat so she could straddle him. Lightness had enveloped her, and she wanted to share it with him. She'd spent the last few days doing everything she could to hold herself back from him. She couldn't tell him she loved him—not yet, not when she didn't know if it was true—but she wouldn't hold back from him, not anymore. She settled over him, and her knee hit the seat belt latch. It dug in just below the kneecap, but she didn't care. She placed her hands on his shoulders and settled her crotch against his. His cock thickened, drawing a quick gasp of pleasure from her. "I know you're rich and all, but I'm still going to work. You—us, this—can't be all that *I* am."

He slid his fingers in her hair and kissed her, a long, deep, slow exploration of her mouth that would curl her hair if she didn't already have that covered. "I expect nothing less. How else are you going to pay for your half of dinner when I take you to Paris?"

She laughed and rocked her hips. He grew harder against her.

He pressed his pelvis upward, holding her waist as he ground against her. "Iz, I want nothing more than to forget everything and make love to you. Here. Now."

She heard the unvoiced "but" and knew he was right. She kissed him one more time, then climbed off his lap. "Let's go finish this." Back in her seat, she buckled her belt and faced the forest road. Reality waited beyond the trees. "We have a crappy day ahead of us, don't we?"

"Yes," he said. His jaw stiffened. The fun was over. "Today could well be our very worst day."

CHAPTER TWENTY-NINE

"I ALWAYS KNEW Nicole was a suspect, but I never accepted it," Isabel said. "Not really." Sadness had crept back into her voice.

Alec gripped the wheel, internally berating himself for leaving Nicole in a position of power here. This too was his fault.

But he'd never suspected Nicole of anything until Thursday night, when he'd created a mental list of people who might have a beef with him as he lay awake and cold on the rotting cabin floor. But at the time, Nicole hadn't even known she wasn't getting the promotion, so why abduct him then? Plus it appeared she'd been doing this for at least a year—maybe longer. Was Vin the first victim? Or one of many?

Chase Johnston had to be another victim. The question was, how long had Chase been experimented on? Had he stalked Isabel of his own accord, or had he been tortured and brainwashed into it?

Alec's memory of killing Godfrey had been buried. It wasn't a stretch to think they were experimenting with mind control.

There was much more to this than Nicole being miffed because she'd been passed over for a promotion, but damn if he could figure out what her agenda was. "She fooled me too. I held her in the same place—a suspect, but not really. She passed the not-loyal-to-Beck test with flying colors. By all accounts, she *hated* Beck. The man hired only a few women operatives and made no secret of the fact it was to keep from being sued for equal employment opportunity violations. She was told point-blank she was a token hire."

"Why did she stay, then?"

"She told me it was because it was just as hard for a woman to get a job at every other private security company. Even Apex has only poached male operatives. I doubt Simon Barstow has made her an offer, and she's the highest-ranked woman in the company."

"So she's probably pissed at Barstow too."

"A reason to implicate him, by using Airwave."

"How would she get her hands on an Airwave weapon?" Isabel asked.

Alec shrugged. "At least half of Apex's top staff has worked either with or for her. Someone might have sold it to her for the right price."

They reached Tamarack, and he drove slowly down the main highway that cut through town. He pulled into an open parking spot directly in front of the ten-room motel. "We'll talk to the agents, then head to the compound."

"Shouldn't we warn Keith about Nicole?"

"I already sent him a text. The message was coded, in case Nicole has access to my phone. She has access to all of Robert Beck's toys, and the phone is one I grabbed from the compound supply locker after my secure one took a swim in the river. I haven't had a chance to get Lee to secure the new phone."

They found FBI Agent Matt Upton in his room. He immediately invited them in.

"We need to speak with you and Agent Crews," Alec said.

"Agent Crews had to return to Anchorage this morning. Your timing is fortunate. I was just about to go to the compound." Upton's gaze landed on Isabel. His face was blank. Unreadable. "I'm afraid, Ms. Dawson, I need to question you again."

Upton's tone had a slight adversarial edge that had been absent yesterday. Unease slid down Alec's spine. He must have read the *Sun* article. "Question her?"

"There's been a new development in the investigation into your abduction. New evidence."

"New evidence?" she asked in an apprehensive voice. "The newspaper article was hardly evidence."

Upton glanced at Alec, then fixed his gaze on Isabel. "I'd like to question you alone."

Alec adopted his command tone. "No."

"You're the victim, Mr. Ravissant. That doesn't mean you can dictate the course of the investigation."

"We don't have time for this," Isabel said. "Just question me now."

Upton shrugged. "Explain to me how Ravissant's blood ended up in your truck."

Her brow furrowed. "Alec's blood was in my truck? That's impossible. I didn't return to my truck after I tended his wound. It was impounded."

"Yes. Impounded before you had a chance to hose out the back and wash away the evidence."

"That's ridiculous," Isabel snapped.

"What I can't figure," Upton continued, "is how you moved him yourself. Who helped you?"

Isabel's face turned a flushed, angry red. "No one. Because I didn't move him—except to get him to the cabin. His blood must've been planted there by whoever abducted him."

Upton stared at her. Finally, he said, "Right now, this case is looking pretty simple. You could easily have an ATV stashed in the woods somewhere. With your truck, you got him to the ATV. From there you got him to the rock where you let him bleed to lend credence to your story. We call that means. You had a beef with Ravissant. That's motive. You knew he was driving in that day, and passing the very woods where you were supposed to be working. That's called opportunity."

"That's ridiculous. Jesus, do you let the *Sun* do all your investigating, or did you just get lucky this time?"

Upton's gaze turned cold. "The *Sun* article has no bearing on the investigation. This is about blood analysis, which came back with a match for Ravissant."

"Alec was never in the back of my truck. Ever. And those woods run along the highway that happens to be the only road into Tamarack. I've done half a dozen timber sale surveys of parcels along that road in the last four months because the DNR plans to sell the logging rights next year. So it's not too shocking or unusual that he or *anyone* going to Tamarack would drive down that road. And I didn't know Alec was coming to the compound. If I had, I might have guessed who he was sooner."

Upton's gaze flicked to Alec's, "Mr. Ravissant, it's no secret you and Ms. Dawson have become involved. Right now, we must consider that this relationship has come about to further Ms. Dawson's real agenda."

"Bullshit!" Isabel said.

"That's a load of crap, Upton," Alec said.

"She wanted the compound shut down, and now it is," Upton said.

"I wanted the compound closed down because no one was investigating my brother's murder! The end goal wasn't a shutdown. *Why* would I do such a thing?"

"Well, Ms. Dawson, aren't you getting an investigation into your brother's murder as well? Yesterday, Mr. Ravissant spent half his interview suggesting links between what happened to him and what happened to your brother."

She looked at Alec. "You did?"

He gave a sharp nod even as he frowned. It was starting to feel like anything he said could be used against Isabel.

"Listen, Upton. I get what you're saying but I didn't do it," she said. "We just came back from the woods. We found the cave!"

Upton cocked his head. "Is that true?" He asked Alec

Again he gave a sharp nod.

Did he believe Upton's scenario? Hell, no. But if he dismissed the allegations too readily, it would just convince Upton he wasn't taking the questions seriously, that he was blinded by his feelings for her.

"Given that the two of you are involved, and you can't be objective where she's concerned, the Special Agent in Charge wants me to bring Ms. Dawson to Anchorage."

Upton's statement only confirmed Alec's concerns.

Isabel stiffened. "Bring me to Anchorage. You're arresting me?"

"Will you go willingly?" Upton asked.

"Later, sure. But right now we need to get to the compound. We found the cave—we—"

Alec shook his head. If they told Upton about Godfrey now, he might arrest Alec. Or maybe assume Alec was covering for Isabel, because he had feelings for her. Which he did. But not because he'd Stockholmed. He needed time. He had every intention of telling Upton everything, but if the FBI agent and his superiors were focused on Isabel, then Nicole could very well get away with whatever it was she was doing.

"If you won't go willingly, I'm authorized to arrest you. We have enough evidence." Upton pulled out a pair of handcuffs.

"Wait! There's no need for that," Alec said

"Again, Mr. Ravissant, you have no say in how this investigation is run. I have orders. The SAC doesn't want you together when it's clear you have feelings for her. You aren't objective and you'll get in the way." Upton pulled Isabel's hands behind her back and slapped the cuffs on her.

Alec's mind raced. He needed time to convince Upton to investigate Nicole. "You don't have to take her all the way to

Anchorage. Put her in the Tamarack lockup while we sort this out. I can take you to the cave. Explain things on the way."

"Put me in the jail! Alec, I'm not a dog that needs to be kenneled."

He gripped her biceps and kissed her forehead. "This way I'll know you're safe while we go after Nicole."

"Safe. In jail."

"What do you mean, go after Nicole? Is Markwell part of this?" Upton asked.

"Yes."

"What evidence do you have?"

Alec frowned. "Absolutely nothing." Hell, they didn't even know if Nicole had been in the cave—if there'd be anything there to tie her to what had happened to him.

"I can't work with nothing, Ravissant. My boss wants me to bring Dawson to Anchorage. If I don't, I need more than vague speculation."

"Do you really think Isabel staged all this?"

"It doesn't matter what I think. It matters what the evidence can prove." His gaze shifted from Alec to Isabel again. "I'll give you one hour. We'll take her to the Tamarack lockup, then go to the compound."

THE CELL DOOR closed, and Isabel watched Upton walk away. Outrage, frustration, anger all bubbled inside her. Very similar to how she felt the last time she'd inhabited this cell.

She sat down on the built-in bunk and rubbed a hand over her face.

She wished she knew what Alec believed. He'd kissed her again before she'd been brought to the back of the post, but his lips had been stiff, the kiss perfunctory.

Who was the kiss intended to fool, her or Upton?

Days ago, she'd feared being charged with Alec's abduction, and this morning she'd been painted the villain by a Maryland newspaper. Now, with solid evidence against her, it was a real possibility.

Alec's memories remained unclear. Even his belief that he killed Godfrey would likely never be proven, given the state of the man's remains. His memories could be written off as a dream, as Vin's had been. They could even claim she'd suggested the memories. Had manipulated him, seduced him so she could get close to him.

Forget that she'd never even heard of infrasound until a few days ago.

She paused in her bleak thoughts. She'd been hit with infrasound three times—two of which happened when she'd been alone, and the third, in the river, Alec hadn't been hit with the same intensity as she had.

It would be so easy for a prosecutor to claim she'd been faking.

But Alec *had* been hit. He'd put a name to it without her suggestion. Surely he believed her.

Every person she'd ever cared about was gone. For ten minutes today, it had seemed possible this thing with Alec could be real. Now she didn't know what to think.

Westover sauntered down the hall. "You sure have gotten yourself in a mess."

She glared at the officer. "I haven't done anything wrong."

"Be original, Isabel. Everyone says that."

She rolled her eyes. "Leave me alone. I'm having a crappy day, and I'm not *your* prisoner."

"Actually, you are. I just received a call from Fairbanks. You missed your court appearance this morning. Your bail has not only been revoked, they want me to bring you to Fairbanks."

"I had a court appearance?" *Shit.* She hadn't listened to the messages from the lawyer Alec hired. Had she really missed something that important? "But Alec dropped the charges."

"No. He paid your bail. He was supposed to withdraw his complaint during your appearance this morning. But neither of you showed. So your bail has been revoked, and they want you in the Fairbanks jail until your next court date."

"When is that?"

"I don't know. All I know is they want *me* to play chauffeur and take you to Fairbanks. As if I have time." He held up a pair of handcuffs. "I need to cuff you for the drive."

"Seriously? Lieutenant, you made me hike five miles handcuffed. Don't make me wear them for a two-hour drive."

"I can't make exceptions." He opened the barred door, and for the second time today, she was handcuffed.

This was hardly the kinky fantasy Alec had offered her this morning. She wanted to say "Tiger" like it was a magic word that would get her out of this situation. "Let me call my lawyer."

"No time. The round trip is going to take me four hours. We

need to get going."

"This is ridiculous, Lieutenant. I get a phone call."

"You were offered a call when Upton locked you up. You refused."

"That's because Alec was here. I didn't have anyone else to call." Alec had said he'd call her attorney. Isabel had yet to talk to the woman he'd hired. "I need to call Alec. Agent Upton is going to be pissed you took me to Fairbanks."

"That's Upton's problem. The warrant for the missed court appearance supersedes his case. Stop arguing. We need to go."

He prodded her down the short hallway.

"Where is Joyce?" she asked as she passed the woman's empty desk.

"Lunch break." Westover grabbed Isabel's backpack from the counter. "She didn't have a chance to log in your stuff before she left. We'll take it and let Fairbanks do the heavy lifting."

They entered the post garage, and Westover locked her in the backseat of the patrol car before depositing her pack in the trunk, then opening the bay door. She looked backward, through the rear window to the main road. It was empty. No sign of Alec or Upton.

Something about this was wrong. It was all too rushed.

Westover circled the car and slid behind the wheel. In minutes, they were on the road, heading west, toward the north highway that would take them to Fairbanks. The Raptor compound was to the east. No way Alec would catch a glimpse and know she wasn't in the Tamarack jail.

"Where were you and Ravissant this morning?"

"None of your business," she said, feeling uneasy.

"Police business is my business."

"It's an FBI investigation."

He grinned into the rearview mirror. "You were looking into Ravissant's abduction, then."

She shrugged.

"I heard someone shot out security cameras in the compound in the middle of the night." He leered at her in the mirror in a way that made her skin crawl. "I wonder what the cameras would have seen."

Given that the cameras had been off before they were shot out, it was strange that Westover knew anything about it. She didn't enjoy being locked in the back of the patrol car as Westover smirked at her.

"Wonder what the voters in Maryland will think about that?"

She bit back her reply. Aside from the fact that they were two consenting, single adults, they were Alec's cameras, meaning there was no crime. No scandal. It was also none of the officer's damn business.

Without warning, he took a sharp left onto a logging road.

Fear shot through her. "What are you doing?"

"Change in plans."

Her mind raced. She knew this road. It was part of a network that branched from Tamarack. The logging roads had been the first roads in the area, then the town grew. Many of the roads connected and intersected, a haven of secret routes for poachers and antigovernment types who liked the anonymity of the Alaskan bush.

She too had used these roads, to sneak onto the Raptor compound. Five minutes later, she was certain. Westover was taking her to the compound.

He must've lied about the court date. Lied about taking her to Fairbanks. He'd sent Joyce to lunch so he could sneak her out of the post with no one the wiser.

She was handcuffed and helpless and too late in remembering Westover had worked for Raptor under Robert Beck, and prior to that, he'd worked for the Defense Intelligence Agency—and rumors had circulated that he'd been involved with developing some "enhanced interrogation" techniques.

He had to be the other man in the cave. The one who'd questioned Alec.

Westover was Nicole's partner. Agent Upton had, at Alec's suggestion, delivered her into her brother's murderer's hands.

CHAPTER THIRTY

AS SOON AS Isabel was settled in the jail, Alec made a beeline for the Roadhouse.

"I hardly think this is the time for a beer, Ravissant," Upton said.

Alec cut the agent a hard stare. "One of my employees quit this morning, and I need to question him. He might be involved." He paused. "I remembered more of what happened last Thursday. I was interrogated in the cave."

"Interrogated? What did they want to know? Details of Ranger ops?"

He frowned. "I don't know. I can't remember the questions." He shook his head. "I'm a candidate, not a senator—it's not like I have real power or access to information."

He shoved open the door to the Roadhouse and immediately spotted Brad Fraser at the bar, nursing a beer. Alec dropped into the seat next to him. "Why aren't you at the compound?"

Fraser tossed him a glare. "I don't work for you anymore. I don't have to answer to you."

Upton settled into the barstool on the other side of Fraser. "Then you can tell me," he said.

"I don't answer to you either."

"You led the team that found Ravissant with Dawson. I have questions."

"I've answered your questions." Fraser stood and dropped a twenty on the bar. "Jenna," he said to the bartender, "I'm heading to your apartment."

"Stop being an ass, Brad, and answer their questions," Jenna said.

He frowned at her. "Babe, I quit for you."

"Yeah, well, I didn't ask you to do that and I think quitting was a huge mistake. So you'd've had to cool your heels in Fairbanks for a few weeks. I'd have been fine here."

"Why did you quit?" Alec asked.

"I couldn't leave Jenna here unprotected. Tamarack is dangerous. Last night a twenty-three-year-old in prime health had a heart attack. Eleven months ago, Vincent Dawson, our best survival-training guide, died of exposure. I've always known Isabel's argument had merit, but no one listened to me."

"You never said—"

"I *did*. It's all in the statement I made during the initial investigation. If you didn't read it, then you didn't care enough to look. I'm done risking my neck for a CEO who doesn't give a shit about the truth."

His words brought Alec up short. Was that how it had appeared? In letting lawyers and investigators look into Vincent's death, did Alec come across as a coldhearted CEO?

"I do care—"

"You didn't give a damn until something happened to you—or until you took one look at Isabel and decided you wanted to screw her. Either way, your reasons for finally paying attention were self-serving."

Alec bristled. Sure as hell, Brad wouldn't be talking to him like this if he were still employed by Raptor. While Alec didn't like what Brad was saying, he had to admit he preferred the honest operative to the obsequious soldier.

"And the way your campaign screwed her in the paper is sickening," Brad added.

"That wasn't me. I've already fired my campaign manager."

"Too late," Brad said. "Listen, there's something rotten going on in the compound. I can't trust the very people I need to have my back. I've been sitting on an offer from Apex for months. Now I'm taking it. I'm just here to convince Jenna to move with me to Oregon."

Jenna let out a heavy sigh. "You know I can't move, Brad. My dad needs me here."

"Your dad can come with us." He took a long drink of his beer, then faced Alec. "If you give a damn about Isabel at all, if you aren't just using her for information or a convenient screw, or a scapegoat for your campaign, you'll get her the hell out of Tamarack. Now. Today. She's hell-bent on justice, screw self-preservation. Someone needs to look out for her. The way I see it, justice isn't going to happen. Not when whoever is doing this has infrasound. Not when they can cause heart attacks in healthy operatives with the flip of a switch."

"Ms. Dawson *is* leaving Tamarack today," the FBI agent said. "With me. Forensics found evidence that ties her to Ravissant's abduction."

"That's bullshit!" Brad said.

"If you have information regarding the investigation, Mr. Fraser, I recommend you stop wasting my time with your gripes and start talking. I'd rather have the right person in custody, than *a* person in custody."

Brad's gaze darted from Alec's to Agent Upton's, then back to Jenna's. Jenna nodded in sync with Alec. "Tell him what you suspect, Brad. Tell them both everything."

The operative took a deep breath. "After Chase Johnston collapsed last night, I called Simon Barstow to accept the job with Apex. I asked about Ted Godfrey—I wanted to know if we'd be working on the same team. He had no clue what I was talking about. Godfrey's not down in Oregon."

"Why didn't you tell me this last night?" Alec asked.

"I wanted to be certain before I said anything. So I made some follow-up calls, but my contacts didn't get back to me until this morning—and you were nowhere to be found. I was about to tell Hatcher what I'd learned, but then I received the Fairbanks ultimatum. Which brings us here."

From Upton's demeanor, it was clear Brad had his full attention. "Who's Godfrey?" the FBI agent asked.

"He's an operative who, according to Nicole Markwell, accepted a position with Apex and quit on Thursday," Alec said.

"But Godfrey isn't with Apex," Upton clarified.

"No. He's missing," Fraser said.

It was time to tell Upton everything. "He's not missing. I know exactly where he is."

"Good. Because he's crooked as shit, and we need to keep an eye on him," Brad said.

"You suspected Godfrey?" Alec asked.

"There's been something off about Johnston ever since Godfrey took him under his wing. Chase was a good kid. Then he started staring at Isabel. Just being strange. I told him to knock it off, and he denied it. But the strange part was, he *really* didn't seem to know he was doing it. I kept telling Isabel it was just a crush, but now…I don't think so. I think Godfrey was fucking with his brain, using infrasound or some other shit that had been in development under Robert Beck.

"Back when Beck owned the place, Godfrey and Westover were tight and teamed up to run lots of the smaller trainings. Knowing Chase's brain may have been fucked with reminded me that Westover once worked for Defense Intelligence. He used to hint at the shit he'd done for DIA. I figured he was full of crap, but now I have to wonder if he really was versed in enhanced interrogation, and if he and Godfrey were working together, screwing with Chase's head."

At the first mention of Westover, Alec felt all the blood in his brain flow straight to his gut.

Isabel.

Alec stood without a word and turned for the door. Upton grabbed his arm, stopping him. "We need more information first."

"She's in danger."

"He'd be a fool to try something now. He'd reveal himself."

"What's going on?" Brad asked.

"Isabel is in the Tamarack lockup while we look into my suspicions of Nicole."

"Nic too?" Jenna said.

Alec nodded. He forced himself to stay and ask the questions, knowing Upton wouldn't release Isabel based on vague speculation alone. "You ever see anything suspicious between Nic and Godfrey?"

Brad shrugged. "He always got the odd assignments—the small trainings, one instructor, of two or three soldier/trainees. Short and intense. Much like Vin Dawson's last training. Those are the fun ones—out in the woods with a small team." He shrugged. "I figured she was playing favorites and it pissed me off. Truth is, I don't like Godfrey because he's reckless, and I swear he likes playing the hostage taker in the scenarios a little too much. We always play it real, per your rules, Rav, but he brought a special level of sicko to the job."

He frowned. "A month ago, we did a dry run in the new shoot house, to block out a new scenario. Chase played hostage and was tied to a chair. I caught Godfrey holding his gun inches from Chase's forehead and dry firing."

"That's a firable offense," Alec said. "Why the *fuck* are you just telling me this now?"

"I reported it to Nicole. Godfrey was put on a two-week suspension, and she said you'd approved the suspension over the firing because we're short on operatives."

"Nic lied. I'd have fired Godfrey on the spot, I don't give a crap how short-staffed we are." How badly had Alec fucked up in leaving Nicole in charge at the compound?

"Anything else?" Agent Upton asked Brad.

Brad paused for a moment, then said, "Search the wine cellar. Nic goes in there a lot, but she's not really a wine drinker, and it would be just like Beck to have a secret room tucked behind his precious wine cellar."

Alec turned to Upton. His body was tight with the need to go after Isabel. "Is that enough?"

Upton gave a sharp nod.

"Go to the compound and detain Nicole for questioning," Alec said. "I'll get Isabel."

"Westover won't release her to you. We'll get Isabel, then leave her here with Fraser." Upton nodded to the former operative. "Do you trust him to protect her?"

Alec met Brad's gaze, then nodded to Upton.

"Good. Then we'll find Nicole Markwell."

"Where's Godfrey?" Brad asked. "Question him. He'll crack long before Nic does."

Alec was about to say Godfrey wouldn't be answering questions anytime soon, when the front door to the Roadhouse opened, admitting a strong gust of wind and the woman who worked for Westover at the Tamarack Post. She had a pinched, anxious look on her face as she met Alec's gaze. "Oh, thank goodness you're still here! He's taken her. She's gone."

Fear unlike anything Alec had ever experienced gripped him by the balls.

"What happened?" Upton asked.

"That ass Westover sent me to lunch—insisted I go, which was unusual for him—but I needed to let the dogs out and was relieved we were going to skip our daily argument, so I went. While I was gone, he took Isabel. She's not in the jail."

CHAPTER THIRTY-ONE

ALEC'S WASN'T QUITE sure he was breathing, yet he must be, because he managed to speak. "Where did he take her?"

"I have no idea! His patrol car is gone. I radioed him, but he didn't respond."

"Can you track his vehicle with GPS?"

She frowned. "The tracking device was damaged a few weeks ago. It hasn't been fixed."

Alec's heart pounded. This was all his fault. He'd suggested they leave Isabel in the jail. He stupidly hadn't suspected Westover. But why did the man expose himself now by going all in? What was his goal? And how did he expect to escape with his life?

Because sure as hell, if the officer hurt Isabel, Alec was going to break his neck—as easily as he'd killed Godfrey.

ISABEL JOLTED AWAKE, unsure what had pulled her from sleep. Then she heard it again. The song. Someone was calling her. Not just someone. Alec. That was his ringtone.

Wait. What was her cell phone doing here?

And where, exactly, was *here*?

She sat up—or rather tried to—and discovered she couldn't move. She was strapped to a bed in a cold, dark room. The only sound was the ringing of the cell phone. The repeated phrases of Carly Rae Jepsen's "Call Me Maybe." The light pop song had been her secret admission she was interested in him when she'd downloaded it, but in this stark, desolate room, it offered only discord and turmoil.

Slowly, the last hours came back to her. The *Sun* article. Finding the cave and Godfrey's remains. Upton's accusations. She'd been locked up. Again. And Westover had cuffed her and they'd driven off. Then…nothing.

She probed the blank spaces in her memory. She'd never really liked Paul Westover, but that didn't mean anything. After all, she'd liked Nicole.

The officer must be involved. He hadn't worked on the compound when Vin was there, but that didn't mean he didn't work with Godfrey and Nicole and infrasound.

She must have been zapped while she was still in the cruiser. She could have passed out with the pain, giving him the chance to bring her here. Wherever here was.

Four concrete walls and a ceiling. They weren't in the cave.

She shouldn't be surprised that they had other locations for their experiments. The cave was probably only for certain special cases. Over the months she'd searched for it, she'd done a lot of research, and understood that caves were ideal for torture and brainwashing because they were disorienting. Sound reverberated in odd ways. Were infrasound waves especially intense inside the cave?

The cave itself, she'd discovered, had felt like an underground cavern. Like being buried alive.

It must have been a nightmare for Vin. And for Alec.

This concrete bunker wasn't much better, but at least there weren't bats clinging to the ceiling. Even so, she had a feeling Alec's and Vin's nightmares were about to become hers.

Footsteps tapped out a rhythm on the floor, the sound echoing as if a person approached from a long corridor. This had to be one of the shoot houses. Or maybe she was inside one of the fake structures meant to emulate a crumbling city street.

That would mean there were cameras here with a direct feed to the compound. Alec could find her if he went to God's Eye and checked the feed for every structure. She had no idea how many structures, how many rooms, how many cameras there were, or if he'd even think to look. But she had to believe he'd find her. She needed a reason to hope.

A person wearing a ski mask with dark, reflective glasses and a regulator of some sort over the mouth and nose paused above her. From the build, she figured the man must be Westover. Did he really think he could hide his identity now? But then, he probably wore the mask for the same reason they'd tortured in a cave, because it was disorienting.

She had to admit, she didn't like her reflection in the glasses.

The man spoke, and his voice was mechanical. Not computerized, the mouthpiece must be a filter that altered the frequency and modulation of his speech. "You're lucky, Isabel, you'll have no memory of this."

She shivered at that. They planned to torture her but considered blanking her memory of the pain a kindness.

"Why are you disguising your voice and face, Westover?"

A sharp crackling noise emitted from the mask. It took her a moment to realize it was altered laughter. He was amused. "Infrasound can interrupt your ability to understand speech, and it's vital you understand so we get the response we need. This filter emits my speech at a frequency you can comprehend while being subjected to the waves. It took us months to figure out the right frequency. Your brother was our first successful filter test. He was able to answer all of my questions."

Her belly turned as she imagined Vin in this position, their test subject as they honed their instruments of torture. "What do you want from me?"

"We want nothing from you."

"Then why are you doing this?"

"Because we want something from Ravissant. You interrupted his interrogation before we got what we needed. It's your fault he killed Godfrey."

He knew she knew about Godfrey?

The mask emitted a low, rumbling sound. A heavy sigh? "We've had this conversation, already, Isabel. I'm tired of it."

"Already?"

"Oh yes. You've already been questioned. You told me everything. You know about Godfrey. You know about Nicole. The only thing you don't know is *why*. That's the word you repeated as you screamed and cried. So much like your brother."

She felt all the blood in her body pull back from her bound extremities. She'd already been tortured? She'd told them everything she knew? "How long have I been here?"

Another set of footsteps entered the room. A lighter step—a smaller person. A second mask and goggles filled her vision. Shorter. A woman's build.

Nicole.

"Five hours," she said, her voice also distorted by the mask. "You were such a good sport, Isabel, this time I'm going to answer *all* your questions. Such a pity you won't remember later."

"You can suppress memories, but you can't erase them. I *will* remember."

A cold, gloved hand caressed her cheek. She flinched away

from the cruel touch. "Oh, sweetie. You said that before too. But you don't remember. And you won't this time either. The only reason it didn't work with Rav was because you interrupted. Once the trance was broken, Westover had to knock him out. After that, there was no going back. He couldn't reset and start over. Your interference meant there was a chance Rav would remember. Too many untested variables we couldn't control. It's why we couldn't abduct him a second time and try again." She tugged on one of Isabel's curls. "Good thing the man has a thing for redheads, or we'd be up shit creek. I didn't know what we were going to do until we were at the shoot house and he freaked about you playing hostage. We can't torture him to get him to tell us what we need, but he'll cave when he watches the video."

"Video?"

"The one we're going to send him. Want to see it?" She picked up a remote from the wheeled cart next to her and hit a button, turning on the monitor mounted to the cart.

The video was black-and-white and blurred, but slowly, the image solidified into crystal-clear high definition. Isabel watched in horror as she thrashed, gasped, and screamed as if she were being sliced open, one slow inch at a time.

There was something horrific about seeing herself whimpering and begging for the pain to stop. She could easily see Vin in her place. Or Alec.

"Stop it!" she shouted when she couldn't take it any longer. She wanted to wipe away the tears that streamed down her face, but her hands were strapped down at her hips. All she could do was turn her head into the cot, but it was covered in cold, crinkly, nonabsorbent plastic.

She didn't want to think about why they used a plastic-wrapped cot, yet her brain still registered that bodily fluids were easily washed from plastic.

"Why are you doing this, Nicole? I thought we were friends."

The cold, gloved hand returned to her cheek. "We are friends, sweetie. I hate doing this to you. But at least you won't remember it. That's my gift to you." Her hand slid from Isabel's cheek and wrapped around her neck. She didn't squeeze, she just rested her hand in a relaxed threat. "As for why, it's simple, really. I want Alec's money. All of it. We tried subtle—going after account logins and passwords, access codes, security questions—everything we'd need to clean him out.

"We were going to transfer his funds to foreign numbered accounts, coordinating the transactions so it would happen right as his assets were being transferred into a blind trust—which he was setting up in the event he wins the election. Because he wouldn't remember giving us the information, he'd have had no idea his assets were vulnerable. It would've been the perfect heist."

Nicole pulled off her mask and glanced at Westover. "I hate this damn thing. It's hot and uncomfortable. I don't know how you and Godfrey could handle wearing it for hours on end. There is no point in wearing it when the subject isn't being subjected to infrasound."

"We need to start another round within four minutes, or she might remember this conversation," Westover said.

"I'll put it on again then." She turned to Isabel and smiled, the same grin she'd flash when they laughed over a beer. "As I was saying… You're the perfect hostage. I don't think you understand exactly how rich Rav is. He has a lot of financial assets that would've been rolled up in that trust, and we would've taken every dime. We'd bide our time, and six months, a year from now, quietly disappear and enjoy his money."

"So you're just a fucking thief?" Isabel's question came out as a snarl.

"Thieves now, but originally we were entrepreneurs. We planned to sell infrasound. I had Russian—and Ukrainian, I believe in taking money from both sides—clients lined up. But then you kept making a stink about Vin and his dreams of the lynx cave, and they balked. It's no good if the victim remembers. But we kept perfecting the techniques. By mixing infrasound with some drugs Westover managed to procure, we were getting pretty good with brainwashing and suggestion. Chase has been stalking you for weeks, not because he wanted to, but because he *had* to. And he had no idea why. But he resisted kidnapping you in the basement, so Westover upped the infrasound frequency. You saw what happened." She tossed a glare at her partner. "It was our one chance to grab you while remaining anonymous."

Finally, Nicole turned off the video, and Isabel's screams no longer provided a horrific soundtrack to the conversation. "When my spy in the DC office told me Hatcher had been hired for the CEO position, Godfrey suggested we kidnap Rav and take his money. It seemed like a fitting punishment. That job should have been *mine*."

"You didn't get the CEO position because you were losing operatives to Apex, and I got the compound shut down because you murdered my brother!"

"Chicken, egg. Whatever. I was content as an operative in Hawaii, but Rav sent me to Siberia. I knew he'd never promote me out of this wasteland, so I seized other opportunities." She had the gall to shrug.

"He sent you here as a promotion! Alaska is the heart of the entire training operation."

"I don't want to train soldiers. I left the Army because they wouldn't let me *be* a soldier. There's little room to advance if you can't play with the big boys. Robert Beck may have been an ass, but at least he let me be an operative. Rav yanked me out of operations and called it a promotion." Nicole reached for the mask. Once it was again over her head, she picked up another item from the cart. It looked like a parabolic microphone. She turned the curved dish toward Isabel. "And I didn't murder your brother. We just tested things on him. In the end, he died all by himself."

Before Isabel could react, she pressed a button on the object in her hand, and Isabel's head began to throb. Her vision blurred. She wanted to puke.

She was going to die.

CHAPTER THIRTY-TWO

ALEC WAS ABOUT to lose his mind. Isabel had been missing for six hours. The compound was now emptied of everyone except Alec, Keith, Ethan, Josh, Sean, Lee, Brad, and Agent Matt Upton, who was now on a first-name basis with the team after he'd been the one to find the panel that opened in the wine cellar, revealing a stark laboratory.

In the lab—which was adjacent to the firing range and, like the range, not under the compound building, but next to it—they found a computer terminal with access to the elevator controls and every security camera that hadn't been replaced by Alec when he took over the company. They also found Isabel's laptop, cell phone, and the notebook she'd used to document her search for the cave. Westover must have seen the notebook when he arrested her Friday morning and taken it when he grabbed her laptop later that night.

At the rear of the lab, there was a short tunnel that cut through the permafrost, connecting the secret room to the forest beyond the concertina-wire-topped fence that circled the compound. Officer Westover had his own entrance and exit into the building that completely bypassed all compound security measures, which explained how he was able to attack both Chase and Isabel and escape without notice while Nicole remained in full view at her desk.

As far as the FBI agent was concerned, the most important find was the lab computer, which had information on infrasound development. As they'd guessed, testing had started under Beck. Westover, already versed in enhanced interrogation techniques during his stint in the DIA, had been in the process of developing tests to determine its uses when Beck was arrested. Godfrey, who'd been a medic in the Army, had been brought on board for his medical knowledge.

There was so much data as they tested different variables and refined the weapon, they'd had to store the information somewhere, and odds were, Nicole wasn't about to give Westover complete control of the data, nor could she keep it on a computer in her quarters or office.

That Nicole didn't grab the computer before leaving meant either she didn't expect them to find the lab, or she didn't care.

Matt had called his superiors at the FBI the moment Isabel went missing, but with the data found in the lab, he'd included the DIA and CIA in the investigation. All agencies would be converging on the compound in a matter of hours, but unless they could help pinpoint Isabel's location, Alec didn't really give a damn.

She was out there with Westover and Nicole, and all the barriers to his memory had crumbled. He knew exactly what they were doing to her.

He'd spent the first two hours after she was taken searching the woods and compound assets where Nicole was likely to take her, while Keith led the search for the lab inside the main building.

After all the shoot houses and training center buildings had been cleared, he'd had no choice but to return to the center of operations. He needed to do what he did best. Strategize. Plan. Run scenarios and predict outcomes.

Nicole's final act before she left the facility was to crash the computer system, using the lab terminal. Apparently, she was the one who'd been attacking the system for months, making it look like it was an external hack that came from Isabel. Now all the camera feeds to God's Eye were offline, and the older security cameras were down as well. They couldn't monitor the shoot houses. They couldn't even access the stored data.

Thank God, Lee had already landed in Fairbanks when Nicole crashed the system. He'd arrived with Sean and Josh an hour later and had slowly been bringing each system back online.

Alec paced the length of God's Eye while Lee worked, fighting the urge to go back outside and search for Isabel.

There were too many places to hide in Alaska.

There was an unsolved Rubik's Cube on the console, part of his ongoing bet with Keith. He had to solve the puzzle in less than five minutes. They'd made the bet four or five years before, and he'd yet to lose—the initial wager was a pitcher of beer, but the double-or-nothing additions over the years probably amounted to Keith owing him a brewery by now. He picked it up. Stared at the squares.

For the first time in decades, they made no sense. He should know exactly the moves it took to shift the orange, blue, and white corner into place without switching any other squares. But his mind was blank. He couldn't visualize the sequence.

He closed his eyes, but that didn't help. All he could see was Isabel. In the firing range. Beautiful, sexy, warm.

With a sharp yell, he threw the cube across the room. It hit one of the dozens of monitors, shattering the screen.

To his credit, Lee said nothing. Other than Alec's ragged breathing, the only sound was the tap of Lee's fingers on the keyboard.

Alec resumed pacing. As far as he knew, they had the numbers advantage. With Godfrey dead, it was only Westover and Nicole they had to deal with, while Alec had Raptor's top operatives on his side. He also had Ethan Quinault, who might not be an operative, but he was an expert marksman. And then there was Keith, former SEAL sniper. He'd rehired Brad, who'd been a Green Beret. Both Josh and Sean had been SEALs.

Hell, even Lee was a fifth degree black belt.

Nicole Markwell and Lieutenant Paul Westover didn't stand a chance.

Except they had a hostage. A woman who meant everything to him.

His cell phone buzzed. He expected it was a message from Keith down in the lab, but the message was from Nicole.

She'd sent a video.

LEE UPLOADED THE video to the large monitor in the main conference room, and the team gathered to watch.

Alec had seen it on his phone several times already, and now he forced himself to watch on the eighty-inch screen as larger-than-life Isabel begged for the pain to stop.

Each shriek was a blow.

My fault.

He'd suggested the Tamarack lockup. He'd delivered her right into Westover's hands. He should have let Upton take her to Anchorage. He should have run off with her himself. There were a thousand things he should've—could've—done, and he'd chosen the single worst option.

Around the room, the men were silent as they watched, most seeing the two-minute-and-fourteen-second video for the first time. At the end, a man wearing a mask and voice distorter demanded ransom. Every asset Alec could turn into cash in twenty-four hours was to be deposited into a numbered foreign bank account. Then Isabel would be released. If Alec paid in less than twelve hours, they'd be kind enough to ensure Isabel would have no memory of her ordeal.

"If you pay late," the masked man said, "she'll live—we aren't killers. Not like *you*. But the torture will get worse with each hour." He paused and adjusted the speaker on his mask, so the eerie, distorted words became sharp and clear. "I know how to break a mind, Ravissant. I will destroy her."

If what Alec suspected of Westover's service with the DIA was true, the man spoke the truth.

Alec would tear him apart.

ISABEL JOLTED AWAKE, unsure what had pulled her from sleep. Then she heard it again. The song was playing. Someone was calling her. Not just someone. Alec. That was his ringtone.

She was in a curved walled room, with small windows in a row along the sides. An airplane. Was she flying somewhere?

Something wasn't right, but it was familiar. This was no déjà vu. Her head throbbed. Her abdomen ached as if she'd heaved every ounce of fluid from her body, twice.

She probably had.

She tried to sit up but discovered she was strapped to the cot. One strap crossed her shoulders. Her wrists were cinched down at her hips. Her ankles were bound as well. She wasn't going anywhere.

A woman sat in front of the bulkhead. When Isabel's gaze landed on her, she smiled and stood, crossing the cabin to the side of the cot. "Oh good. You're awake. Do you want to play twenty questions again, or just cut to the chase?"

"You've been torturing me. Repeatedly." She didn't remember, exactly. It was more the aches in her body and gaps in her memory that told her.

"I have to admit, it's been quite fascinating," Nicole said. "Usually the infrasound testing was Westover and Godfrey's deal. I never even watched. All I cared about were the results. But you, Isabel, you've been special. I wonder if it's because you're a woman. We're made of stronger stuff, you know. We can take higher levels of pain. Westover says your pain threshold is off the charts compared to the men."

Isabel wanted to glare at Nicole, but even that hurt. Blinking hurt. Breathing hurt. "Are we flying somewhere?"

A corner of her mouth kicked up. "No. We're in the airplane hostage simulator. This jet hasn't flown in years."

They were still on the compound. Alec could find her. There was hope. "Why are you doing this to me?"

"I'm getting tired of going over that with you. We're ransoming you. I figure at this point you're worth a lot to Alec, and the more you scream, the more he'll pay. You scream very well."

"Ransom. Wait. You were interrogating him. You were after his money all along. You wanted access to his accounts."

"Very good! You *do* remember!" Nicole gave her a look worthy of a proud mother. If Isabel could lift her arm, she'd punch the bitch, pain or no pain.

"Alec killed Godfrey, and Westover dumped Alec in the woods so I'd find him. Why? Your plan had gone to hell. Why not just kill him?"

"Oh. That's a good question. You haven't asked that one already. Glad to see your brain is holding up after repeated rounds of infrasound."

Repeated? How many times had they done this to her? How many times had they had this conversation?

"If Rav had died, his accounts would have been frozen. We wouldn't have been able to raid them. Westover had to find a way for Rav to live, but he couldn't pull off the car-hitting-a-moose scenario we'd planned, not when Rav had bruises and cuts that couldn't have been caused by the accident. No one would believe it. Plus we weren't sure what Rav would remember. So he dumped Rav in your path, figuring you'd bandage him, then go for help. It was the best we could hope for. You surpassed Westover's expectations by building the travois. Rav might have died if you'd left him—and that would have screwed up our plans big-time. We owe you a debt of thanks. You didn't just save Rav; you saved our asses."

"And now you're thanking me by torturing me."

"Yes, but we've been using the frequencies that result in memory loss—our gift to you. Believe me, you don't *want* to know what you've been through today. Westover is one sick sonofabitch."

Nicole had never been a fan of Westover, and her tone indicated the dislike hadn't been an act to deflect suspicion. Isabel twisted under the restraints, trying to get a glimpse of the main passenger cabin behind her. "Where is he?"

"He's setting up our next location. Right now it's just us girls."

Was Nicole more likely to answer her questions without Westover present? Even more important, without Westover, was she safe from being zapped with infrasound? "Why did he shoot Airwave into my cabin?"

"Westover wanted your computer and notebook. I wanted Rav to bring you inside the compound so I could keep an eye on you—you'd gotten far too close to the cave—plus I wanted to implicate Apex."

"Because Barstow never offered you a job?"

Nicole's lip curled. "Oh, he offered me a job—but I'm an operative, not a whore."

Did Nicole expect Isabel to feel sorry for her? After everything she'd done? Isabel's body ached too much for her to even fake sympathy. "Why did Westover come after us in the river? We weren't anywhere near the cave."

"That was Westover's stupid idea to prevent Rav from letting you search for the cave on your own. He figured if he made it clear you were in danger, Rav would insist you stay inside the building while we planned the training, making you a willing prisoner. Westover didn't expect you both to swim." She patted Isabel's hand. "If it makes you feel better, I reamed him when he told me what happened. Rav could have died."

Where was the woman Isabel had spent hours with in the Roadhouse? How had she hidden her true self so well, for so long? Isabel stared at her, searching for glimpses of the woman she'd laughed and traded stories with, for the soldier who'd seemed dedicated to her job. Maybe, if she hadn't been so lonely and desperate for information, she'd have recognized Nicole for what she was months ago. She cleared her throat to ask one more question. "Why was I attacked in the basement?"

Nicole's mouth tightened and her brows drew together in disappointment. "As I've told you twice already, after Chase failed to grab you, we knew we'd have to take you ourselves. But we could hardly abduct you when Rav had a mercenary army at his disposal. Attacking you in the basement—so blatant after Chase's collapse—made it clear the compound wasn't safe. Rav had no choice but to shut it down"—she flashed a cunning grin—"and send everyone on Falcon away." She picked up Isabel's cell phone. "That's enough questions. Let's see what message Rav left you." She put the phone on speaker.

"I never set up voice mail," Isabel said.

"Don't worry, I set it up for you when I disabled the GPS function."

That not so secret hope wilted before it could fully blossom. Alec's phone guru, Lee, wouldn't be able to locate her based on cell tower pings—because there was only one antenna array in the area—and it was right next to the main compound building.

Alec's voice was crisp even through the small speaker. "You win, Nicole. It takes time to turn assets into cash, but I've spoken with the presidents of three of my banks and have been assured access to twenty-seven million at eight a.m. Eastern time. I just need the deposit account number to complete the transaction."

Nicole frowned and shut off the phone. "By my calculations, his assets—not including Raptor—are worth well over a hundred million, but if the bank is advancing the cash based on stocks and bonds he has yet to sell, they couldn't give him full value." She tapped the phone, her gaze taking a distant look. "I suppose twenty-seven mil isn't bad. I have to split it with Westover, though. Sort of makes me glad Rav took Godfrey out of the picture. It's enough to make this whole ordeal worthwhile. We're giving up on eighteen months of testing and development, plus I'll be forced to leave the US and never come back." The cunning grin returned. "You must give a helluva blowjob."

Isabel bucked against the restraints, more than eager to slug Nicole in the jaw.

Nicole ignored her and reached for the mask on the tray. "Now, it's time to make sure you forget this conversation."

"Why?" Isabel pleaded, sweat dotting her brow at the prospect of enduring more pain, even if she wouldn't remember it later. "You just get annoyed when I ask the same questions again."

Nicole paused and cocked her head, her expression matching one Isabel had seen many times. "You know what, I'm so happy Rav is coming through with the money, I'll give you this one." She winked conspiratorially. "Plus it'll piss off Westover that I didn't follow his instructions, which is always a bonus."

Relief allowed Isabel to take a deep, shuddering breath. She'd only delayed the next round, but at least she wouldn't wake up confused again. With this conversation as a baseline, she'd remember what was going on, and why, which might give her a chance to figure out how to escape.

Nicole gathered items from a cart next to the cot, shoving them into a duffle bag. "It's time for us to join Westover at the next location. We'll send the video we took of you here in a few hours. We need to keep Alec on his toes, guessing where we are. I don't for a moment believe he's just going to give me the money without doing everything he can to get you back first. He might be a good strategist, but he handed over his game plan months ago, and he doesn't know this compound nearly as well as I do. He doesn't really stand a chance."

CHAPTER THIRTY-THREE

A MAP OF the compound was spread out across the conference table. Lee pointed to three structures in the far northeast of Alec's holdings. "We can rule out these structures, because while they have generators and electricity, they don't have Wi-Fi or cell coverage, and they need to be able to access the banks, to be certain the money has gone through."

"They could have a satellite phone," Keith suggested.

Alec considered what he knew of Nicole. "It's possible. But Nicole is tech savvy and more comfortable with computers than telephone transactions. She'll want to *see* the deposits land and move the money quickly. Plus she probably feels secure knowing she locked us out of the LAN and God's Eye cameras. She figures Mothman is in Fairbanks and we're helpless. She has no idea Lee is here."

Lee had already defeated Nicole's bug, but they'd opted to leave it in place until they stormed the position where Isabel was held. Let her think she maintained the upper hand until it was too late.

Four monitors had been set up in the room. Each was paused on a different video.

Four videos. Four rounds of torture. Each one worse than the last.

Brad left the table and approached the second monitor. He hit the Play button and fast-forwarded. He stopped and played a small section.

Isabel's whispered plea for mercy kicked Alec in the chest.

"Sorry," Brad said, and muted the sound.

Only years of training kept Alec from losing his shit. He had a rescue mission to plan and couldn't save her if he lost his focus. He was a razor. Sharp and lethal.

Brad paused the video and zoomed in on the wall behind Isabel. "This bullet pattern. I know it. We ran a training where we hung posters to represent three Tangos in the southeast shoot house a few months ago. We timed how quickly each trainee could get off three headshots. The wall behind the posters was beat to hell after that exercise." Brad pointed to three heavily chipped areas. "This is that room."

Lee studied the map, then pointed. "Is this the southeast shoot house?"

Brad returned to the map and nodded.

Lee drew a red circle around the structure on the map. "I can turn on the cameras there. If they're long gone, it won't alert Nicole we have computer access, and if they're there, we'll see them."

Alec considered the possibilities. "I want a team in position to pounce, just in case they've returned. It would be like her to double back after a place has been cleared. Like the hostage scenarios we run in the shoot houses. And that was one of the structures I searched first."

I was there. Before or after this video was taken?

"If we can determine all four locations," Keith said. "We can have four two-man teams ready to move in."

"One man would have to be solo," Alec said. "We need Lee in God's Eye, working the cameras." He paused, considering the options. "Odds are, they'll be gone, but if each team takes one known location, then moves into position to check out an unknown, we could quickly sweep a few sections of the compound, with Lee activating cameras one step at a time." Alec met Lee's gaze. "Can you work the cameras from God's Eye? It's a lot to take in, usually a two- or three-person job."

"If I'm activating the cameras in waves, no problem. I know the system."

"Good. Let's figure out the other three locations and then identify where each two-man team needs to go from there. We'll do a systematic search."

"We should bring in Sifuentes, Kalla, and Wells from Fairbanks." Keith said. "Then we wouldn't have anyone working solo."

"No time," Alec said. "Besides, I'm not ready to trust them until we're *certain* Nicole and Westover aren't working with anyone else." He met Keith's gaze. He knew the man would object, but really, there was no other option. "I'll search alone."

THREE HOURS LATER, Alec was crouched in the trees surrounding the prove-up. There were no interior cameras in the prove-up cabin, which was why Alec had opted to take this structure after they'd cleared the training buildings. It would be hard for Nicole to ignore the lure of a safe haven without cameras.

They'd been searching for the last two hours, to no avail. Time was dwindling. Soon it would be eight a.m. on the East Coast, and Alec would transfer a massive amount of money—enough to ensure Nic and Westover could disappear and escape justice forever—into a numbered bank account. He had to find Nicole before he made the transfer. Not because he gave a damn about retaining the money, but because he owed the bitch a bullet between the eyes for what she'd done to Isabel.

Alec and Keith had decided on the search teams: Ethan and Josh, Keith and Sean, Brad and FBI Agent Matt Upton, leaving Alec alone and Lee in God's Eye, directing.

It was far from ideal, but it was the best they could do, given the situation, and Alec had complete trust in each man.

He waited until he received the signal from Keith and Sean that they were in position. Because this structure had no cameras, which meant Lee couldn't provide guidance, they'd agreed backup was required. At least the cabin was small and Alec knew the layout. It would take only moments to search it.

As with every building he'd searched in the last two hours, the cabin was empty. But there was one key difference. A still-warm mug of hot chocolate sat on the coffee table.

Alec stopped short, staring at the mug. His heart pounded as the meaning sank in.

They'd been here. In the last hour. Hell, in the last thirty minutes.

Isabel had been here, in the same place where he'd watched her in the firelight and had known, deep down, she was everything he wanted.

He grabbed a lamp from the side table and, with a roar, smashed it into the stone mantel. The ceramic body shattered, sending shards flying in a scatter pattern around the hearth and into the open grate. It wasn't enough. He scooped up the side table and bashed it against the rocks. It cracked and splintered, but it took five solid blows until the table was reduced to a mess of wood fragments.

He roared again as tears of anger, frustration, and fear surged to the surface. He couldn't hold them back any longer.

Isabel had been Nicole's prisoner for sixteen hours. She'd suffered unspeakable pain, and he had no reason to believe Nicole would let her live after he paid the ransom. Her only hope was if he found her before the money dropped.

In the last six days, he'd somehow fallen head over heels in love with her. She mattered to him more than air, and she was suffering. Because of him. Not only had he delivered her straight into the hands of evil, but they were hurting her to break him, because they wanted his money. Because they knew what seeing her pain would do to him.

He was dying inside. He didn't quite understand how his heart was still beating. He leaned his forehead against the mantel and let out the sob that had been building since he first learned Westover had taken her.

Twenty-four hours ago, he'd been in bed with Isabel. He sucked in a painful breath. He'd attempted to count her freckles as she drifted off to sleep, but it was impossible, as one faint orange spot blended with the next in his dim bedroom.

She needed him now, and he was failing her.

"Alec?" Keith said.

Slowly, he lifted his head and turned, meeting Keith's gaze without flinching. He wasn't ashamed for breaking down, and Keith, of all people, would understand, given what had happened to his girlfriend, Trina, only a month ago. "She was here. A half hour ago."

"How do you know?"

He nodded toward the mug on the coffee table. "The hot chocolate is a message. For me."

"What does it mean?"

He shrugged. "Beyond that she was here? I'm not certain."

"Lee's finished rebooting the entire system. He's going over each structure again. I sent the others back to help him. Right now, it looks like they're long gone."

"Not long." Alec picked up the mug and dipped a finger inside. "This is still lukewarm."

"There are a billion hiding places in the woods here, but not a lot of places that have electricity and Internet. And now that Lee's got the system up, if they access the network, he'll know."

"They'll stay away from the Raptor network. Nicole knows it can pinpoint her location."

"There's no way to use Raptor Wi-Fi or LAN without logging in," Keith said. "If they're in one of the compound buildings, Lee will find them."

Alec stiffened as Nicole's plan crystalized in his mind. She'd kept him busy, focused on the compound, blinding him to her final destination. "I think I know where they are."

ALEC AND KEITH circled the meadow and approached Isabel's cabin from the rear. On the surface, it appeared empty. Abandoned.

But Alec was certain this was it.

Nicole would feel so clever, hiding Isabel in her own cabin. It made perfect sense. Remote and isolated, yet with the comforts they needed to complete the transaction and easy egress from the compound. There were two access roads from which to make their escape, or they could take an ATV overland and disappear into the forest.

He and Keith had discussed at length the best approach. The broken living room window left the cabin vulnerable from the front, while the back door not only had a hefty dead bolt, it also had an old-fashioned two-by-four braced across the panel just above the knob. There would be no forcing that door open without a battering ram.

The front was the only option.

They crept below the window and flanked the door with their guns drawn. A slow, quiet test of the knob showed it was unlocked. At Keith's nod, Alec wrenched the door open and dropped down to open Keith's line of sight.

Nicole sat in the center of the couch with Isabel tight against her side. Isabel was bound—her hands zip-tied in front of her—and gagged. The muzzle of Nicole's pistol was pressed casually against the base of Isabel's neck. The blonde bitch flashed her wide, megawatt smile. "Drop the gun, Tiger, and come on in. It took you long enough to get here."

CHAPTER THIRTY-FOUR

TIGER. ISABEL SHIVERED, realizing she must've told Nicole the "safeword" during her interrogation. What else had Nicole asked? What else had she revealed?

"Put your gun on the floor and kick it to me."

Very slowly, Alec crouched and set the gun down. He raised his hands in surrender as he rose then tapped the pistol with his foot, sending it sliding across the wood floor, not in Nicole's direction but to the center of the room. Out of his reach, but out of hers too. If she wanted it, she'd have to take the gun off Isabel and her eyes off Alec. He'd neatly taken the weapon out of play.

He laced his fingers and tucked his raised arms behind his head. "Put the gun down, Nic. You won't see a dime if you shoot her. You pull that trigger and I'll break your neck faster than I broke Godfrey's."

"But Alec, the only thing that's keeping you from breaking my neck right now is the fact that I have the gun on Isabel. I know how lethal you are, even unarmed and barely conscious." She nodded toward the open door. Isabel had caught a glimpse of Keith, but he'd disappeared once Alec stepped inside. "Let's make a deal. Send Hatcher back to the compound, and we can negotiate." She glanced at her watch. "Ten minutes until the banks release the money and you can make the transfer. It would be much cozier if it's just the three of us when the money comes through."

"Three? What about Westover?"

She flashed another grin but said nothing.

A scuffle outside answered Alec's question. A moment later, Westover was shoved toward the open door, blood pouring from his temple. Keith pushed him into the room. "You lose, Nicole. We've got your partner."

The pressure at the back of Isabel's neck disappeared. Before she could draw in a breath of relief at no longer having a gun to her head, Nicole pointed the weapon at her partner's chest and squeezed the trigger.

Isabel lurched forward from the couch as two rapid shots reverberated through the cabin. She dove for Alec's gun and sent it sliding back in his direction.

Westover pitched backward into Keith. Out of the corner of her eye, she saw the pistol glide past the easy chair, out of Nicole's line of sight.

Both men dropped backward through the front door.

"That makes the twenty-seven million all mine," Nicole said.

Isabel rolled, covering the spot where the gun had been, hoping to hell Nicole wouldn't realize it was gone.

Had Keith been shot too?

She faced the woman she'd considered a friend. Nicole's gun was no longer aimed at her. Now it was pointed at Alec.

"You can't shoot me, Nic. Not if you want the money. I'm not stupid. I set it up so the transfer won't go through until I enter my authorization code."

"You'll provide the code." Nicole's voice switched to her command tone. "Isabel, come here."

Isabel twitched, ready to comply. Obeying the woman with the gun seemed like the smart thing. But her racing, panicked brain offered one coherent thought. If Nicole shot Isabel, Alec wouldn't pay her. If Nicole shot Alec, Alec wouldn't pay her. Nicole might have the gun, but she didn't have the power. She wanted the money badly enough to have tortured and played games for the last several days. She wouldn't jeopardize that now, not mere minutes before the transfer. Until the money went through, Alec and Isabel had the upper hand. It just didn't *look* like they did. Obeying Nicole wasn't the smart thing. It wasn't even the right thing.

The gag in her mouth prevented her from speaking, so she raised her bound hands and gave Nicole the middle finger.

Nicole frowned. With Isabel and Alec on opposite sides of the room, she couldn't cover them both. From the look on her face, it was clear she'd realized this too. She'd been so eager to take out her partner, to up her share of the ransom, she hadn't guessed she could lose the power position so completely.

After all, she was still the only person in the room with a gun.

Isabel flicked her gaze to the floor. From her position, she could see the gun mere inches from Alec's feet. Her gaze shifted to Alec's and he gave her the slightest of nods. He *knew*.

She needed to get Nicole's attention so he could get the weapon. Her mind raced. Gagged, how could she get Nicole talking again?

"So was this all about the money, Nic?" Alec asked.

She shrugged. "Pretty much. I figure I've reached my ceiling. There is no more up for me. So I'll take the money and bow out."

"Do you want to know why I promoted you to director?"

"I'll bite. Sure."

"They say those who can't *do,* teach. So I made you a teacher, because sure as hell you sucked as an operative. You don't like to get your hands dirty." He glanced over his shoulder at Westover's feet, which protruded through the doorway.

Isabel's heart squeezed with fear for Keith. The operative hadn't made a sound after he disappeared out the door. "I'm betting shooting your partner was the first time you've done any dirty work during this whole operation. You let Westover and Godfrey be the grunts while you waited for the ship to come in."

"That just proves I'm an excellent manager. But now I'm done. I like nice things and warm places. Twenty-seven million should get me that."

Isabel couldn't join the conversation, so she did the only thing she could think of and rolled again, furthering the distance between her and Alec. With her gaze on Isabel, Nicole wouldn't be able to see him in her peripheral vision.

Nicole shifted the gun from Alec to Isabel. "Where do you think you're going?"

She tried to keep the satisfaction from her face. She made a noise against the gag, as if her bound hands hurt, and rolled again. Nicole wouldn't shoot. Not before the money transfer.

At least she hoped to hell not.

"Stop moving, Isabel."

"Fugh ooo," she said, the closest approximation she could do to telling the bitch off.

Isabel met Alec's gaze. He mouthed the words *I love you,* then dropped for the gun.

Nicole jolted to her feet and spun at the noise, bringing the gun around with her.

Still on the floor, he fired, two rapid shots. Nicole's head snapped backward, then she dropped. Her head flopped to the side as she landed, facing Isabel.

Alec had hit her clean between the eyes.

CHAPTER THIRTY-FIVE

ISABEL WAITED BY the front door of the compound. Anxiety had her rocking back and forth on her heels. Alec and Lee had gone to pick up Keith's girlfriend, Trina, and Lee's fiancée, Erica, from the Fairbanks airport. They were due back any minute. In the meantime, officials from the CIA, DIA, and FBI had gathered in the main conference room, hours early for the scheduled meeting.

Keith was going to be fine. The second bullet had passed through Westover and hit Keith in the ribs. He'd been lucky it had been slowed by the journey through Westover. It had punctured his skin and cracked ribs, but it hadn't reached any vital organs. He'd been playing possum outside the door, plotting his assault on Nicole, when Alec fired the shot that killed her.

He'd wanted to go to the airport, but Alec and Trina both had insisted he rest at the compound.

Footsteps sounded behind her. "They here yet?"

She turned to see Keith. "Not yet." He was pale and very likely working hard to hide his pain. "You're supposed to be in bed."

"So are you."

"I wasn't shot."

"Yeah, well, I wasn't—" He cut himself off, not saying the word.

She let out a sharp, surprised laugh. "Tortured?" she said for him.

His eyes widened. "Sorry. That was out of line."

She shook her head. "No. It's okay. I don't want to make it a taboo subject. If I hide from what happened, it will only give it more power over me. I don't remember most of it, and I'm honestly grateful for that. But if the memories do come back, I don't want to fear them. I *survived*. That's what matters."

He held her gaze. "You did. And you helped take Nicole down."

She nodded. Her only regret about how it ended was what it meant for Alec's political future. The events of the last several days hadn't yet been revealed to the press, and it was hard to imagine he'd get votes when the truth came out. Voters would wonder how sound his mind was after facing torture and how involved he was in the experimentation. There would always be questions about how much he'd known.

On the flip side, with his shot at the senate over, they could date without fear she'd destroy him politically. That card had already been played.

After the debriefing with the FBI, CIA, and DIA tonight, the plan was for Alec to fly home to Maryland tomorrow. He might even withdraw his candidacy. To say that a media circus awaited him when he arrived in his home state was putting it mildly.

"How long have you and Trina been together?" she asked to take her mind off the sorry state of Alec's political future and how depressed the idea of his leaving made her.

"Believe it or not, only a month," Keith said.

"A month?" she asked. "And you're living together?"

A corner of Keith's mouth kicked up. "Well, my town house sort of blew up, so I needed a place to stay." Then he shrugged. "But yeah, it's been fast. Trina is the best thing that ever happened to me." The look in his eye reminded her of how Brad had looked at Jenna. She'd been so relieved to learn Brad was one of the good guys and that he'd helped with the search for her.

A car cleared the main gate and circled the drive. She couldn't help but grin like a smitten schoolgirl. *Alec is back.*

They'd deal with the DIA, CIA, and FBI. And later, they'd return to his quarters and he'd hold her tight. She needed her anchor as she drifted through these unfamiliar waters.

The foursome entered the building, Alec and Lee carrying suitcases for the women. Isabel identified Erica as the dark-haired woman who held Lee's hand, and Trina as the tiny spitfire who bolted through the door but stopped short of launching herself at Keith.

Keith grinned broadly and turned to present his right flank. "This is the side you can hug." Then he scooped her against him with his right arm, lifting her from the floor.

She squealed. "Keith! Put me down! You're going to hurt—"

He planted his mouth on hers, and her complaints stopped.

Isabel turned away from the couple and met Alec's gaze. He smiled and pulled her to his side. He kissed her softly, then led her over to Erica and Lee.

"Isabel Dawson, I'd like you to meet Erica Kesling."

Isabel reached out a hand to the archaeologist who'd made major headlines a few years ago. The press had treated Erica unfairly, and now Isabel suppressed a grimace at the realization they had that in common too.

Erica took her hand, then she cocked her head and said, "Wait a minute. Oregon. Seven or eight years ago. Pipeline survey for a CRM company based out of California."

Isabel searched her memory. Eight years ago, she'd dig-bummed all along the West Coast. She didn't have a good memory for faces, but she did remember projects. "Was that the project with an Oregon Trail site on top of a prehistoric lithic scatter?"

Erica nodded. "Yep. The pipeline company had been caught trying to smooth out the wagon ruts so they could claim the historic site was gone and they could build a road. When the state discovered the damage, not only did they have to preserve the remainder of the ruts, but also they had to pay a buttload in fines *and* for our survey. I hear they went back and did a data recovery on the lithic scatter."

"I was in grad school by then and missed it," Isabel said.

"Me too."

Suddenly, it clicked into place. Isabel had hung back, as was her way, even in the field, not engaging with the other field techs, but the last night of the project, she'd gone out for drinks with the crew and had discussed her grad school plans with another woman who'd been about to embark on underwater archaeology graduate school in Hawaii. She grinned at Erica. "I'm surprised I didn't recognize your name before now."

The woman shrugged. "It was a short project with a large crew. I didn't remember you until I saw your hair."

Isabel touched her curls, which were wilder than usual because she still didn't have a ponytail holder. "Yeah. That's usually the way it goes."

Erica turned to Trina. "Yo. Treen. Come up for air and meet Isabel. I'm pretty sure Keith is going to live."

Trina settled against Keith's good side and extended a hand. "Hi. Just to be clear, I'm not an archaeologist, and I don't like dirt. I like books and oral histories and electricity and plumbing. I'm not entirely sure why Mara and Erica are friends with me, except I make excellent chocolate martinis."

Isabel laughed, a little relieved the woman wasn't ready to

lynch her for causing her boyfriend to get shot.

"Let's head inside to the living quarters." Alec gave both Keith and Isabel a stern stare. "You both were supposed to be resting up for the meeting."

"The officials are already here," Isabel said. "They're waiting in the main conference room."

He frowned and turned to the others. "Why don't you guys take Trina and Erica to your quarters, then join the meeting?"

They nodded, and everyone entered the labyrinth. Isabel gripped Alec's hand as they walked straight to the conference room.

The government officials included two men from the DIA, one from the CIA, FBI Agents Upton and Crews, and their boss, the Special Agent in Charge from the Anchorage office. Everyone who'd been involved in yesterday's search was also present, and Doc Larson had returned to the compound because he'd treated Chase Johnston—who was recovering with a good prognosis in Fairbanks—and was monitoring both Isabel's and Keith's recuperations.

The rest of Alec's employees—those who'd been shipped off when the compound closed—were still in Fairbanks. Isabel dropped into a seat next to Brad and nodded to Ethan, who sat across from her. Sean and Josh flanked the DIA officials. Doc Larson was chatting up Matt Upton.

When Lee and Keith arrived, one of the Defense Intelligence Agency officials stood. "Is this everyone?" he asked.

"Yes," Alec said.

The man crossed to the double doors and pulled them shut. "Good. As you all know, we've been conferring with our colleagues"—he nodded to the guy from the CIA and the FBI SAC—"about the best way to handle the situation and the release of data about what happened here. It pains me and the entire DIA that our former officer, Paul Westover, appears to have been using what he learned when he was affiliated with us to conduct and test research into interrogation techniques and experimental weapons."

The man paced the length of the room. "After reviewing the data found in the hidden laboratory and having examined the cave, we have determined that the best course of action is to classify the events of the last week at the highest top secret security level."

Isabel stiffened, not quite sure what that meant.

"In other words, none of this ever happened. All the data will be destroyed. The remains in the cave have been removed. None of you are to reveal anything you know about Markwell, Godfrey, and Westover's success in weaponizing infrasound waves. Put simply, it's too dangerous. There are several rogue states that would quite literally kill to get their hands on this technology. We at the DIA and my counterparts at the CIA will make certain that never happens, while it's the FBI's job to put out a plausible story to satisfy the people's need for justice."

"What's the story?" Alec asked, his jaw stiff with anger. The DIA was, after all, talking about a cover-up. They were just putting a nicer spin on it.

The DIA official sat down and nodded to the Anchorage SAC, who stood and addressed the room. "It's simple, really, Mr. Ravissant. Paul Westover and Nicole Markwell abducted you with the intention of holding you for ransom. When Ms. Dawson was observed in the area, they panicked and left you. You were unconscious the entire time, which is why you have no memory of your abduction. Several days later, Markwell and Westover seized another opportunity and abducted Ms. Dawson, again for ransom. You and your employees, along with FBI Agent Upton, tracked down the kidnappers and rescued Ms. Dawson. In the ensuing fight, both Westover and Markwell were killed."

Alec shook his head. "It won't work. While this story is close to the truth, it doesn't explain Vincent Dawson's death. You can't admit he was killed by Westover, Godfrey, and Markwell. There's no justice for Vin. No vindication for Isabel."

Isabel met Alec's gaze as emotions flooded her. "But Alec, this scenario is *perfect*. With this story, you can still run for the senate. You could still *win*. You won't have to admit to killing Godfrey. No one will speculate about what being tortured did to you. No one will wonder if you were involved in the infrasound experimentation." She paused. "This story will save your campaign."

"I won't lie to save my candidacy."

"You'll be lying for national security," the CIA official said.

That gave Alec pause, and Isabel pounced. "If we come forward with the truth, not only will you lose, but the Russians will know Westover *was* successful. They'll attempt their own experiments with infrasound. Hell, every rogue state will be after the technology Westover developed."

"I get that," Alec said. "But no one will ever know Vin was

murdered. We need a better story."

She'd suspected she was in love with Alec, but that was the moment she was certain. "The people who matter know. We got justice for Vin. His murderers are dead and can't hurt anyone ever again. I'm satisfied."

It wasn't lost on Isabel that she'd just consented to the cover-up of her brother's murder.

All that was left was hashing out the details of the story, ensuring no one would slip. It was agreed that Alec would make an official statement upon his return to Maryland, adding that the ordeal was personal and he wouldn't take further questions on the subject, and then resume campaigning. The FBI statement would quickly follow, assuring everyone that they were conducting a full investigation to be certain no other conspirators remained. And then they'd hope that the media would tire of the story as no more information was revealed.

Alec could recover his lead and win the election, but much of how it played out wouldn't be in his control.

One thing that could be controlled, however, was not having a liability at his side. Isabel's presence in the campaign would be a constant reminder of the story they couldn't tell, not to mention the newspaper article that painted her as mentally unbalanced—which many people would always believe.

She had no doubt she would reduce his chances of winning.

He wanted to win, and she wanted it for him. The state of Maryland would be lucky to have him, and the US Senate would be a better place if he held a seat. She'd made her decision before she even shook hands with the officials and left the conference room.

At least she and Alec would have tonight for good-byes.

She expected him to remain in the conference room with his employees after the officials left, but instead, the meeting ended and everyone dispersed to their quarters. They all had earned a night off.

He draped an arm around her shoulder as they strode down the winding halls. The compound was quiet. They'd agreed to remain closed for another month, but then the trainings would resume, with Sean Logan as interim director, and she suspected eventually Brad would be named to the top spot.

She wanted to shut down the part of her brain that worried about logistics and cover stories, to set aside for the moment all that had been hashed out during the meeting. She just wanted tonight with Alec.

After they entered his quarters, he pressed her against the closed door and nuzzled her neck. "God, I missed you during the trip to Fairbanks."

"I missed you too." She pressed her lips to his. Tentative. They hadn't done more than hold each other since the shooting yesterday. But she wanted more now. She wanted to forget everything she couldn't remember.

Or, more accurately she wanted to forget there was something she didn't want to remember.

But that wasn't the only reason she wanted him, or even the most important. He made her feel warm, special, and alive. Plus she loved him.

His tongue slid between her lips, and she melted into him, thankful he was ready to move on from cautious touches and take this to the next level.

He pulled back. "Are you sure, Iz?"

She gripped his shirt and held him close. "Don't treat me like I'm fragile. I'm not. I *need* you. Need this. But I don't want soft or gentle. I want hot and fierce."

"You want angry?"

"I'm a little angry. Okay, a lot. But not at you. Never at you."

His mouth covered hers in a deep, hard kiss. His fingers threaded through her curls and twisted, holding her in a tight grip without causing pain.

Yes.

His lips left her mouth and trailed downward, hard, sucking kisses that would likely leave marks. She didn't give a damn. She wanted to ride the edge of rough. She wanted the feel of his hands, his mouth, his body to override every sensation she'd experienced in the last days—even the ones she couldn't remember.

This would be the memory she took away from Alaska.

She began unbuttoning Alec's shirt, but the process was too slow. She gripped the opening and pulled. Buttons popped off, and with satisfying speed, Alec's chest was exposed.

He laughed and scooped her up, heading for the bedroom.

"No," she said. "The marble sideboard."

He changed direction, taking her straight to the named furniture. "It'll be cold."

"And you'll be hot inside me."

He set her feet on the floor and unbuttoned her jeans, then stopped. "Strip while I grab a condom."

She obeyed and was fully naked by the time he returned. He still wore slacks and his torn shirt. Sexy and perfect, and she was about to fulfill the fantasy she'd had that first morning she was here. She opened his fly, and no sooner did she have his thick cock in her hand than he lifted her and set her on the cold marble counter. It was exactly the sensation she wanted—the juxtaposition of hard, unforgiving surface beneath and behind her, with him hot and hard between her thighs.

He slipped the condom on, and that fast, he was inside her. She stretched around him. His first thrust sent intense ripples of pleasure through her.

God, yes. This.

She locked her ankles together behind his ass, gripped the lapel of his open shirt as her head lolled back and bumped against the wall with each thrust. Pleasure radiated from her core, but not the kind that built toward orgasm. For that, she needed direct clitoral stimulation, and she was content to just feel him within her. To have this intimacy. To know her body gave him the intensity he needed.

He loved her.

She could see it in his eyes. In the ferocity of his gaze as he'd stepped into her cabin in the early morning hours and surrendered his gun the moment he recognized the threat to her. In the way he'd held her last night, as she tried to escape into the oblivion of sleep but couldn't—not without a sleeping pill provided by Doc Larson.

And now, as he took her with the edge of roughness she'd asked for.

As if he could read her mind, he grabbed her wrists and held them together above her head, restraining her with one hand, while his other slipped between them and stroked her clit, quickly bringing her to the verge of orgasm. With her hands restrained, she couldn't stop him, couldn't hold back. She had to give in to what he demanded from her body, and she came apart. Her body rocked as the orgasm slammed into her. She came so hard, so abruptly, she cursed. His fingers stayed on her clit, giving no quarter as she bucked against him, trying to pull back, certain she was about to split in two.

His mouth found hers again, and his hard kiss was as inescapable as his fingers. As she rode the wave of what might be the hardest, longest orgasm of her life, she was grateful he made her take it. Midorgasm, the pleasure built even higher, when she would have withdrawn, causing it to end.

The rhythm of his thrusts changed. He groaned into her mouth, and she knew he was reaching his own climax. Impossibly, she crested again as he came with three deep strokes.

Spent, his grip on her wrists went slack, even as the fingers on her clit remained firm. She felt his chuckle—his chest quaking against hers as his lips slid from hers to her neck.

His weight shifted, and she again locked her ankles behind his butt, preventing him from pulling out of her. She felt like she could melt into the marble counter and didn't want him to leave her body just yet.

Without a word, he lifted her and crossed to the couch, sitting down with her straddling him so she could lie across his chest while they both returned to earth.

She propped herself up on her elbows and met his gaze. If only this moment could last forever. If only there was no need for words. No need for him to resume his place in the world. A place in which there was no room for her.

He smiled and tucked a curl behind her ear. "I love you, Isabel."

She shook her head and set her fingers against his lips, as if she could erase the statement. So they didn't have to face it.

She loved him too, but that only made this harder. She cleared her throat. There was no better time or way to say it. "I've made a decision. I'm going back to Oregon."

He frowned, but then flashed a tentative smile. "To finish your PhD? I think that's a good idea but admit I was hoping you'd be able to do the bulk of the work while living in Maryland. I'd assumed your coursework was done."

"Yes. It's all done. My dissertation is ninety percent complete, actually. But I'm not going back for school. I'm going for work. It'll be easier for me to get a job in Oregon."

He scooted up on the couch, sliding from her body. She remained on his lap but was no longer on top of him. Now they were face-to-face. Equals. "You can get a job in Maryland, and it's not like you'd have to worry about money if you don't find anything right away."

"I can't, Alec—"

"Give me one good reason why not. I'd have accepted grad school, but not now."

"I didn't say it was for the PhD, because I won't lie to you."

"Then it can't be because you don't love me, because we both know that would be a lie too."

She stroked his cheek. "I wasn't going to tell you, because I figured that would only make it harder."

"Harder for you to dump me? I hope so."

That was fair enough. She owed him so much more than three words. She wanted to *give him* so much more. Hell, that was what she was trying to do in letting him go. "I love you. And you're the only man I've ever said that to."

His eyes smiled even as he frowned. "Then why the hell aren't you coming with me?"

"It was different when I thought you didn't stand a chance in the election, but now, with the DIA and CIA putting a lid on everything, you have a real chance. But not if I'm by your side. I'm the reminder of everything that could ruin you."

"You want me to drop out of the race."

"No! I think you'd be an amazing senator. I want you to run. I want you to win. But how much would you grow to resent me if I'm the reason you lost?"

"If I can't get elected with you by my side, then I don't want the job. You could never be the reason I lose. *I'm* the candidate. If I can't sell myself to the people of Maryland, it's all on me. It's not my campaign manager's fault, not my advisors, not the volunteers. It would be nobody's fault but mine. It's like planning an op with the Rangers. If the plan failed, there was no one to blame but myself."

"I'm scared, Alec." Even as she said the words, her belly turned. She'd had no idea how afraid she was until she voiced it.

"What are you afraid of, honey?"

"Pretty much everything. Except bears. At this point, bears don't bother me."

He chuckled. "It helps that you carry bear spray."

She smiled and leaned into him, snuggling against his chest. His arms wrapped around her. She could imagine being less afraid if she ended every day like this, and maybe started each day like this too.

With her cheek to his chest, she closed her eyes. "I don't

belong anywhere."

His arms tightened around her. "You belong with me."

She wanted to say no. To walk away without looking back. But what would it be like, on the dig bum circuit in Oregon, California, Washington, and Idaho, knowing she'd walked away from Alec?

He'd—hopefully—win his election. She'd see him on the news nearly every night—because she'd scour C-SPAN if she had to.

"If you don't move to Maryland for me, think of Gandalf. I've grown strangely attached to him. Surely you wouldn't deny me the first cat I've ever thought was tolerable?"

She laughed. Gandalf had slept with them last night. She'd had Alec at her back and her kitty at her front as she closed her eyes to mark the end of the third worst day of her life. Nothing could top losing Vin and her parents.

"Two months. I'll try it for two months."

"No good. That'll get us through the election, but if I win, not to the swearing in."

"Fine. Four months."

"That's not enough either. Life would be in transition, not normal—or whatever normal would be if I'm a senator. I want an eight-month commitment. If I win, that would give us time to settle in to a routine, to find out if we'd really work as a team. Give us until next April."

"You do realize that except for grad school, there are few places I've lived for eight months straight?" He couldn't possibly guess what a big commitment this would be for her.

He kissed her nose. "Yes."

"How do you know that?"

"The background information we gathered on you. I have every address you've ever listed on a government form."

"That's not even all of them. You've probably lived in the same house your whole life."

"No. I bought an estate right before I left the Army."

"Most people buy houses. You bought an *estate*?"

He shrugged. "Originally, I thought I was going to make it into some sort of military training ground—but then Raptor became available, and I bought that instead. So now I have a big old house on acreage in rural Maryland, and no one to share it with. Just think, Iz, Gandalf will love the forest."

She laughed. "Well, okay, then, since Gandalf will enjoy it, I can try Maryland for eight months." Her belly dropped at just saying the words. It was crazy how much this scared her. But at the same time, it was a good sort of scared. Exhilarating. Like a roller coaster.

But mixed with that exhilaration was trepidation. "People are going to talk about how we met—the *Sun* article made sure of that."

"We'll reframe it for them until our version eclipses the tabloid version."

"How will we do that? Tell everyone I zapped you with bear spray?"

"No. We'll point out your brother set us up. It just took a while for us to finally meet."

Warmth flooded her, telling her that she was making the right choice in Alec Ravissant. He'd given the perfect politician's answer, but she knew it wasn't the politician speaking. It was the man. He'd said the smart thing, the right thing, and the truth.

EPILOGUE

Maryland
April

ISABEL STOOD ON the upper veranda and looked out over the garden. It was a show tunes sort of day, crisp and sunny. Cherry blossom time was a little late this year, and Alec's Maryland estate was in full bloom, making it the perfect day for a wedding. If she didn't know it would scare off the guests gathering below, she might belt out a song.

The event had been thrown together in less than a month, but then, once Erica finally agreed to bring their long engagement to an end, Lee wasn't about to give her time to change her mind. Alec offered the estate for the ceremony and party, and surprisingly, Isabel enjoyed helping plan the celebration with Erica. The task had filled the long gap between temporary field projects.

She'd been offered a full-time job at Talon & Drake not long after she moved to the city, but had turned it down, afraid of the commitment. Now, eight months later, she knew Alec expected her final decision.

She'd known her answer for weeks but had yet to tell him. She was waiting for the right moment.

She left the veranda and returned to Alec's bedroom suite, where Erica and her four bridesmaids, Mara, Trina, Undine, and Alexandra, were gathered, putting the final touches on Erica's gorgeous hair.

"At least half the guests have arrived," Isabel said.

The ceremony and celebration were relatively small, less than fifty guests, which seemed about perfect to Isabel. She'd accompanied the new junior senator from Maryland to dozens of political events in the last months, none with fewer than two hundred guests. After that, fifty was downright cozy.

Erica stood, and her gown unfurled. Simple and elegant, she was the perfect picture of a glowing bride. Lee was going to melt when he saw her.

There was a knock on the door. Trina jumped to her feet. "That's probably Cressida. She's bringing champagne for a preceremony toast."

Sure enough, Cressida Porter was at the door. She'd been an intern last summer at Navy History and Heritage Command, where Mara, Trina, Undine, and Erica all worked. Isabel had first met the underwater archaeologist yesterday, but she'd heard a lot about her, especially given the legal troubles she'd had a month ago thanks to a rotten ex-boyfriend.

Accompanying Cressida was Alec. He nodded his head toward the guest bedroom across the hall. "I need to talk to you," he said to Isabel.

She excused herself from the group and followed him into the room. He closed the door and pressed her against the panel.

"You're going to ruin my lipstick," she said right before he kissed her.

She liked that he didn't really give a damn about things like lipstick.

She ran her fingers down his lapels, feeling very sorry that she couldn't rip open his shirt, but it would ruin the tux. He looked great in a tux, and he even knew how to tie his own bow tie, a skill he'd probably learned when he attended Richie Rich's school for loaded boys. It was a good thing, because as a senator, he'd had to don one more than once in the last few months.

Entering his world had been quite the culture shock, but she'd been adapting.

There was less sex in the kitchen than she wanted, because an estate of this size actually required a housekeeper and gardener. Every time she saw the marble counter, she seriously considered the need for downsizing.

"You look gorgeous," he said.

"Thank you. You look pretty hot yourself." She straightened his bow tie. "How are things with the groomsmen?"

"JT is moping because Alexandra wouldn't talk to him, and he's trying to hide how he feels from Lee."

"Alexandra's doing the same thing. I think Erica knows, but she's too happy to let it bother her."

"Lee's the same way." He pulled Isabel tighter against him. "All this wedding stuff is giving me ideas. You know, it's been eight months."

She smiled. "Has it? I hadn't noticed." The lie was so blatant, Alec laughed.

The first few months had been a struggle. Not being with Alec—that was never a struggle. It was the spotlight, the constant attention. That and every forest for a thousand miles appeared to have poison ivy, slapping a high price on long hikes to clear her mind.

Alaska might have bears, but the state didn't have poison oak or poison ivy. And there was no old growth here. Nature somehow didn't feel quite as...*wild*.

She'd also struggled with nightmares. Alec helped her through those long nights, waking her and holding her.

For his part, he'd remembered everything by the time they left Alaska, and he hadn't suffered a single nightmare. He figured knowing he'd killed Godfrey had freed him from being haunted by dreams.

He'd made certain all but one copy of the videos of her being tortured had been destroyed. The remaining copy was on a USB drive in a safe, reserved for if she decided to view it in the hopes it would put an end to the nightmares. For now, she wasn't ready and didn't know if she'd ever want to watch it.

Per her promise, she'd settled in and begun to build a life here, for the first time not planning her exit as she unpacked her bags. When Alec wasn't busy learning his new role as US senator, time with him was her reward for living in this strangely foreign part of the country. She'd learned how to smile for cameras and even occasionally step up to a microphone and introduce him at public events. Since he'd taken office, she'd added talks about archaeology to elementary and middle school students to her repertoire of public outreach activities. But she'd made Mara join her for one of those talks—after all, the woman was married to the US attorney general, while Isabel was a mere girlfriend to a US senator.

The students were far more excited to meet Mara Garrett, and that was just fine with her.

"It's been eight months to the day, in fact," Alec added.

"I've been thinking… It seems like Gandalf really likes it here. It would be a shame to uproot him when he's finally settled in." Even though Isabel had an apartment in the city—a concession to voters who might've had a problem with Isabel moving in with Alec without exchanging vows—they spent more time at the estate, so Gandalf lived here.

Alec's smile lit his topaz-blue eyes.

"And today, JT told me the job at Talon & Drake is still open." She cocked her head. "What do you think? Should I take it?"

"I think it's a great opportunity." He frowned. "But there's one thing left to be settled."

"What's that?"

"Your apartment. I think we should offer it to Chase Johnston when he starts his job at the DC office next month."

She smiled, pleased Chase would be returning soon. She'd gotten to know him well during the months he'd been in the DC area working with the CIA to deconstruct what Godfrey and Westover had done to him. A month ago, that work had been completed and he'd been given a clean bill of both physical and mental health. Alec had sent the young man to his Kauai beach house for much needed recuperation prior to Chase starting his new job at Raptor's home office. "I thought, because you're a public figure, as long as we aren't married, I need to maintain a separate address."

"Exactly. But getting married would negate the need for an apartment." The light in his eyes shifted as he stepped back from her. With his gaze fixed on hers, he reached into his pocket and pulled out a box, then slowly lowered to one knee.

Adrenaline flooded her as the meaning sank in.

"I love you and want to share every facet of my home and life with you—officially. Will you marry me?"

Her heart hammered against her ribs. She didn't know why this moment shocked her so much. It had been obvious they'd been headed in this direction from the start.

He opened the box to reveal the most beautiful ring she'd ever seen.

She'd known since Christmas she'd never leave Alec, but making the commitment legally binding was a giant leap from sort-of live-in girlfriend.

He smiled, undaunted by her hesitation. "I should mention that this ring comes with another piece of jewelry, but you have to accept the ring to get the other." He stood and pulled out a second box. Inside was a diamond-encrusted pendant in the shape of an anchor.

The meaning behind the symbol took her breath away. She'd never been much of a jewelry person, but she wanted that necklace more than any piece of jewelry she'd ever seen in her life.

Alec Ravissant was a brilliant strategist. He knew how to exploit her weaknesses in the most wonderful, diabolical ways.

"Okay. I'll marry you."

He chuckled as he draped the necklace around her neck. He kissed the sensitive skin below her ear after he secured the latch. "I knew it would look beautiful with this dress."

She turned to face him. "Today is Erica and Lee's day. We should probably keep this a secret."

"It'll be hard if anyone notices this." He slipped the ring on her finger.

She studied it, watching it spark and flash as she turned it toward the light. "People will notice. It's beautiful."

"It was my mother's. My dad gave it to me a month after you moved here. If anyone asks, just smile and hold your finger to your lips. They'll get a kick out of being in on the secret, and it won't overshadow the wedding."

She touched the anchor that rested high on her sternum as she gazed into Alec's eyes. The last eight months hadn't been easy, full of transition and discomfort, but they'd also been—by far—the happiest months of her life. "I love you, Alec."

He slipped an arm around her waist and pulled her against him. "I love you too." He kissed her lightly. "Now, we have to decide. Honeymoon in Paris? I know a great little restaurant—"

"Ha! You keep promising me Paris but are too busy to take me. No. I think for our honeymoon we should go to a little cabin in the wilderness. Just you and me. A fireplace. And hot chocolate."

"Sounds perfect, but promise me one thing."

"What's that?"

"No bear spray."

AUTHOR'S NOTE

INFORMATION ON INFRASOUND was gathered from many different sources. The fictional article describing the effects of infrasound on the human body was adapted from the November 20, 2012 *Popular Science* article, "Could A Sonic Weapon Make Your Head Explode?" by Seth S. Horowitz. The full article can be read at www.popsci.com/technology/article/2012-11/acoustic-weapons-book-excerpt. The way infrasound is used in this story is completely fictional.

The Airwave weapon described in *Incriminating Evidence* was my own fictional invention…until I read an article that described a weapon in development that was very similar to how I envisioned Airwave. Information on pulsed energy projectiles can be read at www.en.wikipedia.org/wiki/Pulsed_energy_projectile.

THANK YOU FOR reading *Incriminating Evidence*. I hope you enjoyed it!

If you'd like to know when my next book is available, you can sign up for my new release mailing list at www.Rachel-Grant.net. You can also follow me on Twitter at @rachelsgrant or like my Facebook page at www.facebook.com/RachelGrantAuthor. I'm also on Goodreads at www.goodreads.com/RachelGrantAuthor, where you can see what I'm currently reading.

Reviews help like-minded readers find books. Please consider leaving a review for *Incriminating Evidence* at your favorite online retailer. All reviews, whether positive or negative, are appreciated.

ACKNOWLEDGEMENTS

AS WITH EVERY book, I have many people to thank, this one especially so as it was a work in progress for so long. Thanks to Kris Kennedy, Natasha Tate, and Jennie Lucas, who first helped me plot this book back in 2010, and then again in 2011 (during the plotting group session which shall forever be known as the GH Squee weekend). Thanks to Darcy Burke, Elisabeth Naughton, Gwen Hernandez, and my agent, Elizabeth Winick Rubinstein, who were there for me as I outlined, plotted, and wrote, only to discard my pages and start over again.

Thanks to Jenn Stark, who was ever available to read pages and give feedback when the story veered off-course. Thank you to Gwen Hayes who fed me and talked me through writing the final fifteen thousand words of the first draft. I don't know how I would have finished this book if you hadn't been there. Isabel might have been much more abused if not for your voice of reason.

Thank you to Bria Quinlan, Gwen Hernandez and Krista Hall, who gave valuable (and timely!) critiques of the full manuscript. I appreciate you more than I can say.

Thanks to NW Pixie Chicks Rebecca Clark, Cathy Perkins, Elisabeth Naughton, Courtney Milan, and Darcy Burke, for their wonderful company as I edited this book. Our weekend is always a highlight of my writing year.

To my editor, Linda Ingmanson, and proofreader, Toni, thank you both for your attention to detail, punctuation, and plot holes.

Thank you to my children for tolerating the long drives in Alaska as we explored the setting for this book and for not laughing too hard when I slipped and fell on that glacier.

Thank you to my husband, David Grant, whose extensive research on infrasound inspired the story. When I struggled to pull all the plot threads together, he listened, advised, and poked holes, until I found the way forward. I couldn't have written this book without you. I love you!

About the Author

Four-time Golden Heart® finalist Rachel Grant worked for over a decade as a professional archaeologist and mines her experiences for storylines and settings, which are as diverse as excavating a cemetery underneath an historic art museum in San Francisco, survey and excavation of many prehistoric Native American sites in the Pacific Northwest, researching an historic concrete house in Virginia, and mapping a seventeenth century Spanish and Dutch fort on the island of Sint Maarten in the Netherlands Antilles.

She lives in the Pacific Northwest with her husband and children and can be found on the web at Rachel-Grant.net.